"LET ME BE YOUR SECRET LOVER . . .
I'LL DEVOTE MY LIFE TO
BRINGING YOU PLEASURE."

"You promise me pleasure but not happiness?" Eleanor questioned breathlessly.

"No one can promise happiness to another, however much he may wish it," Simon said softly. "You torment me when you hold me at arm's length and deny me. Put me out of my misery." His burning mouth trailed a fiery path down her throat and his arms tightened about her.

"Please don't! When you press me to your heart I want to . . ." She caught the words back guiltily.

"You consume me," he whispered savagely.

The swift intake of her breath told him exactly what effect he had on her. Eleanor had to fight him and herself both. The feel of his magnificent hands upon her was like an aphrodisiac.

"Let me go!" she said, desperately summoning her anger.

He removed his hands from her. "How ironic that after winning every joust today, I should lose the final one. The only joust that means anything to me . . ."

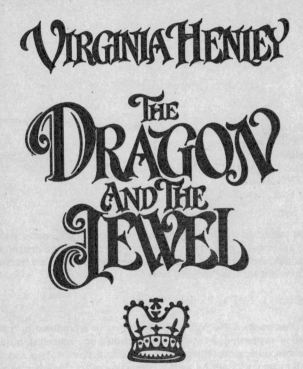

VIRGINIA HENLEY

THE DRAGON AND THE JEWEL

A DELL BOOK

Published by
Dell Publishing
a division of
Bantam Doubleday Dell Publishing Group, Inc.
666 Fifth Avenue
New York, New York 10103

ISBN: 0-440-20624-3

Printed in the United States of America

Published simultaneously in Canada

December 1991

10 9 8 7 6 5 4 3 2 1

RAD

For my grandsons Michael and Daryl . . .
my own precious jewels

PROLOGUE

Eleanor Plantagenet Marshal, Princess of England and Countess of Pembroke, was renowned for her dark exquisite beauty. When her hair was unbound it fell to her waist like a glorious black cloud, its silken tendrils framing a heart-shaped face. Her large, deep-blue eyes were the shade of Persian sapphires, and she was known throughout the land as the King's Precious Jewel. Her clothes and gems were the envy of the entire Court of Windsor where she dwelled, waited upon by an entourage of servants and handmaidens.

Like most girls of seventeen, her thoughts were obsessed by her love for a man. Her passion had known no bounds. She would love him throughout eternity. Her cheeks flushed delicately as she remembered the warm, inviting bed and the Marshal of England's naked body. A soldier's body, wide shouldered, chest covered by thick, corded muscles, deeply bronzed, the firelight accentuating every sinew of his powerful torso. It seemed she had waited a lifetime for this man to make love to her, to perform the hymenal rites that would teach her the secrets of her own sensuality and make her a woman.

But something had gone hideously wrong! William Marshal, Earl of Pembroke, was dead and Eleanor was covered with guilt. The doctors had been unanimous in their verdict. William's heart had burst trying to satisfy the insatiable demands of his young wife. The scandal had been horrendous. The rumors flew fast and furious. It was the talk of the court, the city, the whole country. It was extremely titillating to surmise just how wanton the princess had been to cause her husband, the virile Marshal of England, to expire from excess.

Her mind relived her guilty secrets over and over. She recalled the heightened tension when he had removed her nightgown, making her feel faint with anticipation. His fingers and tongue caressing the tips of her breasts had made her cry out with pleasure. When his fingertips separated the tiny folds of her woman's center to seek the jewel inside, she had been tempted to explore and taste his maleness. When he knelt above her to fill her with his hard, thick manroot, she thought she might die from excitement. Instead it had been William who had died. Eleanor had immediately sworn vows of chastity and perpetual widowhood, but it had not expiated her guilt in any way, nor had it eased her bruised heart from agony.

The Countess of Pembroke was seen only occasionally about the court. She was quietly aloof, speaking with none but her own attendants. It was almost as if she had fallen into a trance with the death of her husband—a trance from which it looked as if she would never emerge.

Eleanor picked up her book and walked languorously down to her private, walled garden. She unlocked the only door, then slipped the iron key into her pocket, secure in the knowledge that none could ever intrude. I'll never get used to this lump in my throat, she thought wearily. I wonder if I shall be upon the brink of tears for the rest of my life. She sighed and thought with infinite patience, It has only been a year. Perhaps in two years or three the tears will dry.

Mother Superior had been pressing her to come to a decision, but Eleanor would not be hurried. I have the rest of my life. I shall decide nothing in haste only to repent at leisure, she cautioned herself. Absently she fingered her braids in which the nuns had taught her to plait three knots on each side. The knots in the left side were for the Trinity: God the Father, God the Son, and God the Holy Ghost. The three on the right were for chastity, obedience, and poverty. I have no trouble whatsoever with the first vow, she told herself, and my obedience improves with practice, but I'm not sure I can live with a vow of poverty. Though I've tried to cast out my love of luxury, I find it impossible. I still adore beautiful clothes and jewels. If I am being truthful, I have not changed one iota. Inside I am still the wild, willful, passionate creature I was when I was five. I've simply learned to hold it all inside and show the world a façade of gentle poise and calm control.

William had donated land and provided money for the Order of St. Bride's convent near Windsor, and she knew that before she took the veil she would have to stay there overnight in one of the cells to see if she could bear to give up her freedom. She was almost convinced she could, for what earthly use did she have for freedom?

In the evening she tried to gather enough energy to go to compline, the seventh and last service of the day. If she took holy orders, how would she last through seven services each day? She asked herself for the thousandth time why she was contemplating the convent, and the answer came back the same: Guilt! Mother Superior insisted her guilt would be expiated, washed away forever, and Eleanor knew she could not live much longer with the crushing guilt.

She rose and took up her jeweled dagger from her bedside table. With unseeing eyes she gazed from the tall windows of the King John Tower. She ran her finger down the sharp blade of the knife. Do it now, do it now, a voice urged her. If she knew she could join William tonight, she would do it without hesitation. Another voice whispered, He has escaped from you . . . he never really wanted you . . . leave him in peace. She cried aloud, "Untrue! Untrue!" Then silently she said, I don't want to live like this. Then she recalled that suicides were purported to spend Eternity in Purgatory. What was the point in exchanging one Purgatory for another? she thought wearily. What was the point of anything?

She dragged herself to the chapel where she spent a whole hour begging forgiveness, then she dully dragged herself to bed. In the morning when daylight crept into her bedchamber, she turned her face to the wall and pulled the covers over her head. She would escape in blissful sleep.

She drifted into a dream where she was hawking with William. They always rode side by side. The crisp air was so invigorating, it tasted like wine. She stood up in her stirrups to cast her merlin and suddenly awoke with a start. The dream had been so real, so tangible that it floated in the air around the bed. What on earth was the matter with her? She'd taken no exercise in over a year. No wonder she had slipped into a decline, not caring if she lived or died. She hadn't hawked with her little merlin from her beloved Wales for what seemed like years. The little hawk had probably forgotten her. She would need a riding dress. Her mind hesitated as she pictured the bold jade green not worn in over a year. She loathed the colors of mourning she'd long adopted.

She'd do it, she decided. She would search out the riding dress and make her way to the mews above the stables. As she impatiently flung back the bedcovers she experienced a strong feeling that she was reliving an experience. Her mind took wing, flying back over the years to her wedding day, when it had all begun. She could remember every minute detail of that fateful day that changed her life so completely. . . .

PART
ONE

1

Princess Eleanor Katherine Plantagenet opened her eyes to the sound of birdsong greeting the dawn. Her heart soared with happiness as she realized that the day had finally arrived. She threw back the covers impatiently and ran barefoot to the polished silver mirror.

She didn't look any different from yesterday. Her black hair was a mass of impossible tangles, the natural creamy color of her skin was marred by too much sun, and her mouth was still set in stubborn lines that clearly showed she got her own way about everything in life. She always would, she decided. Getting your own way was what made life sweet. Some things didn't come as easily as others, but with unwavering determination, and also by making everyone else's life hell, she always got what she wanted.

She had ruled her siblings since she was five years old and was the terror of the nursery. They were all older than she, one was even King of England, but by fair means or foul she bent them to her will. The corners of her mouth lifted as she remembered the day that had set her fate.

Her brothers Henry and Richard, then fourteen and twelve respectively, had a ferret in a sack and were off to hunt rabbits.

"Wait for me!" she cried imperiously, struggling to pull on her shoes over feet still wet from paddling in the fishpond.

"You're not coming, Maggot!" cried King Henry.

"You bugger! Stop calling me that," she screamed furiously.

"I'll tell Nanny you swear," six-year-old Isabella said.

Eleanor looked at her sister with contempt. "She knows I swear . . . you still pee yourself."

Joanna said from the lofty wisdom of her ten years, "We're not to leave the garden. If you go off with the boys again I shall tell on you."

Eleanor snatched up the sack that held the ferret and thrust it at Joanna. Screwing her face into that of a hideous gargoyle, she threatened, "If you tell, you will find a ferret in your bed some dark night."

Joanna screamed, then took little Isabella by the hand. "Come away, she's wicked."

Richard, Duke of Cornwall, cuffed Eleanor across the ear and took the sack from her. "Go and play with the girls, Maggot, you're not coming with us."

She dug determined little fists into her hips and stuck out a belligerent chin. "If you don't let me come with you, I shall tell that you chase the maids and give them belly-burns with your newly sprouted whiskers."

"Maggot-faced little bitch," swore adolescent Henry.

Richard, although younger than the king, was stronger and more dominant. He suddenly threw back his head and laughed. "She's no bigger than a piss-ant, yet she rules the roost one way or another. Come on, Maggot, I'll bet you don't have the stomach for this sport anyway."

In all truth she did not have the stomach for it. She watched in fascinated horror as her brothers slipped the slinky creature down a rabbit hole, then waited with a sack at the other end of the warren for the terrified bunny to pop out. All her sympathies were with the rabbits, and her heart was wrung over the furry brown creatures who went into shock from fear.

Her brothers laughed at her tears and she dashed them away with grimy fingers, leaving rivulets of dirt streaking her face. She felt sick and hurried off in the direction of the palace before they could witness her disgrace herself. To her dismay they followed her, laughing, teasing, and taunting her because she'd allowed them to glimpse her vulnerability.

Henry was golden-haired like his grandfather the great King Henry II, and Richard's head was russet like his namesake uncle Richard the Lionhearted. Eleanor, the baby of the family, was the only one who had inherited the darkness of their father and mother, the hated King John and Queen Isabella of Angoulême. They used her coloring to tease her unmercifully.

Richard said, "Did you ever notice how much the child resembles a black cockroach?"

Henry laughed. "The last one of a litter is always a runt, but she's so little I suspect she's a dwarf."

Eleanor had never felt so miserable. She was nauseated, hot, and tired, and now a pain shot through her heel. She stopped running, took off her shoe, and saw a large raw blister. "Oh, balls!" she muttered, and threw the offending slipper into a bramble bush.

They caught up with her just as the palace came into view. "Someone's just arrived," Richard said.

"It's the marshal!" Henry cried happily, recognizing the device of the Red Lion Rampant on a white field.

Eleanor's miseries dissolved like snow in summer. Saved by the marshal. Oh, how she loved him!

The king and the Duke of Cornwall greeted William Marshal, one of their beloved guardians, a full ten minutes before Eleanor's little legs carried her into his glorious presence. She tugged on his surcoat. "My lord earl, My lord earl!"

He bent and picked her up, then sat down on a stone bench in the shaded courtyard. Her face was now wreathed with smiles beneath the grime. "Sweetheart, you've been crying! Tell William what's amiss."

Henry and Richard exchanged impatient glances. They wanted William Marshal's undivided attention for themselves. He was their father figure, their mentor, and their hero all rolled into one.

"I'm ugly, like a little black cockroach," whispered Eleanor.

Her words startled Will Marshal momentarily, and he fished in a pocket for a sweetmeat while he searched for words to comfort the child. Her eyes lit up at the sight of the sugared mouse, and she sucked it contentedly as she nestled in the crook of his arm to listen to his soothing voice.

"Once upon a time there was a handsome king and a beautiful queen who had a brood of towheaded children. Then along came the last one and, as is often the case, the last was the best. When the king saw how beautiful she was, he was well pleased. She had black silken curls and eyes the deep blue of sapphires. He told the queen, 'She is my precious jewel,' and ever after she was known as the King's Precious Jewel."

"Me!" Eleanor said, having heard the phrase all her life. She looked at Henry and said solemnly, "And I shall marry the marshal and live happily ever after."

Eleanor's mind returned to the present, and she stared at her face in the mirror. In spite of the touseled hair and sunburn, she knew she was beautiful. It had taken four long years to secure her heart's desire. Four years of manipulating her brother King Henry into persuading William Marshal to wed her. An old superstition ran through her mind: "Be careful what you wish for in case it comes true." She laughed at her own silliness. She loved William Marshal with all her heart and all her soul and all her mind. After today he would be hers forever.

Her chamber door was thrown open and a gaggle of nursemaids filed in to prepare their charge for her wedding. Princess Eleanor Katherine Plantagenet was nine years old.

Will Marshal's eyes told nothing of his true feelings on this wedding day. He thought his black velvet doublet emblazoned back and front with the scarlet lions ridiculously ostentatious. His tastes were those of a plain soldier, yet he realized what was expected of the head of the wealthiest family in England. All the Marshals who had gathered for the ceremony had married well. His brothers had wed into the noblest families, his sisters married to the Earls of Gloucester, Derby, and Norfolk.

He sighed. It was only fitting, he supposed, that the head of the Marshals should marry into the royal family. Yet when Henry had offered him Princess Eleanor he had recoiled in horror. He had made the excuse that she was a child and it would take too many years before she could become a real wife to him, but the truth of the matter was he loathed the little girl's mother and feared the princess would become a beautiful, promiscuous replica.

Poor little imp, he thought sadly. What a frightening thought to be born in the image of her father and mother. King John had been the worst King England had ever known and had been hated by all. He had been both venal and vile, and the entire world was relieved that he was dead. Queen Isabella had been a voluptuary at the tender age of fourteen. When his duties took him into the king's bedchamber, her sensuality had disgusted him. She'd been a wretched mother. Before John was cold in his grave and Eleanor one year old, she had abandoned them all and married her previous lover, Hugh de Lusignan, and before the little mite had turned four years old, like a bitch in heat Isabella had produced a litter of three sons, William, Guy, and Aymer de Lusignan. He only prayed to heaven that Queen Isabella's tainted blood had not been passed on to her offspring. What a nest of vipers they could become when they realized the corrupting power royal blood could wield.

He took up two silver-backed brushes and ran them through his thick brown hair, noticing for the first time that it was sprinkled with gray. He had been relieved when Henry's council had rejected the idea of the marriage. Since the Princess Isabella had married the Emperor of Germany and the Princess Joanna had become a queen by marrying King Alexander of Scotland, they also wanted a royal marriage for Eleanor. King Henry had been incensed with his council. He was ever at odds with them, chafing at the fact that he was a boy-king, but a few weeks before he reached his majority of eighteen he again put the matter before his council, informing them that he wished to give his beloved Marshal of England the King's Precious Jewel, Eleanor. He told them in no uncertain terms that if they objected, they would be overruled the moment he became eighteen.

Henry was well pleased with himself this day. The marriage contracts had been negotiated and signed, and the portion Eleanor was to receive from William Marshal was more than generous, amounting to one-fifth of the vast Marshal holdings in England, Wales, and Ireland. Henry had always had a great liking for William Marshal and an even greater liking for his vast fortune.

Henry's brother Richard arrived and without hesitation threw open the door to the king's privy chamber. Followed by half a dozen of his attendants, he filled the room. Richard was old enough to have his own residence and had just returned from his duchy of Cornwall. He put the king in the shade in every way. Not only was he more attractive, taller, and stronger, but the revenues from the vast tin mines in Cornwall were already making him wealthy.

Richard affectionately punched Henry in the shoulder and said, "Well, the little piss-ant is getting her own way again today."

Henry, who had one drooping eyelid, let it close all the way in a sly wink. "You don't think I'd be fool enough to let a fortune like the marshal's slip through my fingers?"

Richard grinned as he reached out to feel the cloth of gold the young king wore. "Is that who is paying for all this lavish pomp and ceremony?"

"No"—Henry laughed—"as a matter of fact, you are. I shall allow you to make me a loan now that you're filthy rich."

"Thanks for nothing!" Richard, who was not really generous by nature, laughed.

Henry sobered. "Christ, Richard, I don't know what the hell I'm going to do. You know I don't have a pot to piss in. It's so bloody unfair—talk about the sins of the fathers being visited upon the son! We had a prick of a father, Richard. The son of a bitch declared England a fief of Rome before he died, which means I owe an annual tribute of a thousand marks—seven hundred for England and three hundred for Ireland. It hasn't been paid for nine frigging years because when I came to the throne I didn't have one piece of gold. Too bad Father didn't get swept out to sea instead of the crown jewels, when his treasure wagons were engulfed by the waters of The Wash."

Richard poured himself ale, but Henry snapped his fingers at one of his attendants who immediately poured him the best imported Gascon wine.

"Have you paid Isabella's dowry yet?" Richard asked.

"Surely you jest! How can I send money to Germany? I'm not the one with a pisspot full of money, you are."

"That's because I don't spend it with both hands like you do. Take this wedding, for example. It could have been a very simple affair. After all, Eleanor won't be a real wife for years. After the religious ceremony the little minx could have been packed off to the nursery and William sent home to his mistress. Instead you choose to put on a lavish show that costs thousands."

Henry's eyes narrowed and his voice became high-pitched. "I was crowned with a simple gold circlet of Mother's and sat down afterward to a tough chine of beef. The *loyal* English barons had *invited* the French in to overthrow my father. The French held every castle from Winchester to Lincoln, and I can count on one hand the men who were loyal to me." He stuck up his thumb. "William Marshal." He stuck up a finger. "Hubert de Burgh." A second finger followed. "Ranulf de Blundeville, Earl of Chester." He pointed to his third finger. "Peter des Roches, Bishop of Winchester." The last and final finger went up. "Falkes de Bréauté, the mercenary."

Richard had heard it all before and knew Henry was obsessed.

"It took these loyal men four years to rid England of the French. Marshal, de Burgh, and Chester paid for it out of their own pockets because I didn't have one gold piece. I swore that when I came into my majority I would make up for it. I'm the bloody King of England! When I throw a banquet it will be a great feast where the greatest men of the realm wear their finest robes and glittering jewels."

Richard threw an affectionate arm about his shoulders. "Then you'll have to do what every other intelligent man does, marry an heiress. Take a page from Hubert de Burgh's book, I certainly intend to. Look at the wealth and lands Avisa brought him and the moment she was measured for a shroud, he was wooing little Princess Margaret of Scotland who was put in his safekeeping. And to make absolutely certain he got her, he fucked her until he got her with child."

"Which royally screwed me! I was negotiating for her sister, Princess Marion, until my council objected on the grounds that Hubert de Burgh would be my brother-in-law. They're just jealous that he was acting regent through my minority and I chose to honor him by making him Earl of Kent. The people love Hubert and so do I."

"And so does Hubert." Richard laughed. When he saw Henry's face twist with anger, he laughed again. "A joke, brother. You know how much I owe to Hubert. He took me under his wing and made a soldier of me. He and William Marshal made it possible for me and you to slip from the clerical leading strings of the Bishop of Winchester."

Henry said, "Peter des Roches made a wonderful tutor. He is one of the most enlightened men of this or any other century."

Richard made a rude noise. "Well, he certainly gained ascendancy over your mind while he installed his relatives and creatures in all the important posts of the household."

"Well, he isn't in control any longer. Hubert and the bishop are at each other's throats. I think it's a wise policy to split my ambitious ministers into two camps. And if either think they can keep me on a leash once I reach my majority, they are in for a rude awakening." He drained his winecup. "Now all I need is money. As soon as negotiations are completed with the Count of Brittany for his lovely Austrian princess, I shall be rolling in it."

Richard, firmly placing his tongue in his cheek, said, "Not when she gets my letter telling her you're squint-eyed and impotent."

Henry took off after Richard and his attendants hurried after him with the magnificent new crown he had just designed for himself.

2

As Princess Eleanor was led toward the altar in the chapel at Westminster, she was almost dizzy from happiness. She was gowned in pristine white velvet, her tiny train trimmed with ermine; upon her cloud of dark hair sat a coronet of snow-drops, and she held a small white Bible.

As she reached the marshal's side, he looked down at her with a grave smile. Her dark-blue eyes sparkled like sapphires as she gazed up at him with adoration. He was the handsomest, bravest, strongest man in the realm. When he smiled his eyes crinkled boyishly and her heart turned over. She opened her mouth to speak his name, but he gave her a little frown of warning to remind her to keep silent until she repeated the vows. She obediently followed his lead and sank to her knees and bowed her head while the bishop droned a Latin prayer over their heads.

She couldn't keep her eyes closed for longer than ten seconds, so she lifted her lashes and saw a black spider making its way across her white Bible. She watched in fascination as the insect walked delicately on its eight legs, then as it reached her thumb it very deliberately bit her. Without hesitation she slapped it into the next world. "You bugger!"

The bishop's mouth fell open and William opened his eyes quickly to see what she was doing. He reached across firmly and took Eleanor's small hand into his. It was freezing and his long, brown fingers wrapped about it to control her, to comfort her, to warm her. After that everything went smoothly. She gave her responses solemnly, from the heart.

William slipped the heavy gold band onto her finger and she clenched her fist tightly to prevent its slipping off. When the long-winded bishop finally pronounced them man and wife, she said ecstatically to William, "I'm the Countess of Pembroke."

He smiled down at her and murmured, "Never have I seen anyone step down in rank so graciously." At the compliment her heart almost burst with love.

The wedding presents were displayed on trestle tables along the entire length of the banqueting hall. The large Marshal family, combining its fortunes in matrimony with the noblest in England, gifted them with magnificent silver plate engraved with the initial M, the finest Venetian crystal, one hundred solid-gold forks, and one hundred sets of Irish bed linen monogrammed with exquisite embroidery.

Since William was the Justiciar of Ireland and owned all of Leinster, a gift of twenty-five blooded stallions and twenty-five blooded brood mares had been shipped across the Irish Sea. The Earl of Chester had gifted them with ten Oriental silk carpets acquired on his last Crusade. Never to be outdone, Hubert de Burgh, Justiciar of England, had fitted out a luxurious barge, painted in the Marshal colors, which rode at anchor a few hundred feet away in the Thames.

The barons too had been generous. They may not have liked their young king, but their respect for the Marshal of England ran deep.

The Earl and Countess of Pembroke sat on carved and padded throne chairs on the dais at King Henry's right hand. The miniature bride was the focus of all eyes as she sat between the two tall men and graciously thanked each couple who came forward. The people captured her interest far more than their costly gifts as she sorted out the Earl and Countess of Derby from the Earl and Countess of Norfolk. The Marshals were certainly an attractive family with their chestnut curls and laughing brown eyes.

William Marshal marveled inwardly at the poise the child displayed as she gravely thanked their guests. There was hope yet that she would grow into a refined lady. He harbored such dread that she might become like her mother that before he agreed to the marriage he stipulated in the marriage contracts how she must be brought up from now on. Alarmingly neglected, she had been allowed the freedom of a wild young animal. First and foremost, her innocence must be guarded day and night. She was to reside at Windsor Castle in a wing that was to be kept separate for females. She was to have her own servants and ladies-in-waiting, and he had asked the Mother Superior of the Order of St. Bride's to supply two nuns to live in her household on a permanent basis.

She was to have tutors to educate her fine mind; she was to be taught to read and write and to speak other languages, as well learn etiquette, deportment, and the womanly arts, which the chatelaine of the marshal's vast estates would need to know.

William doubted that she would be able to hold up through the long, tiring day, even though the banquet was to end at ten o'clock in deference to her bedtime. However, once they were seated at the banquet table, her reserve and poise disappeared and were replaced by an inquisitive, talkative, bundle of energy.

The noisy clamor of the revelers receded for Eleanor as there became only one other person in the room, nay in the whole world.

"My lord earl, you have ridden in tournaments all over the world and never been defeated. May I please attend and watch you?"

Will's eyebrows went up. "Sweeting, I've been defeated many times. Tournaments have been forbidden in England for some time now because of the danger. England needs all her men to fight real battles."

"Then it is high time we had one. I shall command it." Without taking a breath she said, "My lord earl, you are too modest. I know you are the undefeated champion. You know exactly where to thrust in the lance. Will you show me the spot where a man is most vulnerable?" She placed her small hand upon his breast muscle. "Is it here?" she asked, wide-eyed.

William felt alarm rise within him. Surely the subject was unseemly for a child. Gently he removed her hand, murmuring "It's more to the side."

Her hand reached into his armpit. "Here?"

"I will show you the spot sometime when we are private."

Her eyes lit with anticipation and he watched with amazement as she devoured almost as much food as he did. "My lord earl, you have more castles than any other man in the world."

"Well, perhaps not the world, Eleanor," he demurred.

"Well, in England and Ireland and Wales," she said impatiently. "I want to see them all. Will you take me to Ireland and to Wales?"

He tried to discourage her. "I usually only go to these places when there is trouble. I go to fight."

"Oh, yes!" she cried passionately. "Will you take me to the wars, my lord earl, so I may see you ride into battle? Will you show me exactly where you stick your sword in to kill a man?"

William opened his mouth and closed it again, fighting the alarm that rose up within him. "I cannot take you to war, little one. I will not lie to you."

"Won't you, my lord earl? Thank you," she said from the bottom of her heart. "Everyone else does, you know. If I promise not to come to war with you, will you promise to show me how to use a sword and how to stick it in?"

"I-I suppose so," he said faintly.

"Do you promise?" she demanded.

"Yes." He nodded.

"My lord earl, do you have murder holes in your Welsh castles where you can pour boiling oil down upon the enemy? Is it true that the Welsh are so wild and wicked they fight naked?"

"That's the Scots," he said faintly, wondering what on earth he'd let himself in for. Lord God, it would take more than tutors and nuns to civilize Eleanor Plantagenet. He squirmed in his seat realizing to his great dismay that everything about him fascinated the child. Her great sapphire eyes were saucers of adoration as she hung upon his every word. He cleared his throat and picked up his goblet. This was thirsty work.

Eleanor reached across the table to a tall jug of wine and poured a liberal drink for herself. The wine splashed crimson upon her pristine velvet and William couldn't believe his ears. "Oh, balls!" she said, rubbing it and succeeding in making it much worse.

"Eleanor," he began firmly.

She glanced up. "Oh, forgive me, my lord earl, I didn't realize the dancing had started. Oh, 'tis my favorite, the Volta. You will allow me one dance, won't you, my lord earl, please?" she implored.

He was at such a loss that suddenly he grinned. "I could never deny a lass with a yearning heart."

When the assembly saw the good-natured groom was sport enough to dance with the little bride, a great cheer broke out and swept across the floor. William swung Eleanor back and forth in a wide circle, then lifted her high in the air and twirled her over his head until she was giddy with excitement. Everyone joined them on the floor, and each man took his turn partnering the little bride. She was whirled from arm to arm and lifted high by each new dancer, who tried to show off his superiority before the others. Then she was squealing with pure happiness when it was Marshal's turn again.

He shook his head as her brother Richard reached for her. "Enough, you'll have her in a state of collapse."

Richard grinned. "You don't know Eleanor. She'll have *you* in a state of collapse."

William carried her back to her chair and looked down at her flushed face and brilliantly sparkling eyes. The snowdrops had wilted and her coronet sat all askew, but truly she was the most beautiful child he had ever seen. "Shall we just watch?" he suggested.

"Yes," she agreed happily, "I would rather be sitting here with you than anywhere else in the whole world."

William saw her reach for more wine. Just in time he firmly removed the jug down the table and said, "Dancing is thirsty work. I shall go and fetch us some cider fresh from the orchards of Cornwall. Or perhaps there is ambrosia, a honeyed fruit drink. I think you would like it excessively."

"Thank you, my lord earl. I don't wish to be a trouble to you," she assured him solemnly.

William sighed. Trouble was most likely Eleanor Plantagenet's middle name.

When William departed, Henry spotted her sitting alone and brought over a woman of indeterminate age. Though she looked old, her hair was very black and her brow was amazingly unwrinkled. "Dame Margot has been casting my royal horoscope. She predicts that I am to wed next and to a very beautiful princess from a land filled with sunshine. Would you like her to foretell your future, sweeting?"

Eleanor considered for a moment, holding her head on one side. Actually she hadn't thought beyond her wedding. Marrying William Marshal had been an end in itself. The woman's eyes were strange, with the subtle cloudiness of opals. Her voice when she spoke was deep and commanding. "You do not love lightly. Love will dominate your life. It will become a fine madness, an obsession. Love will drive you to take holy vows; love will force you to choose between it and living death. Your steps will lead you to the yawning abyss. On the other side stands a war lord, a warrior god. He is a giant who towers over other men in all ways. He will be England's hero, godlike to the masses and barons alike. You will deny him again and again, but he will laugh at your protests. He will conspire with Fate itself to make you lovers. He shall always emerge victorious. He will be your strength and your weakness, your wisdom and your folly, your hero and your god! His hair will be black as a witch's cat, his eyes like black obsidian."

The soothsayer's spell was broken when Eleanor began to giggle. "Dame Margot, you were right about everything save the color of my true love's hair." Eleanor swept her hand toward the man who approached carrying a large silver jug. "My lord earl, you are just in time to have your future told."

William frowned, wondering what the devil Henry was up to, filling her head with nonsense.

Dame Margot looked at the marshal and fancied she saw the finger of Death reach out from the grave to mark him. Her strange eyes became hooded, and she passed on to the next table where a group of expensively gowned dowagers were likely to treat her predictions with the respect they deserved.

William filled two goblets with the chilled fruit juice and offered a toast to his child bride. He smiled as his youngest sister Isabella danced past.

"Isabella is the Countess of Gloucester, but where is the earl?" she asked.

"Young de Clare is fighting in Ireland. I shall have to join him shortly."

Eleanor watched William's sister intently. "She's the beauty of the family; I like her best."

"Do you?" asked Will, an idea forming in his mind. What a perfectly wonderful example Isabella would set for Eleanor. His sisters had been brought up so strictly. Though she was barely twenty, Isabella was a mature young matron with all the virtues—sweet, pious, modest, meek, obedient, unworldly. He decided to ask her to join Eleanor's household at Windsor until her husband returned.

Eleanor wasn't the only Plantagenet to notice Isabella's beauty. Richard, Duke of Cornwall, asked her to dance and refused to take no for an answer. As he twirled her about, he was mesmerized by the way her delicious chestnut ringlets bounced across her bared shoulders and by the sweet curve of her breasts through the fine fabric of her gown. The way Richard devoured her with his eyes made her quite breathless. He said hungrily, "I would like to see more of you," and she blushed hotly at the double entendre.

"Your Highness, I'm a married lady," she murmured, lowering her lashes lest he see the excitement in her eyes.

"What the devil does that have to do with us, Isabella?" he asked huskily.

A little sigh escaped her lips, then she gasped loudly when his thumbs brushed across the swell of her breasts as his hands rested at her waist. He tried to lead her into an alcove of the hall.

"We mustn't!" she protested breathlessly.

"Darling, we must," he insisted boldly.

Isabella found the king's brother irresistible tonight. He was extremely young, but he was certainly proving himself to be all man, she thought as she saw the swollen bulge of him from beneath her lashes.

He knew that she had seen. "Every inch of me responds to you," he whispered hotly.

A little moan escaped her lips and swiftly he bent his mouth to hers to take it into himself. At such an intimate gesture she melted against him for a moment, unable to help herself. "Your Highness, you mustn't do this in public," she protested, trying to restore a respectable distance between them.

"In private then?" he urged.

"It is impossible," she said, low.

"Difficult but not impossible," he insisted, his eyes fixed on her soft pink mouth. "I know Westminster intimately," he drawled huskily. "Trust me to find us a trysting couch."

She stiffened instantly and stepped back, shocked. The flirtation had been daring, even arousing, but fear flickered across her pretty face. "Your Highness, you mistake me. It is impossible because I am married . . . and a lady . . . not a scullery maid to ease your lust."

"Forgive me, Isabella, but I'm not sure what I feel for you is lust. Is what you feel lust?" he asked bluntly.

"No, of course not!" she said indignantly.

His thumb stroked her wrist. "Your tiny pulse is hammering, your cheek holds the blush of an early rose . . . you are panting, Isabella."

Her lashes swept to her cheeks at her own immodesty, and Richard quickly drew her into a deeply shadowed window embrasure. "Richard . . ."

"Ah, you finally said my name." He brought his lips to hers again.

A tiny sob broke from her and her hands pushed against his broad shoulders. It was an agony to want something and not want it at the same time. His strong hands slipped behind her and firmly brought the lower part of her body to meet his. His swollen manhood pressed into her soft belly and he rubbed against her slowly, rhythmically.

She dare not bring her hands down to his groin to push that part of him away, but braced them instead against his chest. He

was building to a delicious peak against her and could tell by
the way her lips fell open that she was beginning to respond.

By virtue of the bride's tender years there had been no innu-
endos, titillating remarks, or sly winks tossed about as there
were at most wedding celebrations. Neither had the occasion
degenerated into a drunken baccanalia. Promptly at nine
o'clock Eleanor's old nursemaid collected her for bed. She was
surprised that the child made no protest for she knew from
experience that bedtime could be a battle of wills.

William lifted his bride's fingers to his lips and said solemnly,
"Good night, Countess."

She curtsied prettily. "Good night, my lord earl." She was
almost to the top of the staircase where two more maids stood
waiting with candles to light her to bed, when she said to her
nurse, "Will we be sleeping in my chamber, or has a special one
been prepared for the bride and groom?"

The shocked look on her nurse's face puzzled her, but she
didn't expect the slap. "Such wanton words from a child!" the
old servant said repressively. "The marshal is leaving for one of
his own residences."

"No!" cried Eleanor, whirling about and running back down
the marble steps. She saw with her own eyes that the marshal
was preparing to depart. At the top of her voice she shouted,
"My lord husband, don't leave me!"

All eyes swung up to her just as the nurse grabbed her most
ungently. Eleanor's little teeth swiftly bit down until the re-
straining hands were loosed. She ran headlong down the remaining steps, neatly eluding Henry's outstretched arms, and
began pushing her way through the startled guests toward her
goal. "William! William!"

Henry's long legs caught up with her in three strides, and he
scooped her up in firm arms. "Stop it, Maggot," he hissed in
her ear.

She struggled frantically. "William, if you leave, I am going
with you!"

William was discomfited that the child was making a scene.
Henry was handing her over to half a dozen servants, and he
thought it best if he did not interfere. Eleanor was crying inco-

herently now. She was on the verge of hysterics as the numerous hands tried to restrain her.

"William, you p-promised," she screamed. "You promised to show me how to st-stick it in!"

A shocked silence descended upon the hall and then a lone titter was heard. William Marshal was angry now. He strode down the hall toward the distraught Eleanor and her brother, the King of England. "Has no one had the decency to explain matters to the child?" he demanded.

Henry shrugged and the old nursemaid looked at him blankly. William gave them quelling looks and extracted Eleanor from the grip of two servants. He set her feet to the floor, placed her small hand on his arm, and said, "Come, Countess, I shall escort you to your chamber."

Teardrops hung on her dark lashes like diamonds as she gazed up at William from the edge of the bed.

"Sweeting, because of your age you cannot come to live with me. Not until you are older," he explained gently.

"You mean next month when I turn ten?" she asked hopefully.

"No . . . not until you are a grown woman . . . at least sixteen."

She looked at him with wounded eyes. "You don't love me. You don't want me," she whispered.

"Eleanor, of course I want you. The time will pass very quickly. You are to live at Windsor and have your own household. You have so many things to learn before you can become a wife. Your days will be filled with lessons. You will be surrounded by teachers and tutors and nuns."

She looked horrified. "Like my grandmother Eleanor . . . her husband imprisoned her too. My name is a curse!"

"Eleanor . . ."

She recoiled. "Don't call me that!"

William bit his lip to summon patience. "Your grandparents, King Henry and Eleanor of Aquitaine, had a great love story. I shall instruct your tutors to teach you history accurately." He went down on his knees before her to appeal to her. "You are the Countess of Pembroke . . . *my countess.* I want you to be the most accomplished countess England ever saw. I want you to sit a horse superbly, to be able to converse in fluent French, to entertain the crowned heads of Europe. I want you to learn law so that you may sit beside me when I hold courts of dispute. I want you to learn Gaelic so that when we go to Wales and Ireland, the people will love and respect you." He paused to search her face, to see if his suggestions were being comprehended.

They were. "Oh, my lord earl, I shall strive to become perfect so that I shall be worthy of you. First I will polish my reading and writing so that we may correspond and you may judge for yourself the progress I shall make," she promised fervently.

Lord God, how impassioned the child was. "Your older sisters are both gone to be queens and I don't want them to outshine you. You mustn't think of Windsor as a prison. It is a beautiful castle with walled gardens and a great forested park for hunting. Henry is doing much building there so that when he marries it will be a great king's residence. You won't be isolated and lonely there."

"But I shall be surrounded by adults all telling me what to do from the moment I open my eyes in the morning until they order me to bed at nine o'clock."

He thought for a moment, then told her, "I am going to ask my young sister Isabella to come and stay with you until her husband returns."

Eleanor sniffed and wiped her sleeve across her nose. "She's pretty, but she's quite old."

"She's only twenty." Lord God, if she thought Isabella old, she must think him in his dotage. A man of forty wedding a child not yet ten! The whole thing was a farce. Decisively he said, "You shall have some companions your own age. Some little maids of good family."

"May I choose them myself?" she begged.

"Well . . ." He hesitated. "I will select six or eight suitable families and you may choose the three you like best."

"Oh, a mutual decision! See how well we shall deal together, William?"

He let out a relieved sigh. Eleanor Plantagenet could be handled if one used a velvet glove. His eyes crinkled in an indulgent smile. He unfastened his black doublet to bare his chest. Then he lifted her to stand on the bed so that they were the same height. He took her fingers in his big hand and traced his well-muscled ribs. "Right here between the third and fourth rib is a very good place to stick in your sword. It goes straight in to puncture the lung." He raised her fingers to beneath his arm. "Feel that soft fleshy part in the armpit? A downward plunge almost always produces a mortal wound."

He saw the tip of her tongue between her little white teeth as she concentrated on the lesson. He drew her hand to the center of his wide chest until she felt the heavy beat of his heart. "If you drive your sword home here, it is always fatal," he promised solemnly.

"Oh, my lord earl, I do love you!"

3

William Marshal couldn't quite rid himself of a sense of —what was it, guilt, betrayal, unease over his marriage? He had kept the same mistress for some years now until they had become like an old married couple, unremarkable in any way, yet comfortable. The disloyalty he felt, however, was not for his leman, but for the exquisite girl with whom he had fallen in love in his youth at King John's court. Jasmine de Burgh's delicate beauty and innocence had captured his heart, and if he was being truthful she was probably the reason he had never married. He laughed at his own folly. He had been but a youth and stood no chance whatsoever against the bold warrior, Falcon de Burgh, who plucked the flower the moment he had laid his lusty eyes upon her.

In his heart Will had been faithful to her all these years. Whenever he went to Ireland he visited the de Burghs, glad of the deep bond of friendship that had developed. He sighed. Falcon de Burgh had made her completely happy and given her strapping twin sons whose strong sword arms he could depend on whenever there was trouble in that fair isle.

He felt the irresistible pull of Jasmine now and knew he would not be at peace with himself until he had confessed this marriage to her and explained that his motive was due to royal pressure and politics rather than love. Before he left for Ireland, however, he paid a visit to his favorite sister, Isabella, Countess of Gloucester and Hertford.

"It seems you made a very favorable impression yesterday, Isabella," William began tentatively, knowing the sacrifice he was about to ask of her.

Isabella blushed and her lashes fluttered down to her pink cheeks. Her behavior had been disgraceful, and here was the head of the family to rebuke her. "Please, William, let me explain. I intend to return home. We'll never see each other again."

William could not hide his disappointment. "Ah, my dear, that is a pity. Eleanor took such a liking to you that I promised you'd stay at Windsor with her until Gilbert returns from Ireland, but if you wish to return home, you shall do so."

Isabella lifted her lashes. "Windsor?" she asked breathlessly. "Oh, I should like it above all things!"

Will cocked a puzzled brow at the usually sensible young matron who'd just done an about-face. What contrary creatures women were. "Eleanor insists upon having some companions of her own age so I thought you could round up some of the Marshal children and let her make her own selection. She has a mind of her own, to put it mildly, I'm afraid."

"A Plantagenet trait," Isabella said, a secret smile touching her lips.

"Well, I thought that since they are all in London at the moment you could gather together a flock of our little nieces before the Bigods leave for Norfolk and the de Ferrars leave for Derby," Will suggested.

"I'll dash off messages immediately. Eve de Braose and Margery de Lacy are the right age, but then we must not forget Matilda, Sybil, or little Joan."

"You are a wonder. I can't keep them all straight," he confessed, "but I see I can leave it all in your capable hands. What message shall I give your husband?"

"My husband?" she repeated, blushing again. "You are off to Ireland then?" She tossed her chestnut curls. "He spends so much time there I've forgotten what he looks like."

"Poor Isabella. Shall I send him home to you then?"

"No, no," she said quickly, for her husband had been her family's choice, not hers. "De Clare would not be pleased to be sent home to his wife, and I'm looking forward to my sojourn at Windsor."

Eleanor stood in her beautifully appointed reception room at Windsor Castle surrounded by a group of young girls garbed in their finest gowns and jeweled caps. She stared quite rudely at each in her turn, quickly eliminating the only one who was darkly pretty and two others who looked younger than herself. Joan de Munchensi burst into tears. Eleanor knew she did the right thing in eliminating her for she wanted no babies to spoil the little bit of fun she would be allowed.

She sweetly thanked Lady Isabella and said without a trace of guile, "Wouldn't you like to see the new additions Henry and Richard have designed? I think I saw my brother ride in a short while ago. Take your time while I make my choice." Eleanor knew she wouldn't be alone long; a servant, a tutor, or a bloody nun spied on her every waking moment.

She stared at the Marshal nieces. "Do you know how to swear?" she demanded of them.

The little girls all shook their heads in instant denial.

"Well, that's too bad . . . I shan't pick anyone who can't swear," she announced firmly.

Two of them laughed nervously; two others looked as if they were about to burst into tears.

Eleanor looked at the golden-haired one who had laughed. "What's your name?"

The girl curtsied beautifully. "Eve de Braose."

"Swear," ordered Eleanor.

"Damn," said Eve, taking her courage in both hands.

Eleanor's eyes traveled to another pale-haired contender. "And you are?" she asked.

"Matilda Bigod," she answered without a curtsy.

Eleanor's eyes narrowed. "The Earl of Norfolk's daughter? Don't you know any swearwords?"

The girl shook her head firmly.

"Then you must be witless. Your name is a swearword. Matilda B'God," she punned.

Sybil de Ferrars, the Earl of Derby's child, giggled.

Eleanor swung on her expectantly and she blurted, "H-hell."

What a sorry lot, Eleanor thought. Her eyes swept up and down the tallest girl in the room who had coppery red hair and a cheeky face. She knew instinctively this one could swear. "I choose you," Eleanor said without hesitation.

"You can't," said a little mousy creature. "I'm Margery de Lacy. She's only my maid, Brenda."

Eleanor took a threatening step toward Margery. "I am the Countess of Pembroke. I believe I outrank you, even though the de Lacys are noted for their arrogance." She turned a shoulder upon Margery and said to the maid, "Swear."

The girl, who looked at least twelve, said, "Fuck!"

Eleanor gasped with shock, then she turned back to Margery de Lacy. "I suppose I shall have to pick *you* in order to get *her.*" She made her selection swiftly then. "I'll also take Sybil and Eve," she said, not really thinking much of any of them save the precocious copper-haired maid.

Matilda Bigod looked relieved that she had not been chosen to serve the tyrant. When the doors to the reception room were opened to admit a gaggle of chaperons and nuns, she decided to put the ladies wise as to what kind of wickedness seethed in the breast of the youngest Plantagenet.

Lady Isabella did not return for over an hour, but the fresh air must have been most beneficial because when she came to gather up Eleanor's rejects her color was high and her eyes sparkled like stars.

Will Marshal had dined sumptuously at Portumna Castle, the main stronghold of the de Burghs of Connaught. They ruled everything west of the River Shannon while William owned most of Leinster and was justiciar of the whole country. Conditions were relatively peaceful now in Ireland. Of course there would always be clan wars and large pockets of resistance to be put down, but at least the whole country was not in flaming rebellion. That was amazing, considering the untamed nature of the Irish.

Will Marshal gazed across the table at Jasmine, mesmerized as always by her delicate features, lavender eyes, and hair the color of moonbeams. She looked not one day older than the first time he had glimpsed her and lost his heart. Perhaps it was because she was a witch and had the power; now that her grandmother, Dame Estelle Winwood, had passed on to the next world, her power was probably even stronger.

The glow from the candles made a nimbus about her, enhancing her ethereal beauty. Will remembered how irrationally angry he had felt when he learned she had given birth to twin sons, thinking the fragile flower could never survive such an ordeal, but now all he felt for those splendid young men was envy that they were not his sons. They were made in the mold of Falcon de Burgh, dark and strong-limbed, yet their laughing faces were handsomer, not having the darkly forbidding features of their father. It was almost impossible to tell them apart, save that Michael had lavender eyes, while Rickard's blazed with the same green fire as his father's.

They had an insatiable thirst for knowledge of England and had plied William with questions of the king, court, barons, politics, and even its women all through the meal. Finally Jasmine's voice raised in protest. "Enough! You've behaved like louts, monopolizing Will all evening. You act as if you're straight out of the bog . . . uncivilized pair."

Rickard grinned wickedly. "That's because we haven't been polished at court, Mother."

The twins excused themselves, knowing William Marshal would be generous enough to spend the next week answering their questions.

"You walked right into that remark, Jassy," Falcon de Burgh said with amusement. They rose from the table and Jasmine took Will's arm as the three of them repaired to the solar that overlooked the whole length of the lake, or lough, as it was called in Ireland.

"I know I can't keep them any longer. They will grow to resent me," Jasmine acknowledged.

"If only they realized what they have here," Will said, throwing out his arm to indicate the unparalleled vista. "It's like a Palatinate. They live like young princes, with total freedom and without the corruption of the English court. When they fought for me in Offaly last year I knew they were better-trained soldiers than any of Falkes de Bréauté's mercenaries."

Falcon de Burgh poured William a horn of ale. "They must be allowed to spread their wings. They envy you and me because we fought in France and took castles in Wales. We supped with kings and queens, and now we've both married princesses." Falcon's eyes swept possessively over Jasmine. "Have no fear, when they have had a taste of England and Wales, when they have experienced for themselves the greed of the court with its petty jealousies and empty promises, they will return better and wiser men."

"You are right, of course," William said. "When they compare the two lives, they will find one infinitely inferior. They'll go into Hubert's service, of course."

"No!" Jasmine said quickly, then blushed for interfering in men's decisions.

Falcon teased, "She's had one of her visions."

Her lavender eyes darkened to a deeper shade of purple. "My reasons are tenfold! Hubert de Burgh is too ambitious. He flaunts his wealth and position. The barons bitterly resent him. Peter des Roches, the Bishop of Winchester, is a deadly enemy who won't rest until he brings him down."

William said quietly, "It was I who got rid of des Roches. He had too great a hold on the young king and had installed his relatives and creatures in all the posts of importance. He intended to control national affairs."

Falcon de Burgh said, "I agree with Jasmine. I don't want them to go into Hubert's service, though not for the same reasons. Life would be too soft for them. They would become rich and spoiled. I want them to earn preferment . . . to get their lands and castles by rendering loyal service, not receive them as gifts from an indulgent uncle." Falcon grimaced. "I hear now that he is married to Princess Margaret of Scotland they travel about with a long train of knights, men-at-arms, scriveners, confessors, body servants, cooks, barbers, and bloody jugglers —ass-kissers, all."

"Well"—William laughed—"perhaps his train doesn't quite run to acrobats. His influence on Henry and Richard is infinitely preferable to that of Peter des Roches, whose first loyalty will always be Rome. Because of the money owed to the Vatican, the Bishop of Winchester allowed the Pope's representatives to come into England to supervise the collection of funds. The money is paid through Italian banking houses. Florentine financiers have set up moneylending businesses all over London. Almost too late I discovered every church appointment that paid a fat living went to an Italian. There are actually canons who haven't bothered to leave Rome. They were paying clerks starvation wages, and my investigations revealed that over seventy thousand marks had left the country. Meanwhile the king's coffers are empty. England has been drained of money by war debts, Crusades, and greedy foreigners."

"What manner of man has Henry turned out to be?" Jasmine asked.

"That's his trouble, I think. He isn't yet a man though he is nigh eighteen. He's too easily influenced. He is addicted to favorites; luckily it's Hubert at the moment. Oh, he's not cruel and wantonly destructive as his father was, but he's selfish, willful, contemptuous of his barons and advisors, and as a king he is unskilled and unpredictable. It is a pity that Richard wasn't the eldest son. He is a finer man in every way. He's a good soldier, highly intelligent, has a natural charm where Henry's is superficial. The barons look to him to influence the king to fulfill the obligations of his office. Richard also has a genius for building . . ." He broke off, laughing. "I've talked you to death. You must have been wanting to seek your chamber hours since."

Falcon de Burgh stood up and stretched his powerful limbs. "I'll go up, if you'll excuse me, though I'm sure Jasmine has lots more questions for you."

When they were alone she leaned toward him. "Will, is this marriage what you want?"

"No," he admitted. "Oh, Jasmine, I have such a deep fear Eleanor will be like her mother when she grows up."

"I believe your fears are groundless . . . she's never known her mother's influence." They looked at each other, not voicing their inner fears of tainted blood and what was bred in the bone.

Will sighed. "I've insisted she have her own household. Ladies' quarters have been established at Windsor and she's to be constantly chaperoned. I've provided the best tutors and teachers. She even has nuns and Franciscans in her household."

"You are footing the bills for the entire upkeep of Windsor Castle, no doubt?"

"And the Order of St. Bride's." He shrugged. "I would spend any amount of gold to keep her chaste."

Poor little girl, she thought. Jasmine's hand sought Will's. "Don't leave her there too long. The best possible influence on her would be you yourself, Will." She paused. "I would like you to take my sons into your service, Will."

He was almost undone at the great trust she placed in him. "You honor me, lady," he murmured huskily.

"Always," she said, going on tiptoe to kiss him good night.

De Burgh lay stretched on the bed, his arms behind his head. He slept naked and had taught Jasmine to do the same. The green flame in his eyes licked over her curves as she began to undress. "He's in love with you, you know," he murmured.

"Will? Don't be ridiculous. We've been friends since we were at court together." Before she removed her chemise, she picked up her hairbrush.

"Let me do that," he ordered. She came to the bed and absently handed him the brush. The moment his hands tangled in the silken mass of her hair, his erection started. "He loved you then and he loves you now."

She half turned to look deeply into his eyes. "Surely you're not jealous of Will?"

"Oh, I'm jealous all right. Jealous of every man who dares look at you, but strangely I'm not jealous of Will. The poor honorable bastard tries so hard to conceal his love from you."

"He's different from you. He doesn't simply reach out his hand to take what he wants."

Falcon de Burgh made short work of the chemise. "Splendor of God, if I were in his shoes I'd have you on your back in a minute."

"Would you indeed? I seem to recall it took you longer than a minute to have your perverted way with me."

"I'll show you perverted," he said, dipping his head between her legs and running his tongue up the inside of her thigh.

"It will take more than that to thaw me," she teased icily.

"No, it won't," he said with masculine conceit as he spread her center apart with his thumbs and licked the tiny bud inside the soft folds.

She felt herself begin to melt, but didn't want to give in to him so easily. "Stop, I think I'm going to faint."

"I'll make you faint, by God," he promised, thrusting his hot tongue deep inside her.

After a few minutes of such delicious intimate play, it was not nearly enough for Jasmine. "Falcon, Falcon." She knew the cry would bring his mouth up to hers. He loved to taste his name upon her lips. Her fingers slipped down his hard body to encircle his shaft, and she gasped at its size. It never failed to elicit a delicious quiver of fear. He thrust into her hot, wet center, stretching her to the limit, and she went wild with the unbelievable fullness he created inside her. His tongue filled her sweet mouth, moving in rhythm with his hips, and she wrapped her long, slim legs high about his back. Over the years they had learned how to make it last and sustain their pleasure endlessly.

When Jasmine cried out from her release, William Marshal convinced himself it was the cry of a night bird upon the moon-bathed lough.

4

Eleanor Katherine developed an unquenchable thirst for learning. She practiced her writing far into the night until her companions begged her to snuff the candles. The blotted pages she produced gave her such a disgust of herself that she doggedly persevered until her words flowed across the page in beautiful script. Only then did she begin to correspond with her beloved husband.

She was superstitious about the name Eleanor, preferring to be addressed as Countess of Pembroke, but sometimes she went for weeks answering only to her second name, Kathe.

She had a natural ability to learn languages. She soon mastered French, leaving her companions struggling far behind, while she studied Gaelic with one of the Irish nuns. She devoured history and developed a fascination for religion, realizing that the latter had played a paramount role along the path of history, shaping and molding it, sometimes for better, more often for worse. The Mother Superior of St. Bride's began to visit with her, passing on theology and her wealth of nursing skills and knowledge of medicinal herbs. She was a stern, nononsense woman who scoffed at the physicians and the quacks who came to London in noisy droves. She pointed out to Eleanor that only ignorance could account for hanging red curtains about the bed of a smallpox victim, placing coral in the mouth to cure heart problems, or hanging asses' hoofs about the legs to cure gout.

The rich were given powdered pearls, emerald dust, or finely ground gold, and Mother Superior told Eleanor in no uncertain terms the jewels would do the patient more good if they were donated to the church. Eleanor disagreed with Mother Superior on one point. The nun believed that all major ailments came from God and it was sacrilege to interfere, so the two of them enjoyed many lively arguments.

She was soon allowed to be tutored by the Franciscan, Adam Marsh, whenever he visited with Henry. The learned monk soon realized Eleanor's intellect put the king's in the shade.

She learned to play the harp and the lute and to imitate Lady Isabella Marshal's exquisite manners and pretty gestures. William Marshal supplied them with the finest Thoroughbreds from Ireland and falcons and hawks from Wales, and whenever Richard returned from Cornwall, they joined him in the hunt.

As Richard's visits became more frequent, Lady Isabella had begged Eleanor never to leave the two alone. Eleanor realized Isabella loved Richard and sympathized with her lovely companion's plight. Like her own love for William, it must remain unrequited. A lady's reputation must be without blemish. In fact, the very first lesson Eleanor's nuns and chaperons instilled in her was that, without virginity, a girl had no value for marriage. Her husband would repudiate her, ruining her, if he found her unpure.

And so it was that the Countess of Pembroke grew into young womanhood with a vast knowledge of the world, yet not worldly in any way. She grew up innocent and ignorant of all venal matters. In fact, she was the antithesis of her mother at the same age. The only things Queen Isabella had passed along to her youngest child was her breathtaking beauty and an inordinate love of elegant, exquisite clothes in vibrant colors, encrusted with silvery thread or precious gems. Luckily her husband's wealth allowed her the luxury of acquiring anything her heart desired.

* * *

The day Henry turned eighteen he called a special meeting of the council and presided over it. He announced he would assume the full powers of his kingship. Hubert de Burgh, who had been regent up to this day, wisely decided not to earn the king's hatred by thwarting him. In return Henry made him Earl of Kent and told him to set about filling the royal coffers. As a result all owners of land and castles by royal patent were ordered to bring their proofs to Westminster to secure confirmation. A fee was charged and Henry stood to raise a hundred thousand pounds by this plan.

The great barons of England were unhappy and blamed Hubert de Burgh. The Tower of London was in Hubert's hands, and he had resided there a good deal of the time, but now he built a palatial residence that he called Whitehall on a valuable piece of property close to Westminster. He was castellan of every important castle in England—Dover, Canterbury, Rochester, and Norwich. The king gave into his care the great towns of Carmarthen, Cardigan, and Montgomery along the Welsh border. He was sheriff of seven counties that oversaw everything from inquests to tax collection and the revenues came into his enormous purse.

The barons grumbled louder. Hubert blithely ignored them and provided Henry with money to build additions to the Tower of London. They added the Water Gate, the Cradle Tower where Hubert's baby daughter resided, and The Lantern, a new bedchamber for Hubert with a magnificent view of the river. It kept the king's mind from the frustration of his wedding plans. First he had been turned down by the Austrian princess and then by the Princess of Bohemia. He was now considering the Princess of Provence and asked his brother Richard to go and take a look at her, for he was a connoisseur of beautiful women.

When he realized that his reputation for being tightfisted was ruining his chances for procuring a bride, Henry made an effort to pay the dowry still owed to Germany. In return his brother-in-law, the Emperor of Germany, gifted him with three leopards. With them came the idea to create a menagerie at the Tower of London.

*   *   *

Being the premier Marcher Lord of Wales kept William Marshal busy, and the de Burgh twins soon learned that the Welsh were every bit the wild barbarians that the Irish were. William owned vast holdings in Wales. His principal county of Pembroke overlooking the Irish Sea was administered by Welshmen totally loyal to him. The twins were greatly impressed by William's Welsh archers and immediately took lessons to become proficient with the longbow. They were able to inspect their father's castles of Mountain Ash, Skenfrith, and Llantilio. Their uncle Hubert, whom they had favorably impressed, asked them to inspect his new acquisitions at Cardigan and Carmarthen and to give him full reports on the strongholds.

Within the first year they had earned their knighthoods; within the second they had Welsh castles of their own to command. The high craggy cliffs of the County of Pembroke were only a spitting distance across St. George's Channel from William Marshal's Irish holdings in Leinster, and it was nothing for these rugged men to quell an uprising in Ireland and put down insurgence in Wales within the same month.

It was years before Rickard and Mick de Burgh finally set foot in London. Because they were closely connected to Hubert and were among William Marshal's best captains, Henry welcomed them with open arms, hoping to lure them into his own service.

The king insisted his newly returned marshal must see the improvements he had made to the Tower of London. When he arrived Henry and his old comrade-in-arms Hubert proudly gave him the grand tour. Hubert had just shown off his little daughter Megotta in her Cradle Tower, then urged William to visit the menagerie.

As the men descended the stone steps, they saw a barge had just arrived at the Water Gate. Richard, Duke of Cornwall, helped a breathtaking creature adorned in red velvet edged with sable down the gangplank.

"Who is the ravishing beauty Richard is courting?" William asked with appreciation.

The king's high-pitched laugh caused the new arrivals to glance up. "William," Henry said with a laugh, "that is your wife."

Eleanor waved to Henry and called, "We've come to see the elephant." Then her eyes fell on the broad shoulders of the man beside him and her hand flew to her throat. "William," she whispered.

The river breezes snatched his name from her lips and carried it up to the stunned observer. All the other people seemed to recede. He was vaguely aware of Richard helping his sister Isabella Marshal from the barge, but William had eyes only for Eleanor. He was rooted to the spot so she came to him and sank into a graceful curtsy, which sent her velvet skirts billowing out across the gray stones. The crimson color made her seem so vibrantly alive, like an exotic bird of paradise captured for Henry's menagerie and totally out of place in cold, gray London.

"Well come, my lord," she greeted him graciously in soft tones as her deep, sapphire-blue eyes shone with joy.

"Splendor of God, Marshal, I bet you're kicking yourself for wasting your time in Wales while your bride languishes for you in London." Hubert de Burgh gave Eleanor a hearty buss on the cheek. "You are grown into a beautiful woman, my dear. You look exactly like your mother, who at one time was reputed to be the most beautiful woman in the world."

William had to stifle an urge to smash his old friend in the face. He had seen the startled shock on Eleanor's face when de Burgh had handled her, and a rush of protective feeling almost overwhelmed him.

Bluff Hubert kept at her. "How old are you now?" he asked, frankly assessing the swelling curves of her young breasts.

"Fifteen, milord, an' it please you," she said breathlessly.

"It would please any man with blood in his veins. Fifteen is just the perfect age for a bride, I always think." He nudged William suggestively.

Her lashes swept to her cheeks. She hoped William thought so too.

"That is exactly the age of my bride-to-be, Eleanor of Provence," the king announced. "We'll celebrate. Tonight you shall all dine with me at Windsor and I will show you the new wing I'm having decorated for my queen."

William raised Eleanor's hand to his lips and heard Richard

say "Lady Isabella, you must join us; you haven't had a chance to visit with your brother in years."

Isabella blushed and moved forward to kiss William. He smiled at her warmly to thank her for the exceptional job she had done with his countess.

Henry was all boyish enthusiasm as he showed them his menagerie. There were strange shaggy beasts known as buffalo, Barbary apes, lions, leopards, and finally the elephant. Henry insisted upon entering its cage to feed it an apple. "Look! Only look how it takes it to its mouth with its great trunk."

Hubert seemed quite tickled, but Richard caught the marshal's eye and shrugged apologetically as if to say "When will he grow up?"

Hubert was pleasantly surprised to be invited to dine with the king. Usually it was the other way about; Henry's nobles and the wealthier London families were expected to wine, dine, and entertain their young monarch so his own household would not have to bear the expense.

William Marshal looked on with amused tolerance as the king showed them a new diadem he had had designed for his queen-to-be, studded with precious gems at a cost of thousands of pounds. He had also ordered her a complete wardrobe with chaplets, rings, and jewel-encrusted girdles. Henry's inconsistencies were unbelievable; he pinched pennies with one hand and spent lavishly with the other.

A wedding date hadn't even been set, but the Bishop of Lincoln had been dispatched with orders to finalize the arrangements no matter how small the dowry might be. Richard had just returned from Provence and had told Henry bluntly that its ruling family was penniless, although its princesses were every bit as lovely as they were reputed to be. He warned his brother that the Provençals were grasping and so wily they had just married one beautiful princess to Louis of France without providing a dowry at all.

Henry, however, had set his mind on Eleanor, the princess they called "La Belle," and nothing would alter it. The Plantagenets were very open in front of their justiciar and marshal, realizing the two kingmakers knew every detail of their lives since they'd been born anyway.

"Where did the money for all this come from?" Richard asked, indicating the luxury of the newly furbished dining salon where they were eating.

"It isn't paid for. I went into debt," Henry said quite matter-of-factly.

"Well, how the hell do you expect to pay that debt?" Richard asked bluntly, determined to keep his own purse closed this time.

"That's Hubert's problem," said Henry, turning expectant eyes upon his justiciar.

Hubert washed down his beef with a goblet of Gascony wine and said, "Well, the wedding and coronation of the queen are perfectly legitimate expenses. I think a grant of two marks on every knight's fee of land wouldn't be unreasonable."

Richard looked quickly to William Marshal to gauge his reaction because Parliament had to agree to all taxation. "Do you think the council will agree for a queen who will come virtually empty-handed?"

"They will agree," William said shrewdly. "They will think it most advantageous to have Louis of France as brother-in-law."

Eleanor cast him a glance of admiration, and thereafter he was lost to the conversation about him. He was enthralled at the transformation that had taken place. A poetic phrase floated through his mind: Where a rose is tended, a thistle cannot grow. She had been a beautiful child, of course, but she had also been a willful, wild little animal bearing no resemblance to the graceful lady with exquisite manners and regal bearing who sat beside him, softly conversing with his sister about the country of Provence.

When she politely refused any wine, his mind flew back to their wedding day. His lips twitched with amusement as he thought she must have given up drinking since then. She drew his eyes again and again. Simply observing her gave him pleasure. He watched as she daintily dipped her fingers in a bowl of rosewater and dried them on a linen serviette.

Suddenly he realized the king had addressed him, and reluctantly he withdrew his attention from Eleanor and gave it to Henry. "The Bishop of Ferns in Ireland has written to me.

Apparently there is a dispute over land he claims your father took from him. It's a trifling matter of two manors so I think perhaps it would be expedient to give him title if only to shut the old fool up."

"Absolutely not!" said Eleanor, her sapphire eyes blazing. All heads swiveled in her direction. "How dare you ask such a thing, Henry? When you reply to the bishop inform him you cannot disregard the obligations of your office. You cannot play fast and loose with the Marshal of England who laid his life on the line repeatedly to put you on the throne; nor can you slur the memory of his great father."

Henry immediately backed down and William Marshal realized Eleanor was not simply decorative. She had a fine grasp of things and could handle the King of England as if he were an unruly puppy.

Before the hour grew late the Countess of Pembroke begged the gentlemen to excuse her. William, unwilling to part with her until the last possible moment, said, "I shall escort you to your apartment if you will permit it, my lady."

She gave him a playful look. "Ah, sir, only Franciscan monks are allowed into the ladies' quarters of Windsor; you made the rule yourself."

"Rules are made to be broken." He smiled and took hold of Isabella and Eleanor's arms.

"I shall remember that," she teased lightly.

Eleanor was small, of a height that made it necessary for her to look up to a man. It made him aware of his masculinity. William could not help but notice that her breasts were full and pointed, upward tilting. Her fragrance stole to him. He was unknowledgeable about such feminine things, but he knew he liked the scent of her. When they reached Eleanor's apartments William realized they would not be private for a moment. Females were everywhere in abundance—companions, servants, handmaids, and chaperons. Almost desperately he asked, "Would you care to ride with me tomorrow, my lady?"

"It would give me the greatest pleasure in the world, my lord." She sank down before him to bid him good night and he caught the merest glimpse of décolletage, but it was enough to arouse his manhood. Desire flared in his loins momentarily before he controlled it with an iron will. Then she was gone. The females withdrew, permitting the Marshals to speak privately.

"Have you come to take Eleanor to live with you?" Isabella asked expectantly.

William was shocked at her words. "She's only fifteen. What sort of a man do you take me for?"

"You wed me to de Clare at fifteen," she pointed out daringly.

"My dear, he was your own age. I'm past forty . . . old enough to be her father."

"You will always be that," she said softly, lowering her eyes.

Yes, thought Will, more's the pity. Then he was filled with guilt, for he no longer felt the least bit fatherly toward Eleanor.

The Countess of Pembroke pressed closely to the other side of the door listening to the words of the brother and sister. Her hand covered her mouth to prevent a sob from escaping; a lone tear slipped down her cheek. The marshal still did not want her.

5

Eleanor awoke at the crack of dawn and fought the urge to rouse the household to prepare her to ride out with William. Instead she lay quietly recalling his every feature and gesture. His light-brown hair, though clipped very short, had a boyish tendency to curl. His eyes had been warm whenever his glance had fallen upon her. Sherry, she decided; their color was definitely sherry, and she loved the way they crinkled with laugh lines when something amused him. He was stronger, wiser, more mature than other men. He had an air of quiet authority that earned him respect. She would simply die if he did not want her!

She breathed deeply to calm herself. Over the last years she had learned to mask her inner feelings. She had mastered the art of poise so that she was able to present a picture of serenity; no matter that beneath the surface of her calm, her emotions seethed passionately. When she began to grow up she had questioned why she felt so passionately about things and concluded that she was different from others. To Eleanor everything was crystal clear. Her mind was quick and decisive and she knew exactly what she wanted from life. Right and wrong were sharply defined in black and white. She did not like or dislike;

rather she loved or hated with a passion. Her feelings ran so deep that sometimes she frightened herself.

Mother Superior had schooled her to show moderation, but Eleanor never did anything by half measure. She committed fully to things . . . all or nothing . . . life or death. She determinedly pushed away the thought that William Marshal did not want her. He had no choice. They had not simply been betrothed, they had been married, and a marriage could not be broken. She set her goal. By the time she was sixteen he would take her to live with him. She would suppress every fault and strive with all her heart to become exactly what he wanted, rather than being herself.

Her mind made up, she rang for Brenda, the copper-haired maid she had stolen from Margery de Lacy. "I'm riding with my husband this morning. I know exactly what I shall wear, but I want you to help me with this bloody, unruly mass of hair." She had had to stop swearing, of course, and limited herself to cursing only in the presence of Brenda.

All night William had carried a picture of her crimson velvet skirts spreading across the gray stones. Now that picture was wiped out and replaced with the vivid image of her mounted upon a sleek, black mare. Over a white underdress she wore a brilliant emerald-green tabard slit up the sides to the armpits to permit ease in riding. Green boots and riding gloves made from soft leather matched the emerald green exactly, and her silken mass of black curls had been gathered into a gold mesh snood embroidered with emerald jewels.

William said, "You look exceeding lovely this morning, Countess. I have brought you a small token of my affection." He maneuvered his mount close and placed a small brown merlin upon her gloved wrist. "She is from our own wild mountains of Pembroke in Wales, but she has been trained to a lady's hand and will be well mannered, I trust."

"Thank you, my lord; I love presents." Eleanor removed the ornate hood then looked directly into the fierce yellow eyes of the merlin as they challenged each other. After a full minute she murmured, "The pigeons at Windsor will be tame fare for you, my beauty, but someday I shall take you back to Wales." The merlin ruffled and decided to accept Eleanor.

William smiled. When even a winged predator could not resist her, what chance had he? They rode out into the forested park of Windsor with only William's devoted squire Walter in attendance. Eleanor was overjoyed that he dismissed the usual throng of attendants mandatory whenever she rode out.

She was fiercely determined to display her riding and hunting skills, secretly thrilled that she performed for his eyes only. The speed of their horses flushed a covey of woodcock, and they removed the hoods from their hawks and flung the birds skyward. "Which bird do you consider best for hunting, my lord?" she asked.

"Well, the peregrine falcon is the fastest raptor in the entire world. Did you know it kills its prey by striking it hard with a foot balled-up like a fist?"

"No, I assumed it used its beak and talons like other predators. Why are you not flying a falcon today?" she asked curiously.

"The hunting here is unworthy of a peregrine. We'll only bag snipe and such. It's too bad owls are nocturnal; they are much better hunters than hawks. Owl feathers are specially adapted so that owls can fly silently and approach their prey without warning. The leading edge of the feather is downy, which eliminates the flapping noise."

"How fascinating. I love birds, tell me more," she urged, thinking I love the way his eyes crinkle when he glances into the sun to watch his hawk.

"Well, let's see." He searched his mind for some obscure piece of trivia that she'd never heard. " 'Tis rumored that when vultures are pursued by a predator they have a unique defense. They vomit on their predator, and it is said to be so foul-smelling it spoils the appetite of their assailants."

Eleanor's trill of laughter echoed through the glade, startling birds into flight, and they cast their hawks after them.

"I like to see you laugh," William confided. "You throw back your head and let the laughter escape freely."

"Not very ladylike," Eleanor confessed.

"From my observation most ladies cover their mouths with one of those infernal trailing kerchiefs to hide their laughter."

"That, my lord, is to hide their rotten teeth, not their laughter," Eleanor said solemnly. It was William's turn to laugh. She gave him back his words. "I like to see you laugh. You throw back your head and let the laughter escape freely."

"Perhaps we are birds of a feather." He smiled, feeling happier than he had in years.

"Did you know that male and female eagles grasp each other's talons and tumble through the sky?" In that moment she longed for William and her to be eagles so they could cartwheel through space.

When she described the courtship ritual of eagles, he felt unbidden fire snake through his loins. He knew he wanted to mate with the vividly beautiful creature who rode at his side. Yet he also knew he must protect her from his lust until she was old enough to become his wife in more than name.

He felt quite guilty that she had been kept a virtual prisoner at her brother's castle of Windsor for years. It had been necessary while she was still a child, but now that she was almost a woman grown, she should have her own manor and household as befitted the Countess of Pembroke. He owned such vast estates that it would be most ungenerous of him if he did not deed one to her. Keeping her penned up to preserve her innocence would be selfish of him. That had already been accomplished, and now she deserved a taste of freedom. He decided to go over the smaller estates with his land steward and choose something within easy riding distance of Windsor and London.

They had enjoyed each other's company immensely, and he was once again loath to let her go. "I should like it very much if you joined me on a visit to one of my estates. Do you think you could be ready three days hence, my lady?"

"Oh, yes, my lord," she breathed, excited. "In fact, I could be ready in two."

William laughed happily. "Two days it shall be then." When they handed their birds back to the falconer, William helped her dismount. "You are an accomplished horsewoman, my lady."

"On our wedding day you made me promise to sit a horse superbly." Then she repeated word for word the things he had asked of her almost six years before.

A lump came into William's throat when he realized how

seriously she had taken his suggestions to heart. She had fervently dedicated years to master the things that would please him. He felt unworthy. He also felt his years weigh heavy. How intense and enthusiastic the young could be.

After great deliberation he decided upon Odiham, twenty miles south of Windsor. It would be impractical to leave a large garrison of men-at-arms there, but he must make certain that the Countess of Pembroke and her household were adequately protected when she was in residence. With this in mind he selected Rickard de Burgh for the task along with half a dozen of his best men and dispatched them to Odiham with messages for the steward. It would be an easy assignment for them after the fighting in Ireland and Wales.

William brought yet another gift for his countess for her journey to Odiham. It was an ornamental harness and saddle of black Spanish leather, chased with silver. Rows of tiny silver bells hung from the bridle and stirrups. It caused a stir of admiration in the stables as Eleanor's groom Toby saddled her mare.

Although Eleanor had not invited her ladies-in-waiting, but took only her maid Brenda and Isabella's maid, the party traveling to Odiham began to swell as Richard discovered Isabella was going and invited himself along. He took only his squire and page, since William's escort was a company of Welsh archers captained by Sir Michael de Burgh. Richard was in high spirits. Who knows, he thought, perhaps his beloved would yield to him tonight if Eleanor and William had eyes only for each other. God's tears, it had been an eternity since they had been intimate. He rode up beside William and winked at him. "I hope you don't mind my intrusion on this romantic little jaunt, but who better to play chaperon than brother of the bride?"

William flushed. He had had nothing indiscreet in mind and opened his mouth to protest, but Richard winked suggestively and laughed. "Don't worry, my lord earl, I won't play gooseberry." William was relieved when Richard fell back to ride with Isabella.

Eleanor wore striking black and white. The bells on her harness tinkled musically as she came up to ride at her husband's side. "Thank you for the lovely present, my lord. I must be psychic to have chosen this matching outfit. Or perhaps we are beginning to communicate without words."

Will's cheeks warmed. He certainly hoped not. The lusty thoughts she provoked whenever she drew nigh would have made her flee from him in shock. Only last night he had dreamed of her the moment he fell asleep. Probably because he was anticipating their ride today, except in his dream she sat before him. The wind caused her hair to blow and brush against his cheek. Then her warm breath had touched his throat. He remembered he had kissed the eyelids that covered her jewel eyes. It was so sweet and pleasurable, he wished it could have continued through the night.

It did not, however. It was replaced by a second dream, which he remembered now with discomfort. That dream had been hot, sexual, explicit. He had taken her maidenhead, and her cries of pain were soon replaced by cries of pleasure as she writhed beneath him. He felt shame for his lust for a fifteen-year-old girl.

He quickly changed the subject. "You did not bring your ladies along. I assure you Odiham is large enough to accommodate them."

"Eve de Braose and Margery de Lacy are leaving me to be married. They are busy with wedding plans at the moment. Fortunately I've inherited Margery's maid, Brenda, who has elected to remain in my service."

William could hardly credit his little nieces were to be wed. "Eve and Margery are children," he protested.

"They are my age," Eleanor said pointedly. "Their mothers —your sisters—certainly think they are old enough to become wives, if you do not."

Now that he thought about it, he realized he'd given his approval for the matches, but he also recalled their bridegrooms were no more than sixteen.

Behind them Isabella wore a worried frown. "Richard, your boldness terrifies me," she murmured. "If my brother suspects your motives, I will die of shame."

"And I will die of night starvation if you don't yield to me soon. I won't make do with servants and sluts any longer."

"If I yield to you whenever you will, I too may be branded a slut!" she hissed, tossing her pretty chestnut curls.

"Not by me, my heart's desire," he coaxed lovingly.

Farther down the line Brenda had big eyes for Sir Michael de Burgh. Mick was aware of the copper-haired wench's hot glances, and he was not impervious to the invitation he saw writ plainly in those eyes. The darkly handsome knight rode between Richard's squire and Eleanor's groom Toby, who grinned at each other knowingly as if they shared some secret knowledge.

"All right, you two, what's the jest?" Mick demanded good-naturedly.

"Shall we warn him for his own good?" asked Richard's squire, Geoffrey.

"Let him learn the *hard* way, no pun intended. It brings the male conceit down a notch or two." Toby laughed.

"This concerns the fiery wench with the luscious tits, I presume," Mick said.

"She devours men as if they were dessert," Geoffrey said.

"If she had as many pricks sticking out of her as she's had stuck in her, she'd look like a porcupine!" Toby joked.

"An experienced wench can be rewarding." Mick grinned.

Geoffrey's tone changed and became earnest. "There's something wrong with her. She's insatiable . . . can't be satisfied."

"Well, there's a challenge, if ever I heard one," said the virile de Burgh, licking his lips.

"So we all thought until each of us took her on, followed the well-worn path to her bed, and came away almost emasculated," Toby confided.

"Even Richard couldn't give her release; he admits it quite frankly," said Richard's squire. "He had us heels in the air with laughter when he told us of the king's dilemma when she tempted him one evening. Poor Henry couldn't walk for two days, and it was a month before he had an erection again."

De Burgh was one step ahead of his companions. "A wager," he proposed. "Five gold crowns for both of you if she isn't replete and sated by morning. She'll be the one who won't be able to walk."

They took the bet knowing it was the easiest money they'd

ever make. Mick de Burgh slackened the pace of his destrier until the ladies' maids rode up beside him, then he bestowed a speculative smile upon Brenda.

"You are Rick de Burgh," she said huskily, mentally measuring the bulging muscles of his thighs.

"Mick," he corrected, caressing her breasts with his eyes.

"I don't suppose you could bribe the castellan of Odiham to let me have a chamber of my own, do you, Mick?" she asked, her eyes sliding all over him.

"That very thought was uppermost in my mind, sweetheart," he assured her.

William heard the high spirits of his young knights who were only half his age and for the first time in his life he envied them.

The twenty miles from Windsor were soon swallowed up by the travelers, and in less than two hours the pretty turrets of Odiham manor house came into view. It was surrounded by apple orchards whose trees were just budding into blossom. William knew immediately that Eleanor was entranced by it. Her deep-blue eyes sparkled when she was happy and excited, and he wished in that moment he could make them sparkle like that for the rest of her life.

All was in readiness when the master arrived. The housekeeper had set the maids to cleaning and polishing from dawn 'til dusk as soon as young Rickard de Burgh had brought the marshal's message. The steward had brought up the best wines from the cellars and selected two barrels of ale from the small brewhouse. The grooms cleaned the stables and spread fresh straw and hay for the horses. Since there was little for Rickard de Burgh and his men to do save polish their armor and sharpen their weapons, they had gone hunting.

The venison turned on spits alongside lambs and the aroma of roasting pheasant floated across Odiham's flagstoned courtyard to whet all appetites. Before the steward had assigned rooms to all the illustrious visitors, he was richer by several pieces of gold. Not only had Rickard de Burgh's twin brother bribed him to give a saucy maid a small, private tower room that opened onto the parapets, but the king's brother, Richard of Cornwall, had made it worth his while to plenish a large chamber apart from the other females for Lady Isabella Marshal. The steward shook his head at the irony of it. The master and mistress who were legally wed were accommodated in separate chambers.

The household servants of Odiham were well trained. Cool drinks were the first order of business for the dusty travelers, and hot bath water was the next. Mick de Burgh took himself off to the knights' quarters to look for his brother. He thumped Odiham's new captain of the guard with a massive fist and teased, "By the Blood of God, you've got a soft touch here."

Rickard grinned. "Nothing to do save hunt and dice."

Mick grinned back. "I'm glad you're well rested, little brother; have I got a wench for us!"

Eleanor had five maids eager to do her bidding. One tended her bath, another brushed her hair, a third unpacked her clothes and hung them in the woodruff-scented wardrobe. A fourth brought her a luncheon tray with tempting hot meat pasties and a silver dish of early strawberries and cream. They were all dressed alike in gray uniforms with crisp white aprons and lace caps.

They whispered with delight over the countess's beautiful gowns and undergarments. Eleanor had exquisite taste in clothes and knew exactly the vivid shades to wear to enhance her dark beauty. After her bath she chose a peach-colored afternoon dress and tied a matching satin ribbon around her curls in an effort to keep them in order.

William knocked on her chamber door and the maids ushered him in with giggles, then quickly left in a flurry of curtsies claiming pressing duties elsewhere. He raised her fingers to his mouth and brushed his lips across them. "You are so unearthly fair, it takes my breath away," he murmured.

She dimpled, longing for him to put his strong arms about her.

"Come, I'll give you a tour of the manor; it's bigger than it first appears." He retained her hand in his and Eleanor was content. The outbuildings, though small and compact, were numerous. There was a brewhouse, a dairy stillroom, a laundry, a smithy and weapons room, even a small chapel.

William showed her the neat rows of herbs in the kitchen

garden, then led her through the formal rose garden and out into the orchards where little round hives housed the honeybees that pollinated the apple blossoms. She followed his finger as he pointed up to the crenellated roof and guard towers. He showed her the dog kennel where the hounds were kept penned and even took her to a loft above the stables where the hunting birds were housed. "Well, what do you think of it?" he asked seriously, watching her very closely for her reaction.

"I love it. Odiham is quite perfect, I think." She knew that anywhere on earth would be perfect if only William was there with her.

"Come up on the parapets and I'll show you the view," he invited. Once there he stood behind her, lightly resting a strong brown hand on her shoulder. With his other arm he pointed out the various landmarks close by, then he made a wide arc. "Directly to the south is the sea. You can smell the tidewrack if you breathe deeply, and over to the west is Salisbury Plain . . . there where it's so flat, and beyond is Stonehenge."

"How fascinating. I've learned all about it." She looked up at him over her shoulder. "Will you take me to see it sometime?"

He drew her back against him and dropped a kiss on the top of her head. "I would like to take you everywhere and show you everything . . ." His voice trailed off.

Eleanor finished the thought for him. "But you do not have time. Your duties as Marshal of England leave you no time for life's pleasures. I wish it were otherwise, my lord. I wish we could fly away where no one could find us . . . where we could be completely alone and I didn't have to share you with anyone else."

Her impassioned words flattered him beyond measure. From behind he enfolded her in his arms and said against her cheek, "We have this day."

Eleanor would have liked to stay clasped to him forever, but he released her almost instantly and led her downstairs to the great hall. He dispatched a page to summon the entire household, and within minutes the hall filled to capacity.

"Are all your servants in all your manors and castles this well trained, my lord?"

"Oh, this place doesn't belong to me," he told her solemnly.

Her mouth formed an O of surprise, then he whispered, "It belongs to you." He raised his voice then, so that the scores of Odiham servants assembled could hear him. "I want to introduce you to the Countess of Pembroke. We will all celebrate tonight because Odiham now belongs to her. I ask that you serve her as faithfully as you have served me."

A great cheer filled the hall and Eleanor graciously acknowledged their good wishes and their homage. Tears gathered on her dark lashes and William squeezed her hand, hoping he had pleased her. She smiled her thanks to him, but inside she was crying, *William, I don't want your presents, I want you!*

The evening meal in the great hall was nothing less than a banquet. The entire household was invited to the celebration. Even the scullery maids and stableboys drank toasts to the Marshal of England and the king's sister and brother. Odiham had never seen the like. Anyone with a talent for music was encouraged to play for the merry company, then everyone began to sing. Richard's deep voice rang out.

> "Each must drain his cup of wine,
> And I the first will toss off mine."

William persuaded Eleanor that a cup of wine would not be amiss, and soon the laughter almost raised the rafters. After her second cup she seemed to see everyone about her in a different light. Her brother was enjoying himself immensely, yet she could tell he had an air of suppressed intensity about him. His eyes were fever bright with excitement over something—some knowledge or secret. Whatever it was he was hugging it to himself, savoring it. Her eyes were drawn to the knights, who were laughing and teasing the maids. There was Brenda gazing at Mick de Burgh with a look of raw hunger. She could certainly understand her attraction to the handsome Irish knight, but why in heavens name didn't the girl eat something if she was that ravenous?

Suddenly she looked at William's sister. Isabella was the only one of that whole company who was not laughing. She was preoccupied, biting her lips, worried to death about something. Perhaps she didn't approve of William giving away Marshal holdings. Perhaps she didn't want William to take his wife away from Windsor to live with him. Something was wrong. Isabella's food sat untouched. Of course, she misses her husband, Eleanor thought. He's only returned from Ireland once in over a year.

When the trestle tables were cleared everyone stretched his legs, and the company mingled happily as servants rubbed shoulders with royalty as if they did it every day of their lives.

Eleanor dismissed everyone from her mind but William. She watched him with loving eyes as the cook proudly introduced him to her son, and the steward's wife made her curtsy to him. He was such a fine man. He took a genuine interest in his people. He was deep in a serious conversation with his steward when he glanced up and caught her eyes on him. He immediately drew her to his side. "Eleanor, your steward has just been telling me of a dispute between one of your tenant farmers and a stockman. You will sit with me tomorrow while we hold a court. I'm sure there are many disputes that must be settled. I'll show you how it's done so that in the future you can sit in judgment yourself."

He was not treating her as a child, he was treating her as an equal. Her hopes soared.

Isabella approached, nervously twisting a kerchief in her fingers. She seemed determined to attach herself to Eleanor, as if she was afraid to be alone. After quarter of an hour passed she said, "William, I think I should see that Eleanor gets to bed. The hour grows late."

William looked bemused. "Go away, Isabella, Eleanor and I are just getting to know each other. I'm sure I can see that she gets to bed. Bestow your prim, disapproving glances upon Richard, he seems in a reckless mood tonight." William took Eleanor's hand and they left the hall together.

The steward's wife said, "He's besotted with her. I think it was a mistake to give them separate apartments."

"Don't worry, the chambers I assigned adjoin each other, just in case his bed is cold to him," the steward assured her, winking.

"Trust a man to think of that." She slapped his hand away from her bum cheek, but only playfully.

6

When the Earl of Pembroke entered his chambers with the countess on his arm, his squire Sir Walter had just lit a small fire to take the night's chill from his lord's rooms.

"Oh, a fire . . . how lovely! If I could choose, I should always have a fire in my chamber."

"But you can choose," William said, bemused. "Walter, build a fire in my lady's chamber, then take yourself downstairs. The wine flows freely and the company is merry."

When they were alone William drew a chair to the fire for her. "Let's be comfortable. Do you think you could handle a little more wine?"

"Allow me to serve you, my lord. It would give me the greatest pleasure."

He stretched his long legs to the fire and his eyes followed her every move. He had seen her in three different outfits today, and each presented a different Eleanor to him. The black-and-white riding clothes had been striking, but at the same time had been cut to allow ease in mounting and dismounting. Her elegant black riding boots reached all the way to her knees beneath her skirts, showing him she was both practical and modest. This afternoon when she had stood in the orchard in that peach-colored creation he had thought her the prettiest girl in the world, and now as she came forward with the wine, the firelight caught the sheen of her dark velvet gown, which matched the glowing liquid in the crystal goblets. The sophisticated headdress with its fluttering veils and pearls made her look much older tonight, and William dared to hope that in another year perhaps she would be ready.

"If we are to be comfortable, I'll remove this," she said, taking off the headdress. "I hate wimples." Her black hair came tumbling down to her waist in a silken mass and William's mouth went dry. She looked so much younger now, but God help him, so much more desirable. She seemed totally at ease with him, talking with great animation, gesturing dramatically with her pretty hands.

He stared at her in fascination. How could a woman's waist be that tiny, emphasizing the delicious curves both below and above? All his attention was concentrated upon watching her. He had only the vaguest idea of the words they exchanged.

She sat by the fire, leaning toward him eagerly. "Please describe it to me. My tutors are wonderful, but no matter how I beg they won't teach me battle tactics."

William blinked and tried to gather his wits. How in the world had they gotten into this conversation? His eyes fell on the chess pieces set out on a small game table. He set the table between them. "Do you play?"

She nodded eagerly, realizing he intended to use the game of chess to teach her the strategies of planning a battle. William warmed to his subject as she quickly grasped the nuances and subtleties of the game of war. It was two hours before he realized it was past midnight. He sent her to bed. She left with lagging steps, wishing they could have sat up and talked all night.

Eleanor was convinced that William was ready to let her come to live with him as his wife. She felt elated, nowhere near ready for sleep, then suddenly she remembered poor Isabella's haunted look and she felt quite selfish. Decisively she opened her chamber door and made her way to the west wing where Isabella's chamber was situated. At the door she hesitated, concerned lest Isabella was sleeping, then she heard her moan. The manor doors were not the impregnable studded portals that Windsor Castle boasted, and again she heard Isabella gasp and moan. She lifted her candle and turned the knob, when clearly her brother's voice came from within. "I have no intention of leaving. We are going to share a bed. I want to hold you in my arms all night, darling. Damn it, I love you!"

Then she heard another low moan and Isabella's yearning voice said, "I love you too, Richard. Lock the door."

Eleanor was so surprised she almost dropped her candle. She hurried back to her chamber and slowly undressed. She was not displeased that two of the people she loved most felt deeply about each other. She understood Richard's passion. Plantagenets felt passionately about all things. They let nothing stand in the way of what they wanted. Suddenly being alone was too painful to bear. How ridiculous it was to have left William when more than anything on earth she wanted to be with him. Well, that was soon mended, she decided, slipping a white velvet bedgown over her nightrail. He was only in the next chamber.

On the battlements the de Burgh brothers spoke low. "You can go first," said Sir Rickard, "but remember when we change places, I am on guard tonight." He grinned and thumped his brother's shoulder with a mighty blow. "Save some of your strength so you don't fall asleep out here."

Sir Michael jabbed him in the ribs. "I've never fallen asleep on the job yet," he said lewdly. The tower door was opened before he finished knocking. He noticed with amusement that the copper-haired wench was already naked. There would be no games of playful reluctance, no need to coax her to a giving mood. Mick reached out and pulled her into his arms. Her impatient hands were on his chausses, aiding him in the swift removal of his clothes. Never in his life had he dallied with a wench who needed it so badly. While he was still shrugging from his doublet her arms went about his neck and she lifted herself onto his upthrusting erection. Her gyrations began immediately, and he realized they'd never make it to the narrow bed. He took firm hold of her buttocks, planted his legs securely to the floor, and moved her up and down on his engorged weapon. Soon she was doing most of the work. He didn't even need to support her. She impaled herself upon him over and over.

Brenda grunted and groaned but not with pleasure. It was a wild, animalistic mating. A young man as lusty as de Burgh could not fail to respond to the raw sexuality of the female coupling with him. He felt his seed start, tried to hold out longer but couldn't. As a result it spurted up inside of her in hot bursts . . . half a dozen before he was completely finished.

"Mick . . . please . . . again," she begged.

He knew she had not reached her peak and hadn't expected her to this first time. "Yes . . . again . . . hush now," he soothed, lifting her and carrying her to the bed. The moment he was horizontal she was astride his thighs. Quick as a flash of mercury her tongue came out to lick the pearl drops of semen that still clung to him. His shaft suddenly awoke again and filled rapidly. He murmured thickly, "Perhaps if we take it slow this time . . ."

"No, no, Mick, please. I have to have it fast . . . hard and fast . . . please . . . hard and fast."

The wench was almost incoherent in her need. From his experience a girl who could not reach her climax needed stimulation and play. He reached down a strong hand between her legs and slipped two fingers inside her, then encircled her hard little bud with the ball of his thumb. She screamed and writhed, mad with need. She built and built but nothing took her over the edge.

The stimulation was working on Mick much more rapidly. He was hard as marble. Pulling her beneath him, he mounted her with a savage thrust, while schooling himself to make it last this time. He thrust to the hilt, then withdrew all the way, each time stretching her further.

"Mick, fuck me faster, please," she begged.

With a grimace he obeyed her command. The friction he built up with such fast and furious gyrations soon had its inevitable effect on him, and he exploded into her like a volcano spewing liquid fire. All his body's tension melted away, leaving him limp and sated.

Brenda cried out her disappointment as he rolled off her. She came over him again, mounted his thick thigh, and ground her pubis over the hard, bulging saddle muscle. Christ, the wench really was insatiable. She only knew one word: "again." It echoed through his brain, accusing him of failure. He pushed her off his leg and reached for his chausses. "I need some air," he mumbled.

She sat in the middle of the bed, bereft. "You won't come back," she cried.

"Oh, I'll return," he said with grim determination. Mick emerged from the tower room and drew fresh cold air into his lungs in great gulps.

"That good, eh?" remarked Rickard. "Christ, I thought you were never coming out. I'm so hard I could crack walnuts with it." He took off his chain-mail shirt and slipped it over his brother's head. Then he handed him his sword. When Rickard opened the tower door, he fully expected to find the girl asleep, exhausted from his brother's demands. He was delighted when the naked wench flew into his arms and her hand reached down, testing his readiness.

"Oh, Mick, thank you," she sobbed.

"Rick, sweetheart," he corrected, taking her luscious breast into his mouth and sucking hard on the nipple.

Dimly she remembered he had corrected her about his name before. "Oh, God, your name should be Dick, you're so big," she cried thankfully. She unfastened his chausses and slid down with them.

Rickard could feel her hot breath stirring his pubic hair. Her avid hands slid up the back of his legs. "I want it on the floor," she said with a gasp.

"Christ, so do I," he agreed, sinking down and lifting her widespread legs onto his shoulders. In a kneeling position he held her hips immobile in a viselike grip and pumped and bucked into her. Her cries of "harder" and "faster" brought him to a powerful climax, but she clamped the walls of her scalding sheath about him to keep him prisoner inside of her. "Rick, please, please, don't withdraw," she begged.

"My pleasure, sweetheart," he assured her, already semiaroused again because of the girl's insatiable desire for him. Still inside her, he lifted her with him until he was on his feet. Then as he supported her bottom with his hands, she wrapped her legs about his waist and thrust her tongue deeply into his mouth. He walked across the room bouncing her up and down on his cock until she was sobbing with frustration and raking his back with her nails.

"I don't want to be teased, I want to be fucked!"

Rick stretched her out on the bed, towered above her, then drove himself to the hilt. His strokes were deep, lightning fast and savage. She arched her pelvis to meet every one of them, and Rick could not prevent his ejaculation. Though she again tried to hold him, this time it was impossible. He was too flaccid and she far too slippery. "I'm on guard duty tonight," Rickard said hoarsely. "I must go and make the rounds again."

"Promise me you'll come back," she pressed him urgently.

So far he had failed in his mission; there was no way he would quit the field. "I promise," he swore.

The brothers stood shoulder to shoulder on the ramparts of Odiham. "This is no longer pleasure, it's damned hard work. She's like a bitch in heat, writhing on the floor."

"Our reputations are at stake. What the hell are we going to do?" Rickard asked.

Mick squared his shoulders. "Double our efforts, 'tis a point of honor." As he reentered the small tower room, the musky scent of mingled male and female carnality assailed his senses.

"Rick," she purred possessively.

"Mick," he corrected grimly, his nostrils flaring, his mind set upon the battle before him. He would breach the ramparts and accept nothing less than unconditional surrender.

Eleanor stole softly to the door that separated her apartment from the Earl of Pembroke's, knocked politely, and entered before she could be denied. William fitted exactly the night thoughts that drifted in and out of her dreams. Since her childhood he had represented strength, protection, loving arms.

He wore a bedrobe and had been glancing over Odiham's account books, tallying its income. He arose and came forward instantly. "Eleanor, is aught amiss?"

"No, my lord," she breathed. "I-I don't wish to be alone. I have decided to spend the night here with you."

"My dear, that is impossible," he said, stiffening.

"Why?" she asked, knowing full well it was not impossible, for here they were.

"It is wrong," he stated flatly. The sophisticated young woman in the wimple and velvet gown had turned into a child in her nightclothes.

"Why is it wrong?" she questioned in ignorance. "We are married."

"My dearest child, we are married in name only. You are far too young to be a wife." He moved purposely to the connecting door and held it wide for her. "You do understand, don't you, Eleanor?"

Her dark-blue eyes filled with tears and threatened to spill over. Her lips quivered. "No—no," she whispered huskily, "I don't understand at all."

"Oh, sweet, I've made you weep. Don't, please, it breaks my heart." His arms went about her protectively and he drew her closer to the fire and took her into his lap. Why in the name of God wasn't her mother here to tell her these things? Then he repudiated the thought. The last person in the world he wanted to teach his bride about intimacy was Queen Isabella. He sighed and his big hand came up to smooth her unruly curls.

He had no one to blame but himself. He was the one who had insisted she be brought up as pure as the driven snow. He took a deep breath and plunged in. "The difference in our ages is so wide, I feel it would be selfish and unfair to ask a young girl of fifteen to share my bed."

Her eyes were like liquid pools as she trustingly gazed up at him. She thought it would be heaven to share his bed and feel his strong arms about her in the lonely darkness. "I think I would like it. Can we not just try it for one night?" she begged softly.

He licked lips gone suddenly very dry. "Little one, you still don't understand. When a marriage is consummated," he began slowly, praying for words that would not repel her, "a man joins his body, in love, to his bride's body. They become intimate."

She digested this information solemnly for a few moments,

then said, "I don't think I'm too young for that, my lord. I should like to become intimate with you."

In spite of his good intentions, William felt the hot blood flood his loins and he was appalled that his manhood was swelling against her soft buttocks. His mouth was now completely dry, and for a second or two he totally lost his train of thought as her words echoed inside his head. "I should like to become intimate with you . . . I should like to become intimate with you." Why in the name of heaven and hell had he taken her upon his knee? He knew he should push her off before she felt him rising, but she would interpret it as rejection and he knew instinctively that she would more willingly absorb his gentle explanations while he held her in his arms in this warm, intimate position.

She looked up at him with liquid, trusting eyes, her pink lips parted slightly to catch her breath in her effort to spare him her tears. Lord God, it was exactly like the erotic dream he'd had of her last night. Upon waking it had vanished with the dawn, but now that his senses had been stirred, it came flooding back to him. In the dream he had taken her upon his lap and gently freed her breasts from the confines of her bedgown. Seeing them bared for the first time had been especially thrilling because he was aware that no man had ever done this to her before. He had drawn out his play, stroking and fondling, then cupping and weighing them in his palms, and finally lifting them to his hot mouth to tongue and suck the rosy nipples until they rouched and hardened into rosebuds.

Eleanor shifted her weight slightly in his lap and his shaft began to throb and rear with a will of its own. He came back to his senses when he realized with horror his hands were at the opening of her bedgown. In desperation he reached for a thought that would effectively cool his lust. A picture of his young wife's mother flashed into his head. Amazingly, Isabella's image worked its magic for him. In less than ten seconds his shaft shrank back inside its cowl, limp and harmless.

Further explanations were obviously necessary. "Eleanor," he said gently, "when a man and woman's bodies join, he plants his seed in her and she has a child."

A great dawning light came into her face. A mystery had just been solved for her.

William added firmly, "And fifteen is too young to become a mother. I think even you must agree with me, now that I've explained it."

Yes, she really did see that she would have to wait until she was sixteen.

As he brushed away her tears with gentle fingers, she said, "I'm sorry, William, I simply wanted us to spend the night together like Richard and Isabella."

He put her from his knee. "Wherever did you get such a sinful notion?" he demanded, scandalized. "You must never, ever say things like that. Such a falsehood would create a royal scandal and ruin my sister."

"It's all right, William," she hastily reassured him, "they commit no sin, they love each other."

"They what?" he ground out, realizing Eleanor had innocently exposed her brother's attempt at seduction. William flung open the door. "Where is my sister's chamber?"

Suddenly Eleanor realized she should have kept her mouth shut. William was scandalized and was clearly determined to vent his anger on his poor sister. He strode into the west wing of Odiham and she had to run to keep up with him.

Breathlessly she cried, "My lord, I was mistaken. If it is wrong, then of course they aren't spending the night together."

Isabella lay against Richard's heart. "Beloved, never fear, I will cherish you forever." His fingers stroked her silken shoulders tenderly, trying to erase the guilt he had forced upon her. Suddenly someone was crashing a shoulder against their chamber door, and with disbelief Richard saw the wood splinter. He sprang from the bed naked and snatched up his sword, thinking Odiham had been attacked. William Marshal charged into the room like an enraged bull. Eleanor followed, her face as white as her velvet bedgown.

"Bones of Christ, what have you been doing to my sister?" William thundered.

"The same thing you've been doing to mine," Richard shouted angrily at the undressed pair who had just invaded his chamber of love.

William advanced, ignoring the sword. "I should kill you for
that remark. Unlike you, I know how to keep a check on my
lust. My brains aren't all in my prick!" He turned accusing eyes
upon the woman in the bed clutching the covers to her nakedness, looking striken as if she wanted to die. "How could you
break your vows . . . commit adultery?" he asked in outrage.

Richard lowered his weapon. "She had no choice, William.
Isabella is blameless. I forced her."

"You are no better than your filthy father!" William spat, not
caring that he blackened John's memory in front of Eleanor.
He had an almost uncontrollable urge to put his hands about
Richard's throat and snuff the life from him. "Your father lost
all his continental possessions because he was addicted to having a woman between his legs day and night!"

"Nay!" cried the woman in the bed. "Richard loves me."

"A man will say anything so a woman will let him fuck her,"
shouted William, who had never used such language before a
woman in his life. He glared at Richard. "You are the governor
of Gascony, the only corner of France that remains to us. 'Tis
time you departed for that country and began governing!"

Richard was stung, yet he could not deny the truth of the
marshal's words. "William, I do love her. I want to marry her."
His voice was solemn and sincere.

"You've both conveniently forgotten de Clare. 'Tis a Plantagenet habit to steal other men's wives."

Richard stood his ground in the face of William Marshal's
rage. He said quietly, "We've been in love for five long years
and controlled our need all that time. Tonight's romantic atmosphere pushed us over the edge. I beg your pardon, William, I
have abused your hospitality and brought dishonor to the
woman I love. I shall relieve you of my odious presence within
the hour. Gascony is where I should be. An ocean between us
will keep me from temptation, but I charge you to lay no blame
upon my sweet Isabella."

After Richard quit the chamber, William turned accusing
eyes upon his sister. "You were supposed to be a moral example
for Eleanor. By God, if you've tainted her with your carnality . . ."

"Stop!" Eleanor cried. "Isabella is the gentlest, most respectable lady I've ever known. If it is a sin to love, then I commit it every day of my life, for I love you beyond reason, William. I can understand her need for Richard's strong arms for I have the same need. You may think it wicked, but I would give anything to share your bed. However, for better or for worse, I am yours and I will obey you in everything. Good night, my lord earl!" She swept regally from the room.

William ran his hand through his hair and said in a more subdued tone, "I seem to be the villain of the piece. I'm sorry, Bella, I never knew your marriage to young de Clare was a loveless match." He laughed shortly, but there was little amusement in it. "These Plantagenets are the very devil. Their passion borders on madness."

The knights and servants had the great hall to themselves the next morning for the king's brother had taken himself off in the middle of the night and the Earl and Countess of Pembroke kept to their apartments—separately, to everyone's astonishment.

Brenda had slept late but had awakened with a healthy appetite. She strolled into the hall in time to see the handsome de Burgh swallow the last mouthful of his breakfast. He smiled at her with his lazy grin, amused to see her slip down on the bench beside him almost purring like a contented cat.

"Good morning, Mick," she drawled languidly, her eyes half closed with sensual memories of her satisfying night.

"Rick," he corrected solemnly.

Brenda looked slightly confused. She stretched her arms above her head languorously and said, "I could have sworn on the ride from Windsor yesterday you told me your name was Mick de Burgh."

"Do I hear someone taking my name in vain?" drawled a tall knight as he folded his legs beneath the trestle table beside her. She turned at the familiar voice and her eyes widened in recognition. Then her eyes flew back to the other knight who was grinning from ear to ear. "Allow me to present my twin, Sir Rickard de Burgh."

Rick winked at her wickedly. "Oh, I've already had the pleasure."

As realization dawned on her, her hand flew to her mouth. Then when she saw the devilish looks on the young knights' faces, she began to giggle.

When the Countess of Pembroke walked into the hall, she was greeted by roars of laughter.

"I fail to see what's causing such a fit of hysterics, unless it's because I received no bath or breakfast tray this morning."

Her husband's knights were on their feet immediately in respect for the beautiful princess.

"Forgive me, my lady, I thought the Odiham maids were looking after your needs." Brenda slipped from the hall, almost running into William, Earl of Pembroke, as he arrived to break his fast. As he glanced down the room he felt a seering jealousy that his wife was flanked by the devastatingly handsome sons of Falcon de Burgh. William crushed down his jealousy. It was an emotion he could not afford to indulge. Jealousy led to lust, and he had sworn to keep himself in check for at least another year. Richard's behavior with his sister was clouding his judgment. The de Burghs were knights of honor in whom he had every faith. They would protect his wife's virtue as diligently as he himself would.

The moment she saw William, Eleanor came down the room to meet him. She could not let the events of the night spoil things between them. She loved him with all her heart, and he must be most fond of her to have generously deeded Odiham manor house to her. He would not allow her to curtsy to him, and when she raised her dark lashes he saw there would be no awkwardness between them.

"You haven't forgotten your promise to teach me how to hold court, my lord?"

He smiled down at her. "It is a pleasure to have such an eager and intelligent pupil. I pledge that I shall never forget a promise to you."

Eleanor's heart soared. She was the luckiest lady in the world to have William Marshal for husband.

7

Llewellyn, self-styled King of Wales, looked down from the lofty heights of his impenetrable stronghold on Mount Snowden and saw that Hubert de Burgh was building a formidable fortress at Montgomery. He knew how the de Burghs' had conquered half of Ireland, and he swore the avaricious Norman bastards wouldn't do the same to Wales. Hubert de Burgh already had more castles than flies on a dog turd and Montgomery stuck in Llewellyn's craw. He was damned if he would swallow the insult.

He began to incite his people to rebellion. The men who ruled England began immediate preparations for war. King Henry couldn't wait to get his first taste of battle. His wedding plans were pushed to the back of his mind in his excitement to take up arms and teach the uncivilized Welsh a lesson.

Richard came home from Gascony bringing his fighting men. The Gascons had proved impossible to control; the counts and viscounts of each region were bitterly contentious. They burned towns and ravaged the countryside, and Richard's meager resources were not strong enough to keep the rampaging nobles in order. Richard had fought beside Hubert de Burgh before and relished the idea of a full-scale war. As well, it would keep him from the temptation of Isabella Marshal de Clare.

Thoughts of Eleanor were erased from William's mind as well. This is what men were born for, to fight, to kill, to hold what was theirs. The importance of women was insignificant when compared to that of glorious war. A few barons who held castles in Wales joined the fray, but a great many of them, envious of Hubert de Burgh's power and wealth, refused to spend their money or risk their men.

The aging Earl of Chester owned lands not only in Wales but also in so many counties of England that he could quickly gather a great army of men. He finally came forward to pay the enormous fee for confirmation of his lands and titles, and Henry welcomed him with open arms.

On the eve of his departure for Wales, Rickard de Burgh took quill in hand and wrote to his parents in Ireland.

Once again Llewellyn is inciting his people to rebellion. We march our men into Wales at dawn to snuff out the flame before the whole land ignites into an inferno of burning destruction. Uncle Hubert inadvertently set the spark by building a fortress at Montgomery, which as you know lies at the foot of Llewellyn's hallowed Mount Snowden.

I am surprised at the jealous envy the barons are openly displaying against Hubert. Since there is naught they can do about his wealth, they are doing their best to undermine his power. I suppose it is human nature to covet and hate one who has risen so high who was not born into the nobility. I must own, however, that Hubert is guilty of flaunting his wealth to a marked degree, seemingly oblivious of the gathering storm of grumblings against him, which grows ever louder.

You would not believe the high state in which he dwells at the Tower of London. He lives on a far grander scale than the king; his entourage of sycophants, body servants, musicians, scriveners, almoners, and confessors almost outnumbers his knights and men-at-arms. His vanity has grown apace with his girth, and he rides forth in polished chain mail and bright silk scarves. He owns so many castles he has lost count, and wherever his household travels they can repair by nightfall to his own lodgings. All his business is carried out by Stephen Segrave who is ambitious and without many scruples.

For his daughter Megotta's fifth birthday, Hubert gave her five manors in Sussex, Leicestershire, and Lincolnshire. He employs great armies of men, stewards, seneschels, yeomen of the ewaries, larderers, cooks, grooms, blacksmiths, carpenters, and villeins to till the soil, all wearing the iron badge of de Burgh about their necks. The number of armorers alone necessary to cover the backs of his men-at-arms and forge steel chausses, shields, prickspurs, and two-edged swords is legion. A feeling of dread for Hubert nags at me. I hope I have not inherited mother's second sight. She calls it a gift, but I consider it a curse.

My own lord, William of Pembroke, probably commands more knights and men-at-arms, and is doubtless wealthier in estates, yet he does all unobtrusively and makes few enemies. I thank God you had the foresight to urge us to his service. He is a Spartan man with the tastes of a soldier. He made me castellan of Odiham whenever Lady Eleanor, Countess of Pembroke, is in residence. I regret to say they still live entirely separate because of her tender years, but she is a beautiful lady and I much doubt me if he will be able to resist her charms much longer.

When we return from Wales the royal wedding will take place immediately. It is too bad you cannot talk Mother into coming for the great celebration and for the bride's coronation; after all, she is King Henry's cousin.

I write also for Mick. When he dips his quill, it is not in ink, I assure you.

The devastator of England swept down from his fastness with fire and sword, his battle helmet crested with a fierce wolf. It took all the armies of King Henry, William Marshal, Hubert de Burgh, and Ranulf of Chester three long months of hard fighting to quell the uprising that had spread like wildfire. William Marshal's vast storehouses from Chepstowe to Pembroke were emptied to victual the entire army before Llewellyn was brought low enough to beg for terms.

Richard of Cornwall and the marshal were thrown together in battle frequently. At first they were not on speaking terms, but grudgingly William was forced to admit that Richard was a brilliant strategist as well as a brave and valiant knight. He took his hand in a renewed pledge of friendship and hoped that Fate would arrange the future to someday make them brothers-in-law.

All had conspired to keep young King Henry out of the fray, but when it came time to negotiate terms of peace, Henry insisted upon riding out with the Marshal of England. William was appalled at how easily the crafty Llewellyn manipulated his young monarch, but he kept a wise silence. In exchange for a yearly gift of goshawks, falcons, and Welsh bowmen, Henry agreed to make Hubert de Burgh raze his castle at Montgomery.

When King Henry arrived back at Westminster, the business of England, neglected for three months, threatened to overwhelm him. He ignored the scores of petitioners and complainants clogging the halls, declaring that the only important matter he would attend to was his wedding. He made one exception, however. Simon de Montfort, younger son of the Sovereign Prince of Southern France, demanded an audience. The de Montfort men were reputed to be the greatest warriors on the whole continent. They were war lords who had fought on Crusades, conquered the country of Toulouse, and were a continual threat to Louis of France.

Henry was closeted in his office behind the exchequer, issuing orders to his chamberlain in charge of ceremonial matters. "I want the streets of London cleaned up, aye, and its moral tone. Get rid of the whores, stop the drinking and loose living. Forbid games in the churchyards. I want cressets of oil placed at every street corner for illumination."

The chamberlain was nodding, but he wondered where he would get the money for all this. Richard of Cornwall walked into the office to interrupt them.

"Henry, are you aware that Simon de Montfort has been cooling his heels for two days, waiting to see you?"

"The war lord?" asked Henry, not able to conceal the awe the very name de Montfort inspired. He turned to the chancellor. "Find him and usher him in immediately."

"Nay, Henry," Richard protested, "let's not receive him in this dark cubbyhole you call an office. He's descended from the great Robert of Leicester. He has more Anglo-Norman blood than we have, for Christ's sake."

"The throne room?" Henry suggested.

Richard shook his head decisively. "Invite him to your private apartment. He's kin to us. We want to extend the hand of friendship . . . he would make a deadly enemy." Richard instructed the chamberlain and added, "See that the steward attends us to offer hospitality and provide refreshment."

When Simon de Montfort entered Henry's apartment, the king's mouth literally gaped open. The war lord was the largest man he had ever seen. His actual height was six feet four inches, but when anyone described him they invariably said he was six-and-a-half-feet tall. His torso was so well muscled his clothes could do naught to disguise his magnificent physique. He had the dark beauty of the Southern French and his eyes were a magnetic, jet black.

Richard's eyes held only admiration, while Henry's flickered with fear. The war lord had come armed into the king's presence because none had had courage enough to ask for his weapons. It was only when Simon de Montfort smiled and held out a massive arm that they realized he was a young man, not much older than the king.

His voice was deep-timbered as it rumbled up from his massive chest. "Congratulations, sire, I hear you are just returned from a successful campaign in Wales." Simon had shrewdly guessed the weaker of the two brothers was the king.

Henry laughed nervously, flattered to receive a compliment from the champion warrior. "If I'd had a sword like yours, my lord, I might have vanquished the foe sooner."

Simon immediately unbuckled the double-edged weapon and presented it to Henry. Not wishing to slight the Duke of Cornwall, he untied the knife strapped to his thigh. It was no jewel-encrusted showpiece, but a deadly dagger, ten inches in length, its handle lovingly bound in leather so that when gripped by a strong palm it became an extension of the hand that wielded it. As they drew the weapons from their sheaths, all three men shared a moment of zeal that only glorious battle could generate. They tasted bloodlust on their tongues and experienced such a rush in their veins they all three became sexually aroused. The young men laughed because they knew their momentary reaction was mutually shared.

Simon did not wait for the king to address him. "I am here to offer you my services."

"You would swear fealty to me?" Henry asked in disbelief.

"What do you seek in return?" a more astute Richard asked.

"Only that which is mine by right," Simon said in an implacable voice. "My family came with the Norman conquerors and fought at Hastings. My grandsire wed an English heiress and became the Earl of Leicester. When your father lost Normandy to France, it became necessary for my father to choose which king and country to serve. When he elected to serve France, King John confiscated all his lands and honors in England and put these estates and the earldom of Leicester in the hands of Ranulf of Chester to be held in trust for us. You have just reconfirmed Chester with my earldom, and I am here to formally protest it."

Richard was well versed in the ancestry of the Norman nobility. "I agree the earldom of Leicester belongs to Simon de Montfort, but that is your father, I believe."

"My father was killed in battle wiping out the Albigenses from Toulouse. My elder brother has just been appointed Constable of France. Since I do not wish to spend the rest of my life at my brother's throat, we came to an agreement. I renounced all claim to the continental possessions of the family in exchange for whatever I could salvage in England."

The Plantagenets could only admire his blunt honesty. He did not dissemble, but asked outright for what he wanted.

"And if you do not get what you want by asking?" Richard inquired.

A wolfish grin spread across Simon's face. Henry interpreted. "You take it."

"I am a soldier of fortune. I stand before you without money, land, or title. What I do have is ambition—and I am in a hurry," he added with a disarming smile.

The steward came in accompanied by two servants laboring under trays of food. Richard was thankful the man had sense enough to order something substantial, for their guest must surely have an enormous appetite. Simon accepted their hospitality and the three were seated at a table laden with meat and game, accompanied by fresh baked loaves and tankards of good English ale.

"If it was in my power I would restore your earldom today, but it is not so simple," explained the king. "Chester wields enormous power. I cannot offend him by demanding back your lands and title, at least not yet. But Ranulf of Chester is no longer a young man. When he dies, I will see that what is yours reverts to you. I'm sorry it seems so hopeless."

Simon quaffed his ale, seemingly unperturbed.

"Why do you prefer England to France?" Richard asked baldly.

"I always felt my father chose the wrong country and I am obsessed with the notion of regaining all that he lost." He looked into the eyes of both men. "You must be obsessed by a similar curse."

All their lives they had been ashamed of what their father had lost, and in that moment the secret ambition to regain Normandy and Aquitaine burst into flame. Their victory in Wales had made Henry turn his eyes upon France, but Hubert de Burgh and the Marshal of England were totally against war.

Simon confessed, "Your grandsire, Henry II, served as my role model. He was a mere count, but his ambition rode him relentlessly until he became not only King of England, but ruler of Normandy, the Angevin provinces, and the fair Aquitaine. Although I admire the way he took whatever he wanted, his real genius lay in ruling. He was the great lawmaker. His vision was crystal clear. He transformed the whole judicial system from the superstition and corruption of the dark ages." He paused, then laughed. "Forgive me, when I get on the subject of Henry II I get carried away."

"I'll arrange a pension of four hundred marks if you enter royal service," Henry offered.

Simon almost choked on his disappointment, but had enough common sense to accept the king's offer. He would make his own success. "I command a hundred knights—I shall send for them at once."

"Hold, the Count of Brittany has declared war on France and has asked for my help. Since your men are yet on the continent, I will send you. Because de Burgh and Marshal are against fighting in France, I was going to refuse aid to Brittany. Now by a stroke of good fortune you have provided me with the means of joining the fray. I'll give you messages for the count."

Henry had taken fire with the idea and looked to his brother for his support.

"If we are going to do it," Richard said, nodding in agreement, "now is the time, while there is so much unrest in France." Richard could be cool, calculating, and close-mouthed, but silently he recognized before him the perfect man to control Gascony. Simon de Montfort's father had been known as the Scourge. When the war lords descended upon a region, they soon cured its dissension with severe medicine. Their methods might be stern, relentless, even cruel, but they were amazingly effective. Yes, thought Richard, we have much need of a warrior such as Simon de Montfort.

"I'll order Hubert de Burgh to raise an army whether he likes it or not," Henry said firmly.

"I'll rally the barons if you'll give me command of them," Richard suggested, with the arrogant confidence of youth.

Simon de Montfort recognized immediately that the King of England was easily led and recklessly impulsive. A war against France to regain Normandy could never succeed unless it was meticulously planned and mounted on a full scale. Simon shrugged. He would wrest personal victory from this campaign regardless of its outcome for Henry III.

8

La Belle, Eleanor of Provence, landed at Dover with a great train of knights and servants. They had only the clothes on their backs, and even Eleanor's trousseau consisted of gowns made over from her mother and sisters. And yet the lowliest of these Provençals with patched elbows arrived with such a superior attitude they sneered at everything English from the weather to the culture, or lack of it, as they never tired of pointing out.

Henry rushed to Dover to escort his bride the fifteen miles to Canterbury where they were to be married immediately by the archbishop. The king was enthralled by her ivory skin and dark golden hair. Plantagenets never did things by half, and so completely in character, Henry fell wholly in love with the sophisticated beauty who set about to enslave him and hold him prisoner for the rest of his life.

Though the Provençal court was poor, it was the center of European culture, literature, and music. Eleanor had her own Court of Honor for troubadors and a Court of Love for her knights, and the entire cavalcade was boistrously noisy and rang with youthful laughter.

Henry and his court had never seen anything quite like it. It seemed their reason for living was to extract the last drop of pleasure from each day and then begin afresh after dark with all the tempting pleasures of the night.

Eleanor, Countess of Pembroke, was excited. She loved the pomp and pageantry of the royal court of England, and this was the first royal wedding she had ever attended. It was the first ceremonial occasion where she had appeared in public as the Countess of Pembroke, and she fervently hoped it would convince her husband to think of her as a woman.

The Marshal of England rode ahead of her on a massive gelding he used for ceremonial occasions. She followed mounted upon her new white palfrey, flanked by Sir Michael and Sir Rickard de Burgh. All wore white capes bearing the marshal's device of the resplendent Red Lion Rampant.

William knew their attendants would make a brave show, but ever a practical man, he had charged the de Burghs with Eleanor's safety. He would be busy with his duties as marshal to the king, and Canterbury was no fit place for a decent young lady unless she had the constant protection of two strong sword arms at her back.

Inside Canterbury Cathedral she had been far too short to see over all the heads of the bishops and clergy, the choirboys and the incense swingers. She had not yet had a chance to get a good look at the beautiful princess who had just become her sister-in-law. The magnificent music still echoed inside her head as she rode forward behind her husband to greet the mounted cavalcade of King Henry and his new bride.

Eleanor's heart was bursting with love and pride for her brother. They had always been very close, and she fervently wished for him great joy in his chosen marriage partner. As she came face to face with the royal couple, her eyes first met and held those of Henry. Love poured from her to him as they held each other's gaze for long moments. She thought he had never looked more handsome in his entire life, proudly holding up his golden head wearing his golden crown. He of course was inordinately proud of his beautiful young sister whose vivid loveliness took men's breath away.

They smiled at each other, their smiles widened to grins, then they laughed aloud with pure unadulterated joyousness.

The splendor of the newlyweds was dazzling to the eyes. Each was clothed from head to foot in gold. Eleanor's eyes reluctantly left her brother's as she looked upon Eleanor of Provence for the first time and she thought, How lovely she is. No wonder they call her La Belle. Her hair is dark, burnished gold, and matches her cloth-of-gold gown exactly. Eleanor wanted to welcome her with love, but when she smiled into the bride's eyes, the girl simply returned a haughty stare. Eleanor's heart went out to her. Oh, dear, she is nervous of all the trappings of kingship and the very thought of becoming queen very shortly is probably frightening her to death. Poor lady, I shall have to offer her my friendship and encourage her to be brave. This country and all these people must be so overwhelming to a fifteen-year-old.

Eleanor would have been astounded had she been able to read the thoughts of her brother's bride. So this is the infamous little bitch who has ruled the royal roost since she was five years old. This is the King's Precious Jewel. Her eyes swept William Marshal from head to foot and envy gnawed at her throat. Though his hair was graying and he was past forty, by God he was all man. The bride was not inexperienced in these matters. Her regal sister-in-law was flanked by two of the handsomest young studs she had ever seen, and she vowed in that moment to wean Henry from any love he felt for his sister. If she had *anything* to say in the matter, and she intended to have *everything* to say, she would reduce Princess Eleanor's influence to nil.

The sun came out upon the dazzling couple in gold, and for a brief moment Rickard de Burgh was blinded by the glittering spectacle. He closed his eyes and swayed slightly in the saddle. When he opened them the beautiful bride was transformed. He experienced a strange vision. The day was no longer sunny. The young queen was in a barge on the River Thames. She was being pelted by stones to drive her back to the Tower of London. The cheering throng had changed to an ugly mob that called her harridan and witch. Rickard de Burgh put a hand to his head, blinked rapidly, and once again golden royalty sat before him in glittering splendor, acknowledging the cheers of joy from the throng. Rickard shuddered for he knew at his heartroot he had been allowed a brief glimpse into the future.

One of William Marshal's duties was to see that the king and court, his new bride and her long train of attendants were delivered the fifty miles to London with all possible speed and safety. At the close of every year the pilgrims marched to Canterbury. This year, because of the royal wedding, there was such a crush of visitors, the town was literally bursting apart at the seams. They traveled into the town by three roads, from London, Dover, and Winchester, and these roads were thronged with humanity. They came on foot, by donkey, or on horseback. Great ladies traveled shoulder to shoulder with invalids, pilgrims, prostitutes, rich men, poor men, beggarmen, and thieves. Canterbury was a wall-to-wall religious bazaar where every citizen knew this was the season to make a killing, to fleece the visitor and live off the profits for a whole year.

The clamor for food, drink, and bogus religious souvenirs was surpassed only by the jostling for a place to sleep. There was no longer room at any inn or private home or stable. People slept six to a bed or in spoon fashion on floors of taverns or churches. Many lay outdoors in churchyards or under hedgerows, and the whores, thick as fleas on a dog's back, serviced their customers standing up in doorways or lying on tombstones.

The court also had to cope with crowded conditions, for the gracious rooms of the priory at Christ Church were the only place fitting to house the nobility.

Eleanor left Isabella Marshal and her maids to cope with the logistics of securing a chamber and plenishing it, while she rushed off to congratulate the bridegroom. Henry and his bride were the only ones lucky enough to have a private chamber, but even this room would remain crowded to the rafters with courtiers and servants until the groom rid himself of the wellwishers around midnight.

When Eleanor arrived she flew into Henry's open arms, and he swung her about, laughing. "Hello, Maggot, what do you think of my beautiful bride?"

"Congratulations, love, she is wondrous fair. I hope you live happily ever after." She had removed her white cape and her gown was spectacular. It was crimson velvet embroidered with the golden leopards of the House of Plantagenet. Her black cloud of hair was fastened back by two great golden leopards with jeweled emerald eyes.

Henry set her feet to the carpet and she glanced about, seeking a familiar face. She encountered only Provençals, most not even bothering to speak English, but the men had seen her exquisite beauty and crowded about her with speculative eyes.

"Let me introduce you. This is my wife's uncle, William, Bishop of Valence." Before William could kiss her hand, he had been shouldered aside by his brother, who was younger and handsomer. "This is my wife's uncle, Peter of Savoy."

"A pleasure to meet you," she murmured, her dark lashes sweeping her cheeks. Suddenly her eyes flew open again for Peter of Savoy had lifted her by the waist and kissed both her cheeks. Before her feet touched the rug again another uncle was admiring her openly, his eyes fixed upon her cherry-ripe lips.

"Amadeus," Henry said indicating Peter's brother, and greatly impressed by these Provençals with their good looks and fabulous easy manners. "And this," Henry said with great pride, as if he were producing a rabbit from a hat, "is their father, Thomas of Savoy."

Thomas assessed Eleanor's breasts and raised his eyebrows to the king. "My sister Eleanor, Countess of Pembroke."

Henry's bride suddenly appeared at his side and ran a possessive hand up his arm. She pouted her lips. They were so close that Henry could not resist kissing the tempting mouth. "Surely there is room in your heart for only one Eleanor?" she asked prettily.

"Of course, my darling," said Henry, slipping an intimate arm about her and hugging her to his side. She glanced at Peter of Savoy, the handsomest of her uncles and the one who knew her intimately. When she saw the look on his face, the dislike she had formed for her sister-in-law turned to instant hatred. Henry had a fatuous look on his face as he said, "Eleanor, may I present to you the Queen of England?"

Though technically she would not become queen until she was crowned in a few days, Henry had made the introduction in a way that made it necessary for Eleanor to curtsy. She did so graciously, but she got the distinct impression that this impoverished young woman was looking down her long nose at her. "You may rise," the bride said coldly, looking through narrowed eyes. Then her face transformed as she looked at her new husband adoringly. "Henry, at my coronation when we ride into London I want you to let me have the two men who guarded your sister today."

Eleanor's voice became crisp as she explained matters to the newest member of the family. "That is impossible. Henry cannot let you have the de Burghs. They are the Earl of Pembroke's knights."

The bride drew herself up to her full height, which made her considerably taller than Eleanor. "Did you say *impossible*?" she said acidly. "Henry is the *king*. He can do *anything* he wishes." She bestowed a dazzling smile upon him, bathing him in adoration. Her eyes promised rich rewards for his generosity.

Her words echoed his own thoughts. He was the *king*. He was sick and tired of being told what he could and could not do. His hand slipped higher upon her waist until the back of his fingers brushed against the swell of her breast. "The de Burghs will be honored to flank you in the procession from the Tower of London to Westminster."

Eleanor bit her lip. With a few well-chosen words she could have cut her brother down to size, but she loved him too much to shame him before these arrogant Provençals. She glanced at the queen. Thou shalt not covet thy sister's knights, she thought irreverently.

Later when she enjoyed a few moments with William before he rushed off upon his endless duties to the crown, she explained matters to him in a humorous way to avoid a breach between her brother and her husband. If the Earl of Pembroke thought Henry was ordering his men about and playing king again, he would soon explain the facts of life to him. "Lud, I was glad when the girl took her covetous eyes from my gown. I feared she would order me stripped before that litter of Savoys."

His eyes gleamed with amusement. "I met only three uncles, Eleanor," he corrected.

"Only three, you say? I could have sworn someone said

Thomas of Savoy had sired a baker's dozen of the damned foreign fellows." She smiled at him. "Well, never mind. She may have my guards . . . she may even have my gown, but if she sets her eyes upon you, William, I shall scratch them out."

Splendor of God, when his beautiful young wife said things like that to him, desire snaked through his loins before he could control it. It was a moment before he could conjure up her mother's image, which was the effective device he had learned to use to rid himself of a painful erection. He would have to use the services of a whore to rid his body of its demands. He had never had so many erections in his life, not even in his lusty youth. Then inevitably he felt shame for his lust.

He deliberately turned his mind to his duties. The accommodations in Canterbury were totally inadequate. He would have to ride to Rochester tonight to see firsthand that the vast numbers of Provençals who had accompanied the queen would be better housed. The sooner he got them out of Canterbury the better, for at the moment it was trying to cope with a population twice the size of London's and every thief, cutpurse, pickpocket, and penny-whore was trying to separate the visitors from their money before the religious charlatans did so with their fake saints' bones and bottled martyrs' blood.

He left his men patrolling the streets, for he knew when this many people were crowded into one place, knifings, fights, and murders were inevitable.

9

The cavalcade rode to London for the crowning in easy stages where Richard of Cornwall had held supreme authority while his brother King Henry had traveled to Dover and Canterbury. He knew his brother trusted him totally with the crown of England because he had no ambitions whatsoever to steal it and wear it.

He was secretly appalled at the lavish coronation that had been planned. The whole month of January had been set aside for spectacles and pageants, and anyone in England who had ever had a remote connection to the nobility had arrived for the crowning of the queen.

Richard had discovered that the king had forced his rich nobles to lend him money to pay for this lavish spectacle and that the London guilds had been "persuaded" to open their purses to provide expensive wedding presents. Richard shook his head in disbelief. His brother and he were alike in being able to pluck gold coins from thin air, but his own acquisitive Norman fingers hoarded his wealth, while Henry's hands scattered gold to the winds as if he were able to acquire it like King Midas.

La Belle Eleanor sat her palfrey, flanked by Sir Michael and

Sir Rickard de Burgh. They rode directly behind the king. Because of her insistence at having the twin brothers upon her right and left flank, they had already earned the hatred of her ambitious uncles and the rest of the arrogant Provençals.

The Tower of London was the first stop on the long procession to Westminster. At the Tower she rode up beside the king and her guards fell back among the queen's train. La Belle wore a glittering, tight-fitting gown; its sleeves lined with ermine. As she positioned her horse beside Henry's, he smiled across at her. "You are very beautiful today. I hope you won't find this too tiring . . . especially since we didn't get much sleep last night."

Her eyes were heavy-lidded, her mouth sensually full-lipped. In a throaty voice she said, "We can sleep when we're dead." She was so much more woman than he had expected. They had set sail on a sea of carnality where he would have willingly drowned to satisfy her.

"Three hundred sixty men and women are to greet us on horseback and welcome you to the City of London. Each couple will present you with a cup of gold or silver." The men wore cloth-of-gold tunics; their wives were adorned in fur-trimmed cloaks. Beginning with the Lord Mayor of London and his wife, the couples rode forward bearing their cups of precious metal. Hubert de Burgh, England's justiciar and castellan of the Tower of London, had arranged for one hundred eighty young pages and squires to act as cupbearers. One by one they came forward to pipe their thanks on the queen's behalf and carry the precious cups into the Tower for safekeeping. La Belle decided it was a waste of precious metal and wondered how soon she could have some of them melted down and fashioned into objects of adornment.

When this ceremony was concluded, the glittering cavalcade moved slowly down The Strand toward Westminster. The entire route had been hung with silk banners, and at each and every corner trumpeters blew a fanfare as they approached.

The Londoners' cheered this dazzling young beauty who had come to their king so he might beget heirs upon her body. The crowds went mad in an excess of ecstacy, scattering colored confetti and dried flower petals.

The highlight of the whole glorious day for the new bride
was not being anointed by the archbishop, nor receiving the
blessing of God the Father, God the Son, and God the Holy
Ghost. The thing that sent the blood rushing to her fingers and
down to her very toes was that sanctified moment in the abbey
when the crown was placed upon her burnished gold hair and
she became Queen of England. She felt the incomparable rush
of power. It was stronger and more potent than anything she
had ever known before. It surpassed sexual gratification in its
thrilling impact, making her breasts tingle and her abdomen
ache intensely. To her great amazement she felt herself climax
and she became wet and sticky between her legs.

The banquet that followed was the greatest feast ever laid out
in history. Henry had suffered the burn of humiliation at his
own humble crowning, accompanied by the stringy joint of
beef, and he had been determined that Merrie Olde England
would make up for it now.

During the long winter, or season of the devil, as it was
known, everyone existed on salted meat and smoked fish, but
the spring had arrived early this year, providing lambs, kids,
and calves to add variety to the vast platters of roast oxen and
venison. Strong-fleshed peacocks, swans, and herons filled the
banquet tables. Thousands of eggs had gone into the puddings
and pastries to tempt the nobility and provide lavishly for the
thousands of Londoners who packed the gardens and roadways
around Westminster.

The consumption of fish was tremendous, the varieties too
numerous to count. Sturgeon, conger, mullet, mackerel, floun-
der, salmon, and plaice vied with great piles of shellfish, oys-
ters, shrimps, and crabs as well as crayfish, eels, and lampreys.

Wine flowed freely and none of it was domestic, which
Henry feared the Provençals would think inferior. The most
expensive kinds imported from Guienne and Gascony and
sweet Spanish muscatel were served to the guests by none other
than the Lord Mayor of London.

The nobility performed their hereditary parts in the ritual,
but the wedding train of the bride overflowed with so many
foreigners who looked down their long, thin noses at the na-

tives, totally ignoring the age-old precedence of rank with high-handed disregard for the long-established pecking order.

The bride's relatives filled the head tables as if it were their divine right to do so, and Henry was so flattered by the attention they lavished upon him, he realized happily he much preferred their noisy, laughing company to that of his staid English aristocracy. Tedious English ballads now gave way to more robust ones:

> "You say the moon is all aglow
> The nightingale is singing,
> I'd rather watch the red wine flow
> And hear the goblets ringing."

Henry thought the Provençals witty, clever, and sophisticated. Surely they were the most beautiful young people God had ever created. He couldn't believe his own luck in attracting and attaching them to his court.

William Marshal enjoyed showing off his beautiful wife. He was extremely proud of the accomplished, elegant young lady she had grown into and knew that perhaps only one more year would be necessary before she became a woman . . . his woman. She always managed to stand out from other females, and this coronation banquet was no exception. Everywhere was cloth-of-gold or gowns fashioned from material of threaded gold. Eleanor wore deep royal purple, her sleeves lined with heliotrope satin. A priceless chain of amethysts long enough to wrap about her neck twice and still encircle her waist made her blue eyes turn a mysterious shade of purple.

When her brother Richard approached them, Eleanor watched the pink roses ever-present in Isabella Marshal's cheeks blossom to dark red. She knew they had not seen one another for months, yet it was painfully obvious how they still felt about each other. She lifted her mouth to her husband's ear. "William, dance with your sister and I shall dance with Richard." William squeezed her hand. Already he loved her dearly. She was so quick to size up a potentially explosive situation and defuse it.

She laughed up at Richard. "Did you enjoy playing king?"

"You little maggot, you know I hated every minute of it. I'll be so bloody glad to get back to work sounding out the barons about war with France."

Eleanor groaned. "Bugger war, 'tis all men think of."

"Then I wish to God Henry would spare it a thought. With what he's spent today, we could have mounted a full-scale assault to regain Normandy. He's handing out gold marks, tracts of priceless land, castles, and even pensions to these grasping Provençals. Christ, with my own ears I heard him promise Thomas of Savoy a groat for every sack of English wool that will pass through his territory. Her relatives are legion and I think he's determined to reward every last one with a royal post. There's one been named King's Special Harper and another he's going to put on the roles as King's Versificator. I swear if Henry had any brains he'd be dangerous."

"Don't be too hard on him. He's in love. You can't blame him for trying to impress her . . . she's very lovely," said Eleanor.

"That's generous of you, sweeting; most women dislike each other," Richard said.

"There shall be no rivalry between us whatsoever. Look, here she is dancing with Henry; don't they make a magnificent pair?"

The two couples faced each other. The queen looked at the exquisite purple gown and amethysts. Henry spoke. "Eleanor . . ."

Both beautiful young women replied, "Yes?"

The queen gave Eleanor a look that should have felled her. Then she turned her face to the king and said, "We cannot both be called Eleanor. I have decided only the queen shall be Eleanor. You will have to be called something else. What is it your brothers call you—Maggot?" she asked sweetly.

Richard was shocked and almost jumped to his sister's defense. Then he hid a smile as he realized the maggot was perfectly capable of looking after herself.

Eleanor drew herself up to her full height, less than five feet and said regally, "I am the Countess of Pembroke and you may address me as such. I have always loathed the name Eleanor

. . . it is hideous. You are most welcome to it." She took Richard's arm and swept off.

He bent low to whisper in her ear, "I'm so relieved there is no rivalry between you."

"Bloody foreigners . . . I'm up to my gorge in them. Too bad we'll have to put up with them a whole wretched month before Henry sends them packing."

But Henry did not send them packing. He allowed the hangers-on to stay. Not only that, but more flocked over every day like a skein of geese honking into England. Henry listened to William of Valence as if every word were a pearl of wisdom. He immediately created Peter of Savoy the Earl of Richmond and gave him a valuable piece of land along the Thames in exchange for three symbolic feathers. He gave Amadeus land that he promptly sold.

They all sang homesick songs for their beautiful sunny Provence, but they didn't go back. Though King Midas was heaping gold upon his wife's relatives, he never had anything left over for his English subjects who paid the bills, not even kind words.

The English conceived a hatred for the Provençals that grew daily. After only three weeks a great council was called, and the barons most emphatically affirmed that no changes were to be made in the laws or methods of government.

The subject of Princess Eleanor came up again and again in conversations between the king and queen. "Each time your sister puts in an appearance, she is wearing different jewels."

"Darling, those jewels didn't come from royal coffers, I can assure you. They are gifts from her husband. The Marshals are probably the wealthiest family in England," he explained.

"Henry, I am the Queen of England. It is ridiculous that your little sister be allowed to outshine me. Why don't you give me the gold and silver cups stored in the Tower? I have goldsmiths and jewelers showing me their designs every day, begging me for my custom."

He cleared his throat. "Well, actually, I've had an offer for some of them. I really do need the money, Eleanor."

"Those clowns! If they are rich enough to buy our possessions, they can afford to give you the money you need!"

His voluptuous young wife always managed to make her demands at the end of the day preparatory to their going to bed. She gave him a sidewise glance from beneath her golden lashes. "Henry, why don't you help me remove my stockings? I feel in a most giving mood tonight." She reclined upon the bed and ran the stockinged sole of one foot up her other leg. Her skirt fell back to display the golden treasure between her legs.

As Henry's fingers strayed from her garter to a more tempting object, she stroked his swollen groin with her toes. "If I can be generous," she said throatily, "why can't you? You are the king, for God's sake, and I am your queen. If we put our minds together as well as we put our bodies together, we should be able to come up with some arrangement that will satisfy me." She ran the tip of her tongue over her lips. "You know that when I am satisfied, all my attention can be concentrated upon satisfying you."

He had already learned she was capable of teasing him, holding out against him until his part of the bargain was accomplished. "There is an honored custom known as Queen's Gold. It's a percentage of the fines levied on the Londoners. I see no reason why we cannot reactivate this custom, which has been out of use for many years."

His words worked like magic to open her legs wide and allow him to indulge his fantasies to the full. As he moved vigorously back and forth upon her, she gave vent to her own fantasies of luxurious excess. Surely fines could be levied on these Londoners with the thinnest pretext; if the Queen's Gold hadn't been paid for years, she was probably due a fortune in back payments of the tribute. She would look into it immediately. If the sheriffs of London balked, she would have them imprisoned. She was the Queen of England and she would be obeyed.

It was not enough, however, to have as many jewels and gowns as Eleanor Plantagenet. Secretly she wanted the regal beauty brought low. She thought it ridiculous that the young princess lived in a wing of Windsor Castle that was off-limits to men. She would have ousted her immediately if she had not learned that William Marshal's money was used for the upkeep of her apartment and servants.

It rankled her that Eleanor's virtue had been guarded so

jealously and that the young woman was reported to be still virgin. Because of her own experiences she had some doubts about the girl's innocence. An entertaining plot was hatching in her prurient mind that would put an end to speculation.

She recalled vividly the look on Peter of Savoy's face the first time he beheld Eleanor. It told her clearly that he thought the girl breathtaking and worth the great risk involved for a little dalliance. One afternoon when the newly created Earl of Richmond was lounging about her apartment indulging himself in her most expensive wine, she appealed to him in a way she knew he would not resist. "Peter darling, I have a wager for you."

He raised a lazy brow, not too interested. He'd just been created an earl, he was having plans drawn up to build a lavish dwelling he'd call The Savoy along the Thames. He had the use of any of the women at court, even her if he took the trouble to insist, so what did she have to offer?

" 'Tis said the prim little Countess of Pembroke is still virgin, but I don't believe she still has a cherry!"

Peter's attention had been engaged. "There is only one way to find out . . . pluck the cherry!" He laughed.

"Precisely, then I shall be right about her and the others wrong," the queen said smugly.

Peter applied himself diligently. He managed to be present whenever the dark beauty left her female sanctuary. In the stables he managed to shoulder her groom aside and assist her into the saddle. She thanked him coolly, politely, but he received no sidelong glances inviting him to dalliance. His little game of seduction had begun to excite him. He was beginning to believe she really was innocent. She seemed unawakened, unaware of innuendo or suggestive conversation that made more experienced young females blush or giggle.

The queen discovered that the princess, Lady Isabella, and her younger companions were going into the woods of Windsor to pick wild blackberries. She ordered her Court of Love, as she called her beautiful young male and female attendants, on an impromptu blackberry-picking expedition, and when she met up with her sister-in-law insisted they make a family affair of the outing.

The leafy glades were conducive to titillating games where couples eventually drifted off to secluded bowers. Peter of Savoy garbed in forest green never took his eyes from the Countess of Pembroke. She wore a pale-green summery gown that made her seemingly disappear among the trees, and he realized how well camouflaged they would both be.

He bided his time patiently and eventually his patience was rewarded. With a basket over her arm Eleanor gradually moved off from the others. He stalked her silently, taking time to carefully select a lovely place to corner his prey. "May I help you fill your basket, demoiselle?" he asked in heavily accented English.

She glanced up quickly like a startled young doe, but when she saw who it was no hint of fear showed in her eyes. "It is madame, sir, as you well know," she rebuked him lightly with a smile.

"Ah yes, *chérie*, but though you are married you are still . . . how do you say . . . a maiden."

"Would you prefer we converse in French, sir?" Though she knew Henry had created him Earl of Richmond, she could not bear to give him his title.

"Ah no, *chérie*, I must learn your native tongue. Perhaps you will be kind enough to instruct me? In return there are perhaps things I could teach you."

"I can do better than that; I can provide you with a tutor," she offered, deftly sidestepping his invitation.

He threw her such a hungry look she feared for her blackberries. His eyes were on her mouth. "Do you think your fruit is ripe enough for the plucking?" he asked playfully.

"Of course it is." She reached into the basket and held her hand out to him. "Taste it," she invited.

Peter took her hand, raised it to his mouth, took the berries with his lips, then very suggestively bit her fingers. She snatched her hand away from him, thinking What strange customs these foreigners have. She held his eyes with her sapphire gaze trying to fathom what he was up to.

He inched closer to her. Then very deliberately he reached into her basket and lifted a luscious blackberry to her lips. If she licked his fingers it would be the signal he was looking for, longing for.

She studied his face for a moment then very deliberately bit her teeth down into his hand.

"Peste!" he swore. "What the hell was that for?"

"The queen sent you to spy on me," she told him quite openly.

For a moment he thought she knew exactly what he had been sent to find out, then it dawned on him she had no inkling of the sexual connotation implicit in biting, licking, or sucking fingers. His eyes darkened with desire as he realized she was untouched after all.

"Why does she hate me?" Eleanor asked bluntly.

He threw back his head and laughed. " 'Tis not hatred she feels, but jealousy."

"But why?" Eleanor asked, baffled.

He shook his head regretfully. How could he explain to her that she was more delectable than any blackberry; that a man would give his soul to taste her innocence and awaken her senses so that she would suck the black juice from his fingers seductively?

A hunting horn sounded and through the trees came a party of young knights on horseback. The carcasses of two stags with great antlers were slung on poles carried by their squires. When the queen saw that the hunting party was headed by Rickard de Burgh, she hailed him.

Rickard dismounted. The rest of his men followed suit and graciously bent their knee to their sovereign queen. "I shall ride back to the castle with you, Sir Rickard, I've had enough of this boring, bucolic pastime. You may help me mount," she said, her hot eyes devouring him.

"Your Highness, forgive me, but I am bloodied from the hunt."

Queen Eleanor licked her lips and stepped close. "I don't mind a little blood . . . or sweat on a man. Labors that are sweated over give most satisfaction," she said suggestively.

As he lifted the queen into her saddle, he saw the Countess of Pembroke approaching with Peter of Savoy. The man had a possessive hand at the small of her back that made the muscle of Rickard's jaw clamp painfully. He would never have dreamed to take such a liberty himself even though he considered himself her personal guard. He searched Eleanor's face to see if the hated Savoy had distressed her in any way. Though she was neither flushed nor covered with blushes, her stiff little back and grave demeanor told him the man's attentions were odious to her.

The newly appointed Earl of Richmond threw him such a smug look of satisfaction as he helped himself to the fruit in Eleanor's basket that de Burgh knew he was attempting seduction.

Sir Rickard was on the horns of a dilemma. If he went to William Marshal with his knowledge, it would create more bad blood. There were already hostilities between the English and the Provençals, especially the favored Savoys. This could result in open hatred flaring out of control. If he went to the princess with a warning, it could rob her of some of her innocence. Somehow he could not bear the idea of Savoy tainting even her thoughts. He would handle the matter himself and take a subtle revenge.

He allowed two days to pass, then he sought out Peter of Savoy. "My lord earl," he said with a sober countenance as if he disapproved of the mission he had been sent upon. "A lady, who must remain nameless, wishes to become more intimately acquainted."

"Can this be true?" said the Earl of Richmond, taken by surprise.

"She is most interested in your offer of friendship, my lord, but her position demands the utmost discretion, if you understand me."

"I understand perfectly. You must reassure her on that point. I will make myself available at any time or place the lady will name."

De Burgh bowed with grimly compressed lips. At their next encounter de Burgh looked more grim than ever. He uttered few words, as if more would surely choke him. "Tomorrow night at the hour of eleven. I will come for you."

Peter of Savoy nodded eagerly, his mind already selecting an expensive jewel with which to charm the lady. At the appointed hour the two figures moved silently through the shadows of Windsor Castle. Just inside the women's wing, which Eleanor occupied, Rickard de Burgh paused outside a heavily studded door and held his finger to his lips. The arrogant Earl of Richmond nodded his thanks and entered.

"Poor Peter," said Rickard, half to himself, "you'll have your night's work cut out for you with Brenda." He had to wait until he was outside the bachelor knights' quarters before he could let out the laughter that almost choked him.

10

Peter des Roches, the Bishop of Winchester, who had been the king's guardian until Henry had tired of the leading strings and turned to Hubert de Burgh, returned to London. Henry welcomed him like a long-lost father. Winchester had a score to settle—or two scores, to be precise.

Hubert de Burgh and William Marshal had made the mistake of a lifetime when they had schemed to rid King Henry of Winchester's influence. He had worked hard to gain ascendency over the youthful king. He had placed his toadies in key positions and was ready to rule England when the two military leaders had seduced an impressionable Henry away from him. He had withdrawn to Rome to save face, but during his years of absence his ambition and his need for revenge had become an obsession, until there was no deed too foul for the ungodly bishop to contemplate.

The timing of his return was brilliant. His wealth and his hospitality would be extended to these greedy Provençals. The queen and her uncles would rule Henry, and the Bishop of Winchester would own and rule the Provençals.

He immediately invited King Henry and his court to spend Easter and later Christmas at Winchester. Henry had spent his boyhood Christmases there, joyous holidays filled with snow-ball fights, presents, and feasting, with only lip service paid to religion.

Henry immediately accepted because Winchester was a wealthy diocese and would bear all the festive expenses. He could not see that behind Peter des Roches's learning and charm was venality. He picked up the expenses now, so that he could reap a king's ransom down the road. There was not a shred of generosity or inner grace in the man.

Winchester had a bastard son, Peter des Rivaux, under his wing, and he was determined to secure a position of power for the young man. At the end of each day's celebrations for the new queen, the two Peters met to discuss their strategy.

"I think I have found the means by which you can bring Hubert de Burgh to his knees," Peter des Rivaux said.

Winchester's sausagelike fingers stroked his beard and his eyes gleamed with his lust for revenge. "Hubert has friends in high places because he appointed them to those places. He chose the chancellor as well as the treasurer of the royal household. Don't tell me they would be disloyal to him," Winchester said doubtfully.

"No, but his right-hand man is ambitious without being too scrupulous. I have paved the way for you to recruit him. I have informed him that, unlike de Burgh, you wish to remain in the background, but if he can bring us proofs of Hubert's malad-ministration and diversion of funds, those proofs would be worth their weight in gold."

Peter des Roches studied the jewel in his great thumbstall ring. "I'll speak with him. A promise of gold is enough to whet his appetite, but I have found there is nothing like the promise of a title to enslave a man. Hubert de Burgh is justiciar . . . I think it only fitting we hold out the carrot of 'justiciar' to this Segrave if he can help us depose our enemy."

"Your other enemy is another kettle of fish entirely. The Marshals have such old wealth, even their servants are loyal. The Earl of Pembroke is never ostentatious. The people love him, the barons respect him, and even the Plantagenets do his bidding."

Peter des Roches ground his teeth. He had an aloof and

superior manner and knew the English hated him. "His wife, Princess Eleanor, is a Plantagenet. There has never breathed a Plantagenet who was not vain and ostentatious."

"You are right, of course. She is vividly beautiful and the Earl of Pembroke keeps her in the lap of luxury, her every whim fulfilled. She has a maid called Brenda—a little slut who would make a perfect spy for us if only she could be placed in the marshal's household."

"Yes, it is overtime that he took Eleanor to wife. If the sanctimonious bastard had ever used the tender flesh of a young girl he'd know what he was missing. I'll speak to the maid. She must urge Eleanor to put a stop to this separate-household nonsense."

The grimace that passed for a smile made the Bishop of Winchester's eyes disappear in little fatty folds. "When we find the Achilles' heel of our enemies, their destruction will be inevitable."

The following day Peter was able to point out Brenda to his father, who lost no time approaching her. When the Bishop of Winchester's eyes looked deeply into hers and he suggested he would like to hear her confession, she was filled with dread. How did he know her shameful secrets? She had never felt shame that there was a well-worn path to her bed, but now suddenly the night of fornication with the de Burgh twins, which had led her to use multiple partners, caused bright spots to burn her cheeks and her conscience cried out for the balm of confession and absolution.

She curtsied low and kissed the bishop's ring. "I shall make my confession in the chapel after compline if you will make time for a sinner like me, my lord bishop."

"My child, I shall fill you with the Holy Spirit," he promised silkily.

Brenda spent a wretched afternoon wrestling with her conscience until finally she wished only to be free of the whole sordid business. If her behavior became public knowledge she would be dismissed without recommendation, but if she confessed all and begged for absolution, surely a man of God, pledged to silence, would wash away her sin and cleanse her.

Inside the confessional the atmosphere was close and hot.

Brenda's hands began to tremble and a trickle of sweat ran between her breasts. The Bishop of Winchester finally opened the upper half of the door, made the sign of the cross, and bade her confess her sins.

As her words came tumbling out, they had such an erotic effect upon the bishop that his nostrils began to quiver in an effort to pick up her woman's scent. The close, warm confines of the confessional often afforded him the telltale musky odor, which stirred him to erection. The favorite part of his calling was the confessional booth where the deepest intimacies could be shared in the utmost privacy. The sex of the sinner mattered little to Winchester. Inside this little box he enjoyed total power and control over the penitent, and it was like an aphrodisiac.

In a tight-voiced little whisper Brenda explained, "You see, my lord bishop, it is almost impossible for me to get release . . . and that is why I am so guilty of the sin of overindulgence."

Peter des Roches smiled into the perfumed darkness. "My child, I know exactly what you need. I am an instrument of God. Through me you shall receive fulfillment. I shall unlock the door between us and you will come into my cubicle." When she heard the click of the latch, she moved through the opening quickly and quietly. His unorthodox instructions hinted at some dark but sinfully pleasurable secret practice that she could not resist.

His robes smelled of incense as he lifted them and began to handle himself. "I shall fill you with the Holy Ghost." His plump hands lifted her skirts and underdress, and he began to stroke the cleft between her buttocks. In all her vast experience she had never felt anything that aroused her so swiftly.

His thumb ring, which boasted a ruby the size of a pigeon's egg, was hinged open to reveal a whitish powder. "Inhale some of this Holy Host and lick up the remainder," he instructed. He handed her his purple sash. "Use this to muffle your cries when I mount you."

She was reduced to a quivering mound of fecundity when he anointed her with Holy Oil and plunged his erection into her. Her need was so great that her low moans echoed about the confessional despite the silk sash. He used the thumb that boasted the enormous oval ruby both uniquely and skillfully, and before he had completed a dozen strokes he felt her spasm so violently, he spilled hot and high into her chalice. Her release in such a holy place was so intense she almost fainted.

This holy man had indeed brought her a little piece of heaven. "And the beautiful part is, my child, it works every time," he promised soothingly.

She could hardly speak. "Every time?" She gasped with disbelief.

He knew in that moment she was his, body and soul. She would do *anything* he asked of her.

11

William Marshal lived at Durham House when he was in London. It was situated on the bend of the Thames just up from Whitehall. Compared to most town houses it was immense, with bachelor quarters for his knights, a tiltyard, an armory, a washhouse, a buttery for keeping the wine cool, storage sheds, and a large stable.

William had just come from a meeting with four barons. They were livid. The king had recently promised to do nothing of importance without asking the barons' counsel, and now he was handing out titles and land like a man possessed. They felt Henry was treating them as if they were slaves to provide money for his foreign friends.

The sun had set by the time his squire helped him remove his chain-mail vest and brought him food. William ran his fingers through his clipped, curling hair and said, "I'm expecting female company tonight. When she arrives send her up."

He had not taken a woman since he'd been in Wales, he remembered as he stepped into his bath. In fact not since the day he had been reintroduced to his lovely child-wife. He'd recently married off his mistress of years, a discreet lady older than himself, to a wealthy goldsmith. A just reward for her loyal service, but perhaps he would have been wiser to keep her a trifle longer.

A picture of Eleanor sprang into his mind as she had stood upon the Tower water stairs in her crimson gown. It was a vision that came to him again and again. He cursed as his body reacted to the mere thought of her. He was annoyed that he needed the services of a whore. Then he sighed in resignation. He'd spent hours jousting in the tiltyard that morning to rid his body of lust, but Eleanor was ever in the forefront of his mind. All he needed to provoke an erection was a glimpse of the color crimson.

Eleanor sat alone in her bedchamber at Windsor. The lump in her throat almost choked her as she clenched her fists and absolutely refused to let herself cry. Not enough that her privacy was destroyed, the queen added insult to injury by starting a whispering campaign about her.

The queen thought it her right to waltz through the Countess of Pembroke's apartments at any hour simply to compare them with her own, which Henry had redecorated in his favorite green and gold. Thankfully she preferred her own. Eleanor had heaved a sigh of relief. Then her rooms had been invaded by those uncles . . . those Savoys . . . those foreigners!

Finally her temper had snapped and a whole roomful of people had felt the sharp edge of her tongue. The queen came in and caught the echo of her tirade. She had gone on tiptoe to the handsome Peter of Savoy, now Duke of Richmond, and whispered something amusingly cruel. He had laughed and murmured to one of his brothers, obviously repeating the queen's witty remarks. Thereafter whenever she was about the Provençals she saw them speaking behind their hands, rolling their eyes and laughing. Finally in desperation she took Brenda aside and demanded to know what was being said about her.

"My lady, do not ask me," Brenda pleaded. "Whatever she says stems from jealousy. I had it from one of her maids that she was in a continual rage because you set the fashion for dress at court. Rumor says she is demanding that Henry pay for her clothes to be imported from Paris so she will outshine you."

"Brenda, do not becloud the issue. I asked you what was being said about me."

Brenda sighed. Eleanor was one of those people to whom you could not lie. She decided to tell her everything. "They are whispering and laughing because your husband refuses to take you. They say he uses your age as an excuse to keep you from his castles and from his bed. They say his mistresses are legion, that he has had a liaison for years with Jasmine de Burgh. They say that your brother paid the marshal to enter into this marriage of convenience."

The blood drained from Eleanor's face and her throat closed as she whispered, "Leave me." She sat unmoving in the fading twilight until it was dark. Then suddenly she wrapped herself in a dark cloak, pulled the hood up, and slipped down through the grounds of Windsor Castle until she came to the barge sheds.

When she ordered her bargemaster to take her to Durham House, he was alarmed that she intended to go abroad at night without so much as a maidservant to accompany her, but he reasoned that since she was going to her husband's house, he would make no protest.

They sailed past the ships lying at anchor in the Pool of London, under the great bridge, and past the lights of the city before her barge pulled into the water stairs at Durham House. Eleanor pulled her hood close and hoped there would not be many servants about at this late hour. When she entered the reception hall, however, she encountered William's squire. She was quite relieved when he did not detain her, but waved her upstairs to William's private quarters.

She had never been in the house before and so opened the first door at the top of the staircase. It was a large, comfortable chamber with an inviting fire crackling on a marble hearth. It drew her instantly. Chilled from her ride on the river, she opened her cloak to let in the delicious warmth.

William's voice came through an open door in the adjoining room. "I'll be with you in a minute. Why don't you take your clothes off by the fire where it's warm."

She turned in amazement. Had he said "take your clothes off" or "take your cloak off"? And how could he possibly be expecting her? He came into the chamber with only a towel wrapped about his middle and stopped dead in his tracks. "Eleanor, what in the name of God are you doing here at this time of night?"

"I-I'm sorry William, I didn't realize you were bathing. Your squire sent me up here as if I was expected," she faltered.

"You were the last woman in the world I expected," he assured her.

She stiffened. "That is painfully obvious. It's all true then. You don't want me. Your women are legion. Marrying the king's sister was a political move, a marriage of convenience."

"Splendor of God, what are you saying?" he demanded. In three strides he was across the room and she was in his arms. His mouth swooped down to taste hers before he could stop himself. Though Eleanor had never been kissed before, she had spent a lifetime imagining what it would be like when William embraced her and touched his lips to hers. Her eyes closed and her arms reached up about his neck encountering the bared flesh of his chest and shoulders.

He lifted his mouth from hers and said huskily, "Darling, I've never wanted anything as much as I want you this moment. Who has been filling your ears with lies?"

"Oh, William, I can't bear it. They are whispering and laughing at me because you don't want me. I have no privacy; they have invaded my rooms."

"Sit down while I dress. I shall come immediately and lay down the law. Henry is being totally irresponsible to let them run loose like a pack of unruly dogs."

"No . . . William . . . please, let me stay here with you."

"Eleanor darling, we've been through all this before. We agreed and I thought you understood that you are far too young to be my wife in anything but name."

She pulled away from him and forced her eyes from the superb musculature of his chest. She sat down primly before the fire and chose her words carefully. "My lord earl, it is obvious you are expecting your mistress, so I will be brief. I do not ask to share your bed since you make it plain I could never satisfy a man of your age. All I ask is that you take me to live as your wife. If we must maintain separate apartments and be married in name only, then let us do so under the same roof so that I am not the laughingstock of the court."

William ran his hands through his hair distractedly. He wanted to scream at her that he had been expecting a common whore. That he needed the services of a whore because of the lust she aroused in him. He wanted to warn her how close he'd come to ravishing her. If she'd been wearing crimson, he would never have been able to bring his lust under control. But he could say none of these things to her. He burned with shame. He had been naked and awaiting the services of a whore when his innocent wife had come upon him. When he crushed her mouth beneath his, he had known immediately she had never even been kissed before.

"Eleanor, if you will return to Windsor tonight, I shall come for you tomorrow with all honor. You are the Countess of Pembroke and you will reside with me wherever I go from this day forward. We will stop their wicked tongues from wagging. There shall be no hint that we will have separate bedchambers for now. When I decide to make you my wife in the flesh, it will be our business. Our *private* business." He smiled at her. "Is that acceptable to you?"

She flew into his arms again. "Oh, thank you, William. I do love you so very much. I promise you with all my heart I will be no trouble to you whatsoever. I will sleep at the opposite end of the house so I will never, ever disturb you."

He sat naked by the fire long after she had taken up her cloak and departed. Only someone that innocent could believe her presence would not disturb him. Something inside him told William he must do the thing properly. He was the most unostentatious man, but he knew the immature royal couple could be impressed easily by a show of wealth, so he set aside his innate good taste for a show of theatrics.

Only two days since he had been aboard a vessel from Russia to purchase sable skins. He had been disturbed to see a small white bear chained inside an iron cage so confining it could not even stand. He would purchase it for Henry's zoo. He went along to the Templar's Countinghouse near the Palace of Westminster where the banking of the country was carried on. A great deal of Marshal treasure from the East was stored there for safekeeping as well as prizes and trophies he had won at tournaments in his youth. He was looking for something that would impress the new queen.

When he saw the ornate dressing table fashioned from bronze with its tiers of tiny compartments for hairpins and other such women's fripperies, he shuddered. The built-in candle holders surrounding its mirror had dangling prisms and its carved legs tapered down to carved animal-claw feet. When he noticed the matching seat was fashioned in the shape of a throne, however, he looked at the table with speculative eyes. He decided to gift the queen with it as a small revenge for the indignities she had shown his countess.

With tongue in cheek he actually sent heralds ahead to announce his arrival at Windsor and to alert the king and queen that this day marked a momentous occasion. He asked his Welsh archers to wear full armor as a special favor to him, and since the queen coveted the twin sons of Falcon de Burgh so much, he had them and the rest of his knights don their white cloaks emblazoned with the Red Lion Rampant.

At the last moment he remembered the full-length cape of white Arctic fox he'd ordered made for Eleanor's sixteenth birthday. He would drape the exquisite Norwegian fur about her today while the weather was still crisp. In a couple of months when she turned sixteen the weather might be too warm for her to enjoy it.

William also took along a score of servants to pack Eleanor's clothes and household furnishings and transport them to Durham House.

The trumpeters blew their fanfare as the Earl of Pembroke dismounted and greeted the king and queen and the gaggle of courtiers who had flocked out into the courtyard to view the marshal's cavalcade.

Eleanor threw open her casement window high above the courtyard to see what was causing the uproar. She gasped with pleasure as she caught sight of William and realized his intent. When his voice floated up to her, formally announcing to the King and Queen of England that he had come to take unto himself his dearly beloved Countess of Pembroke, her heart almost burst with joy. It was not by chance she had chosen symbolic white, faintly resembling a wedding gown, in which she would go to her husband.

Henry, who reveled in the power of kingship, laid the queen's bejeweled hand upon his arm and led the way to the throne room. He could not conceal his delight as the bear, *sans* cage, was led in on a long chain. "What do you think of the name Bruin?" he asked the crowd of youthful Provençals, and the ass-lickers they were flattered him into thinking it a most original name indeed.

The household steward was dispatched to ask that the Countess of Pembroke attend the king. A Plantagenet to her very bones, Eleanor arrived with her handmaidens in attendance, all Marshal cousins, and all gowned in pristine white. She arrived in time to see the bronze monstrosity presented to the queen. It was now freshly polished, its throne seat sporting a royal purple cushion. She curtsied low to show her respect for her husband, and he immediately raised her, kissing her upon both cheeks, his humorous eyes laughing down into hers.

"For one hideous moment I feared that was a gift for me," she murmured, low, keeping her face perfectly straight.

"No, my love, this is your gift," he said. Turning to Rickard de Burgh, he took the garment the knight carried over his arm and enfolded her in the crimson-lined white fur cape. His large hands squeezed her shoulders to show her his pleasure, and she gifted him with a smile of adoration to show her deep appreciation for the trouble he had taken today.

Now that Eleanor's departure was imminent, Henry suddenly became very possessive. He had become all prudish and proper and threw the Marshal of England a look of downright disapproval. "I realize you have been legally wed for many years, but I'm not sure my baby sister doesn't still need my protection. She is overyoung to be a wife in anything but name, I think."

The queen spoke up immediately. "Henry enjoys his little jests. He knows his sister and I share the same name as well as the same year of birth, and believe me, I am more than a wife in name only."

Henry's frowns turned to smiles. If this arrangement pleased his Eleanor, he was ready to sacrifice his sister, and by the evidence of his own eyes, Eleanor was a most willing sacrifice.

Actually, now that Henry thought about it, his baby sister had changed completely from the little terror she used to be. She had applied herself to her lessons in an effort to please William Marshal, and the young woman who had emerged was both poised and educated. He felt a small pang of regret for the willful, passionate child who had changed herself to please another. His glance fell upon his wife and he realized he'd done much the same thing. Was it worth it? he wondered.

William accompanied his countess back to her apartments where he thoughtfully gave each of her ladies-in-waiting a thank-you gift of jewelry. His young nieces were not unmindful that their uncle William had provided dowries generous enough to contract great matches for each of them.

"I know you have been happy here with Eleanor for I know just how generous she can be, but now you will be free to go forward into the future your parents have planned for you. I hope Eleanor's passion for life has rubbed off on each of you a little." He dropped an affectionate kiss on the top of her head, and her unruly black curls tickled his cheek.

"I have brought extra servants to take the drudgery out of your packing. Feel free to stay here as long as you wish, but rest assured when you are ready to return to your homes, my men-at-arms will give you safe escort."

He looked at his sister Isabella, saw the worry in her eyes, and said to Eleanor, "If you will excuse us, I would like a private word with Lady de Clare." In her chamber he patted her shoulder in a fatherly manner. "Do you suppose you can go home to Gilbert and give it another try? If it is untenable you may come and live with Eleanor. We will still live separately, you know. This circus today was for the benefit of the jackals."

His sister looked so infinitely sad, he tried to cheer her. "You can be proud of all you have accomplished here with Eleanor and with the Marshal nieces. Today they made the queen and her Provençal ladies resemble overripe peaches who had hung against a sun-drenched wall so long they had begun to rot."

"Oh, William, I had forgotten how outrageous your wit

could be." She smiled at him. "I believe you are a match for Eleanor."

"I doubt that," he admitted ruefully. "What's your decision?"

"I have decided to go home," she said with finality. "If only I didn't feel this disloyalty . . . this betrayal."

"Gilbert need never know; will never guess."

"I wasn't speaking of disloyalty to Gilbert, but to Richard," she admitted hopelessly.

"My dear, if you have it that bad, there is little hope of reconciliation."

"William, what has made you so understanding?" She searched his face.

" 'Tis simple enough. I've fallen in love. How ironic that my morals prevent me from making love to her."

"William, she is as you wished her to be, ignorant in the ways of men. But lately she has shown a great curiosity and asked me many pointed questions. Naturally I preserved her innocence, but rather than have her learn from some sluttish servant, I wish you would relax that damned rigid code of honor and satisfy her natural curiosity in a loving, wholesome way."

"Well, she will celebrate her sixteenth birthday very shortly. I shall think about your advice, Isabella, but trust me to know when the time is right to make her a wife in every way." His sister didn't know him very well, thank God. His damned rigid code of honor was Eleanor's protection, for his thoughts of her were far more carnal than wholesome.

12

Brenda insisted upon staying to supervise the servants from Durham House as they packed Eleanor's beautiful clothes. The Countess of Pembroke shook her head in amazement at the transformation that had come over the girl lately, very likely due to fear that she would not be included in the new household. Not only had she become very attentive, but she had actually started to go to confession twice a week!

Brenda sought out the Bishop of Winchester, who was at his dinner, but when his servant told him who was at his chamber door he told him to admit her.

"I have been expecting you, my child. Events are unfolding exactly as they should." He wiped his mouth on a square of linen and dipped his sausagelike fingers in a bowl of rosewater. "Keep your eyes and ears open and your mouth closed. I want to know everything about the Marshals, no matter how trivial you may think it. A good place to start would be William Marshal's squire. He will be loyal, of course, but remember he will be a fountain of privileged information." Peter des Roches smiled. "Once you get your hands on his balls, you should be able to squeeze out any information." He was twisting the thumbstall ring with its enormous ruby until Brenda's attention was fixed upon it with longing.

"Tell me, my child, do Eleanor's ladies-in-waiting go with her or do they return to their homes? They are all Marshals and I have an interest in every Marshal who ever drew breath."

"They are all returning home, my lord bishop. Even Isabella de Clare, which greatly surprises me."

"Why so?" he asked with narrowed eyes.

Brenda focused on the ring, her mouth totally dry with her need. She had to moisten her lips before she could speak. "She loves Richard of Cornwall. She and Gilbert de Clare are like strangers."

Winchester's eyes disappeared into the creases of his smile. "You should have told me this before. I want to know everything," he emphasized.

"My lord bishop, Windsor is some distance from Durham House. How will I make my confession?"

"I am at Westminster every Sunday, well within walking distance of Marshal's town house."

"My lord bishop . . . I need absolution." She damned him silently for making her beg.

"Of course you do, my child. Go straight through that door and I shall be with you in the flesh directly."

After Brenda had gone, Peter des Roches lost no time seeking out Richard. "It has been many years since you spent the holidays at Winchester, Your Highness. For old times' sake I hope you will come at Easter."

The king's brother was filled with martial zeal and a thirst for war with France at the moment, and he had little time or thought for matters ecclesiastic.

"With my own hands I placed the crown upon Henry's head when he was only nine and you but seven. You had the makings of a king, my boy, but you never seemed ambitious for power."

"Make no mistake, my lord bishop, I am ambitious for power. It is only my brother's crown I do not covet," Richard stated.

Roches smiled. "So, the lessons I taught you as a boy found fertile ground. Then alas I was cast aside and your favorites became illustrious soldiers like Marshal and de Burgh, which is right and proper for impetuous youths. But now that you are older you should come to realize the vast power wielded in the name of religion. The church controls half the wealth of this world, and with enough money even a crown can be purchased. Tell me, does the title King of the Romans appeal to you?" The Bishop of Winchester's eyes disappeared inside his smile. "When you were a boy you came to me with all your problems . . . I can still solve some of them for you, you know. You are the only Plantagenet unmarried, and yet I know you long for sons." He paused and Richard was on his guard immediately. "If your fancy fell upon a lady who had the impediment of, say, a husband, the church has the power to remove that impediment."

Richard knew the wily old swine had sniffed out his desire for Isabella Marshal de Clare. Surely to God she hadn't let out their secrets in the confessional booth? Still, he'd never dreamed of taking steps to have the church dissolve her marriage, but if he was hearing correctly, Winchester was offering to do this for him.

"My lord bishop, I should be both grateful and generous to any man who helped me fulfill my ambitions."

"Are you having any luck urging the barons to take up arms?" he asked silkily.

Christ, Richard thought, he has a fat finger stuck in every pie. "The barons who have interests in Normandy and Aquitaine need no urging. 'Tis the rest I must convince. I assume you are against war?" Richard asked point-blank.

"There, you see how little you know of me. In times of war there are fortunes to be made, ambitions to be realized, hungers to be satisfied, and old scores revenged. It is only when evolution speeds up into revolution, or peace erupts into war, that the old order can be swept aside to make way for the new."

Richard excused himself. The man made him feel unclean. He still remembered a day when he was about eight when he had knocked those sausagelike fingers from his genitals. He had often wondered if the old swine had made advances to Henry.

Richard had the support of Ranulf, Earl of Chester, and though Hubert de Burgh had had enough fighting with the French to last him a lifetime, he could always be counted upon to obey the king, reasoned Richard. Hubert had even stayed loyal to their father, King John. If he could stomach that prick, he would certainly hold his nose and obey Henry.

The mercenaries, led by Falkes de Bréauté, were paid to fight wars. They did their job well and were willing and eager, but that was because England was not at their heartroot. They'd be willing to fight for anyone with the gold to purchase their services. If the fabric of England was torn asunder by war, it mattered naught to them. He could number on one hand the barons who would go to France willingly. He could count on Fitz-John, Fitz-Walter, Peter de Mauley, and Philip d'Aubigny. Richard knew that William Marshal held the key to success or failure. If he could get Marshal on their side, then the Earls of Norfolk, Derby, and Gloucester would fall into line as well as the influential de Lacys, de Warennes, de Clares, and de Ferrars. Tomorrow he would pay a visit to his sister at Durham House. If he could convince Eleanor, William would be clay in her hands.

That night, however, William Marshal was in the throes of a dilemma. It had taken only a few days for Eleanor to get settled. She was adored by the household servants, and they bent over backward to make it easy for her to take over the role of chatelaine of Durham House. He found he enjoyed her company more than he had ever dreamed. She was fascinating, witty, enthusiastic, sensitive to his moods, and more alluring than a courtesan. If he spent time with her, desire raged through him like wildfire. On the other hand, if he avoided her company so that his blood stayed cool and his thoughts were rational, he was utterly miserable without her lovely face smiling up at him or her sapphire eyes challenging him over a game of chess. Whenever her laughter floated to him he was drawn to her side, like a moth to a flame. Finally he stopped fighting with his inner voices and gave himself up utterly to the pleasure of her company. He faced the fact that a casual whore would now be impossible. If his wife's closeness and the scent of her made his body's needs too painful to bear, he would simply have to masturbate. It wouldn't kill him and he certainly wouldn't be the first man to have to resort to such unsatisfactory measures.

After the evening meal Eleanor would have withdrawn to her own chambers, had not William watched her longingly as she moved toward the stairs. "If you'll stay down here and keep me company for a while, I'll build up the fire for you," he bribed.

"Would you care to play a board game or I could play the lute for you, my lord?"

"Sweet, you don't need to entertain me constantly. I just want to be with you," he said, sitting in an easy chair.

She picked up a bowl from the sideboard and took a copper pan from the wall. "We can roast chestnuts and talk," she said, sinking to the rug at his knee.

He watched her profile against the backdrop of the orange flames. He would have sold his soul to the devil in that moment to be an eighteen-year-old youth again. He would push her back on that rug and undress her with impatient hands, then he would worship her with his young body and make love to her until dawn.

She peeled a hot chestnut with nimble fingers and held it to his lips. "Once upon a time you told me my grandfather and grandmother had a great love affair. No one has ever enlightened me."

He could not resist touching her and reached out a hand for an unruly black tendril of hair. It curled about his fingers possessively, and he sighed his contentment. As he began his tale she leaned her head against his knee so that his hands could play with her hair or wander wherever else they wished to stray.

"Your grandmother, Eleanor of Aquitaine, was married to King Louis and was the reigning Queen of France when your grandfather, the lowly Count of Anjou, was sent on a mission to the King of France. Henry was so vigorous, horses fell beneath him. He was so ambitious and such a great war lord that he made himself King of England on the thinnest connection to the throne. When he laid eyes upon Eleanor of Aquitaine, he lusted for her. He knew he would need a queen to rule England with him, and his choice fell upon Eleanor.

"They were true opposites. He was a soldier, rough, unpolished, coarse in word and deed, while she was beautiful, cultured, educated, and seductive. Never mind that she was almost a dozen years older than he, never mind that she was married to another man who was king of a great country. In his blunt, direct way Henry told Eleanor he would have her and without hesitation told Louis he must divorce her. Of course Louis was outraged and refused.

"That didn't stop Henry." Here William paused. How could he put the rest of the story to her delicately? He could not. Henry II hadn't known the meaning of the word "delicate," and of course this was what had attracted Eleanor's passionate nature. The story would lose its impact if he put it delicately. He continued. "He deliberately seduced Eleanor of Aquitaine, bedded her again and again until he got her with child. It caused the greatest scandal of the century, but he achieved his goal. Louis divorced her immediately and Henry made her Queen of England, and begat five sons and three daughters upon her. They were mad for each other. Eight children in less than a dozen years."

"So it was only years later when their passion cooled that he imprisoned her?" Eleanor asked.

"Their passions never cooled. When he took a mistress, the fair Rosamonde, and she gave birth to your uncle, William of Salisbury, Eleanor was so jealous she spent a lifetime getting even with him. She fed the fire of ambition in her sons until they pulled their father down for the crown he wore. He confined her to her own castle to protect himself."

"Then I think their passions cooled, my lord," Eleanor said, caught up in the tale.

"Their love cooled, but not their passions. They still shared a bed. Half her children were born after the affair with Rosamonde."

"I don't think he married her for love—he married her to further his ambition. I have never heard anything so calculating in my life. He was a vile man . . . and she no better to have committed adultery with him. They deserved each other."

"I shouldn't have told you," William said ruefully.

"Of course you should!" she said, laughing up at him. "William, you mustn't shield me from the truth. They were wicked and worldy—but very well matched. Who could ask for more?" she said almost wistfully.

He came down to the rug and brushed the back of his fingers across her cheek. "Eleanor, I want to take you to Chepstowe and Pembroke. I love Wales. I want you to love it too."

"Oh, William, will you really take me? I've longed to see it for years."

"You are the Countess of Pembroke. I'll take you home." Now he peeled a hot chestnut and held it to her lips. "You may not be quite old enough to be a wife and mother, but I've decided you are old enough to be courted." He lifted her against his heart and very gently touched his lips to hers.

When Richard arrived at Durham House, he found it a hive of activity. It was obvious preparations for a journey were being made, but Richard could not locate the marshal in either the armory or the knights' quarters. He was amazed to find him helping Eleanor select warm traveling clothes. Richard rolled his eyes to the rafters. "You've already got him in leading strings. I thought you had more brains than to involve your husband in women's affairs."

Eleanor laughed, pleased to see her brother at her home. "Richard, I'll get you refreshments. We had ale from Kent delivered just this morning."

William held his tongue. He knew her brothers loved her dearly, but they must learn to respect her.

Richard said, "Don't hurry back, Eleanor, I have business of the realm to discuss with the marshal."

"In that case the Countess of Pembroke must remain. From now on all my business will be conducted with Eleanor at my side. She has the ability to learn faster than any Plantagenet I've ever met," he said pointedly.

"I stand reprimanded," said Richard, more bemused than ever that his sister had the Marshal of England wrapped about her little finger. He put forth his most persuasive arguments for war with France, stressing that the main objective would be to regain any small part of the territories his father had let slip away. He then gave the marshal a list of the men who would stand with them and, saving the best 'til last, he said, "We already have Simon de Montfort aiding the Count of Brittany. He has sworn fealty to Henry."

"Simon de Montfort?" Eleanor was unfamiliar with the name.

"I am impressed," said William, then he enlightened Eleanor. "He is a war lord, a legend, probably the greatest warrior of our time. He is reputed to be a giant—like a massive fighting machine."

Richard laughed, remembering. "He dwarfed Henry and me. His arms and legs resembled young oak trees; no wonder he is fearless. When the war lord descends upon a region, his methods are so severe and relentless none can withstand him for long."

Eleanor repressed a shudder. "The Frenchman sounds odious."

William said, "He is only half French, heir to the earldom of Leicester. You surprise me, Eleanor. I always understood you to have a fatal attraction for soldiers," he teased.

"Not soldiers in general, my lord, just one soldier in particular," she said, thinking him the most gentlemanly soldier in the world.

William turned back to Richard. "Even with the mighty war lord on your side, you will have your work cut out for you. You must convince the men of the Cinque Ports, also people like Surrey and Northumberland."

"My Lord Earl, if you are with us, the others will follow suit," Richard said with the confidence of youth.

"My guess is all will commit grudgingly. You'll get either a token of money or men, not both, and only as little as the barons can get away with. The campaign won't succeed because victory over France will require full commitment."

"The king will order men to arms," Richard began.

"Will he indeed?" William's mouth was grim. "I will go into Wales and Ireland and *recruit* men, not order them. Soldiers forced to fight are a liability in battle, not an asset."

"Again I stand corrected. It is just that Henry has already ordered Hubert de Burgh to gather ships at Portsmouth to transport men and supplies."

"Hubert always did fear the danger of opposing his king,"

William said. He did not need to add that the Marshals always did what was right and honorable, not what was expedient. "You will both need to school yourselves to patience. Men won't leave the fields until the harvest is in, so we have months to recruit. I intend to take Eleanor to Wales in any case. I don't suppose she'll cavil at going to Ireland as well."

She cast him a look of gratitude and he winked back at her. Richard caught the byplay and decided these two people longed to be alone with each other. He saluted the marshal and thanked him most sincerely for his commitment. Then he bowed formally to Eleanor and, raising her hand to his lips, murmured, "Adieu, Countess."

William grinned at her when they were again alone. "I do believe he was finally showing respect for the Countess of Pembroke."

Eleanor laughed happily. "The word 'Countess' almost choked him."

It had already become their custom to spend the hours between the evening meal and bedtime alone together. William pulled out his well-worn maps and charts and spread them out for Eleanor. "We'll make a sailor of you. How would you like to go overland one way and take ship the other?"

She leaned against his shoulder as they scanned the parchments. "Have I told you how much I like being married to you, my lord?"

He slipped his hand about her waist and squeezed her. "Not nearly enough, Eleanor Marshal. You plan the journey; I'll trust your instincts entirely."

Her finger traced the maps and charts and her brow wrinkled in concentration as she plotted the journey, rejecting her first thoughts and starting afresh. He pulled up a stool and watched her for the sheer pleasure of it. She gave him so much, he could never give enough back. So this was love then—wanting to give only pleasure to the beloved; constantly searching your mind for love tokens that would bring a smile to her lips or a sparkle to her eyes. He deeply regretted it had come so late in life, but since his heart's desire was Eleanor who was so much younger than he, it could have been no other way. He was grateful it had come at all.

When he saw the corners of her mouth lift in triumph, he knew she had decided exactly how it would be. "Since spring comes very late to your wild Welsh mountains, I think it would be best to sail to Pembroke first and then Ireland. At the end of the summer we can ride across Wales to Chepstowe and return to London only when we can tear ourselves away. When the harvests are being gathered in is the happiest time of the year, and fodder for the horses will be plentiful. Food as well if you recruit your army. I shall be generous and offer to put you up the first night at my estate of Odiham. That's approximately halfway to Portsmouth where I know you anchor most of your ships."

Unable to keep his hands from her long, he came back to the map table. Placing his fingers beneath her chin, he raised her face so that he could look into her eyes. "Enchantress, do you have the power to read my mind, or has marriage to me made you more intelligent?"

"Your head swells apace with your male conceit," she teased.

"My head isn't the only thing that swells," he murmured, but the look of incomprehension she gave him made him curse his male vulgarity. He could enlighten her. He could take her hand and gently guide it to his male center. Sooner or later he would have to put an end to her innocence. The trouble was he loved her exactly the way she was. He couldn't bear to despoil her quite yet. Her innocence was the most precious gift she could bring him, and he would savor her to the full. She was on the brink of discovery. He would not rush her first delicious, delicate steps down the road to intimacy. He would do everything in his power to preserve the magic, the mystery, the silent promise of love's fulfillment.

He cleared his throat and went back to the plans for their journey. "All our households are fully staffed with servants so we won't need to take any except maids for you, of course, but I'd advise you to take as few as possible. From my experience women slow you down when you are traveling and they are notoriously bad sailors. If I know you, you'd end up nursing them through seasickness."

She would not argue with him. All men had such poor opinions of women. She'd change all that, but of course it would take time. "I won't need to take any maids along to slow us up, my lord."

"Could you really manage without?" he asked, his face alight with hope.

She teased, "If I need the services of a maid, I'll just ask Rickard de Burgh."

"You will ask me, madame. The de Burghs will have enough to do in Wales making the annual inspection of their own castles and their father's." He watched her face closely. "Sir Rickard is a handsome young devil—are you attracted to him?"

She looked at him, uncomprehending for a moment, then saw the vulnerability written on his face. "William, he's just a boy."

Her words made his heart sing, and Eleanor hugged the wonderful knowledge to herself that her husband was jealous of her.

13

Brenda lost no time reporting to Winchester that the Marshals were planning a journey to Wales and Ireland. This immediately confirmed to him that the Earl of Pembroke was supporting Henry and was off to recruit. He was disappointed.

The bishop had hoped for a clash between the king and the highest peer of the realm. He was ready to step in and fill the void an estrangement would have created. However, he could see clearly that his political ambition would remain in limbo forever unless he took steps to remove the obstacle that blocked his goals: the Marshal of England, who had been his bête noire for years. The man had no vices that could be exploited, and even though impressionable Henry shifted his loyalties about like a weathercock, his respect for William Marshal remained steadfast. Now was the time to lay plans that would lead to outright elimination. He could never become the power behind the throne while the Marshal of England lived and breathed.

"Is the countess to accompany him?" the wily bishop asked.

"Yes, I have never seen her happier, though he hasn't yet taken her to his bed," reported Brenda, unable to comprehend such abstinence.

"If they were intimate she would be privy to his every move, his every thought, and I'm sure you would have no trouble relaying the information to me. I have a powder that I want you to sprinkle on the earl's food, not unlike the stimulant I provide for you. This, however, stirs an insatiable desire in a man, a craving that must be satisfied. You know what that is like. The marshal will soon have Eleanor in his bed and will be casting glances your own way, I shouldn't wonder. However, I caution you to wait until you are in Wales before you use it. The effect will not be nearly so efficacious when traveling and taking meals at odd hours," Winchester lied.

"My lord bishop, I don't know how I will manage without you. I need to cleanse my soul with confession at least once a week." Brenda moaned.

"Marshal's old squire Walter is training a new squire by the name of Allan. He is in my employ and a most apt pupil. I will instruct him to serve you in any capacity." He wished to reveal as little as possible to this slut. It must never be proven there was any connection between Allan and himself. He would give instructions to eliminate the wench once the other impediment had been removed. He smiled to himself as he recalled how Allan had revealed himself in the secrecy of the confessional booth as a child murderer, thereby placing himself entirely in Winchester's power as a pawn in his political games. The booth certainly had its diverse uses.

When Brenda learned that she would not be accompanying Eleanor to Wales, she was overcome with disappointment. Learning that the new squire, Allan, was also being left behind improved her mood considerably. After Brenda invited him into her bed, she was delighted that he had been tutored by Winchester regarding her needs. She confided, "Allan, the bishop gave me an aphrodisiac for the earl. I almost sprinkled some into your wine tonight. How lovely that you don't need it."

Allan blanched visibly at her words. Christ, surely the wench wasn't naive enough to think Winchester had really given her an aphrodisiac. The stuff was unsafe in her hands. "Since you do not accompany the countess to Wales, the powder will go to waste. Give it to me. I will doubtless need it on occasion if I am to fully satisfy a lusty wench like yourself."

He would do the deed himself. It was unsafe merely to put the stuff into a decanter of wine. He had no idea if the powder worked at once or needed to be ingested over a period of time before it took its toll. The entire household could not become sick or die at one and the same time; poison would be suspected immediately. He would put the powder away for safekeeping until the marshal returned from Wales. In the meantime he would become indispensable as a trusted household servant.

Eleanor fell in love with Wales and its magnificent mountains, crystal lakes, and virgin forests. She was able to show her husband her proficiency in Gaelic, and he was so impressed by her feel for the Welsh people and their language that he insisted she sit beside him while he transacted all his business. She presided with him when they held courts of justice, and he asked her help in handing down judgments and sentences. Her fine hand appeared beside that of her husband on all legal documents as she signed Eleanor, Countess of Pembroke.

She accompanied him while hunting and hawking, and his knights soon learned that William wished to help her mount and lift her from the saddle himself at day's end. They were both happier than they had ever been in their lives and indulged in loving little rituals. As he reached up his arms he would murmur, "Are you my girl?" and the back of his hands would brush against her breasts.

She would blush and lower her lashes. "William, you know I am."

"Good, then I think I'll keep you for one more day," he would tease, and brush her lips with his own.

She learned so many things from her mature husband. He taught her patience and showed her how to look beyond the obvious to seek the truth. He allowed her complete freedom in running the households and made it possible for her to draw any amount of money she desired. The theories she had learned of being chatelaine of a household with hundreds to feed were now put into practice, and her influence was evident in the improved quality of the meals, the efficiency of the servants, the cleanliness of the castles, and the luxurious warmth of the chambers.

She made a smooth transition from Wales to Ireland, visiting as many as two-thirds of the Marshal manors in Leinster. To Will's delight the Irish, who were more obstreperous than the Welsh ever dreamed of being, took an instant liking to his beautiful wife.

The de Burgh twins went home to Connaught to recruit men-at-arms from their father, and for the first time in years Will was free from the siren call of their mother, Jasmine. Eleanor's fears about the legendary enchantress were also laid to rest, since William showed no inclination to visit Portumno.

Their summer had been perfect, then suddenly as they were about to return to Wales the aging Bishop of Ferns showed up breathing hellfire.

William Marshal, as was his habit these days, received the bishop with Eleanor at his side.

"I want no Plantagenet present. My business with you is a private matter," the old man thundered.

"My wife is the Countess of Pembroke. She is a Marshal now and as such is privy to all Marshal business," William stated flatly.

"Your father cheated me out of two manors," the old man charged, warming to the subject and shaking his fist in anger. "I asked King Henry to return them to me and got nowhere. I ask *you* this time."

"My father was incapable of cheating, my lord bishop, and since the man has been dead for over ten years I fail to see why you keep harping on the matter. The church is notoriously greedy for land. I have borne the upkeep of my Irish manors for years, generously subsidizing them through times of famine. If I ceded them to you undoubtedly you would cut the timber, sell off the livestock, and the tenants would find themselves without a roof over their heads. Once and for all time my answer is no," said Will.

The Bishop of Ferns turned purple. Livid, he began threatening excommunication, which would be ineffective without the Pope's consent. Then the bishop looked upon Eleanor Plantagenet with raw hatred. Her exquisite beauty whipped him up to the point where he became overwhelmed with the need to destroy. He pointed his long, bony finger and placed a curse upon them where they stood. "The Almighty Marshal family will end! In one generation the name shall be destroyed. You will never share in the Lord's benediction to increase and multiply. You and your brothers after you will die without issue and your inheritance will be scattered. All shall come about by one year from this day!"

Eleanor listened to his outrageous curse with two spots of crimson burning upon her cheeks. Will would not smite down the old sinner because of his age, but finally she could bear no more. She lifted her riding crop and flew at the old man. "Get out! Your curse is absolutely meaningless to us. I swear by Almighty God that before I am twenty I will have a houseful of children! I, the Countess of Pembroke, will negate your wicked curse."

Late that night Will awoke to hear Eleanor sobbing in the next chamber. He went to her and gathered her into his arms. "My darling, I had no idea the old fool would upset you this much. Don't cry, sweet, I can't bear it."

She clung to him, wanting to be reassured that a bishop's curses could not touch them.

"Sweetheart, he was trying to intimidate me into relinquishing the land. These tactics of hellfire and brimstone work very well in a country steeped in superstitions."

She buried her face in his neck and whispered, "I want to prove him wrong . . . I want to have a baby. Give me your son, William, please."

He closed his eyes and held her against him so tightly she could not breathe. She was too young, too small. If she died in childbirth he would die without her.

"Eleanor, I cannot risk getting you with child until the fighting in France is done. You must see that it would be totally irresponsible of me. If I was killed you would be left alone to bring up the child."

"Oh, Will, don't go to France. I am so afraid for you!" Her sobs increased.

He tried to humor her. "You fell in love with me when you were five only because I was a great soldier. I was your hero because I could wield a sword better than other men. On our wedding day your admiration for me knew no bounds when I showed you the vulnerable spots to stick in a sword."

"I'm sorry," she whispered. "How you must hate tears. They are a pitiful woman's weapon designed to rob you of your strength, and I swore I would never resort to such tactics."

He lay down beside her and she rested her cheek against his shoulder. He stroked her hair, loving the alive, almost crackling feel of it beneath his fingers. "Let all your foolish, fanciful fears slip away. Ireland can do that to you. There is an otherworldliness about it. Once the melancholy grips you, it is difficult to shake. Let's go home."

"Will, don't leave me," she begged.

"Hush now. I'll stay right here until you sleep," he comforted.

But that wasn't what she meant. "Will, don't *ever* leave me." She shivered uncontrollably, and he gathered her close and kissed her eyelids, tasting the salt tears that still clung to her lashes. The warmth of his body and the all-encompassing love in which he surrounded her gradually relaxed her until she was lulled to sleep.

Before he could tear himself away from her, he gazed at her for a full hour. His eyes devoured the black cloud of hair spread across the white pillow, the dark shadow of her lashes that formed crescents on her high cheekbones, the lovely full mouth, cherry-ripe and oh so tempting.

He eased the covers from her and his reaction was immediate and marked. He held his breath as he unfastened the ribbons of her sheer nightrail to allow an unimpeded view of her swelling breasts. He throbbed as he imagined himself taking a luscious pink nipple into his mouth to suck. He could almost taste her.

His swollen phallus moved of its own free will as if seeking the entrance to Paradise. Very gently and carefully he moved closer to her to allow its tip to brush against her silken thigh. He quivered with the delicious sensations her nearness aroused. He knew he could wait not one instant longer for her to touch him, so he took her hand and laid it upon his manhood. Her fingers curled in her sleep and he closed his eyes, imagining exquisitely erotic manipulations.

He sighed deeply. Fate or the gods had entrusted her to him.

He felt like Hercules must have felt when the mythic Zeus was testing him, though the difficult task of protecting Eleanor from his growing lust was like Hercules's twelve labors rolled into one.

William Marshal recruited an army of about 250, and along with England's other nobles gathered at Portsmouth. Henry put too much faith and money in the hands of his new relatives. When Hubert de Burgh, who was supposed to be in charge, saw the fiasco too many chiefs was creating, he complained bitterly but was always overruled. The treasury was depleted before enough vessels were provisioned, and the Bishop of Winchester was at Henry's elbow the day some of the casks were accidentally broken open. Instead of holding weapons and supplies they were filled with stones and sand.

Henry rushed at Hubert calling him an old traitor, and William Marshal had to stand between them until tempers cooled. Marshal and de Burgh knew in their bones the venture against France would fail. They lacked men, ships, arms, money, and most of all the will to fight, but it had now become dangerous to oppose the king and the powerful Provençals.

Henry's army went ashore in Gascony, the safe southwest corner of France that still belonged to England. Simon de Montfort, who had helped the Count of Brittany take back his country from the French, immediately joined King Henry and put forth strategic battle plans. Henry ignored his advice. He was willing to let de Montfort risk his life and men on the front lines, but he would not commit his entire army in a concerted effort.

The young Provençal knights spent their time drinking and wenching, and Henry seemed content to parade through the safe reaches of the territory that still remained under English control.

William Marshal's Welsh and Irish joined Simon de Montfort's men in the heavy vanguard fighting. They scored victory after victory, but Henry brought in no reinforcements, not even to hold the land gained. The men at the front could not conquer new territory today and hold on to what they had taken yesterday without backup.

William was impressed by Simon de Montfort. The six-and-a-half-foot giant certainly lived up to his reputation as a fierce war lord. He had never seen a man in such superb physical condition. All other men suffered by comparison, even himself, William admitted. But de Montfort had more than strength of body. The marshal recognized his natural abilities of leadership. He was a brilliant strategist and always fought with an eye to his men's safety. He never asked a man to do aught he was not willing to do himself. He always took the lead, and his men trusted and loved him enough to follow his magnificent example.

William and Simon spent many hours together in campaign tents after the day's fighting. Here he got to know the man behind the soldier. Simon was candid and forthright about his ambition, yet William doubted he would ever sacrifice his honor for expediency. He was a true, worthy, and valiant knight.

Simon knew his men by name. He was completely fearless, especially when it came to removing his wounded men from the field. He was so quick and strong, it was easier for him to carry out wounded singlehanded than to send in two-man teams.

William Marshal poured Simon de Montfort a leather horn of ale and sat down by the campfire. Simon's deep voice was troubled. "Cite me for treason if you wish, but the king has no more idea about winning wars than a bloody pack mule."

William agreed with him. "We both know only a decisive thrust would have been effective. He listens to the wrong people these days. I've managed him for years. I let him think my ideas were his own and led him down whichever path was best for England, but now we will all suffer from the false council of those who have him by the balls. Relatives!" he spat.

Simon laughed. "Are you not his brother-in-law?"

"Aye," William acknowledged. " 'Tis a wonder he turned out as well as he did with John for father. I tried to be a father to them all, but I was off fighting so much. If only Henry had Richard's guts and Eleanor's brains, he might have made a good king."

" 'Tis hard to believe he's descended from the great King Henry II. Surely it gnaws at his throat that his grandfather ruled an empire three times as big as that of the King of France. He believed what I believe," Simon de Montfort said firmly, "you can become what you behold. Henry II wrested England, Brittany, and Normandy from Henry I. He inherited Anjou and Touraine from his own father, Geoffrey of Anjou, and he acquired Poitou, Gascony, and Aquitaine by marrying Queen Eleanor." Simon shook his head in silent admiration.

"He was an extremely ambitious man—a great leader. That's what we lack today, strong leaders," William lamented. "Hubert de Burgh would rather wear silk scarves and ornamental armor than the real thing. Ranulf of Chester grows old. The barons have no strong leader to unite them and oppose the vicious influence of men like the Bishop of Winchester and the greedy Savoys."

Simon seconded his hatred of religious leaders. "They take holy orders only because it's an easy path of preferment. Personally I have always opposed the Pope's influence, especially in matters concerning England."

"You have strong views, de Montfort, but you are right, of course. I believe you have the qualities of a great leader. You have rare ability and a resolute mind, and from our conversations I know you have political foresight. You see more clearly than a native Englishman the genius of the old English institutions of law Henry II laid down."

"I?" de Montfort asked. "What about you? The Marshals are the uncrowned Kings of England, and 'tis rumored you control half its wealth."

"I'm tired of being a leader. I'm tired of King Midas giving my gold to his favorites, but most of all I'm tired of fighting this losing war. All I want is to go home to my beautiful wife and start a family of my own."

Simon de Montfort laughed. "There aren't many men who are in love with their wives. Most are glad of war so they can escape from marriage."

"I've little experience of marriage," Will admitted. "The king's sister was a child when we wed. There is a vast age difference between us." He shook his head. "I feel she is being robbed of her youth, married to an older man."

Simon kept a wise silence. The marshal sounded vulnerable

tonight, as if he looked mortality in the face. Simon tried to visualize William's wife. He pictured a vain, spoiled princess who had in all probability already been unfaithful to the older man. "Get her with child," he advised.

William smiled ruefully. "I'm forty-six years old, I must act before it's too late." He set down his empty cup. "They are finally sending us reinforcements. Chester is supposed to arrive tomorrow. You would enjoy talking to him. He was one of King Henry II's brilliant young leaders forty years ago."

Simon got to his feet. "Chester holds my earldom and lands in England. I intend to have them back. I intend to be Earl of Leicester before I'm much older."

William Marshal gazed into the campfire long after Simon de Montfort retired. It had not been a threat exactly, rather a statement of fact. The marshal did not doubt for a minute that Simon would soon be Earl of Leicester.

It was indeed fortunate that Henry had sent reinforcements, for Louis of France had called together his entire army to pit it against the war lord Simon de Montfort and the Marshal of England. That day the beautiful vineyards of the wine country were turned into battlefields, the earth stained by blood, not grape. The fighting was hot and heavy, yet though they soon became covered with dust and sweat and blood the combatants were easily identified by the sleeveless surcoats covering their armor and emblazoned by their coats of arms.

Simon de Montfort towered above all, wielding a long sword in one thickly muscled arm and a battle-ax in the other. His black stallion was both fierce and massive, standing a full thirty hands tall and trampling everything in its path. He was a fearsome sight to the enemy, vanquishing some by intimidation alone. Usually an enemy hesitated before engaging the giant and in that moment of hesitation was lost.

His two squires Guy and Rolf, who were father and son, fought at his back. They enjoyed the reputation for bravery this gave them, but in truth fighting at de Montfort's back was just about the safest place on a battlefield. For the last half hour Simon had focused his attention upon Ranulf de Blundeville, Earl of Chester. Though aging, he had put up a valiant fight, surrounded as he was by the French. If he was killed in the melee, Simon would be Earl of Leicester. He wanted the lands and title so badly he could taste it upon his tongue mixed with the metallic taste of blood. Then Chester went down and Simon's heart leapt with a feeling of what . . . triumph, hope? Surely nothing so base. Simon forced his horse into the fray, needing to know if Chester was already dead or just wounded. The knot of French fell back before his maddened warhorse and blood-drenched weapons, and there, almost beneath his hooves, lay the Earl of Chester.

A pair of blue eyes, icy with fear, pierced Simon's black orbs from either side of Chester's nose guard. Simon's bloodlust was up and for one second he realized how easy it would be to snuff out Chester's life. His horse could trample the life from the earl, he wouldn't even have to stain his weapon. Then the red mist cleared from his brain. That was not the way he wanted to fulfill his ambitions. He would never taint his honor with a deliberate act of cowardice. He would attain his goals by dint of his own ability; by fair means, never foul ones. In a flash de Montfort was off his destrier and lifting the old earl into the saddle. He thwacked its rump with the broadside of his sword and swung about savagely to dispatch two of the enemy into eternity. His squires closed ranks about him fore and aft, but it took thirty minutes of heavy combat for the three men to clear a path to the perimeter of the battlefield to reclaim Simon's mount. He recognized his destrier before he saw Chester. However, as his powerful hand snatched up the reins and he vaulted into the saddle, Chester, his pitted face still gray from shock, shouted up to him, "You saved my life—I owe you a debt."

Simon knew he had to get back into the battle before his sword arm stiffened, but in that moment he sensed his destiny stared him in the face. "I am the rightful Earl of Leicester—you owe me that, nothing more!" He wheeled his great stallion back onto the field of battle.

At dusk when the fighting had ceased and the clang of battle had subsided to pitiful cries and low hopeless moans of those with mortal wounds, Simon de Montfort saw William Marshal struggle from the field with a soldier in his arms. Simon strode forward and lifted the heavy burden from his arms. "I think you are too late. His limbs are stiffening." Simon deposited the body in a field tent. There was an English arrow in the Irish soldier's back. "Who is he?" Simon asked angrily, feeling tragedies like this were the result of blatant carelessness.

William Marshal swallowed the lump in his throat. "It is Gilbert de Clare. He is . . . was my sister's husband." He knelt and with amazingly gentle fingers removed the fatal arrow.

"Do you suspect foul play?" Simon asked bluntly.

"By the bones of Christ, I hope not," William said grimly.

Marshal and de Montfort felt only frustration when they were recalled to Gascony. They were holding their own against insane odds, but once they withdrew from the front lines the territory they had regained would be swallowed up by Louis's army. Moreover, the English and Irish would look as if they were retreating.

When they were ushered into the king's presence, they tried to hold their frayed tempers when they learned he was suffering from a bad case of dysentery. "This campaign was doomed to failure before it was even begun," Henry lamented. He was looking for a scapegoat and there had been plenty to whisper one man's name in his ear: *Hubert de Burgh*. Henry looked at the marshal. "Well, go ahead and gloat. You were another who had his mind set against this venture." Henry's eyelid drooped noticeably and the gripe of his distended bowels made him petulant. "Your father's terms were too easy when they drove the French from England. He should have demanded Louis's head."

The marshal stiffened. He was used to Henry's whining thanklessness, but when his criticism was directed at the old Marshal of England, it was too much for him. He gripped the handle of his sword until his knuckles turned white. De Montfort thought his control was magnificent. "You are ill, sire. You should return to England."

Henry nodded, the insults he'd just uttered forgotten. "I ordered Richard home to smooth my path with the barons. They'll be livid that all the money is gone without regaining one acre of land."

Simon de Montfort almost choked. He had helped regain

Brittany for its ruler and would have regained Aquitaine for Henry if he'd given him a free hand and agreed to a full-scale decisive thrust. "Leave me your army, sire, we may yet be able to claim victory. I have never accepted defeat in my life!"

"Chester came to me this morning. I don't know how you did it, but he is ready to hand over your English lands. I need your support in England, Simon—at least one of my barons will be loyal." Henry groaned and rubbed his gut. "I need my wife. I've done nothing but regurgitate and defecate since I took that camp slut to my bed."

They could hardly keep their smiles of satisfaction from their faces. There was a God after all. As they walked back to their men to see if camp had been set up, William Marshal felt an overwhelming sense of relief. Though it was galling to admit defeat, this ill-fated war was over. He looked up at Simon. "Congratulations, you said you would soon be the Earl of Leicester, and I didn't doubt it for a minute." Who would have thought Simon shrewd enough to manipulate old Ranulf into relinquishing the title? He was also relieved that Richard had returned to England already. Therefore it was unlikely he'd had a hand in Gilbert de Clare's death.

14

Back in England the barons who had borne the cost of the French campaign were demanding a reckoning. The King's council had decided that as soon as he returned they would draw up a document for Henry to sign, reaffirming the Great Charter. He needed their loyalty and their money to rule effectively, and they felt it was time they put him on a leash.

At the end of the month all the leaders sailed home except William Marshal. Henry left him in charge of getting the men-at-arms and horses back to England. The marshal didn't mind; at least he knew the job would be done properly.

William felt excitement building up inside of him. He wouldn't have believed it possible to miss someone as much as he'd missed Eleanor. Her father, King John, had been right about one thing: She was a precious jewel. He loved her above all things. Her sixteenth birthday had come and gone six months past and he would wait no longer. She was with him from the moment he closed his eyes at night until dawn when he awoke in a sweat and an agony of need.

William put Rickard de Burgh on the first troop ship with instructions to stay by the Countess of Pembroke at all times to keep her safe. He entrusted the knight with a love letter—the first he had ever written in his life.

My Darling Eleanor,

Though it is sad for England that the fighting in France is over, it is happy for me personally. I rejoice that I shall soon be with you and fervently hope you welcome my return to London.

I thank God in his Heaven that I allowed you to persuade me to take you with me to Ireland and Wales. I cherish the memories of the months we had together. To me they were the most precious of my life. If I close my eyes I can see you step from Richard's barge at the Tower. When you sank down before me your crimson gown spread across the gray stone steps and you took my breath away. I think that was the moment I fell in love with you.

William lifted his quill and closed his eyes. Instantly she rose up before him, but she was in his bed naked, save for the cloak of her silken black hair. When she reached out to touch him, he groaned. He opened his eyes quickly, cursing that his body had again responded to the mere thought of her. What a bloody fool he'd been not to make love to her before he left. Then suddenly he was glad that he had not. The anticipation gave him unbelievable pleasure, and the ultimate experience of intimacy still lay ahead for both of them. He would hint at it in order to prepare her.

If the master bedchamber at Durham House does not suit, you must redecorate and refurnish, or we can choose another chamber when I return. I count the hours until I see your lovely face again. I know that Heaven blessed me the day you became my beloved Countess of Pembroke.

Forever,
William

When Richard, Duke of Cornwall, returned to Westminster, he was asked to join the Bishop of Winchester in the chapel. He would rather have avoided him, but Henry had restored Win-

chester to a position of power. He was now the Treasurer of the
Royal Household. Richard was annoyed that Henry had confirmed him in that position for life, but he was both alarmed
and angry when he learned that Henry had been witless enough
to give Peter des Roches custody of the king's personal seal.
Richard decided to beard the lion in his den.

"My lord bishop, now that I am returned from France you
may give the king's seal into my hands for safekeeping."

A superior smile touched Winchester's mouth. "I trust the
matter we discussed was handled to your satisfaction, your
Highness?"

Richard was puzzled. Surely the wily bishop hadn't been able
to obtain an annulment for Isabella de Clare in so short a time?
He dared to hope. "Do you speak of the annulment?"

"We spoke not of annulment, we spoke of removing an impediment, your Highness," Winchester carefully pointed out.

"Are they not one and the same thing, Peter?" Richard
asked, at a loss.

"Annulments can take years. Apparently you are unaware
that Gilbert de Clare, the Earl of Gloucester, fell in battle."

Richard was speechless. How often had he lain awake and
wished the man dead? Now this oily swine was hinting that he
had arranged his death because Richard had asked him to do
so. Jesu, Winchester had him by the balls! He could have his
heart's desire but not without paying a heavy price.

If Isabella ever got wind of this, her love would turn to hatred. His concern for Isabella took precedence over who had
possession of England's seal. Did she know she was a widow?
Had the lands and titles of Gloucester been confirmed upon her
son Richard? He must go to her immediately. She would protest that she was in mourning, but he would convince her to
marry him as soon as he received Henry's permission and the
council approved the marriage.

When Richard arrived at Gloucester, he saw that Isabella
Marshal de Clare already knew she had been widowed. Not
only the castle, but the city of Gloucester was in full mourning
for its young earl.

Draped in black from head to toe, Isabella received him
stiffly, surrounded by her castellan and her faithful de Clare

servants. He had visited her there only once before, and it too had been an emotional trauma for him. She had fled Windsor and he rushed after her demanding a reason. When he learned she was carrying his child, their world had been turned upside down. She begged him never to show his face there again and because he loved her, because he wanted no scandal attached to her, he had departed that same day so that de Clare's servants could carry no tales to their earl.

This time, however, he would not be banished. No impediment stood between them, and his resolve was taken. He ignored the disapproving glances he received from the mournful household servants. Damn it all, he was the Duke of Cornwall, and royalty had its privileges. Almost he began to mouth condolences, then he changed his mind.

When he raised his voice, eyebrows also were raised, but the time was past for him to play out his role in the shadows. "The Countess of Gloucester and I have matters to discuss in private. Please see that we are not disturbed." He stared them down. Her ladies were the first to depart, her male servants were slower. Richard saw her stricken look, saw her small figure sway. He was beside her instantly. "I am taking you upstairs."

Her pleading eyes beseeched him, but he put a firm hand at the small of her back and propelled her forward. Isabella took him into the solar. It was beyond her to flaunt convention and invite him into her chamber. She whispered urgently, "Richard, you should not have come to Gloucester. You know how servants gossip. Their curiosity will know no bounds."

"Their curiosity will soon be satisfied when they learn you are to be Duchess of Cornwall."

He picked her up and held her against his heart. She sobbed against his shoulder.

"I love you so much. I can't bear to see you in these black draperies."

"I'll have to be in mourning for a full year," she said helplessly.

"Like hell you will. Didn't you hear me say we will be married?"

"Richard, we cannot marry until I'm out of mourning. Even then it may cause a scandal."

"Scandal be damned." He took the black wimple from her head and threw it on the floor, then he threaded his fingers through her lovely chestnut curls and held her immobile while he kissed her.

She clung to him desperately, having no strength to deny him. "I'll wait for no mourning." Then he smiled down into her gentle eyes. "Every fortune-hunter in England will beat a path to your door once they learn you are a widow." His fingers went to the fastenings of her gown and she was shocked that he would take such liberties in the solar. "The servants," she protested.

"I've already sent a formal request to the King and council that we be married immediately," he explained, his hands persisting in their quest.

"There is no lock on the door," she cried in alarm, pulling her gown back up to cover her naked shoulders.

With an impatient sigh Richard went to the door and jammed a high-backed chair beneath the latch, then he turned and came toward Isabella with such resolute intent, she could deny him no longer.

Simon de Montfort assumed Ranulf of Chester was the most generous man breathing. As he rode through the English countryside with his hundred men at his back, he felt more English than French. This country was a rare jewel with its verdant pastures dotted with fat sheep and cattle. The peasant farmers contrasted greatly from their European counterparts. They were adequately clothed, their wives and children plump and happy, their homes sturdy wooden or stone structures thatched with mud and wattle.

Simon was inspecting his newly acquired estates. Though the king hadn't formally ceded him the lands and title of Leicester, that was only a formality. The estates were spread over a dozen counties, and he found the same thing at every one he visited. They had all been willfully mismanaged. The stock had been driven off and sold, the timber cut and the game depleted. Each and every demesne was in a state of impoverishment, contrasting starkly with the surrounding estates. The revenues in no way equaled the costs.

He smiled grimly as he realized Chester had unloaded an almost insurmountable liability from his back. Simon wasted no time laying the facts before King Henry.

"My dear Simon, the solution is simple. You must do what every other English baron has done, marry an heiress. Your own grandfather became Earl of Leicester by marrying a great heiress. My brother Richard is about to marry de Clare's widow, who just happens to be a member of the wealthy Marshal family."

Simon felt it was the time to marry though no lady held his attentions. An earl needed a countess to run his households and provide him with children. He was a practical man with few romantic notions. Marriages were forged for the advantages they brought to a man. A wife brought land and estates, and her dowry paid for the upkeep of those castles and holdings.

"I have no objections, Sire. I will be happy to accept any lady you propose," Simon replied.

"Zounds, I would arrange it in a minute if there was an English heiress wealthy enough to restore all your estates, but the truth is rich widows are so coveted, they are often abducted and forced to the marriage bed."

Simon thought to lighten the conversation by a half jest. "I have no objection to force, all I need is a name."

"I have a dozen heiresses who are still children," Henry suggested.

"I need money now, Sire, I cannot wait for a wife to grow up and her father die before she comes into her inheritance," de Montfort pointed out.

"Oh, you simply borrow from the moneylenders against your future prospects," Henry explained, totally familiar with negotiating loans. "The only drawback, of course, is that you wouldn't be able to breed sons until the little girls were at least fourteen."

The mere suggestion of the six-and-a-half-foot giant mating with a fourteen-year-old child was so ludicrous both men dismissed the idea. "We'll have to look outside England. From the rate you kill men off in battle, France must have a goodly share of wealthy widows. What about Mahaut, Countess of Boulogne? She's middle aged, but eager I wager."

Simon swallowed hard. Middle age was a euphemism; she was an old woman.

"I'll send a dispatch to William Marshal today. He can negotiate it before he returns home."

Simon thanked the king coolly and wished to God he'd never asked for the audience. Not that he was a sentimental idealist where marriage was concerned. He was a realist and he was ambitious, but the thought of taking Mahaut to wife made him want to run to the nearest brothel and lay the prettiest whore he could find.

When Rickard de Burgh handed Eleanor the letter from William, she was overjoyed. She knew he would be among the last to return home because of his duties as marshal and was determined to exercise patience.

When she read the love letter, however, her heart fluttered and the rosy blush that touched her cheek stayed there for days. She was more excited than any bride. After six long years of yearning and dreaming, her life's wish was about to be fulfilled. Her spirits rose, her eyes sparkled brighter, her laughter came more frequently, and she broke out in song day and night.

Peter des Roches and his bastard son, Peter des Rivaux, who now spent more time in Westminster's Exchequer than Westminster's Chapel, had called in the king to tell him the treasury was empty. This was nothing new to Henry, but a new twist was added. They convinced him that his poverty was due to Hubert de Burgh. He had been the cause of the expensive war in Wales, and his mismanagement of the French campaign had caused it to fail. Moreover, his right-hand man, Stephen Segrave, had now brought them documents that proved Hubert had also mismanaged his position as Justiciar of England and was a master at diverting funds. They told the king that Hubert should be dismissed from office.

"But Hubert is a peer of the realm," Henry protested, half afraid of the military man who had done so much for him when he was a boy.

Winchester sneered. "There are no peers in England."

Henry had grown quite used to foreign disparagement of

everything English. Winchester's voice was now added to the Provençals'. All told him, "You are the king . . . be firm . . . let them know you are the king. Don't give in an inch to these English traitors!"

"Before I dismiss Hubert from office, I want William Marshal's advice," Henry said, holding firm for once.

The Bishop of Winchester was hard-pressed to lay any fault at the marshal's door, but his natural cunning made him devious and unscrupulous. "We all admire the marshal, but sometimes, Sire, you overburden the poor man. You've left him to clean up the mess de Burgh created in France. Now as soon as he returns you want to lay the problem of de Burgh squarely on his shoulders. Being a king carries grave responsibilities. Sometimes you must do your own dirty work, rather than always expecting the marshal to do it."

"You are right, of course," Henry said, ever ready to change his tune when opposed. "I will ask Hubert de Burgh to account for all funds that have passed through his hands. Then when the marshal returns he can weigh the facts fairly."

Peter des Roches wanted to strike him, but he controlled himself and pressed from another direction. "Very wise. You will then see for yourself the mismanagement in every area. No new sheriffs have been appointed, the stewardship of all royal houses has been used to siphon off thousands of crowns. I suggest you appoint Peter des Rivaux as your first minister in custody of wardships and chief justice of the forests. Bribery and outright fraud are draining the royal coffers of every penny. If we put a stop to it now, you will soon have money to burn, which is only right and proper for a king."

Henry would give him no arguments there.

Hubert went by barge from the Tower of London, where he resided, to Durham House. The Countess of Pembroke received him graciously. "My lord, William is not yet returned. Henry has sent him off on business to Boulogne."

Hubert collapsed into a chair like a sack of grain. Eleanor could see something of import was troubling him heavily. "Your nephews are here, Hubert. Can they be of help to you?"

she suggested, and sent a page off with a message for the de Burgh twins.

Sir Michael came from the stables where Marshal's returning Welsh archers would be housed that night. As soon as he saw Hubert he was concerned. "What's amiss?"

"Mick, I've just received this official document from the treasurer." He glanced at Eleanor, uneasy before her for the first time in his life.

She stood up immediately. "I'll leave you gentlemen to your business. I'll send the steward for ale." But the de Burghs didn't even hear her. She encountered Rickard coming up the stairs of the family quarters. "Rickard, your uncle is here. He's in trouble. If he needs you, you have my permission to pledge him your service."

"Thank you, my lady. Whatever it is, I will inform you fully before I do anything." She touched his arm. She knew she could count on this man if she was ever in danger. He had pledged to her and he meant it with all his heart.

Mick was trying to calm Hubert, but when Rickard arrived and saw the royal command in writing, bearing the king's seal, he knew it was the start of the bad times he had foreseen. "This is only one step away from being charged with treason. It won't blow over, it will get worse," he stated.

Mick cast him a look that clearly told him to shut his mouth, so Rick gestured for his brother to move off a few steps so they could speak in private.

"It will be horrendous, Mick. I've foreseen it. He must be warned."

They looked into each other's eyes for long, stretched-out moments, then, convinced, Mick nodded his agreement. They stepped back to Hubert. "Anything of value, deposit with the Knights Templars. We can do it after dark tonight. Don't be too trusting of those in your employ. I think probably someone is being paid to betray you. I know there is treachery being planned in high places . . . I feel it. I think Mick should go to Ireland and warn Father—such is the strength of my premonition. I would go myself but I am pledged to keep the Countess of Pembroke safe for William. I know there is danger coming to her too. I see her weeping rivers of tears."

The ruddy color always present in Hubert's craggy face had drained away. "Your mother has true visions of the future. I believe you, Rickard, but surely being married to the Princess of Scotland will protect me."

Rickard shook his head. "They will use it against you." He did not add that he would be accused of seducing Princess Margaret in hopes of becoming King of Scotland.

Hubert clutched Michael's doublet. "Go tonight. Tell Falcon to bring his most trusted knights. I command whole armies of men, but have none I can trust implicitly, it seems."

Sir Rickard sought out Eleanor. He would not unduly alarm her, even though he had promised to inform her fully. "Hubert needs Mick's services for a few days."

She searched his face. "Hubert seemed undone over a letter from the treasurer. I believe the Bishop of Winchester holds that office."

"That is correct, my lady." He would not lie. "He has been ordered to account for all funds that have passed through his hands."

"That's ridiculous, like saying they don't trust him. Would you like me to speak to Henry about this?"

"The document bore the king's seal, my lady. I thank you for your concern but prefer to keep you clear of this matter. William would have my b-my brains," he amended quickly. He smiled at her to banish her worries. "The marshal is on his way home—I know these things."

"You have the second sight like your mother, Jasmine." It was a statement, not a question.

"You know of my mother?" he asked in surprise.

She smiled at him wistfully. "Jasmine is my cousin, though she was a woman grown when I was born. Her supernatural gifts and her beauty are legendary. She is an enchantress who stole the hearts of many men: my father, the Earl of Chester, William Marshal. The queen has spitefully thrown her name at me many times, and somehow I was always afraid to ask William because in my heart I believed it could be true."

"My mother belongs to Falcon de Burgh body and soul. She and Will Marshal are friends, just as you and I are friends."

Their hands touched in a silent pledge. "Thank you, Rickard. I sometimes feared she would always stand between William and me like an ethereal specter."

As soon as dark descended, Eleanor had more unexpected company. Her brother Richard arrived with her husband's sister Isabella in tow. Isabella was most hesitant, but Richard led her forward with an insistent hand at the small of her back.

Eleanor was tongue-tied for a moment. Should she offer condolences or congratulations? Finally she did both. "Isabella I'm so sorry that Gilbert de Clare died in battle, but I'm happy that you have Richard to share your life now."

"Eleanor, you won't mind if Isabella stays with you until our wedding? This way I'll be close enough to see her in the evenings where she's well chaperoned. I swear, all she can utter is 'What will people say?'"

"Oh, Eleanor, he overrules me on every point. I'm supposed to be in mourning, but he has announced our wedding plans to the world! He wouldn't take no for an answer. So I agreed, thinking it could be a quiet affair, but it's all getting out of hand," she wailed.

"We have absolutely nothing to hide. The King and council have approved it and the people of England love royal weddings. Only look at the month-long celebration for Henry and his queen."

Isabella was trembling. "I'm afraid of what William will say."

"Damn it, woman, he'll be pleased as punch to have me for brother-in-law. Besides, Maggot here has him wrapped about her little finger. You'll smooth our path with William, won't you, love?" he coaxed his sister.

She blanched, remembering the last time they'd all been under the same roof. "Of course Isabella is welcome to stay at Durham House. We'll face William together."

"Oh, Lord, whatever must the de Clares think?" Isabella worried.

"Darling, their mourning for their son will not blind them to the fact that your marriage will link them directly with the royal family. They know their grandson Richard can only benefit from our union. I'll get Henry to confirm him as Earl of

Gloucester. We can afford to be generous and let the de Clares have him for a year." Richard embraced her and kissed her upon the mouth to stem any further protest.

Eleanor sighed and gave them the privacy they craved. She was now torn between wishing William would speed his arrival or delay it until after the wedding. Eleanor invited Isabella to share her bedchamber so they could talk.

"Isabella, what is it like to sleep with a man?"

"Oh, Lord, William still hasn't shared your bed?" Isabella asked with disbelief. "Well, you may find it strange at first after sleeping alone all your life. But I love it. I love the feel of a man in my bed. I love his hairiness; I love to feel the weight of him."

Eleanor's eyes were like saucers as she listened to the intimate details.

"I don't know how we've managed all these years. Once you've been intimate it's almost impossible to abstain."

"You mean the night you spent together at Odiham was not the first time?" Eleanor asked.

Isabella blushed hotly in the dark as she confessed. "It was the night you were wed to William, when you were nine." She could not bring herself to confess that it was the first time they'd ever laid eyes on each other.

"That's almost seven years," said Eleanor, her quick mind drawing conclusions. "Then the child you bore . . . oh, Isabella, that's why you named him Richard!"

"Oh, mother in heaven, Eleanor, never breathe a word, I beseech you. Nobody must ever know! Richard and I were irresistibly attracted to each other. Though Gilbert was Earl of Gloucester and we made our home there, he spent most of his time in Ireland on the de Clare estates. I was so much alone, so lonely when I met Richard. You know how strong he can be. I just fell into his arms. I never intended for Richard to find out about the child. I retired from Windsor before I started to show, but Richard came after me and learned of my plight. Gilbert insisted on taking the child to the de Clares to be brought up in Ireland. I didn't dare refuse lest he become suspicious. To be deprived of my baby seemed like a fitting punishment for the sin I'd committed."

"Oh, Isabella darling, how can you think of yourself as sinful? If I know Richard he'll get the boy from the de Clares and he'll give you another baby to make up for your loneliness."

"I can't believe in less than a fortnight we'll be married. I keep thinking something will happen to spoil it."

"Hush. In ten days you will marry a prince, then you will become the mother of a prince and you will live happily ever after. William is on his way home and we too will live happily ever after." Eleanor hesitated for a few moments, then she took courage and whispered, "Isabella, how can I make William take me to his bed?" He had seemed on the verge of doing so many times, but it had never happened. "How can I make him give me a child?"

"Eleanor, I promised William I would let him teach you these things. He likes the idea of your being innocent."

"I'm not just innocent, I'm ignorant!" Eleanor protested.

"Well, men are visually stimulated. If you let him see you in a state of undress, nature will inevitably take its course and that control on which he prides himself will melt like snow in summer."

"And when nature takes its course, as you so delicately put it, what does it feel like?"

"I-I-I think it depends upon the man. I hated it with Gilbert, but with Richard it is so overwhelming, I can't describe it. But I think it is all connected to a man's strength. If he's strong enough, dominant enough, you can give up your control to him. A woman can let herself go completely, give herself to him utterly, and he will take you to Paradise. Your senses are heightened. Together you go higher and higher until you experience 'the little death.' "

"It sounds almost mystical," Eleanor said wistfully.

"Oh, it is, but not at first, darling. The first time it hurts terribly and you bleed a little."

Eleanor giggled nervously. "Pain . . . blood . . . little death . . . I can hardly wait! No wonder William has been trying to protect me."

"Oh, darling, everything will be wonderful for you. Just trust William and he'll make it an experience you'll never forget."

15

Two days later Eleanor and Isabella were in the solar with a dozen seamstresses and maids. The entire room was strewn with material and gowns, coifs and wimples, nightrails and bedgowns, all for Isabella's trousseau.

"Your wedding gown must have a train, Isabella. 'Tis the latest fashion, and just think what a delightful picture it would create to have two little flower girls holding it up as you walk down the aisle at Westminster."

"Perhaps two of Richard's pages would be better. Boys are better trained," suggested Isabella, now totally caught up in the preparations.

"Perhaps you're right. I know when I was a little girl, I would have made a disaster of it. I created a fiasco at my own wedding."

"I remember it well," said a man's voice from the doorway.

"William!" Eleanor cried, dropping the bolt of peach silk she was holding and rushing into his arms, unmindful of the roomful of women.

He laughed, pleased with her response, but gave her only a chaste kiss upon her forehead. "Durham House has been like a bachelor's residence for so long, I thought I was in the wrong place," he teased, his eyes devouring her.

For a moment she panicked as she realized he had caught them red-handed preparing for a wedding to which he hadn't yet consented. She placed her hands upon his chest in supplication and, looking up at him, said, "Let me explain. Your sister is staying with us until . . . until . . ." She struggled with her explanation, then her eyes widened as Richard stepped into the solar.

"I thought I'd save you from a beating," he teased, his eyes going to Isabella.

She came forward on knees weak as water. "He knows, then?"

"I'm not such a scurvy lout I don't know my duty, you know. I formally asked for your hand the moment William stepped off his ship."

"You're not angry?" Eleanor asked anxiously.

"I would have been damned angry if he *hadn't* declared himself, now that Isabella is free."

Eleanor leaned against her husband, weak with relief.

"Sweet, I need a bath, I came directly from the ship."

"Oh, my lord, forgive me, you must be starving."

He looked at her hungrily. "As soon as I'm bathed and changed I must go straight to court. I haven't reported to the king yet."

"I'll fetch you a tray. Henry can wait," Eleanor said, disappointed that he would leave her so quickly.

"Why don't I take you two beautiful ladies to court with me?" William suggested.

"Oh, lovely!" Eleanor agreed instantly. "I'll wear my new jeweled girdle with my dagger stuck in. It will make the queen sea green with envy."

At Westminster William closeted himself with the king for a couple of hours, bringing him up to date on affairs in the various regions of France and the continent. He had borne the heavy cost of victualing the vessels for the men and horses and knew he stood little chance of being reimbursed. He had also reached into his own pocket to pay the soldiers' wages but didn't burden Henry with the problem. He'd present an accounting to the treasury and wait patiently for his money.

"Gascony shouldn't be left without a ruler, Henry. They are so like the Welsh and Irish it is uncanny. They are contentious to a man. Order should be established there once and for all. The petty nobles are at each other's throats, raiding each other and stirring up so much shit the very air is foul."

"Would you consider being senechal of Gascony, William?"

"To be frank Henry, I don't want it. My men are on their way back to Ireland and Wales. Give it to somebody who's ambitious, but for God's sake let it be a man who can rule with an iron hand. Some of your nobles hanging about the court these days are too limp-wristed to masturbate!"

"Simon de Montfort!" Henry declared.

"An excellent choice, but he'll need more than the four hundred a year you allow him. He has a hundred men to support. Which brings me to the matter of Mahaut of Boulogne. The countess was most eager for the union, but unfortunately she is a friend of King Louis's mother, Blanche of Castile. They forbid Mahaut to hand over her estates to a man in the service of the English king."

"Damn their interference. De Montfort is desperate. He goes deeper into debt each week."

"I took the liberty, Sire, of sounding out Joan, Countess of Flanders. Her late husband left her great stretches of land and castles topping Flanders's ridges. Her parks are stocked with deer and her baileys are filled with blooded stock. She is older than Simon to be sure, but not so old as Mahaut."

"Good work, William. I'll appoint him senechal of Gascony and let him do his own wooing." Henry dismissed the problem from his mind. "So, in a week's time marriage relates us again. Let us join our wives and I'll tell you of the great feast we have planned. There will be over ten thousand dishes to choose from."

William groaned and wondered whose purse would bear such extravagance. He knew it would not be Henry's.

On the short boat ride from Westminster to Durham House, William slipped his arm about Eleanor's waist and drew her close. "You grow more beautiful with each day," he murmured.

"I missed you so much, William. I thought you'd never return. Whenever the loneliness became too much to bear, I relived the happy times we spent in the mountains of Wales."

He kissed her temple. "I'll take you back there," he promised.

She was sorry the ride ended so quickly, but she kept her hand firmly clasped in William's as they left the barge at the water steps and walked slowly up to Durham House. Almost as soon as they entered the foyer Isabella bade them good night and disappeared up the stairs. William caught Eleanor in his arms and drew her close. "Why the devil did you invite my sister to stay here? I was looking forward to being private with you."

She took his hand and led him through the darkened house to the cozy salon where a low fire still burned upon the hearth.

"It's very late," reminded William, as he took a chair before the glowing embers.

"Are you going to send me to bed like a little girl?" she asked, crawling into his lap, "Or are you going to start treating me like a woman?"

"I'd like to keep you 'til dawn, if you're willing."

"I'm willing," she said, low. "Tell me all about France and the battles you fought. I think Henry learned his lesson about jumping into war."

"If you think I'm going to waste our precious time together discussing war, you are grievously mistaken. And speaking of lessons, it is time you taught me how you like to be kissed."

She laughed happily. "I know nothing of kisses, 'tis you who'll have to do the teaching."

He began by gently pressing his lips to her eyelids and the tip of her nose. Then he moved to the corners of her mouth and felt them go up in a smile of pleasure. He cupped her face in strong hands and lifted it as if receiving a sacrament. As her breath mingled with his, a shudder of desire rippled along his spine, and he cautioned himself to go slowly and not frighten her. He kissed her for an hour—gentle kisses, soft kisses, short quick kisses, and long, slow, melting kisses. Never once did he try to part her lips with his tongue and intrude into her soft, exciting mouth.

Eleanor realized just how much she had been missing. She liked to be kissed excessively! She loved his closeness and the delicious warmth of his body. His gentle lovemaking in no way threatened her, rather it tempted her to boldness. She reached out to undo the buttons of his doublet, then she slipped her arms inside to caress his naked chest. He gasped with pure pleasure as she rested her soft cheek against his bare flesh. His manhood was so swollen he longed to free himself from the confines of the tight material, but knew it was too soon. Considerably more foreplay would be necessary to arouse Eleanor's virgin body.

William's fingers found their way to the neckline of her gown, then very slowly he began to undo enough tiny buttons to allow him to slip his hand inside her bodice. His large hand cupped the rounded fullness of one delicious breast and she sighed with pleasure. "Though it is Isabella's wedding, it is I who feel like the bride," she whispered breathlessly.

"Sweet, sweet, and so you shall be the bride. When the archbishop says the words over them, we'll renew our vows to each other."

"How lovely," she said dreamily. "I don't remember our vows, I only remember touching your bare chest."

His thumb caressed her nipple and it ruched into a tight little bud. "Oh, don't." She gasped, so he stilled his fingers and contented himself to simply hold her breast in his hand. She yawned and relaxed against his hard body. She murmured drowsily, "I'd like to sleep with you holding me all night."

William was in an agony of need. His erection brushed against her firm young buttock until its sensitivity pulsed with every heartbeat. He allowed himself to hope. Perhaps now was a good time to initiate her deeper into the mysteries of lovemaking. She was so relaxed, so warm and responsive, the opportunity was heaven-sent.

Still tenderly cupping her breast, he slipped his other hand beneath her thighs and stood up from the chair. His doublet fell open to the waist and he lifted her against his heart. Her arms glided up about his neck and she murmured, "Where are you taking me?"

"To bed," he said huskily. A chair simply wouldn't suffice

for what he had in mind. His mouth was dry with the anticipation of undressing her and seeing her completely naked for the first time. He ascended the stairs slowly, savoring every moment, brushing her soft mouth with his.

His shaft was rigid and its pulsing tip rubbed against her bottom on every step of the staircase. His imagination took fire. He would light the candles so he could see her loveliness. He wanted to watch every expression on her face as his fingers stroked the uninitiated cleft between her legs. The ritual taking of the hymen could happen only once in her lifetime, and he wanted her to see him worship her with his eyes, his lips, his whole body.

In her chamber he lay her upon the bed and removed his doublet. Then his fingers located the candelabra on the bedside chest. Soon the soft glow of candlelight illuminated her in a pool of beauty. His hands stole to the bodice of her gown. He opened it and slipped it from her shoulders. As her breasts were exposed to his fevered gaze, he bent to kiss the swell of each delicately tinted globe. Her scent made him reel with desire. Suddenly a sleepy voice inquired, "William, whatever are you doing?" His eyes flew to the other bed where he realized to his great dismay his sister was sleeping.

"Peste!" he swore, and Eleanor put her fingers to his lips to silence him.

"William, go away." Isabella yawned her protest. "Surely you haven't come at four o'clock in the morning expecting Eleanor to satisfy your needs."

"Of course not," he said stiffly, "I was just tucking her into bed. Go back to sleep, Isabella."

At breakfast Eleanor came in and touched her husband's shoulder as he sat at table. "My lord, can you ever forgive me?" The look on her face was so penitent, he burst out laughing and gathered her onto his knee. She kissed him. "You weren't amused last night."

His lips nuzzled her neck. "When we rid ourselves of our uninvited guest, I'll keep you abed for a week."

"Promise?" she teased, her eyes changing color to a deeper blue.

His hand sought her breast through the material of her pretty gown. " 'Tis better this way. After the wedding, after we renew our vows at Westminster, we'll have our honeymoon. No groom was ever more in love or eager than I." His hands tightened on her body and he crushed his mouth down on hers.

"William!" protested Isabella, coming into the breakfast room. "Your continual demands will exhaust the child." Her face was pink with embarrassment. "I swear, you're acting like an untried boy."

"That's exactly how I feel when I touch Eleanor." He winked outrageously at his wife and she laughed happily.

"You'll have to excuse me, love, I've business to attend to," he said, pushing his chair back from the table.

"William, you never rest. You had to dash off to see Henry the same day you arrived home, and I know you took no rest last night. Now your duty is again beckoning."

"Are you hinting that I'm getting old, that I'm overtaxing my strength? Surely you don't want me to sit in the chimney corner in house slippers, do you?"

"Of course not," she protested indignantly. "It's just that I thought you might get fitted for new clothes for the wedding. The fashions have changed dramatically since the Provençals swarmed over the court. The very latest thing is a particolored cotte."

"I will do many things for you, my darling, but dressing like a court jester isn't one of them. We'll let the Savoys imitate peacocks and bantam cocks, while the Marshals remain soberly out of fashion."

"Speak for yourself, sir! Isabella is having a six-foot train on her wedding dress while my gown is a state secret to prevent copying."

"Sweet, you always make other women look dowdy. The Countess of Pembroke is famous for being the best-dressed lady in England."

She went up on tiptoe to kiss him. "That's because of your money and my good taste."

He resisted the urge to fondle her pert breasts. "We are a well-matched couple. Seriously though, I promised Rick de Burgh some time this morning."

"Oh, of course. Hubert fancies himself in trouble, I think. Go and straighten everything out."

He smiled to himself. She was growing up in so many ways, but she still had the childlike belief that he could right the wrongs of the entire world.

When Sir Rickard explained the seriousness of Hubert's position, the marshal was outraged. "Christ Almighty, I knew there would be trouble the moment Winchester returned. He hates the English with a vengeance and will be in his glory pulling one of us down from a high place. Well, I rid Henry of him once, now I shall have to rid him of Winchester again."

"Have a care for your own person, my lord earl. I appreciate whatever you may be able to do for my uncle, but it must not be at too great a price to you and yours."

Rickard de Burgh was mindful of his "curse." He sensed danger to William Marshal, but he felt only a vague disquiet. There was nothing he could warn him about directly.

"Damn Henry and his obsession with favoritism. He's so shortsighted he can't see he's setting his English barons against the foreigners. If it's allowed to continue it will split England asunder. If it leads to civil war he'll have the shock of his life. His only adherents will be fops in particolored cottes!"

"Mick has slipped over to Ireland to warn my father," Rickard said.

"When Falcon arrives my castles and men are at his disposal," William said.

Rickard's eyes widened at his lord's generosity. "I hope it isn't necessary for my father to come, but we thought he should be made aware of the danger to Hubert."

"He'll come," William said grimly. "He's a de Burgh—scratch one and you scratch all! Did you examine the document closely? Are you certain the seal on it was the king's?"

Rickard de Burgh nodded. "Hubert will be pulled down as surely as his castle at Montgomery."

"Not if I can help it," William said, clenching his jaw firmly.

Henry was delighted to see the marshal back at court so quickly. "William, it was my idea to move the court from Windsor to Westminster for the wedding. Even so I'm not sure the banqueting hall will hold all the guests. I want you to bring Eleanor; I've set aside an apartment for you in one of the towers. Richard and Isabella's bridal suite will be in the opposite tower. England will have two princesses after the wedding. I think it most romantic to lodge princesses in palace towers."

William held his patience, wondering if Henry would ever grow up. "Sire," he began, forcing himself to use the royal title, "I'm here about our friend Hubert de Burgh."

Henry blinked rapidly and denied any part in the business. "As treasurer, Winchester needs an accounting. 'Tis none of my doing."

William looked him straight in the eye. "The document bore your royal seal."

"I gave it into the treasurer's keeping—I cannot be expected to carry out all the business of the kingdom myself. I have to delegate responsibility."

"You what?" William thundered, de Burgh's plight momentarily forgotten in the enormity of the offense of a King of England letting his royal seal be used by another.

Henry had the decency to flush. " 'Twas only a temporary arrangement while I was in France. Now that I'm returned Winchester will give it back."

"He will place it in your hands this day. I shall accompany you now while you go to retrieve it."

"I can't just go and ask him to give it back," protested the king, feeling like a reprimanded schoolboy.

"Sire, you can and you will," William said implacably.

The king and the marshal entered the Treasury Office together. William waved aside Peter des Rivaux who had recently been appointed king's first minister. "We are here to see Winchester," William said, not bothering to hide the contempt he felt for Winchester's bastard.

When Peter des Roches came into the room, he scented danger. The marshal and Winchester were like two dogs with raised hackles; the king, a bone between them. Since Henry did not take the initiative, William said, "The king is come for the royal seal." Then he added as an afterthought, "And since I'm here I might as well be repaid for expenses incurred in the French campaign." He threw down a detailed accounting for the money he'd laid out, smiled blandly, and said, "I'll take it in gold."

The hatred inside the room was palpable. Winchester played for time. "It will have to be tallied and verified. It will take time." His sausagelike fingers spread in a placating gesture.

"The accounting is exact; the king will vouch for my honesty."

To avoid an open confrontation, Winchester had no choice but to surrender the seal and the gold. As William walked from the Exchequer with the king, he said, "Henry, Hubert de Burgh remained loyal to your father even when I turned against him. He helped secure the throne for you, and almost single-handed he held Dover against the French. More than that, he has been your dear friend. I sincerely hope you plan no treachery against him, nor allow others to do so."

"If Hubert has not betrayed me, William, I pledge you no harm shall ever come to him."

"Had he wished to betray you, you would never have obtained the kingdom."

"I swear to you that I will do nothing without your advice, William," Henry pledged.

William was satisfied for the moment. The wedding festivities of Henry's brother Richard were all that would occupy the king in the coming week. Once the great celebration was over, William would see to it that Hubert de Burgh was exonerated from any blame.

Peter des Rivaux and Peter des Roches were unable to stomach the insult they had just been made to swallow. With narrowed eyes Winchester said, "Obviously the powder was never used on Marshal. The girl cannot be counted upon. 'Tis time our young squire Allan earned his pay."

16

The evening before the wedding was spent packing the bride's clothes and the magnificent wedding gown with its six-foot train. All had to be transported to Westminster where the bridal suite had been prepared in the tower for Isabella and Richard.

Since it was her second marriage, she had chosen material in a heavy cream color, but that was the only concession. The gown was far more elaborate than Isabella's first bridal dress had been. All the servants at Durham House lent willing hands to pack the bride's belongings carefully. Then they would do the same for Eleanor and William since a suite in the other tower had been set aside for the Earl and Countess of Pembroke.

Eleanor could not resist trying on her gown one more time before it was boxed up in its protective wrappings. The maids aided her with its many petticoats, then lifted the gown of silver tissue over her head. She smiled secretly at her reflection in the mirror because she knew the queen and her ladies had copied the deep jewel tones she usually wore. Tomorrow, as usual, she would stand out from the other women like a swan midst a gaggle of geese.

Something drew Eleanor's eyes to the doorway where William stood transfixed. The admiration upon his face was so marked she hadn't the heart to scold him for glimpsing her gown before the morrow. He looked regretfully at the number of women present and said, "I had hoped for a few private minutes of your time tonight, but I can see how busy you are."

"William," she said warmly, "only wait a moment while they divest me of my gown and I'll come with you." She cared not a whit that she took his arm and accompanied him from the chamber dressed only in her petticoats.

All he could think was that tomorrow night he would be the one to divest her of the silvery gown. His voice was all husky as he looked down at her and said, "You look like a wedding cake or some such delicious confection."

"I am as excited as a bride," she confided.

He hugged her to his side and whispered, "You are a bride."

Her eyes in the shadows were like deep pools. Impulsively he said, "I bought you sapphires to match your eyes. I was keeping them for a bridal gift for tomorrow night, but they will look so lovely against your silver gown, I'll give them to you now."

They moved through the shadowed halls of Durham House to William's rooms, where he opened a drawer in his bedside table to give her the jewels. The candlelight reflected against the deep-blue gems as she opened the case, and tears of happiness blinded her. "When we return to Durham House, I'll be sharing this chamber with you," she whispered.

He had her in his arms in a flash, the precious sapphires momentarily forgotten as they fell to the bed. He kissed her eyelids, her temples, then found the sweet lips she offered up to him so trustingly. With a little groan he sat down in a bedside chair and gathered her into his lap. "My little princess," he murmured, tenderly stroking her hair.

She laughed softly, "Tomorrow night I shall be a princess in a tower."

He gazed into her uplifted face, marveling at its dark beauty. "Henry still has a childlike love of fairy tales," he said indulgently.

Against William's hard chest she said breathlessly, "Childish qualities in a man are not becoming. Oh, William, I am so thankful you are a real man who is mature in every way."

Her words inflamed him, tempting him to take the male's aggressive initiative in their lovemaking. The swell of her breasts was revealed by the delicate petticoat she wore, and his hands could no more have stopped exploring their secrets than his lungs could have stopped breathing or his heart stopped beating. "I thank God you feel that way. It eleviates my worry for you." The back of his fingers trailed against her throat. "You are so very young, I sometimes feel I am sacrificing your youth," he whispered huskily, "and yet you display such maturity when we hold courts of law and you help me decide policy, I forget your tender years."

When their mouths fused and the kiss deepened, she thought her very bones would melt from love. He tore his mouth from her with a ragged cry. If he was as mature as she believed, he ought to be able to control himself for one more night. Eleanor deserved to have their marriage vows reconfirmed and sanctified in Westminster Abbey tomorrow. She deserved to rejoice at the great royal banquet that would follow. Then she would feel truly a bride, and he a bridegroom.

His huge bed, however, was only inches away from where they sat immersed in love play. William was so hot, he felt his blood was on fire. He fought a losing battle; his brain's logic pitted against his body's needs. Eleanor moved against his strong shoulder and suddenly felt his hard manhood pressing into her soft thigh.

She reached down shyly to touch him and he jumped as if he had been scalded. He was on his feet in a flash, taking her hand and urging her from the dangerous proximity of the bed. "This chamber is too temptingly private for propriety."

"I love your chamber. Your strong imprint is stamped upon everything in the room. In fact, that's what I like about Durham House. Every room is a reflection of your personal taste."

He hugged her to his side as they left the chamber and wandered along the high wall that faced the River Thames. The breeze blew a tress of her silken hair across his cheek and his hand tightened on her waist.

"It will be full moon tomorrow night," she said dreamily.

"A lover's moon," he promised as the sound of a mournful

ship's horn floated up from the wide river and a gull screamed into the darkness.

Below in the courtyard, Rickard de Burgh was about to enter the knights' quarters. He threw one last apprehensive glance at the moon before he turned in. What was it about a full moon that brought events to a climax? Something could hang intangibly in the air for days until the moon waxed full, then suddenly babies were born, the old and sick departed the earth, and men lost their tempers to spill blood. He shook his head to dispel his unease and lifted the latch.

Across the sea in Flanders, Simon de Montfort gazed at that same full moon. All in all he had had a most successful month. He had soon curbed the contentious Gascons. First he had obtained a two-month truce with Louis of France, then he set about to break the power of the nobility. The medicine he made them swallow was so severe, his hand so firm and thorough, a sudden peace descended. Next he had settled the strife that was tearing apart the Bordeaux region by imprisoning the noble troublemakers, incarcerating them in a secure dungeon with a severe seven-year sentence.

This freed some time for him to secure the favor of Joan, Countess of Flanders. He had steeled himself against disappointment before they met, so he was not distressed to find her plain of face and thick of figure. He knew he should be flattered that Joan was attracted to him the moment she saw him, for she made no attempt to hide the pleasure that transformed her face every time her eyes alighted upon him. She was more than amenable; she was downright eager.

He had bedded her almost immediately, and this day the marriage contract had been signed in the great library with its impressive collection of literature. Joan had many castles in her dower, whose baileys were filled with blooded stock. As he gazed at the moon he caught himself sighing heavily. He knew he would have many regrets, for he was a romantic at heart, but he could not afford to have anything stand in the way of his ambition.

Simon was an honorable man who intended to do his best to make Joan of Flanders a good husband. She was older than he, but she was an old-fashioned sort of lady who would obey her lord in all things. Though she was a countess, she never asserted her opinions or interfered in what Simon considered men's business. Indeed she had shown herself to be most grateful for the honor he did her. He stretched his long limbs before his eyes left the moon, but not before he had heaved one last heavy sigh.

At dawn two great carriages arrived at Westminster from Durham House. One brought the bride Isabella Marshal with all her wedding trappings and the other brought Eleanor. She had wanted to ride, despite the unusual dampness of the summer morning, but Rickard de Burgh exchanged words and a frown with William and she was urged inside the carriage. She noted with amusement that Sir Rickard never left the side of her carriage until it arrived at Westminster.

Her maid Brenda and William's younger squire, Allan, took charge of the luggage, but Sir Rickard insisted upon escorting her to the tower where she and William would spend the night after the wedding festivities. The tower suite consisted of two rooms, one atop the other. The sitting room on the lower level held a small dining table, comfortable easy chairs, and a welcoming fire. The bedchamber above on the upper level had a door that led out onto the crenellated battlements.

Rickard inspected the tower suite so thoroughly, Eleanor cocked an eyebrow at him and teased, "Aren't you going to look under the bed?"

The tension left his face for the first time that day as he laughed. "A nameless fancy nags at me, but all is in order here. The Earl of Pembroke is all the guard you need. My time would be better spent at my uncle de Burgh's elbow this day, I think."

The passageways between the two towers were crowded with attendants and servants fetching and carrying everything from food to firewood and from beer to bathwater, and confusion reigned.

The Marshal cousins were all present. Six of the younger boys were to carry Isabella's train while the older girls who had been Eleanor's companions were to scatter rose petals. The female chatter of the reunited young women was loud enough to make the men cover their ears and send the pages running for ale and wine.

Eleanor bade Brenda to hasten her dressing so she could go help Isabella with her bridal gown. Her own gown of silver tissue set off her sapphires to perfection, and she had chosen to wear a silver crown atop her silken, black curls. Her friends all gasped in admiration as she arrived in time to lift the creamy lace wedding gown over the bride's stiff petticoats.

Isabella cried out her protest as the two Plantagenet brothers came into the chamber. "Sire," she scolded the king, "you are not supposed to let the bridegroom see me before the ceremony."

They were in such high spirits, however, they were ready for any mischief. Richard looked especially handsome. His royal-blue doublet with matching hose had its sleeves slashed and heavily embroidered with gold thread. His russet hair curled as wildly as Eleanor's, and the bride's heart turned over in her breast that at last she would have her heart's desire. Richard laughed and squeezed her about the waist. "Not even a king could keep me from you today, sweeting."

Eleanor looked from one brother to the other. As usual Henry suffered by comparison. The king had chosen a white satin suit that did little for his blond coloring. Because of his excitement one eyelid drooped noticeably, and he thought it hilarious when a page spilled wine upon one of the flower girls. She threw her basket of rose petals at the boy and the king joined in, throwing flowers and whooping with laughter.

It took William to bring order from chaos. "The bride must be at the altar before the hour of noon or you won't be able to receive the sacrament," he warned Richard. "Do you have the ring, Sire?" he asked Henry, which sobered him instantly, for indeed he had forgotten it.

Isabella cast her brother a look of gratitude. Eleanor sponged the wine stain from the little maid's dress and instructed the young boys exactly how to gather up and carry the bride's train.

* * *

Across the channel in Flanders the marriage of Joan and Simon de Montfort was disrupted by more than a glass of spilled wine. De Montfort, although usually abroad before daylight, had made an exception this morning. They had arisen late and he had taken a leisurely breakfast with Joan. He was about to make an excuse that would enable him to be outdoors on estate business when messengers from King Louis arrived for the Countess of Flanders.

She flew into such a dither that Simon could hardly credit her agitation. She begged him so earnestly to repair to the library while she received the king's men that he took himself off. He did not know exactly what was said to Joan, but he had a damned good idea when she burst into the library, snatched the wedding contract from the desk, and with trembling hands threw it on the fire.

She hissed, "If they find any evidence, they will arrest me." She had gone deathly pale and looked ready to faint. They had been wed in her own chapel so it would be simple to silence her priest.

Simon strode out to confront the two soldiers who wore the army uniform of the King of France. As he opened his mouth to demand an explanation, Joan's high voice gushed forth. "Ridiculous rumors have reached the king that we are married . . . that a marriage contract has already been signed. I shall go to Louis myself and assure him that no such marriage has taken place."

She poured the soldiers refreshment and said, "The Earl of Leicester and I are friends, intimate friends to be sure, but I would not dream of remarrying without my king's permission. If you will excuse me, gentlemen, I will prepare myself for the journey."

De Montfort was torn between routing them from his castle or keeping a wise silence. He bowed and followed Joan from the room. Upstairs he found her trembling and in tears. "Forgive me, forgive me, my lord. I am in love with you, Simon, but Louis will crush me if I give you possession of my lands. Women have so little control of their own lives. I dared to hope I could choose for myself, but it is not to be."

Joan began to sob and he enfolded her against his massive

chest. In a ragged voice she said, "I know I shall regret this moment for the rest of my life." She tipped back her chin to gaze up into Simon's magnetic black eyes. "You are a magnificent man." Her knees turned to water just looking at him. "For one tiny space of time you were mine. Thank you, my lord, for being so gallant to me."

The enormous relief he felt that proof of the marriage had been erased told him that he had had a narrow escape. Fate had snatched him from the jaws of matrimony because his destiny lay elsewhere. He was convinced of it.

At Westminster, however, Isabella Marshal knew she was about to fulfill her destiny. It took a full thirty minutes for the bride and her attendants to wind their way along the passages of Westminster to the doors of the abbey. The church was filled to capacity with the large Marshal family, the nobles of England, and the vast number of relatives and friends of the queen.

Before she entered, Eleanor thought Isabella looked slightly daunted. Whether it was the long aisle she must maneuver or the thought of becoming a princess was not clear, but Eleanor went up on tiptoe to kiss her cheek. "We are doubly sisters—first I married your brother, now you are marrying mine."

Isabella's sweet smile made her face radiant and Eleanor knew why Richard had fallen in love with her. Eleanor slipped into the abbey and walked proudly to the front pew, which was reserved for the royal family. The queen cast her a look of pure venom as she saw the silver tissue gown and silver crown, but Eleanor didn't even notice. She had eyes only for William who stood at the altar steps with Richard. He would not be able to join her until he had given the bride away. A small shiver crept over Eleanor as the dampness seemed to emanate from the cold stone walls.

The smell of incense almost overpowered her, but when the pure voices of the choirboys filled the vaulted chapel, it was so beautiful it lifted her heart. Her spirits rose and her moment of disquiet passed. At last the Archbishop of Canterbury asked, "Who giveth this woman to this man?"

William's sure voice gave the response. "I do." He placed his favorite sister's hand into that of his friend, Prince Richard Plantagenet.

From the moment he joined his wife in the front pew, everyone receded for Eleanor and William. He took her small hand in his and immediately his warmth entered her body. They looked into each other's eyes as they silently repeated the solemn vows intoned by the archbishop. William remembered the little girl who had sworn when the spider bit her, and a wave of protectiveness swept over him. He would cherish her forever.

Eleanor gazed up at him, wanting more than anything in the world to believe that what she saw in his eyes was love. The great Marshal of England hadn't wanted her, hadn't chosen her, and so she had set out to make him proud of her. For years she applied herself diligently to her lessons, curbed her impulsive behavior, even stopped swearing. She had become a lady. Oh, she was exactly the same inside—her passions seethed wildly in her royal blood—but she had learned patience, even shrewdness. Though she was cursed with a quick temper, she had learned to curb it. By hard work and sheer determination she had molded herself into the kind of young woman of whom a great earl could be proud. She clung to his hands as William whispered, "I love you." It had all been worthwhile! She would make him a perfect wife.

The festivities began at two o'clock in the banqueting hall and lasted ten full hours. Ten thousand dishes had been prepared by order of the king, and the tables groaned beneath platters of roast boar and oxen, fat geese and plump plover. Fishcarts had been rushed from England's largest ports, piled with turbot and herrings, shellfish, eels and lampreys. The forests of Windsor had provided venison and enough meat to fill a thousand savory game pies.

King Henry loved to entertain with high jollity and hilarity. Today all was done with magnificence. Gleemen sang "To English Ale and Gascon Wine." The steward had never worked so hard in his life as he watched the squires, assisted by the pages, carry the platters, mets, and mazers to the tables. As the trenchers were being cleared away, the guests were entertained by the very latest craze, a mystery play.

As Eleanor's eyes scanned the vast assembly with amusement, she pointed out to William that the guests were divided into two camps closely resembling enemies who were about to go into battle. The current holders of the ancient earldoms, such as Chester, Kent, Norfolk, Northumberland, and Derby, fraternized only with the noble Anglo-Norman families and the old English bishops, such as Chichester, Lincoln, and York. The ceremonial robes of the men and the quiet good taste of their ladies was in stark contrast to the other camp.

The Provençals, most of whom were related to the new queen, were dressed in the very latest fashion, some of which had been imported from the continent. Compared with the sober taste of the Normans, the Provençals preferred gaudy, exaggerated fashions, and it seemed that all eleven of Thomas of Savoy's offspring vied with each other for center stage.

The influential Bishop of Winchester hid his devious venal personality behind a mask of learning and charm. He had shrewdly chosen to befriend the Poitevins, Gascons, and Provençals who were now taking over all the lucrative posts.

When the trestle tables were pushed back against the walls to make room for dancing, the queen and her cohorts took pleasure in making loud comments and laughing at the clothes of the English ladies. When Eleanor saw young Eve de Braose close to tears, she decided to join the fray. Without effort, her tongue could cut a strip from any female foolish enough to disparage her or any lady belonging to her husband's family. At least half a dozen of the queen's maids wore the saucy new-fashioned pillboxes with tiny veils. Eleanor drawled to the bride, "I wouldn't be caught dead in one. They look for all the world like the little hats that musician's monkeys wear to collect coins."

Isabella tried her best not to laugh and Eleanor noticed with relief that Eve's chin went up and she decided not to cry after all. The queen, to be different, wore a new fashion that was actually most flattering—a wimple that surrounded and framed the entire face. The bride said generously, "The new wimple is a lovely fashion. It makes a lady's face look like a flower."

Eleanor's lips twitched. "A cauliflower?" she questioned, and the ladies surrounding them went off in peals of laughter, to the great consternation of the queen and her court.

William squeezed her hand under cover of the cloth and she

felt a moment of shame at her pettiness. She would not mar this day by indulging in silly, feminine jealousies. She bestowed a dazzling smile upon him and, still handclasped, they rose to join the dancing.

William's eyes never left her face. In fact, he gazed at her so hungrily she became flushed with sheer pleasure. Though the females turned up their long noses at Princess Eleanor, the male Savoys did not. She decided to bestow only one dance apiece upon them for the sake of politeness, but when Peter of Savoy's conversation became deliberately titillating, she wished she had not partnered him.

The very feel of his hands made her want to shrink from him, and his bold leer made her lower her lashes to cover the contempt in her eyes. Rumor had it that he had gotten two young maids with child, and Eleanor fervently wished the dance would come to an end.

"Now that your elderly husband has returned from France, you will have to play the faithful wife for a time, but should you fancy the services of a younger man, I guarantee you satisfaction."

She almost made a cutting remark about the crop of bastards he was sowing, but decided not to even engage him in conversation. She would make it very plain that she much preferred to be partnered by her husband or her brothers.

When Richard spun her about she asked, "When are you leaving for Cornwall?"

"As soon as I can extract myself from the endless entertainments Henry has planned."

Eleanor laughed indulgently. "He's really outdone himself this time. I'll bet he's in hock up to his neck. You are obviously escaping before he presents you with a bill for your own wedding."

Richard bent his lips toward her ear. "Actually I'm spiriting Isabella away so we can get on with the business of making babies. I intend to produce a son before Henry."

The corners of Eleanor's mouth lifted in a mischievous smile. "Me too!"

Amusement shone from his eyes as he admired his beautiful sister. "By the tears of God, I bet you will do exactly that."

17

Since anyone who was anyone had secured rooms for the night at Westminster, the "bedding" didn't take place until well after midnight. Richard and Isabella took it all in good sport, both secretly relieved that the bride would not be stripped naked to prove she went to her marriage bed without blemish as she would have if she'd been an unwed virgin.

Eleanor hung back thinking perhaps Isabella would prefer to have her sisters accompany her to the nuptial tower, but William's sister took hold of Eleanor's hand and begged, "Please come with me—you're the only one who can control Richard and Henry if they start being outrageous."

Eleanor cast her husband an apologetic glance and left the table with Isabella. As he rose to follow her a pain nearly cut him in half. It started at the top of his stomach, slashed up through his diaphragm, and stabbed into his chest wall and heart. He sat back down abruptly and sweat broke out upon his brow. Bones of Christ, he'd never experienced chest pain in his life except from battle wounds. What was amiss? He sat still for a minute, thankful none had observed his plight, then slowly, experimentally he tried to stand. The excruciating pain had gone as quickly as it had struck.

He trailed after the noisy crowd of revelers through the heavily shadowed passages of Westminster, wondering if the pain had been caused by something he'd eaten or if it came from his heart. When he arrived at the nuptial tower, it was bursting at the seams with merrymakers who had clearly imbibed too much good English ale and Gascon wine. He craned his neck to see over the crowd but could not see Eleanor. Then her voice came to him clearly as she admonished, "No more wine for Richard, Henry! Isabella doesn't want an unconscious bridegroom."

Eleanor felt a hand touch her bottom. She whirled about and looked up into the lecherous face of Peter of Savoy. Her hand flew up to strike his cheek and she shuddered with revulsion. His eyes narrowed in his handsome face and she knew she had just made an enemy. God's feet, they were all so immature, she couldn't bear their company one moment longer. She pushed her way from the room and heaved a sigh of relief as William's arm reached out to extract her from the crowd. She leaned against him gratefully, knowing that the moment she had been awaiting all her life was here at long last.

William plucked a torch from its wall bracket to light their way to their own tower. She hoped that Brenda and Allan were not waiting for them. She had told the maid and squire they could have the night off as she and William wished to be completely private.

She watched William's strong hand place the torch in a cresset at the door to their tower suite, and as they entered the lower chamber a feeling of shyness overcame her. She hurried across the room to the fire, which burned low on the hearth, then suddenly began to plump up the cushions on the chairs and straighten the ornaments upon the mantel shelf.

William's eyes softened as he saw her straight little back. He came behind her and reached up to remove her silver crown. As she whirled about to face him, he saw the tiny flicker of apprehension and his heart skipped a beat. "Don't be afraid, love," he whispered.

Her apprehension melted away. "Oh, William, I'm never afraid when you're with me, I'm only afraid when you're not with me."

He kissed her nose. "Perhaps you're not afraid, but you are suddenly shy." He smiled down at her. "You go up . . . I'll give you all the time you need."

As she climbed to the upper chamber she was suffused with warm, delicious happiness. She loved him with all her heart and all her soul and all her mind. She removed her silvery gown and petticoats and washed her hands with rose-scented water. She took up her nightgown made especially for this night. It was made of sheer lavender sarcenet, which floated about her body as lightly as thistledown. She shook out her raven hair until it hung in silken waves about her bare shoulders.

William would surely come through the doorway any moment. She quickly turned back the covers on the wide bed and ran her hand over the pristine white linen embroidered with roses and crowns.

William sat below in front of the fire, his brows drawn slightly together. Surely he was not so old that he was having heart trouble? He dismissed the idea quickly. He was perfectly all right now. Eleanor's extreme youth was making him feel his years. Nothing must spoil this night for her, he decided firmly.

The minutes stretched out as Eleanor sat in the bed, propped against the pillows. Why didn't he come? Perhaps he had fallen asleep. No, he was being thoughtful and giving her time to compose herself. Her thoughts flew to Isabella and she remembered the night she had seen her in bed with Richard. He had been so eager she experienced a moment of longing. Surely William hadn't changed his mind? What had Isabella said when she asked her how to get William to consummate the marriage? "Let him see you in a state of undress and nature will take its inevitable course," Isabella had advised.

Finally Eleanor could sit still no longer. She put aside her shyness and slipped down the shadowed stairs to the chamber below. William's eyes widened with pleasure at the sight of her, all thoughts of himself wiped from his mind. The light from the fire silhouetted her nakedness through the sheer nightrail, and his breath caught in his throat as he feasted on her lovely curves. Desire snaked through his loins as he stood to open his arms and she flew into them.

She buried her face against his shoulder, her heart overflowing with happiness at the hunger she'd seen written in his eyes. His lips traced a molten line against her throat as his hands crushed her against his hardness. His hot mouth teased her ear and his husky whisper sent a shiver of delight down her spine. "Let me carry you up to bed."

Halfway up the dark stairs the pain cut into him again. He stopped, drew in his breath, and by sheer dint of will banished it from his chest.

Eleanor raised her head from his shoulder. "What's wrong, am I too heavy for you?"

"Heavy?" He laughed. "By the tears of God, I hope you don't think me too old and infirm to carry my bride to my bed?"

She joined in his laughter. What a ridiculous question to ask a champion. Wasn't he William, the great Marshal of England?

Again the pain vanished as quickly as it had come and he wasted no time even thinking of it. He lay Eleanor gently upon the bed. "You won't mind if I don't snuff all the candles? I'm starved for the sight of you."

The pink of her cheeks deepened as she replied, "I want to see you too." She watched him with breathless curiosity as he divested himself of his doublet, shirt, and finally his chausses. His legs were thick with corded muscle and between them his groin was covered by chestnut hair.

So, this was what a naked man looked like, she thought. Then she amended the thought. Not all men looked this splendid. William was no ordinary man. When he reached out a strong hand to remove her lavender nightgown, she thought she might faint from the heightened tension of the moment. The gown whispered to the carpet and the bed sighed as William's full weight came upon it. He gathered her to his heart tenderly, anticipating the feel of her satiny skin against his hard body. She gasped with pleasure. God, how she loved the feel of this man—his heat, his weight, his hairiness!

His fingers closed over her breasts. "Sweet, sweet," he murmured, caressing the rosebud tips with his thumbs until they ruched, then touching each one with the tip of his tongue.

"Ohh," she cried out in pleasure. His palms sought the silken place beneath her breasts as he lifted them to his mouth. He caressed every inch of her as he explored her loveliness. His kisses took her breath away and her heart sang with the dizzying thought that she would never be separated from him again. They would share the same bed for the rest of their lives and there would be no other loves for either of them, ever.

"My little love, how long I have waited for you."

For her too the wait had been endless, but well worth every moment. He curbed his need, schooling the heated blood in his veins so that he would not ravish her. She was his precious jewel whom he had vowed to cherish. "Did I tell you how very beautiful you looked today?" His hands moved ever lower, but he caressed each new place, knowing that lovemaking was completely new to her.

On an intake of breath she answered, "Yes, you make me feel utterly lovely. The sapphires you gave me were the bluest I have ever seen."

"Not so. They pale in comparison to your eyes. They are like deep pools—I could drown in them," he whispered as his fingertips separated the tiny folds of her woman's center to seek the jewel inside.

A thrill ran through her body as a result of William's touch and also at what her own hands encountered. She let them stray and play about over his muscles, then set her mouth to his shoulders and chest and rib cage to kiss and taste him.

He slipped a finger inside her then held it still so that she could become familiar with the sensation. She cried out, then quickly apologized for he hadn't really hurt her.

"Sweet, cry out as much as you like. I'll try to be careful, but the first time there will be pain." Slowly he began a stroking motion with his finger, seeking to produce a little moisture to make her first penetration more bearable. After a prolonged manipulation she arched into his hand. "Mmm . . . William." Her soft mouth parted as the first spark of sensual pleasure was ignited. He quickly crushed her lips with his in a demanding kiss that told her better than words that there was much more he wanted from her. They were bathed in an aura of love and longing and need as if sealed in a cocoon that separated them from the whole world. Their bed was so intimate a place, they could do anything to each other, privately, secretly. This was paradise.

She reached down to touch the hard insistence against her thigh, and they both jumped at the shock. "Don't! Don't move your fingers, love, or I am lost," he explained hoarsely.

"William . . . you are so big, so rigid." She faltered, a note of fear creeping into her voice.

"Don't be afraid, my darling. It is better when I am extremely rigid and hard. Penetration is easier that way, trust me."

"I do, William," she said simply, ready to yield all control to her beloved husband.

He knelt above her, loath to hurt her, but he was too far gone for further loveplay.

Eleanor was in a passion of conflicting emotions. She had never wanted anything more in her life; she had never wanted anything less in her life!

He whispered, "Forgive me, Eleanor," then it was done. She closed her eyes and a little scream escaped her lips as the pain and fullness spread inside her like a burning sunburst. It took her a moment to gather her scattered thoughts. Truly it had been more pain than pleasure, but she loved the closeness of their bodies and knew he still impaled her. William lay fully upon her, his great weight engulfing her. She remembered screaming, yet he too had cried out as if in pain. He lay motionless now. So this was "the little death" Isabella had spoken of. It was indeed a mystical experience.

William's weight became too much for her and she tried to ease her position slightly. She found that she could not move, however, and said softly, "William, you are hurting me."

He made no reply, no sign whatsoever that he even heard her. He had fallen asleep. She must rouse him. His ear was not too far distant from her lips and she cried his name, "William! William!" A small wisp of fear curled in her body. He was not asleep, he was unconscious. Tears of God, if only she weren't so ignorant. Could the hymenal rite cause a man to faint?

His crushing weight prevented her from breathing properly. She took quick shallow breaths as a feeling of dread penetrated her brain. Her mind screamed its denial of what she feared, telling herself over and over that if she just endured it a moment longer, all would be well.

She did not know how long she lay imprisoned beneath him before she lost control and began to scream, but the next thing she knew Rickard de Burgh had entered the tower chamber from the ramparts and was lifting William's body off her.

De Burgh stared in horror at the naked princess, her virgin's blood staining the snowy sheets and the dead body of the Earl of Pembroke, Marshal of England. He groped blindly for Eleanor's bedrobe. "My lady, my poor sweet lady," he whispered.

"No, Rickard, no. Help me, sweet Jesus, help me! He cannot die; I won't let him die!" She enfolded William's naked body in her arms, sobbing wildly.

"Eleanor, he is gone, we cannot bring him back."

She recoiled from his words. "Don't call me that, the name is cursed!"

Firmly he pried her from the body of her husband and forced her arms into the velvet bedgown.

"Fetch a physician—fetch the king," she cried hysterically.

"If I fetched the angel of death, my lady, he could not give him back to you. Quickly, Eleanor, before these rooms are overrun—what happened? Was William ill? Did he drink wine left in this chamber?" Rickard demanded suspiciously.

She shook her head, her face paler than death. Rickard had sensed danger to Eleanor, not William. If only he could have done something to prevent this tragedy. He had no option but to break the news of the sudden death, but prayed that no blame would touch this innocent lady. He drew the bedcovers over the blood-spotted sheet and murmured, "You should have a lady to attend you." He didn't think she even heard him. He left her desperately clutching William's cold hand.

Soon the tower bedchamber was filled with shocked relatives, clergy, and physicians, while more spectators gathered in the chamber below. The king's face was tinged with gray and he was indelicately sick in a corner. Two physicians had examined the body and were interrogating Eleanor.

"Tell us exactly what took place when you retired," the king's personal physician ordered accusingly.

Eleanor pressed the back of her hand to her mouth in an

effort to speak coherently. She managed to whisper, "William carried me up to bed and we . . ." Her voice failed her.

"He carried you up that steep staircase?" the physician asked in disbelief. Then he turned to his fellow. "How old was the marshal?"

"Forty-six years old," he supplied. They both looked at Eleanor. "And you are?"

"Six-sixteen," she answered. "Almost seventeen," she amended.

"It has been less than a year since the marshal took you to live with him?" the accusing voice persisted.

Eleanor could only nod.

"Tell us honestly, Countess, do you have a young lover?"

Her eyes sought out Rickard de Burgh, but he knew he must not jump to her defense or they would be condemned as lovers. She shook her head mutely, misery washing over her in waves.

"How many times did you insist he perform his marital duties tonight?"

What were these men raving about? she wondered as her grief threatened to overwhelm her. She pressed her hands over her ears and cried, "Henry, make them stop!" But the king had gone to pieces over the loss of the man who had been like a father to him. He cried openly and the queen and the Savoys were lavishing their sympathy upon him.

The king's physician announced to the room at large, "It is obvious that marriage to a sixteen-year-old proved too much for the aging marshal. His heart burst trying to satisfy the demands of his young wife. If I had only known the Earl of Pembroke suffered heart trouble, I would have supplied him with a piece of coral to hold in his mouth at all times."

Eleanor heard a rushing in her ears and for a moment everything went black. She stretched out a hand of supplication to her brother Richard, but he was entirely taken up with his bride's grief over losing her brother.

The physician's verdict was avidly repeated among the guests who had been present at the wedding, none of whom would have missed being present at this fatal drama for the world.

Brenda stared across the room at Allan. Everyone was in shock save the squire. His face registered no surprise whatsoever. In fact, he wore a look of smug satisfaction as if he was inordinately proud of some great accomplishment. All through the wedding feast she recalled how he had hovered at the marshal's elbow, serving him food, refilling his goblet, and now the marshal lay dead.

As Allan caught sight of Brenda, he read the suspicious thoughts plainly writ upon her face. The girl knew too much. His instructions were clear. He must leave no untidy thread dangling that could connect him with Winchester. At his last encounter with the bishop, it had been brought forcibly home to him that if he did not swiftly carry out his end of the bargain, his own life would be forfeit. He motioned with his head for Brenda to follow him out onto the battlements. It was easy to slip out unnoticed, for just at that moment they tried to remove the marshal's body from the tower chamber.

Suddenly Eleanor sprang to life. "Don't touch him—don't anyone dare to touch him!" She looked like a wild woman as she blocked their approach to the bed. "Get out!" she screamed. "Every last one of you, out!"

The king and queen led the exodus, followed by the Savoys, the bishops, and Richard and Isabella. The two physicians remained, condemning her with looks of outrage. She stood her ground like an avenging angel. "Out!" she screamed.

They knew they had little choice. She was suffering from a bout of Plantagenet madness. They had seen it happen to her father many a time.

She threw the bolt upon the door, then went back to the bed. This was all a nightmare. Presently she would awaken and all would be well. Guilt engulfed her. She sank to her knees, took his hand between hers, and pressed her cheek to it. "My God, William, what have I done to you?" she asked. The last words he had said to her were *"Forgive me, Eleanor."* Lord God, who would forgive her? She bathed his cold hand with her tears. Over and over inside her head the words repeated, Don't leave me, don't leave me, don't leave me.

Out upon the high walls of the palace Brenda confronted Allan like a terrier with a rat. His deadly fingers snaked about her throat before she could utter her accusation. Instantly she joined the dance of death. She brought up her knee sharply to jab him viciously in the testicles. The moment his hands released her throat, she butted him in the chest with her head, sending him backward over the parapet. She drew in a labored breath to ease her bruised throat, and before she released it she heard a sickening thud on the flagstones below.

She slunk back into the shadows, fear almost immobilizing her. Never would she breathe a word of what she suspected. Allan had tried to murder her on orders from Winchester. She must get away.

When the gray dawn arrived, the body of the insignificant squire had been spirited away by unknown hands. The disappearance of the lowly servant and maid was overshadowed by the grave tragedy that had touched the lives of the highest in the land.

18

The Marshal of England lay in state at Westminster. His young widow, looking like a wraith, was in deep shock. She had not let his body out of her sight, but had polished his armor herself and placed his favorite sword in his hands. When she had brushed his hair, she wondered when it had turned from chestnut to gray.

Now she stood vigil beside the catafalque draped with the Red Lion Rampant as the nobility came to pay its respects. Later the people of London would be allowed in, but at the moment the royal family, the Marshals, and every member of the clergy within a fifty-mile radius were crowded into the abbey.

Henry came, supported by his gentlemen, but he could not bring himself to draw close. Eleanor watched numbly as her brother's eyes filled with tears and he turned away. Silently she spoke to William, feeling that he could still hear every word that was uttered and know every thought that entered her head. She knew she would be able to bear it so long as they were together. She firmly closed her mind and refused to think about the burial.

The aging Archbishop of Canterbury intoned a prayer for

William's soul, and the Bishop of Chichester tried to comfort her with some trite religious twaddle. Her heart hurt. With every beat she felt its aching soreness. She hugged the pain to herself, loving the exquisite torture. She needed to suffer.

Peter des Roches, the Bishop of Winchester, made the sign of the cross upon William's brow, and Eleanor flinched when his sausagelike fingers touched her husband's cold flesh. As the Marshal brothers and sisters and cousins filed past, they looked at her coldly. She fancied the members of the wealthiest family in England were thinking that he would still be alive if he had not married her. Eleanor burned with guilt, for it was what she herself believed.

The queen came next with her inevitable entourage of Savoys in tow. She bestowed a pitying look upon Eleanor and said, "Never fear, my dear, we will find you another husband."

Eleanor stiffened and said quietly, "I shall never marry again."

The queen laughed and the sound offended Eleanor's ears—offended her very soul. She was outraged that she would say such things within William's hearing.

"Next time you shall have a younger husband." She bent close. "Peter of Savoy has already spoken for you," the queen said with a coy glance at her old lover.

Eleanor cried out, "I shall never marry again! I swear an oath of chastity! I take the vow of perpetual widowhood!"

The Archbishop of Canterbury and the Bishops of Chichester and Winchester immediately stepped forward to sanctify the vows that the Countess of Pembroke swore so fervently. They had her hand upon the Bible before the echo of her cries had stopped reverberating through the arched sanctuary. She took the vows gladly, wholeheartedly, but wondered why she felt such a disgust for bishops. Then she remembered Ireland and the curse of the Bishop of Ferns. "The Almighty Marshal family will end. In one generation the name shall be destroyed. You will die without issue and your inheritance will be scattered." Eleanor's hands stroked her abdomen. "Please God, let me be carrying William's child," she begged.

The Countess of Pembroke collapsed after a thirty-hour vigil. The Mother Superior of the Holy Order of St. Bride's was called upon to nurse the grief-stricken young widow. Eleanor was taken by barge the short distance to Durham House. It housed a vast number of servants, each and every one devastated by the sudden loss of their beloved Earl of Pembroke.

She was nursed around the clock by the Mother Superior and the two nuns who had lived in her household since she was a child. At one point she became delirious and they feared for both her life and her sanity. The house was kept silent, each room draped in black; the entire staff was in mourning. It seemed to rain for weeks. When Londoners looked up to observe the darkened windows from the Thames, it seemed the very stones of the stronghold wept with sorrow.

Eventually she could no longer escape with the excuse of illness and reluctantly left the sanctuary of her sickbed. No one called her Eleanor now, they called her the Countess of Pembroke, which comforted her. The ghost of William haunted every room. The tasteful furnishings of Durham House evoked poignant memories.

She was always chilled until she found William's mole-colored velvet doublet and put it on. She wore it often, stroking the soft fabric absently, lost in thought. When the pain became too great to bear, she slept in it.

Within three weeks she was ousted from her haven when Richard Marshal came from Normandy where he had administered the family estates. Now that William was dead he had come to take over the estates and offices of the wealthy Marshal family. This younger brother was a stern and resolute man who harbored a suspicious resentment against all Plantagenets.

The Countess of Pembroke had no option but to appeal to the king. Henry was shocked at his beautiful sister's appearance. He feared her outrageous wrath at the prospect of losing Durham House, but none came. She was so subdued it worried him. "Henry, it doesn't matter," she said quietly. "I am heartsore to live there without William."

Richard Marshal had already confronted the king. Henry had been rubbing his hands together at the thought of acquiring the Marshal holdings, for when a man of large possessions died without male heir, his estates passed to the Courts of Chancery and the king benefited. Richard Marshal, however, pointed out that since William had no son, he was the heir and had the legal papers to prove it.

"I have no liking for these young Marshals," the king said petulantly, yet he knew he could not afford to offend so wealthy a family. Money was power. He would willingly sacrifice Eleanor's portion of Marshal holdings to keep the peace, since she did not even seem to be aware that she was entitled to one fifth of everything, not only in England, but also in Normandy, Wales, and Ireland.

"You shall come back to Windsor," he said firmly, wondering how he would tell her that Thomas of Savoy now occupied her old apartments.

She smiled sadly and murmured, "There is room for only one Eleanor at your court. I ask only peace and quiet and privacy."

Henry saw a solution to his problem. He took her hand in his. "You shall have your own court. You can have Father's old residence way back in the Upper Ward where you can enjoy complete privacy. Our grandfather built those apartments with stone brought all the way from Bedfordshire. The King John Tower is rectangular and behind all, I believe there is a walled garden with only one key."

She squeezed his hand gratefully and murmured, "Thank you, Henry. The entire staff of Durham House has begged me to keep them in my service." He was relieved that he did not have to pay for her servants. He stared after the small figure as it retreated. Gone was the girl whose eyes flashed like brilliant jewels. Gone was the sister who cuffed him over the ear to reprimand him. Gone was the princess who ruled the Plantagenet roost.

On the same day that William Marshal was buried, the Bishop of Winchester, on the king's behalf, commanded Hubert de Burgh to surrender all the royal castles in his possession to Stephen Segrave. To add insult to injury, Segrave was named the new justiciar. When Hubert could not account for all the funds that had passed through his hands, all his personal possessions were taken away. They caught him fleeing and put him in the lowest dungeon of the Tower of London, while upstairs his sumptuous apartments stood empty.

Falcon de Burgh accompanied his son Michael back to England. He sailed up the Bristol Channel accompanied by two dozen of his finest fighting men. As they rode the hundred miles to London, de Burgh hoped his journey from Ireland would prove unnecessary, but when they arrived in the capital and learned that Hubert was no longer Justiciar of England, that he had been arrested and that his greatest ally William Marshal was dead, Falcon de Burgh knew he had not a moment to waste. They took rooms at the Bag O'Nails Tavern in Wapping on the edge of the Thames. Under cover of dark, Falcon sent for his son Rickard.

Rain pooled on the floor as Rickard de Burgh flung off his drenched cloak and strode toward the welcoming peat fire. "Father, Mick, thank God you are come."

Falcon de Burgh saw the green fire in his son's eyes, exactly like his own, and knew his visions had foretold the disaster. "I brought men," Falcon said, low. "We'll use the back room to decide our plans, but if there's any dirty work to be done, I'm the one who'll do it—I know how."

"I suspect the marshal was poisoned," Rickard said in a low, intense voice.

"If he was, he must have been in the way of someone's insatiable ambition. He must have opposed this persecution of Hubert. Neither of you must be seen to champion your uncle. In fact, I want both of you to go into the king's service."

Mick grimaced. "That would rankle. His lack of character is pitiful. The way his loyalty swings about is like a bloody weathervane. Hubert and William were his favorites. They were both like the father he never had and look where they are now."

Falcon held up a scarred hand. "I don't want you on the losing side. If someone had balls enough to poison William Marshal, the younger Marshals' lives aren't worth a pinch of pig shit. You will learn more if you are in the king's service. Henry is weak, not evil. Someone is manipulating him." The three men grinned for the first time. "All right, *everyone* is manipulating him."

Rickard said, "The king is inconstant as are all Londoners. They are whispering vile untruths about Hubert. I've already heard it rumored he poisoned the marshal and that he used black magic for his evil hold over Henry."

Mick said, "The next charge will be that he seduced Princess Margaret, hoping to become King of Scotland."

Falcon said, "London isn't England. It's like the tail trying to wag the dog. England will remember it was Hubert who freed them of the French."

Rickard scanned his father's dark, forbidding features. "Will you free him from the Tower?"

"How and when you need not know," he replied, "but I think I'll take him to sanctuary at the church in Devizes."

"Excellent choice!" approved Rickard. "Devizes Castle was where King John kept young Henry for safekeeping, was it not?"

Falcon nodded. "He was taken from Devizes and crowned. Let's hope the choice is not lost on him."

Mick asked, "Isn't Devizes just north of Stonehenge?"

Falcon nodded absently. It had been at Stonehenge that he had glimpsed his enchantress Jasmine for the first time. His blood stirred, then his heart sank. How the hell would he ever tell her that her dearest friend Will was in his grave?

By the time de Burgh and his men got to Hubert, he had already been tortured. He had been forced to sign a paper turning over everything the Knights Templars held for him. There was gold, plate, jewels, and over a hundred high-standing cups of precious metals elaborately decorated with uncut gems.

Falcon de Burgh fed him, tended his wounds, and turned him over to the priests at the church in Devizes. He withdrew his men to his wife's castle of Salisbury to await developments. They were not long in coming. Mercenary soldiers under Winchester's orders dragged Hubert from sanctuary and fastened him to the wall with triple shackles in Devizes' dungeon.

Outraged, Falcon de Burgh informed the Bishop of Salisbury, then rode immediately to the Bishop of London and informed him that sanctuary had been violated. The two bishops together with the Archbishop of Canterbury descended upon Westminster.

When Henry spoke to Winchester he was actually wringing his hands. He hated confrontation and usually took the path of least resistance.

"You are the king!" Winchester argued. "Why do you allow them to give you orders?"

"They have told me in no uncertain terms that the barons are outraged; that I must listen to my English peers."

"England has no peers." Winchester sneered, using one of his favorite phrases.

"My council has informed me that they have no evidence of murder or witchcraft against Hubert," Henry insisted.

"Then it is high time you appointed a new council," Winchester advised.

Henry thought this a brilliant suggestion that he would set about implementing immediately, but it did not solve his immediate problem. He said flatly to Winchester, "Unless I restore Hubert de Burgh to sanctuary, the bishops and the archbishop will excommunicate me. They will place me under an interdict as they did my father. I have no choice."

Winchester smiled. "By all means return him to the church. Simply surround it with a heavy guard so that no food is allowed in. He will shortly come out of sanctuary of his own free will."

"How brilliant you are, my lord bishop."

"Speaking of brilliant, Sire, wait until you hear the plans we have made for the Christmas festivities at Winchester this year."

Three men sat in the smoky recesses of the backroom at the Bag O'Nails. Falcon de Burgh's mouth was grim as he argued with his son. "Mick, if you ride with us, you may never be able to return to London and the king's service."

"I care not! The stench of this court sickens me. Foreigners get every preferment anyway. After this I'm for Connaught, a place where de Burghs rule, not Plantagenets!"

Falcon raised a brow, black as a raven's wing, to his other son, Rickard.

Quietly he answered, "I pledged to William Marshal . . . I still feel pledged to the Countess of Pembroke."

His father searched his face. " 'Tis hopeless to love her when she has taken the vow of chastity."

Rickard closed his eyes for a moment. "I have no illusions in that direction. I regret she took the vows because I would like nothing better than to see her cleave to a strong man who will protect her. I will see the year out in the king's service. By that time I think she will have taken the veil. If and when she does, I will feel free to return home to Ireland." He grinned suddenly at his brother and father. "But if you think I'm going to deny myself the pleasure of cutting Hubert's guards to ribbons and hanging their balls from the nearest oak tree, think again!"

Half of Falcon's men took Hubert's child and wife, Princess Margaret, north for safekeeping. The king would never have dared to persecute Margaret for fear of bringing the wrath of Scotland down upon England. However, accidents happened all too frequently these days.

Falcon de Burgh chose a moonless night for his operation. The second reason he'd had for choosing Devizes as sanctuary for Hubert was its proximity to the Bristol Channel where his ship lay at anchor. A quick sail across the Severn would carry Hubert into Wales where the king's writ could not reach.

It was a hard and bloody fight for the de Burghs were outnumbered two to one, but Falcon knew they had the advantage of surprise and he also knew the mettle of his men. When dawn broke upon the castle of Devizes and the mists swirled about the empty ramparts, it was as if both prisoner and guards had vanished from the face of the earth. Again there were rumors of black magic, but most tongues decided discretion was the better part of valor.

The next evening Sir Rickard de Burgh was offering his services to Henry while openly flirting with the queen. At the same hour Falcon was on his way back to Jasmine. Mick realized his father spoke the truth when he said, "Every battle is won before it is ever fought."

PART
TWO

19

Eleanor, Countess of Pembroke, had been widowed for more than a year. At first her name had been upon every malicious tongue. The misdeeds of her redheaded maid had been added to her own, and the sex scandal had amused the court of Windsor for months on end.

However, as the months drifted into a whole year, interest in the pale young woman waned and even the lusty, promiscuous Savoys ignored her existence since her vows had made her inviolate.

The queen no longer taunted her with jealous jibes, for where was the fun in tossing a cutting remark when it received no answering invective? The crowning glory of her sister-in-law's hair was tightly braided, and the queen's burnished gold tresses now had no rival. Queen Eleanor reveled at the way things had turned out. She had sworn to wean everyone from the princess's camp and fate had done most of the work for her. Soon the doors of the convent would close behind Eleanor Plantagenet and she would never have to spare her another thought for the rest of her life. From that day forward she would be the reigning beauty of England.

It had taken a whole year to accomplish his goals, but with

Hubert de Burgh and William Marshal out of the way, Peter des Roches, the Bishop of Winchester, was in a position to exercise full control over the realm. He and his illegitimate son, Peter des Rivaux, took custody of all wardships, all forests, took over stewardship of all the king's houses and appointed all new sheriffs. Authority was not delegated but brought under central control. Officials in Westminster offices managed the affairs of the whole country, while foreign mercenary soldiers enforced the law. It was tyranny—organized control.

Winchester kept the barons from consolidating with each other by a vicious whispering campaign, and so it was left up to the bishops to look after England's interests. The powerful Bishop of Lincoln, who held the largest see in England, persuaded the Earl of Chester to tell the king that the counsel he was getting from Winchester was a danger to the realm because he estranged the English king from his English subjects. Suddenly, however, the aged Earl of Chester died, and it seemed that every voice which championed the English had been silenced. The English barons had no leader. At one time they looked to Prince Richard, but at the moment his only interest was in minting new coins of the realm, a venture that consumed all his time and interest.

Henry was elated at the moment. All the dreary business of the realm had been lifted from his shoulders, giving him more time to spend with his vivacious young queen and her fascinating, fun-loving court. He shared in the profits his brother Richard was reaping from the minting of new coins, and Simon de Montfort had brought peace to Gascony. Henry called Simon home to invest him as the Earl of Leicester. As the Earl of Chester was now deceased, he decided to be generous with Simon and give him all the lands around Leicester that came with the ancient title.

Simon de Montfort was shocked to learn that Hubert de Burgh had been pulled down from the lofty heights of Justiciar of England and fled to Wales. Chester's death he accepted at face value, not only because he benefited from it, but also because Chester had lived to be a good age. The thing that shocked him the most, however, was the death of William Marshal. Though it had happened well over a year since, no word had reached him in Gascony. The last news he had had of the Marshals was that Richard had married William's sister. Simon wondered briefly if news of the marshal's death had been hushed up.

King Henry feted Simon, took him to Winchester for the unbelievable Christmas festivities. Much to Simon's chagrin, he realized that he had been chosen as the new favorite. Hubert and William had been father figures to the young king and Simon soon realized he was being cast in the same role. Though he was the king's age, he was so much more mature both in body and intellect that Henry looked up to him and revered him.

Simon was appalled at the way the country was being ruled. De Montfort loved almost everything about England. He was a true Anglophile, becoming more English than an Englishman born.

At New Year's, Henry was most generous with de Montfort and gave him title to lands in Coventry near Leicester. De Montfort was burdened by heavy debts from fighting Henry's battles in Gascony, but he was farsighted enough to see that owning land meant wielding power. Amazingly no one seemed to resent the favor being heaped upon the newcomer, possibly because the queen had taken one look at the young Apollo with his dark, compelling beauty, and decided she would make him a "Queen's Man."

Simon took his men to Leicester and Coventry to see to the administration of his new holdings. From past experience he knew he must take a firm hand in running his households if he was ever to get out from under his mountain of debt. The king and queen allowed him to go only because he had promised to come back into their service when the court returned to Windsor in the spring.

Simon kept his ears open for whispers about William Marshal's death and questioned his two squires about rumors. Guy, who kept company with the king's younger knights, avidly repeated the stories that had circulated after the marshal's death.

" 'Tis common knowledge his young wife killed him."

Guy's father Rolf asked bluntly, "How?"

"He was an older man who married a young girl. He didn't

take her to live with him until she was about fifteen, then he didn't last a year!"

"What do you mean, he didn't last a year?" Rolf asked, puzzled.

Guy winked at Simon and explained to his father, "You know, he wore himself out in bed trying to please her."

"Bullshit!" replied Rolf. "The marshal was my age, he wasn't an old man."

"Too old for the insatiable Plantagenet princess apparently. He died on the job!"

Rolf looked at Simon for confirmation. De Montfort nodded. "I've heard the same stories."

The look of disbelief on Rolf's face was replaced by one of admiration. "He died fucking—what a way to go!"

The squires couldn't help laughing even though they knew de Montfort had held the marshal in high esteem. "You should hear the tales they tell in the stables about a red-haired maid of Princess Eleanor's," said Guy.

"I hear lots of tales, but I'm not gullible enough to believe everything I hear," Rolf said repressively.

"These tales must be true. Men seldom admit their cocks are lacking in virility. This maid was so lusty it took six men to satisfy her." He winked at his father. "Six Englishmen, that is; I wonder if she ever tried a French prick?"

Simon mused, "It seems at this court the morals of the ladies, be they maid or princess, leave much to be desired." He turned his destrier over to Rolf. "Saddle my other horse. I think I'll fly my falcon in Windsor forest." Simon de Montfort went above the stables to get his bird.

"You shouldn't talk like that in front of his lordship," Rolf reproved his son. "I know he's the easiest man in the world to talk to, but you forget he's now a great earl." He removed the saddle, bit, and bridle of the black stallion and began to rub him down. "A red-haired wench, did you say?"

Guy laughed, "Tie a knot in it," he said as he brought Simon's hunter from its box. "She hasn't been seen at Windsor in over a year!"

* * *

Once Eleanor's firm hand fell upon the jade-green velvet riding habit in her wardrobe, she could not wait to see how the vibrant color would change her appearance. When she stepped in front of her polished silver mirror, she shuddered with distaste at the ugly braids. She quickly unplaited the pious knots and brushed her hair into a wild mass of curls, then hunted for a jeweled net to complement her outfit and confine her unruly, waist-length tresses.

The mouths of the grooms and falconers had fallen open when the beautiful young princess demanded her horse be saddled and her merlin unhooded and jessed, but in their hearts they were pleased to see that she was again taking an interest in life.

Eleanor filled her lungs with fresh air. This was the first time she had ridden in over a year, the first time she had cast aside her mourning garments. Outside again, enjoying the solitude of nature, she marveled that four seasons had slipped by without her noticing their passage. She gained a more balanced perspective of how her small existence fit into the scheme of things. Though Eleanor Plantagenet Marshal's heart had been broken, the world had not come to a crashing stop. The birds still sang as sweetly, the trees that had towered there for hundreds of years still spread their branches to the sunlight, the butterflies still fluttered about the pallid violets at the edge of the stream and that stream trickled along until it became a brook, then widened into a river whose current swept it out to sea. For the first time in over a year she allowed herself to become immersed in something other than grief.

She'd lost the confining net from her hair hours ago as she'd galloped beneath a low-lying branch in the vast forest of Windsor. She had truly forgotten how invigorating it could be astride her mare with the breeze whipping her black tresses into an impossible tangle.

For a small moment in time she had allowed her guilt to drop away as she took pleasure in the cool, green solitude of the woods. When she cast her little merlin she was not surprised when it missed its first prey, for the small hawk had been sadly neglected. It did not return to her hand until she cast the lure several times, then when she stood in her stirrups and flung it high a second time, it brought down a pigeon.

Instead of bringing its prize to her hand, it flew to a high branch and devoured the pigeon. Eleanor did not get angry at the merlin. It was her own fault for flying her so seldom. The hawk had half forgotten her training and had reverted to her natural instincts.

Eleanor's cheeks were filled with roses as she gazed upward at the defiant little rebel. Suddenly she heard a sound like a whistling and to her horror saw a sleek peregrine falcon thud into her merlin with its great talons. The tiny gray bundle of feathers dropped from the tree like a stone.

Eleanor dismounted in a flash and picked it up from the grass, hoping it had only been stunned, but she saw with dismay its throat had been torn open. A cry of deep hurt was torn from her own throat. This was the little merlin William had given her; brought all the way from their beloved Wales. Suddenly all the quiet reserve left her and the floodgates opened. She fell to the forest floor cradling the limp little bird, sobbing uncontrollably.

Simon de Montfort signaled his falcon and it immediately returned to his hand. He tied its jesses to his saddlebow and dismounted. With one massive hand he lifted the jade-clad figure from the ground, saying "Hush, child, hush. Don't break your heart. What's done is done. What can't be undone must be accepted, child."

"I'm not a child . . . I'm a woman!" raged Eleanor, her eyes blazing with hatred.

As he set her on her feet he saw that indeed she was a woman. A pair of tempting breasts thrust upward from her riding dress, and a pair of eyes like rare jewels glistened with tears in the most breathtakingly beautiful face he'd ever seen. "Forgive me, *chérie,* I thought you were a child because you are no bigger than a . . ."

For one unbelievable moment she thought he would say cockroach or piss-ant.

"You filthy swine! 'Tis not I who am small, 'tis you who are a bloody giant!" Eleanor saw him through a red mist of rage. She was angry at the world in general and this odious male in particular. Her eyes fell upon the falcon secured to his saddle. "I'll kill the son of a bitch," she screamed, and lunged toward the predator.

It stood its ground fiercely and tore open her embroidered glove with its talon.

Simon dragged her away. "You will not! Control yourself, you foolish little wench."

"Then I'll kill you, you filthy whoreson!" She twisted in his massive arms and raked her nails down his cheek.

He dropped her on her arse without hesitation. "Who are you?" he demanded. "You have a mouth like a cesspool."

Her eyes glazed threateningly. "I don't give out my name to any bastard who asks."

De Montfort's black eyes narrowed. "That's enough, English, control yourself!"

"You are the one who needs controlling, you and that damned vermin you call a hawk."

"That, English, is a peregrine falcon, the fastest, finest bird of prey in the world."

"I hope you both rot in hell," she shouted, her breasts heaving from her shortness of breath.

"I should teach you to curse in French, it sounds so much more civilized."

"You? You? Teach *me* anything? *Fais de l'air,*" she cried, telling him to get lost.

Again his eyes narrowed, but she ignored the warning. "English, I think I'll teach you some manners," he threatened as he took a step toward her.

"Don't call me that," she warned. "Pigs can't teach manners."

"Someone should have taken you over their knee when you were a child. You shouldn't speak to your betters in gutter language."

"Don't call me that!" she screamed. "You . . . you Frenchman! You filthy foreigner! You come over here with your superior airs, with your unmitigated gall, and take over. You're thick as scum on a pond. Don't ever dare to lay a hand on me, Frenchman—you're not fit to clean my boots!"

Suddenly he began to laugh at himself. She had exactly the

same quality as all the other beautiful things he admired—wild
orchids, dragonflies, peregrine falcons—things so exquisite that
it was hard to get enough. He had a fascination for wild things;
a desire to make a connection with them. He wanted to get
close, to touch, to possess. "I'll stop calling you English if
you'll tell me your name," he offered.

"Go and rot!" she spat.

He shrugged. "I already know much about you."

"In a pig's eye!" she swore.

"I can see that you are some important man's fancy piece
and that you are far too beautiful for your own good." As he
looked her over, Simon felt his balls tighten and his shaft fill.
He had an urge to remove her clothes to see if her body was as
exquisite as her face. He knew he could span her waist with his
hands. She was so small, in fact, he wondered if she would be
able to take his great shaft, which pulsed with desire from just
looking at her.

His throat went dry. Somehow the contrast in their size
acted like an aphrodisiac on him. His vast experience with
women told him that satisfactory coitus could be achieved only
if she became fully aroused. Lord God, how pleasurable it
would be to bring her to such a peak.

She shrieked with chagrin. "Oh! You are a mountain of conceit. You see yourself as tall, dark, and handsome, but I see you
as a monster, a giant, a freak!"

Her mare shied nervously, but before it could bolt Simon
grabbed its bridle and thundered, "Stay!" The horse trembled
uncontrollably but it obeyed the authority in his voice.

Eleanor blazed angry as fire. "You might intimidate my
mare, but you don't intimidate me!" She recalled that the giant
Goliath had been brought down by a stone and looked about
her for a missile. She bent to snatch up a rock in each hand, but
he clearly saw her intention and clamped his great boot on her
long hair, effectively pinning her to the ground.

For a moment she was bereft of speech. Her eyes traveled up
the muscled column of his leg that resembled a young oak tree.
As he towered above her she realized for the first time the
powerful strength he held barely in check. A tendril of fear
curled inside her as she took in his height and breadth. He

could snuff out her life with his bare hands without even exerting himself. His impossibly broad shoulders strained the fabric of his doublet as he stretched his muscles. She shivered delicately and said in a small, hurt voice, "I cannot believe you would crush my hair beneath your filthy boot."

He took her shoulders into his powerful hands and dragged her up against the solid wall of his hard body. "I could beat you to a jelly and enjoy every minute of it, English," he told her with relish. With punishing fingers he wrenched the stones from her grasp and flung them an impossible distance. He turned his black, obsidian eyes upon her and held her mesmerized with his compelling gaze.

How had she ever dared to curse him, to challenge him? she wondered desperately. What a foolish mistake it had been to scratch him and threaten him with stones. His dark, forbidding face promised punishment, and she wondered wildly what in the name of heaven and hell he would do to her.

"I shall soon discover your identity. I shall find out whose mistress you are, and when I do I shall buy you from him."

He was a madman. "Women cannot be bought and sold," she whispered.

"Can they not?" He flashed her a look of triumph and withdrew his hands from her.

She took courage the moment he removed his iron grip. She knew she must say something that would allow her to escape. "I am a married woman." She lifted her chin and gave him a small defiant look. "My husband shall own my heart forever."

His own heart plummeted at her words. He stiffened and the muscle in his jaw clenched like a lump of iron. She retrieved the little merlin from the ground and led her mare off with the pride of a pantheress.

Eleanor, Countess of Pembroke, had awakened from her trance.

20

A few evenings later Simon de Montfort sat between the king and queen at supper. They had a surprise guest in the person of Robert Grosseteste, the Bishop of Lincoln. His was the largest see in England, comprising Lincoln, Leicester, Buckingham, Bedford, Stow, Northampton, and Oxford. He was an unrelenting critic of the king, and Henry hoped the presence of the Earl of Leicester would divert the bishop's attention.

Lincoln and Simon de Montfort hit it off amazingly well. Both men had a profound understanding of science. They believed in stern measures for putting an end to rebellion and treachery, and Lincoln had been known to lop off the head of an abbot or prior as he traveled about his monasteries.

He and Simon had been engaged in a two-hour conversation before dinner in which they discovered how much they had in common. The bishop was totally against England sharing revenues with Rome, as was Simon. He also opposed Italian priests in his territory because they couldn't speak English, which made perfect sense to Simon. This was the bishop who had abolished the Pagan Feast of Fools and put an end to games in churchyards.

Henry was delighted that the bishop befriended de Montfort, but bit his lip in annoyance when Lincoln brought up the reason for his visit the moment they sat down to dine. Simon watched and listened with interest as the stern bishop said bluntly, "Sire, you have put forward the name of John Mansel for prebend of Thane. He is unacceptable. He is nothing more than an acquisitive royal clerk."

Henry had proposed Mansel because Winchester wanted him in the post. "My dear bishop, he has a natural ability with figures and an affinity for paperwork. I assure you he is an excellent choice."

"Sire, we need men who put England's interests before their own, like de Montfort here. Mansel is unacceptable to me."

"My dear bishop, I am not the only one who thinks he should become prebend of Thane. The members of my council have already approved him."

"My dear Majesty," Lincoln said implacably, "if you persist in this, I shall have recourse to excommunication. I may even have to put the royal chapel at Westminster under interdict."

Henry retreated.

Simon missed nothing.

Lincoln leaned forward and winked broadly at Simon who did a creditable job of masking his amusement. The Bishop of Lincoln had just taught him a valuable lesson in dealing with the king.

The young queen accidentally brushed her hand against Simon's thigh and murmured an apology. The sidelong look she cast him told him plainly it had not been accidental and that she quite enjoyed pawing him.

Henry turned petulantly away from the bishop and engaged Simon in conversation. "I hope you have found much to amuse you at court. The queen's ladies will be fighting each other for your favors. Has your fancy fallen upon any one yet?"

Simon shook his head. "I like spirit as well as beauty."

Henry grinned and looked pointedly at the scratches on Simon's cheek.

Simon laughed as he fingered the gouge. "A little wench, prideful as a cat, spat and clawed at me."

"I used to have a sister like that. She was a little blackhearted devil, a true imp of satan. I miss her."

Simon asked, "Isabel?"

Henry didn't understand. "I beg your pardon?"

"Your sister Isabel who married Frederick of Germany?"

"Heavens no, she was a sweet-tempered child. I meant Eleanor. Since William Marshal died the change in her is appalling. She swore a vow of chastity on her husband's bier and turned into a recluse. I think she's about to become a nun."

More conflicting stories about Eleanor Plantagenet, thought Simon. He'd heard her called everything from the Whore of Babylon to a nun. Neither picture appealed much to Simon.

He could no longer ignore the queen's overtures. "Would you care to dance, your Highness?" Her sensual body language told him she had a more voluptuous nature than King Henry, and he shrewdly speculated about which Gascons received her favors.

The king had asked the war lord to take over training the men in his personal service, and Simon had spent the morning trying to master a weapon that fascinated him, the longbow. He pondered on why it was a more effective weapon in the hands of the Welsh. His idol, Henry II, and Henry's Norman knights had been experts, and Simon thought it imprudent to allow the weapon to fall from favor. He soon discovered he had a natural ability with the longbow, probably because of the great length of his arms and legs. He could draw the bow with ease and had no trouble hitting his mark. All he had to concentrate upon was improving his speed. He stopped to watch the knights practicing in the quintain yard and shook his head. Their skills with the sword left much room for improvement. Tomorrow he would have them remove their chain mail and padded gambesons. There was nothing like exposed bare flesh to improve a soldier's agility.

He walked toward the Upper Ward, admiring the older buildings of Windsor that Henry II had designed. From the tail of his eye he saw a small figure walking on the northern terrace and was certain it was the beauty he had encountered in the forest. Without hesitation he followed the dark-haired girl and saw her insert a key into a door and disappear behind a fifteen-foot wall.

Scaling walls wasn't too much challenge to a six-and-a-half-foot man. He stood atop the stones for a moment scanning the beautiful garden to gauge which place she would choose to sit, then lithely dropped to the lawn and stretched his long legs out before him as he sat down upon a stone bench beside a fountain.

Eleanor's gown was an acceptable mourning shade of lavender, her hair was severely plaited into knots for the Trinity, chastity, poverty, and obedience. She lifted the trailing frond of a weeping willow and rounded the fountain, then she stiffened with disbelief as she saw a man sprawled before her.

"You!" she cried with dismay. "You bribed the gardener to let you in. You will leave at once. This is my sanctuary."

"I came over the wall, English," he said, grinning.

"You lying oaf!" She caught her lip between her teeth, for what she had almost screamed at him was "Balls!" Until their last encounter she hadn't used such profanity in many years and was determined not to allow him to destroy her dignity again. She clung to her temper, but when she saw how much she amused him she felt it dangerously slipping away.

"How old are you—sixteen, seventeen? Why in the name of heaven do you need a sanctuary?" His laughing black eyes mocked her.

"Because I am in mourning for my husband," she whispered sadly.

His dark eyes became suspicious. Last time she had told him she was married, now she said she was widowed. Could he believe her? "I'm sorry, English. You don't seem old enough to be a wife, let alone a widow."

Her temper snapped. "Don't call me that, you filthy Frenchman!"

"Supply me with a name and I'll stop calling you English."

"Katherine," she replied, giving him her middle name.

"Kathe," he murmured, making the name sound like a caress. "Allow me to introduce myself. I am Simon de Montfort."

Her eyes widened. "The war lord?" she asked doubtfully. She had assumed he was one of the queen's relatives. William had spoken to her of Simon de Montfort, calling him the world's greatest warrior. Some of her fear departed. If he was the great knight, his code of chivalry would prevent his harming her. "Your reputation as a soldier is clearly undeserved," she said with contempt.

Simon's eyes widened in turn.

She continued coolly. "You disregard the first rule of battle. If your enemy is superior, avoid her."

Simon threw back his head and his deep laughter rumbled up from his chest. "You have wit. We shall deal very well together."

She was alarmed at the noise he was making. Blood of God, no one must ever know she had had a man in her private garden. She said icily, "We? We? Get it through your thick skull there is no 'we.' Nor can there ever be a 'we.' Now, sir, if you are any sort of a gentleman you will never again violate my solitude."

"I am no gentleman, as you will soon learn, but then, Kathe my little hellion, you are no lady." He repeated, "We shall deal very well together."

"I am a lady," she insisted passionately. " 'Tis you who bring out the very worst in me!" Tears gathered in her eyes of sapphire. "The little merlin was a gift from my husband; I cherished her."

Simon felt a prick of shame. He had noble qualities and usually treated the gentler sex with gallantry. Somehow Kathe had lit a spark deep within him and he knew he wanted to possess her. He thought bleakly of the unpalatable heiress he would likely have to wed. If he could possess this delectable little wench, his days would be filled with laughter and his nights with sensuality.

His fingers flashed like quicksilver to capture a tear from her cheek, then he actually tasted it before he ran across the lawn and vaulted over the wall.

Eleanor sat stunned. She didn't know which had astonished her the most, his intimate gesture or his athletic ability. What she did know was that her thoughts were in disarray, her temper in chaos, her poise shattered, her tranquility vanished, and her heartbeat accelerated.

* * *

On Fridays the Countess of Pembroke tended the sick at the side of Mother Superior. The head of the Order of St. Bride's was very pleased with her pupil. She had led her down the path of salvation and knew in her very bones that Eleanor was only a step or two away from taking the veil. She had learned obedience, and her nursing skills with the poor improved every week.

She had even taken to wearing the white habit of a novitiate when they went to tend the sick. Today they went outside the confines of Windsor, down to Thames Street where a peasant woman had reportedly been in labor all night. A small group of mounted knights rode up Thames Street toward the main gateway to Windsor and politely reined in their horses to let the nuns pass.

Simon de Montfort's mouth gaped open as he saw Kathe, swathed in religious robes, enter the humble home of a peasant. Beside him he saw young Rickard de Burgh frown at him. Something told him Sir Rickard had more than a passing interest in the girl. For the moment he kept silent, but he was determined to get to the bottom of the puzzle.

Inside the small chamber Eleanor helped Mother Superior ease the swollen young woman onto a clean sheet. They heated water and Eleanor bathed the girl who moaned in agony. She was cold and clammy and had a dirty gray pallor from her vigil. Eleanor could see that her strength was spent and that if something was not done immediately, she was going to die.

Mother Superior lifted her rosary and began to pray. Eleanor kept silent for a full minute then said urgently, "Mother, you must do something."

"I am doing something, my child. I am praying," she reproved Eleanor solemnly.

"Praying is not enough . . . we must do something more practical, we must help her."

Mother Superior was deeply shocked. What on earth had come over her pupil? The passive, malleable girl who had learned meekness and obedience had been replaced by an imperious Plantagenet princess who was practically issuing orders. "All pain, affliction, and suffering come from God. It is sacrilege to interfere," she said repressively.

"What rubbish!" Eleanor cried. "Move aside."

Mother Superior fell back in alarm. She must not lose her hold over the young countess at this late stage.

Eleanor opened the young woman's thighs to examine her. A doubled-over limb of the child protruded from the cervix and simply wedged there when Eleanor tried to coax it further. Eleanor had attended birthings only since she had visited the sick with the St. Bride's nuns. Up until this last year she had not even known how children came into the world. Common sense, however, told her that while the birth canal was blocked, nothing would happen other than death for both mother and baby. She washed her hands in the heated water, then began slowly to press and force the doubled limb back inside the mother.

The young woman was almost beyond protest and her color had become an alarming bluish hue. Eleanor's hands were extremely small and delicate, and she was able to manipulate the child into another position. Suddenly she felt its round head push into her hands. Then the rest of the baby slipped out with a gush of blood and body fluid.

Eleanor wrapped the little bundle tightly in a swaddling blanket and wiped the mucus from its tiny nostrils and mouth. Mother Superior now took over extracting the afterbirth and giving the new mother a restorative herb tea.

Outside in the pale sunshine Mother Superior could see for herself the transformation in Eleanor. It was as if she had awakened from her sleepwalking and her strong will, so long dormant, was reasserting itself.

Eleanor's usually generous mouth was set in thin disapproving lines, so quickly Mother Superior said, "We must talk. You have questions and differences that must be addressed, my lady." Mother Superior hid her alarm. Eleanor had been like a ripe damson ready for the plucking; now she was like a young colt that bolts at the sight of the stable door. "Come to the convent with me now."

Eleanor shook her head. "I shall come this evening when my emotions have had time to settle down."

"As you wish, my lady."

* * *

Simon de Montfort had put the King's Guard through their paces. Though they had practiced their swordplay stripped to the waist, the sweat ran off them in buckets. Most of the knights had received at least one nasty gash before their sloppy fighting was corrected. An exception had been Rickard de Burgh.

Simon de Montfort complimented him on his skills as the two men walked to the bathhouse. The female attendants laughed when Simon had to double up his legs to fit his great frame into a wooden tub. Simon and Rickard exchanged rueful glances for the women who tended them had faces like rusty buckets. "We will soak for a while," de Montfort said, dismissing the servants. When they were alone he said, "Your brother did not come into the king's service after the marshal's death?"

Sir Rickard shook his head. "There was that bad business with our uncle Hubert. It was an insult to the de Burghs that Mick would not swallow."

Simon nodded. "After serving with William Marshal I could hardly stomach service with the king, but now that I see you are here, it feels better." Simon held Rickard's eyes with his magnetic black stare. "I've heard the ridiculous rumors concerning William's death. We both know he was fit enough to service ten women. How did he really die?" Simon asked bluntly.

"I suspect he was murdered, but I have no proof. It happened after the wedding banquet when Richard married William's sister."

"Poison." Simon nodded grimly. "Is that why you took service with the king, to learn more?"

De Burgh shook his head. "Not really. As you can see for yourself Henry is a puppet of Winchester and Winchester is too powerful to pull down. Nay, I pledged to the Earl of Pembroke and I still feel pledged to Eleanor, Countess of Pembroke."

Simon was surprised. "By all accounts she sounds like just another wanton Plantagenet."

Rickard stiffened and de Montfort thought he resembled a dog with raised hackles. He put up a hand. "Easy, man, I did not mean to offend you."

"The talk about the countess was vile. William must be spinning in his grave. She was no more than a child; an *innocent* child," de Burgh emphasized. "The marshal saw to that. He paid for an all-female household from the time she was nine. He established the convent of St. Bride's so the nuns could teach her. The day he died, I had this premonition of danger to Eleanor. I stayed close by. She and William were housed in one of the towers at Westminster. When I heard her screams in the night I ran into their chamber. William was dead when I arrived." De Burgh hesitated, for he'd never before breathed a word of what he was about to divulge. "My lady was imprisoned beneath his body; she is very small. I lifted him off her and saw that he had taken her virginity."

"Splendor of God," de Montfort murmured.

"The physicians came in with their prurient questions and blamed her for William's death."

"You didn't defend her?" de Burgh asked in a nonaccusatory tone.

"They were insinuating a female with her appetite must have a lover. If I had championed her, I would have condemned us both."

De Montfort nodded his understanding. After stepping from the wooden tub, he vigorously toweled himself. Rickard reached for a towel. "When the Countess of Pembroke takes the veil, I will probably return to Connaught."

"Henry said his sister was about to enter the convent. I've never seen her," Simon said.

Rickard gave him an odd look. "That was the Countess of Pembroke you stared at this morning—the lady in white with the Mother Superior of St. Bride's."

21

Eleanor walked through the cool halls of St. Bride's, past the cloistered, windowless cells where the nuns slept until she came to the chapel where she knew she would find Mother Superior. The head of the order had been watching for her and took her into a small classroom she used for teaching. She had rehearsed what she would say and spoke up quickly before Eleanor could take the offensive.

"What you did this morning was commendable. Though it is our prevailing belief that all affliction comes from God and must be borne, I think you may have much to teach us. There is much to be said, I think, for exhausting every avenue before we give one up to God."

She had taken the wind from Eleanor's sails. Eleanor said, "Well, I am relieved that we have come to an understanding about my beliefs because they are strong. I could never reconcile myself to closing my eyes and praying while there was yet a breath of life. I believe that even when the mother dies, the life of the child should be saved."

"My dear countess, that is one of our firmest beliefs. If there is any hint of danger to a newborn life, we believe in putting that life before the mother's."

"Well, again I must disagree with you. A man can try for another child each year, but I hope he would not try for another wife."

Mother Superior was not about to argue Catholicism with her or she would certainly lose. "My dear, your hands have special healing powers. They are so small and delicate. I know that if the Earl of Pembroke could have seen you save that mother and child this morning, he would have been very proud of you."

Eleanor lowered her lashes to hide her pain and Mother Superior pressed home her advantage. "I know how deeply you mourn and I also know the panacea for that pain lies with the order. It was instinctive for you to swear the oath of chastity and take the vow of perpetual widowhood. I think you are ready to move forward. I think you are ready to wear Christ's wedding ring."

Eleanor looked alarmed. "Oh, no, William's ring is quite enough, thank you."

Mother Superior bit her lip and murmured, "The ring is merely a symbol. I think you are ready for the vows of obedience and poverty."

Eleanor shook her head. "I have many doubts. I know I am not ready yet. I am only just recovering from the shock of my husband's death. I loved him more than I loved my own life."

"I believe you *are* ready, my dear. You have come such a long way in the years I have known you. You are not the same child, not the same young woman you were."

Eleanor looked deeply into her eyes. "Inside I am exactly as I was in the nursery. I feel everything passionately. Inside I still swear and curse. I am probably the most vain woman you will ever meet, and I have an insatiable thirst for beautiful clothes and jewels."

Mother Superior grew alarmed but hid it behind a calm mask. "All that will change when you take the veil."

"Inside I will not change, because I do not really want to," Eleanor confessed.

"I want you to come next week and stay in a private cell in the cloisters. I want you to experience the quiet, the peace and tranquility before you decide. Will you do that for me, Eleanor?"

"Yes, Mother Superior."

The older woman dipped her fingers in the holy water and anointed Eleanor's forehead with the sign of the cross. "Go with God, my dear."

Eleanor took her book to the walled garden, but her eyes read not one line. She was lost in reverie over the decision she must make. She did not believe she would make a very good nun, but if William would have approved of her taking this step, she would do so without hesitation or regret.

Simon stood concealed where he had been awaiting her for hours. He stayed where he was to observe her. The splash and murmur of the fountain mingled with the piping birdsong as the willows nodded in the gentle wind. She sat frowning, musing, white chin resting upon white arm. She was dreamy-eyed and languid, and he gazed enraptured upon her beauty.

He saw how her black curls were kissed with red highlights from the sun. Then he saw her lift her eyes heavenward, brimful of dreams. He wanted to be part of those dreams. He did not fully understand why he was drawn to her so strongly, he hadn't reasoned it out; he only knew a compulsion that his destiny beckoned. He stepped forward boldly now. "You are Eleanor Plantagenet." It was a statement, not a question.

She gasped, startled at the intrusion upon her solitude. "If you know I am the Countess of Pembroke, you also know I am inviolate. I must never be seen alone in a man's company."

He grinned. "That's why the walled garden is perfect for our meetings. None will ever see us; none will ever know."

"I will know!" she cried. "We must never meet again."

"Rubbish," he said forcefully. "Why did you not tell me who you were? There must be no subterfuge between us."

"There is no 'us,' I thought I made that plain the last time you intruded," she cried.

"Quietly, sweetheart." He put a finger to his lips. "If you rave and shout we might be overheard and our secret discovered." He made the words "our secret" sound so illicit, she blushed. His heart skipped a beat for he knew the blush was the result of his nearness.

The crowding sensations and racing thoughts made her quite breathless. Simon looked at her speculating exactly how long this wooing would take him. She lowered her lashes as he stretched out upon the grass beside her. She could not see his face but she was acutely aware of his hands as they grasped his knees. They were large, strong, and brown, and for some inexplicable reason she found them unbearably attractive.

She glanced away from them, but she found again and again her eyes returned, gauging the length of the fingers, the breadth of the square palms, and noticing how the crisp black hairs curled on the backs below his thick wrists.

He was content for the moment to just look at her. She was exquisite. The curve of her cheek, the stubborn dimpled chin seemed to make a heart-shaped frame for the full lips that he longed to mold against his own hot mouth. The delicate curve of her black eyebrows would arch above eyes like deep-blue pools, if she ever got the courage to look at him. "Why did you tell me your name was Kathe?" he demanded savagely, and he was rewarded by her startled glance.

"Katherine is my middle name. I hate the name Eleanor, it is cursed!"

He went on his knees before her, capturing her hands between his, scattering her parchment across the grass. "Eleanor is a magnificent name, a queen's name!"

She stared mesmerized at the attractive hands that had seized hers. Her heart beat so loudly, surely he would hear it.

"Your grandfather, Henry II, was England's greatest king, and Eleanor of Aquitaine, whom you were named after, was her greatest queen. It is a magnificent legacy, not a curse!"

"I loathe and detest the name," she said defiantly.

"Rubbish," he said. "I shall call you Eleanor until you learn to like it." His bold, black eyes taunted her. "Perhaps I'll call you Kathe when I make love to you."

She snatched her hands from him and struck him in the face.

He was pleased to get such a hot reaction from her. "I am only teasing you." His eyes were alight. "Does no one ever plague you to make you laugh?"

"Not for years," she answered sadly. "My brothers teased me unmercifully, calling me a cockroach and piss-ant, because I was so little," she explained.

"You informed me that you were not little, I was a giant, remember?"

The corners of her mouth went up. "And so you are a bloody giant."

"Well," he bargained, "I'll admit to being oversized if you'll admit to being undersized." His thoughts were so lustful he had to fight the urge to lay her back in the grass and ravish her. He retrieved her pages. "What do you study here, day after day?"

"Gaelic. William taught me the beauty of the Celtic languages. I became quite good at them."

"I'd like to learn," he told her. "Say something in Gaelic."

She lowered her black lashes. "*Sim,*" she said softly.

His black brows drew together then he suddenly smiled. "*Sim* . . . that's Gaelic for Simon, isn't it?"

She nodded.

"Lend me the book and I'll learn Gaelic for you."

"It takes years of application; 'tis a very difficult language."

"A wager. Next time we meet I'll converse with you in Gaelic."

"Impossible," she said.

"Then you won't mind wagering a kiss," he answered.

"There will be no next time, there will be no kiss," she said primly.

He towered above her. "Now you have challenged me, Eleanor, and I have never lost a joust in my life. A kiss is the forfeit I shall demand."

"Not on the lips," she said quickly.

Simon threw back his head and laughed. "Not on the lips," he agreed. "How long is it since you laughed?" he asked, his eyes on her mouth.

"You must know how long," she said sadly, filled with memories of William. "Simon, I think you should know that I am contemplating entering a nunnery. This has just been a game of make-believe. We must not see each other again."

Her words made him furious. "I won't allow you to do any

such ridiculous thing. Splendor of God, William must be spinning in his grave!"

She stiffened. "What do you mean?"

"In France I fought side by side with the marshal. At night in our tents we shared our thoughts. The great difference in your ages appalled him. He feared he was sacrificing your youth. Splendor of God, Eleanor, his soul will never rest in peace if you lay the reason for entering a convent at his door. You are not yet eighteen years old; don't sacrifice your life to the church!"

"I have such doubts," she admitted gravely.

"You are likely being coerced to go against your nature."

She shook her head at her great dilemma. "I loved William so very much. My life is over anyway."

"Rubbish! Your life hasn't yet begun. I have no doubt you loved him. He was a fine man, but he would run mad if he knew you walked here with his ghost. He would want you to be vibrant, passionate, have children. If you want to do something for William's memory, stop sleepwalking. Come out of your trance and find his murderer—avenge him!"

"I killed him!" she cried.

"I shall have to prove to you that making love does not kill a man."

"No one would murder the Marshal of England. My brother the king wouldn't allow such an evil thing to happen," she said indignantly.

"If Henry ruled England, I agree with you that he would not let such things happen, but Henry does not rule England. He bends to whichever will is stronger than his own at any given moment."

Eleanor was angry. "Be damned to you, that's treason."

"Well, probably politics are beyond a woman's grasp."

"You arrogant French swine. I've had the finest of educations. My grasp of politics is comprehensive."

He said savagely, "Swine I may be, but I object to being continually referred to as French. I am descended from the same Norman nobility as the Plantagenets. I am the Earl of Leicester."

He looked so threatening she felt afraid and had to take her courage in her hands to continue the game of parry and thrust. "You say the name Plantagenet as if you hold it in contempt."

"Your grandfather was my idol. The name has fallen from grace since his time. It is within your brother's power to restore England to glory. While he has his youth and health he should strive to bring peace and prosperity to his kingdom, instead of setting his barons at each other's throats. His policies of advancing foreigners over Englishmen breed only jealousy, greed, and discontent. A man has it in him to become what he beholds. You have to do your very best on good days knowing there will be bad days on which you'll do your worst. The king fritters away his birthright, toadying to his wife's relatives. Henry spends money he doesn't have to get things he doesn't need, to impress people he doesn't like."

"Are you quite finished, de Montfort?" she said icily.

"I've only just begun," he threatened, allowing his eyes to wander down to her impudent breasts and back up to her mouth. "I much prefer it when you call me Sim."

"Please leave, de Montfort," she requested.

He sighed. "Ah, well, we shall call each other Kathe and Sim when we make love."

She stood and raised her hand to strike him. He encircled her wrist with ease to stay the blow.

"Never strike me again," he said in such a quiet, menacing voice, she feared for one awful moment he would snap her wrist like a twig. In reality he was astounded at her courage. She actually had enough daring to attack a six-and-a-half-foot man. Such a passionate female was a treasure beyond compare.

"If your grasp of politics is as comprehensive as you claim, you will know I speak the truth, if you will but pause in your headlong sacrificial dash to the convent." He swept up her book, rustled the pages to taunt her, then winked at her audaciously.

She sat a long time after he had taken himself over the wall, her mind going over and over the things he had said. Splendor of God, had she been in such a deep slumber she'd never suspected irregularities in William's death?

*　*　*

Two nights later Eleanor bade her serving women good night and entered her private chamber atop the King John Tower. She removed her gown and bathed her arms and face with rosewater, then pulled aside her bedcurtains to reach for her nightgown. Simon de Montfort lay stretched out on her bed with his arms behind his head.

"Oh, bugger." She gasped.

"Very pretty language for a nun," he whispered.

"I'll scream," she hissed.

"You won't," he whispered. "You are too big a coward to be caught with a man in your bedchamber."

"How on earth did you get in here?" she hissed.

He pointed to the tower window and grinned.

She groaned. "What do you want?"

He rolled his eyes, just thinking of what he wanted. Her petticoat revealed much more of her high-thrusting breasts than he'd seen before, and he was enjoying her predicament immensely.

He eased a hand into his doublet and carefully brought forth a handful of ruffled feathers. "I brought you these orphaned creatures," he said, holding out his hand. On his big palm sat two tiny screech owls. "I know you love birds. Perhaps you could keep them in your garden where they'll be safe from weasels and foxes."

"I cannot even keep out a wolf," she murmured. Diverted for the moment, she emptied a gilded casket of its jewels and gently placed the owls inside. "Ruffles and Truffles," she murmured softly as she touched a finger to each tiny head.

"I knew you would be an angel of mercy," he whispered.

"Merciful to them perhaps, but not to you. Get out!" she hissed.

He shrugged his massive shoulders and walked toward the door. She ran to him quickly and grabbed his arm. "Not that way," she whispered in distress. "You are a devil!"

He nodded at her assessment, his black eyes glittering with amusement. "We were meant for each other. The devil and the angelic nun," he teased. Again he reached into his doublet. "I brought back your book . . ." His whispered words hung in the air. In disbelief she stared at him. He had learned some Gaelic and had actually come for his kiss.

"I won't give it!" she whispered.

"Don't give it—I'll take it."

She was trapped. She knew she must get rid of him before they were discovered, yet she also knew he would never leave until he got what he wanted. She hesitated for long moments as he towered above her. The tension in the room grew unbearable. "All right," she said resolutely as she lifted her cheek and closed her eyes.

Her bare shoulders were cupped in his warm hands, his dark head dipped low, and she felt his hot mouth in the deep valley between her breasts. Her eyes flew open and she gasped. "What are you doing?"

His lips moved close to her ear. "You said not your lips, so I kissed your heart."

A great shudder ran down her back all the way to her knees. She knew not if it was a result of his warm breath on her neck or his romantic words. She could hear his husky voice over and over saying "I kissed your heart, I kissed your heart."

He felt her tremble and saw her eyes liquid with apprehension and knew he had plagued her enough. "Good night, my Eleanor," he whispered as he threw one leg over her windowsill.

The Earl of Leicester had chosen his bride. Eleanor Plantagenet was going to be the Countess of Leicester. He knew full well he would never have her consent. Her previous marriage vows were sacred to her. Forevermore she wished to be known as the Countess of Pembroke. While he had lain in wait for her, his eyes had fallen upon the letter at her bedside. He read it without hesitation and discovered it was a love letter from William Marshal. For the first time in his life he doubted himself. How could he overcome the idealized love she still bore her dead husband? She lived on memories of the time they had shared together in Wales and Ireland. She had made it plain there was room in her heart for only one pure love. Simon had never known vulnerability before. Eleanor was his Achilles' heel. His resolve hardened. He was living flesh and blood . . . he would banish all ghosts. He doubted he would ever be able to control her mind, it was far too strong. Too, he guessed she was willful in the extreme, and he would not have her any other way. However, he intended to control her somehow.

His fertile imagination had already pictured her in every state of undress, in every erotic position known to man. The sight and scent of her inflamed him to such a degree she had almost become an obsession. Whenever he closed his eyes her image was there on the inside of his eyelids. He envisioned what it would be like to undress her slowly, uncovering her ripe young body to worship with his hands and his mouth. He knew a savage hungry craving to touch her, smell her, taste her. What was this fatal fascination he felt toward her? Was it her exquisite beauty? Was it because she had committed her love so deeply and irrevocably? Was it the erotic titillation that she was almost a nun? Or did the vows of chastity make her such forbidden fruit he knew he must pluck, taste, and devour her? The answer to every question came back yes.

The thought of her delicate, small form was irresistible to him, and he would know no peace until he had joined his powerful body to hers. If only he could make her desire him as he did her. Perhaps he could pander to her senses and enslave her body. If he could make her crave his caresses, make her need his lovemaking like a drug, even if it was all in secrecy, he would be more than halfway home. She would never enter the convent. If her own good sense did not stop her, he would.

Becoming her lover would be much easier than becoming her husband, however. There was this barrier of her vow of chastity to overcome. He flashed his wolf's grin in the darkness. When Henry II had decided to possess Eleanor of Aquitaine, she had been married to the King of France. Henry II had always been his role model. There was a very simple way to get a woman who was unobtainable.

22

👑

King Henry was overjoyed. He received a letter from his mother, Isabella, asking him if the three sons she'd had with Hugh de Lusignan could come to England for a visit. He replied immediately, insisting his young half brothers come and make their living in England.

William de Lusignan was the eldest, then Guy, then Aymer who was still a boy and an acolyte in the church. When Henry began planning a lavish banquet to welcome them, his queen became alarmed. Up until now her relatives had received all the rich plums that fell from Henry's trees. Now she saw clearly there would be inevitable rivalry between "King's Men" and "Queen's Men."

She took the news to her uncle Thomas of Savoy and urged him to send for his youngest son, Boniface the Handsome, who was also in the church. The queen knew better than any how easily her lamb Henry could be fleeced. She had no doubts that the avaricious de Lusignans would make their fortune.

On Friday as usual Eleanor donned her white robes and spent the day aiding the sick and poor about Windsor. When they had finished their charity work, Eleanor returned to the convent of St. Bride's with Mother Superior. She shared a simple meal with the nuns, accompanied them to the chapel for evening prayer, then Mother Superior led her through the cloisters to a windowless cell.

The floor was stone, the walls whitewashed, the only decoration a crucifix. The cell contained a long, wooden bed and a table that held only two items, a Bible and a candle.

"Good night, my dear. You must read your Bible before the candle burns low for there are no windows and you will be in total darkness when it is gone. The cell on either side of you is empty, for it is only when we are alone with God that we find our inner strength. This night will be like no other. Spend it in prayer and meditation. I have every faith that in the morning you will emerge transformed."

Eleanor sat on the end of the bed a long time staring at the small candle. Simon de Montfort's words echoed in her mind over and over. She hadn't really needed him to tell her that the convent was out of the question. She had known it in her heart all along.

She faced the facts squarely. She loved William and would always love him, but becoming a nun would not bring him back, nor would it remove the guilt she suffered over his manner of death. What could not be cured must be endured.

Lines by the Persian poet Omar Khayyám ran through her head. "The moving hand writes, and having writ, moves on. Not all your piety nor wit can cancel half a line, nor all your tears wash out a word of it."

Her grief had made her seek a route of escape, and just as suicide would have been wrong, so was becoming a religeuse. Eleanor knew she was lonely. Up until she was nine she had enjoyed the rough and tumble of her brothers, but once she'd had her own household, all her energies had been devoted to learning and preparing for the day she would become the marshal's wife. It had been a solitary existence, for her temperament had little in common with that of the young Marshal nieces. Even her maid Brenda had deserted her.

William had been her life's goal and the moment she had achieved that goal, she had lost it. The queen had become an effective barrier between Eleanor and her brother, and there was not one member of the court she could call friend.

She sighed as the candle guttered and extinguished itself. There was no profit in feeling sorry for herself. She would inform Mother Superior of her firm decision at dawn and then she would begin to rebuild her life. She would attend more court functions. She would visit her beautiful estate, Odiham. She could even visit her beloved Wales. What was there to stop her?

She held her breath in the pitch black as she heard a slight scraping noise and fancied she heard a muffled footfall. As she listened there was only silence and total blackness, but the noise had sounded as if someone had entered the cell from the one next door. She rose and, with arms extended before her, explored the darkness. "Who?" she breathed softly, frightened.

"Sim."

She thought she must be hallucinating. This could not be happening, but her outstretched hands suddenly touched real live flesh and blood. She blushed hotly in the dark for she had touched him on his male part. He took her hands gently and felt them ball into fists as she whispered, "How did you get in here?"

With his mouth close to her ear he whispered, "I took the hinges from the door and waited in hiding."

"Why?" she demanded as softly as she could.

"To make you change your mind about entering this convent. Blood of God, if you want a religious experience, I'll give you one."

What in the name of God would she do? "We mustn't speak . . . our whispers will carry on the still night air." Inside she was raging at him, but she knew she would have to vent her anger upon him later, in a much more suitable place.

"I know we cannot speak or see, but we have our other senses. We can still hear and smell and touch."

She was so alarmed when he drew her to the bed and sat her beside him that she went faint. If he tried to rape her she would scream, no matter what sort of scandal it caused. Her single experience with sex had been an horrendous one. She would never go through it again. Uncontrollably she began to tremble.

Slowly Simon began to realize the enormity of her fear and agitation. He had fully intended to take advantage of the setting to awaken her senses and make her body respond to his. The sensual darkness and the fact that she would be unable to voice her objections had inflamed his imagination. Now, however, he realized what she needed most was to lose her fear and feel secure.

She did not need his passion just yet, she needed his strength. As he reached for her, she pushed against him strongly, but was amazed to find him as immovable as a mountain of granite. She withdrew and turned her back upon him to show him her righteous indignation. How could he be so high-handed and devious as to select a place where her silence was guaranteed?

With firm hands upon her rigid shoulders, he turned her to face him, then took her small hands into his large ones, squeezed them comfortingly, and simply held them. She railed at him mentally, trying to withdraw again, but he would not allow it. She closed her eyes in frustration, her mind darting about for avenues of escape from this man's attentions. There were none. She would simply have to endure him.

She withdrew from him mentally because he made it impossible for her to withdraw physically. She vowed never to capitulate. However, his warmth soon began to seep into her, and after half an hour her trembling subsided. Though she tried to keep her thoughts from him, it was impossible. She learned exactly what it felt like to wage a losing battle against the war lord.

As he stroked her hands with the ball of his thumb, she recalled how unbearably attractive were his big, brown hands. Slowly he raised one of hers to his mouth and kissed each finger with reverence, then repeated the process with her other hand. He was slowly, silently overwhelming her with his presence.

When he had her completely gentled, he raised a tentative finger to her face. Gently, tenderly, he traced her brow, her high cheekbone, her dimpled chin, and finally the curve of her lips. She caught her breath with disbelief. Simon de Montfort was a warrior, a war lord. His hands had been trained to kill, yet they were the gentlest hands ever to touch her.

How could hands so huge be so sensitive? His fingers stroked her hair, brushing it from her brow and temples, then played with its springy curls. As he brushed the backs of his fingers against her cheek and throat, she remembered the crisp black hair on the back of his hands and fancied she could feel it against her skin.

His attitude was so nonthreatening that gradually her fear left her and was replaced by a feeling of thankfulness that she did not have to spend the dark, lonely night in solitude. Again he kissed her hand then raised it to his face. He separated her index finger from its sisters and laid it upon his brow. He smiled with satisfaction as she began to trace his features, outlining his straight nose and muscled jaw. She recalled that his hair was blacker than a witch's cat and that his eyes also were magnetically black.

Gradually she became aware of his scent. When she tried to define the warm, manly aroma she identified leather, sandalwood, and something male and dangerous. Its combination was pleasing and evocative, setting her curiosity to wondering if the scent came from his garments or his body. He should not be there with her doing these things. She should be angry as fire and yet she found when she could not rail at him, storm about and throw things, her anger was nonexistent.

Simon propped the pillow against the bedhead and leaned back against it, stretching his long legs out before him. Then gently he moved her so that she leaned into his massive chest, and he held her in the curve of his arm. Eleanor had never felt so safe and warm in her life. The total blackness hid the sin they committed, and she wished the night could go on for days. It felt so right, surely this was the way it was supposed to be between a man and a woman. She had needed this closeness all her life. Why had it come too late?

She closed her eyes and rested her cheek against his shoulder. She would enjoy it while she could. To hell with scruples. This intimate privacy would flee with the dawn, but for now she was clasped against his heart and there was nowhere she would rather have been.

Slumber must have claimed her, for when she drifted back to consciousness she was appalled to find he cupped one of her breasts in his powerful hand and his lips rested against her temple. She tried to struggle, but his strength held her absolutely immobile. Through the material of her robe she could feel the fire from his hand, or perhaps it was he who felt the fire from her breast. She managed to move her hands so she could press them against his chest, but she found Simon de Montfort was an immovable object. She felt the great slabs of muscle beneath her fingers and, as if they had a curiosity of their own, her fingertips began to trace the rigid contours of his chest, shoulders, and arms.

When she was a little girl, the thing that had attracted her to the Marshal of England was his great strength as a soldier. She felt weak all the way down to her knees as she realized the arms that held her now were those of the greatest warrior of their time.

Simon fought the urge to be naked. This time he knew he must be content to feel her soft curves through the cloth barrier and let her do the same. In a way it heightened his desire. Their tactile sense of touch grew so acute, he hoped her body too yearned to be naked. The silence was thick with unrequited need. Uppermost in their minds was the knowledge that they only had 'til dawn. In the blackness his nostrils flared with the scent of her. His rising excitement sent the blood beating in his throat.

Eleanor was becoming aware of a secret side to herself that until now had been unknown and unexplored. She knew it was this man who had reawakened her mind, but now it was as if her body too was being awakened. In the pit of her stomach was a taut feeling as threads of desire were stretched to their limit. Her breasts ached with the need for . . . she knew not what. Her legs were weak and the secret place between them tingled and tightened tensely.

Simon felt consumed. She had provoked every sense of his body so that he felt his blood pulse in his ears, his throat, his chest, even the soles of his feet. His shaft had turned to marble hours ago, and for a moment he feared he would stay in that unbearable condition for the rest of his life. His inner clock warned him that he must depart before they were discovered. He knew it was the hour before dawn, but how could he tear himself away from her when he hadn't even tasted her?

His hand slipped up beneath her hair to hold her head still for his kiss. His lips brushed hers twice as he noticed with deep pleasure how he affected her breathing. Then his mouth claimed hers, branding her forever as his woman. The kiss was everything—fire, war, life, death, love.

At first her mind screamed at his boldness. My mouth, my reputation, my honor, my God! Simon de Montfort's mouth was like heaven.

He rose from the bed and took her with him. His arms had tightened so that as she stood against him she could feel all the strength of his body, the heavy shoulders, the powerful legs. He lifted her in a last embrace so that her feet swung clear of the floor. When he removed his arms, her loss was so great she almost collapsed.

She groped behind her and sat upon the bed. The quality of the silence in the cell told her she was alone. During the next hour her emotions swung wildly from denial, assuring herself he must have been a dream, to fury—how dare he have taken advantage of her stay in a convent where she could do nothing but silently submit to his will?

She gasped and jumped as her cell door was unlocked, but she realized it was morning. She could not bring herself to go to the communal room where the nuns performed their ablutions. Instead, with a firm resolve she sought out Mother Superior to inform her of her decision.

"Eleanor, I hope His arms reached out to you to gather you to his flock."

For a moment Eleanor did not realize Mother Superior was speaking of God. She fought the blush and failed. Then she lifted her chin and took control of the situation. "Mother Superior, I have made my decision and it is quite final. I shall not be entering the Order of St. Bride's. I am totally unsuited to a life of poverty and obedience. It is simply not in my nature." She bit her lips guiltily thinking that chastity was not in her nature either. "I shall still tend the poor and the sick wherever I may be, but I need not become a nun, nor wear white robes to perform works of charity. I needed a season of mourning before I could heal. It is time for me to reenter the world."

As she spoke, Eleanor watched the face of the head of the

order. Not only did it show great disappointment, it showed dismay, fear almost.

Mother Superior's voice cracked as she said, "We need a deal of money to carry on here now that the Earl of Pembroke's support is gone."

Eleanor went cold. Even the church did not want her for herself. All this pressure and persuasion had been for the Countess of Pembroke's lands and money, not for the immortal soul of Eleanor. Well, the jest was on them for the avaricious Marshals had not yet ceded her one acre.

In a businesslike manner she stood up and said, "I shall look into the deed for this land and convent. I shall also wish to see your account books. When they are ready have Sister Mary bring them to me."

When she arrived back at her apartments in the King John Tower, she sought out Bette, a round comfortable woman servant who had followed her from Durham House. When Eleanor gave her a dazzling smile, the look of anxiety left the woman's face.

"Bette, be a love and fill me a bath. Oh, and you can have these white robes burned," she said as an afterthought.

Bette returned the dazzling smile. It was not her place to tell the Countess of Pembroke what she should do with her life, but she certainly had not approved of her becoming a bride of Christ. "King Henry sent a squire looking for you, my lady. I asked him what it was all about an' he said summat about all your brothers cummin' to live here. I didn't know you had more brothers, beside Henry and Richard."

Eleanor's mind flew to her mother. She barely remembered her. She'd seen paintings of her mother, of course, and heard whispers of her wanton behavior. She'd given her former lover sons only nine months apart and had started producing them before Eleanor was one year old.

Eleanor chose a gown of sunny yellow. As she walked along the wall that overlooked the quadrangle and tiltyard she was amazed to see over a hundred men naked to the waist, engaged in ferocious practice with the broadsword. Towering head and shoulders over the other men was the unmistakable figure of Simon de Montfort who seemed to be in charge of this barbaric melee. Her eyes widened as she noted the dragons tattooed upon his massive forearms. She had caressed those dragons without even knowing of their existence.

She was relieved to see that his black eyes looked right through her with all the indifference in the world, as if they had never met, and, of course, hers tried to do the same. She glanced up and saw that Henry watched from a high window. When he saw her he beckoned her up eagerly.

"Eleanor, how wonderful to see you out of mourning." He ran forward to take her hands.

"Well, I thought I had better tell you I have decided against the convent."

"Oh, I can't tell you how happy that makes me. More wonderful news—our brothers are coming home!"

She eyed his joyous enthusiasm with tolerance. "You mean our half brothers."

"Oh, don't tell me you are displeased like my wife," he begged her.

Eleanor brightened. "Oh, isn't the queen overjoyed? Well, certainly I am not displeased. It will be very interesting to meet the other half of the family."

"Oh, Eleanor, what fun it will be to have our three young brothers live here. Only think of how much I'll be able to do for them. I've a letter here from William telling me of a tournament he enjoyed. I've decided to plan a tournament for when they arrive."

"I thought they were banned in England because of their danger."

"Oh, they were, but I rule England now and I shall unban them." He walked to the window. "Come here, I want to show you something."

Eleanor placed her small hands on the stone windowsill and leaned out.

"Do you see that giant down there? That is Simon de Montfort, the new Earl of Leicester. He is like a fighting machine. Knights are riding in every day for a chance to be trained by the great war lord. Undoubtedly he will emerge champion of my tournament. He is like a magnet; he draws fighting men. He will gather for me the largest army England has ever known."

As she looked down into the quadrangle she knew that never in her life had she seen so superb a man. Those same forearms tattooed with the images of dragons had embraced her all night. His heavy, dark brows slashed above his deep-set black eyes, his wild black mane flowed about his broad-shouldered frame that revealed unmistakable raw strength.

"You'll help to hand out the prizes at the tournament, won't you, Eleanor? It will in no way compromise your holy vow of chastity and widowhood, my dear. You have no idea how much it means to a champion to receive his reward from a real princess."

"Of course I shall," she assured her brother. "I was not meant to be a recluse." Her smile flashed like sunlit gold. "I must see to my wardrobe, I don't even know what the latest fashions are. I must wear something to make the queen grind her teeth in chagrin."

"Little Maggot," Henry said happily.

23

The lists for the jousting and the stands for the spectators were built in Windsor's Great Park, which lay beyond the walls of the Upper Ward. The fields about bloomed with colorful silk pavilions and it seemed half of England descended on Windsor.

Henry gave a banquet to welcome his brothers. Eleanor attended out of sheer curiosity. To her delight she discovered that one of the serving women from Durham House, Dame Hickey, was an excellent seamstress whose husband was one of London's finest tailors. The couple had labored long and lovingly over a new wardrobe for Eleanor. Fashionable gowns now were flowing and feminine and were made from exquisite material imported from Syria and the East. Transparent silk sarcenet was used for trailing sleeves, veils, and mantles of honor that floated from the shoulders. Silks were interwoven with gold thread and brocaded in flower designs. Baudekin, a six-threaded samite from Syria, glowed as if the rays of the copper sun had been caught and imprisoned in it.

For the banquet Eleanor chose a gown of pink and mauve. Its many layers of transparent silk were embroidered with flowers and butterflies. A transparent head veil held in place by a

gold fillet over her forehead did not conceal the beauty of her
silken mass of black curls.

As Eleanor approached the dais that was reserved for royalty, Queen Eleanor's face registered shock and annoyance. Obviously her sister-in-law had tired of playing nun and was out
of her drab widow's weeds. The queen's eyes narrowed as she
thought, Well, at least her vow of chastity prevents any men
save her brothers or the clergy from even approaching her.

Eleanor smiled sweetly at the queen as her eyes swept over
the profusion of scallops bordering her shoulder mantle, which
were repeated in the overlong train. Her eyes lit with amusement as they fell on the boy page at the queen's elbow who was
puffed up at the importance of carrying her Majesty's train.

Henry's welcome, however, transformed his face as he spied
his sister. "Sweeting," he exclaimed excitedly, "these are our
brothers!" He stood back to display them like rare treasure.

Guy and Aymer were tall young men who resembled each
other in size and coloring. She noticed they did not possess the
handsome looks of Henry or Richard and though they were
younger than herself, they had a worldly air that could only
have come from overindulgence. When her eyes fell upon William de Lusignan, the eldest of the trio, they widened in astonishment. She could have been looking into a mirror. He was
small, had a profusion of shining black curls, and only his cruel
mouth could prevent him from being described as beautiful.
She stared in fascination as he gesticulated with pretty hands
and exclaimed in a feminine voice, "*Ma petite chou,* how devine
to meet you at last. You are so ravishing our mother would hate
you on sight. Dearest heart, please say you will partner me at
dinner. If I do not learn the name of your tailor I shall simply
die." He tossed his head and his jeweled earrings glittered as
they caught the light. Earrings, begod!

He is more like a sister than a brother, Eleanor thought with
distaste. William was so talkative she learned more than she
cared to of her brothers. They had brought their dogs and all
their servants and even had their own musicians. "Henry is
going to find me an heiress," he confided to her. "Aymer, the
baby, decided to go into the church. The livings are so good

and preferment comes quickly, Henry has assured him he is on his way to a fortune."

"Is Aymer a priest?" she asked, appalled at the way that young man was ordering about the squires who served the high table.

"No, no. He's only an acolyte. He hasn't taken holy orders yet because he is only fifteen."

"I see," Eleanor said faintly, thinking she had never seen anyone less suited to holy orders.

"Tell me, dearest heart, do you make your own lip rouge? Dare I ask you for the recipe?"

Eleanor was relieved to see that Richard and Isabella had arrived. She scanned Isabella's waistline quickly and raised her eyebrows in a mute question. Isabella kissed her and whispered, "Nothing definite, but I'm keeping my fingers crossed."

Richard hugged Eleanor and said gruffly, "God's nightshirt, it's good to see you looking so recovered. We were all very worried about you."

"Well, now you can worry about the rest of the family. Richard, do you realize Henry has organized this great tournament just to please William de Lusignan? Have you seen him? He looks as if a strong wind could knock him over, let alone a champion holding a lance." She bent toward him confidentially. "The other two look like they would benefit from falling from a high horse, but someone's going to have to protect Wee Willie."

Eleanor need not have worried for the undersized William. He was one of the most viciously cruel men to ever draw breath. Cruelty to animals especially excited him, and he found the atmosphere surrounding a tournament where horses screamed from lance wounds or swordthrusts particularly exhilarating.

Isabella joined the other members of the Marshal family who had arrived for the tournament. Her sister had brought her daughter, and of course all the young Marshal cousins formed a merry group. They made a point of ignoring Eleanor, which both puzzled and hurt her. One of the Marshal cousins was Matilda Bigod who had always disliked her intensely, but Eleanor was dismayed to see her husband's sisters turn their heads away from her. She took Isabella aside to voice her concern. "Your sisters and their daughters are pointedly ignoring me. They still blame me for William's death."

"Oh, darling, of course they do not. It's all to do with money. They resent that you are claiming a fifth of the Marshal holdings."

"I've received nothing yet. They are like a pack of damned vultures. Bloody rich Marshals!"

Isabella put up her chin. "The Plantagenets are every bit as avaricious as the Marshals. Henry thinks he should get all that belonged to William because he died without an heir, and Richard is claiming a fifth because I am a Marshal and entitled to it."

So, Eleanor thought, it is every man for himself. While I sleepwalked for eighteen months, they divided up the pie. She would go to Henry and demand an accounting. She must know what she would inherit. He was surrounded by his newfound brothers at the moment, enjoying himself immensely playing indulgent father.

Eleanor's eyes moved on to the queen, who was surrounded by her own fawning Savoys. She had been preening and flirting outrageously as she idly popped sweetmeats into the mouth of the page who occupied a stool beside her. Suddenly the little page set his goblet of wine upon the dais and vomited. It sprayed all over the queen's train, and he received a sharp slap for his efforts. There is a God after all, thought Eleanor, biting her lip to keep from laughing aloud.

Suddenly the amusement was wiped from her face. Simon de Montfort's black eyes had been studying her. His gaze was impersonal, as if he found nothing to distinguish her from any other woman. Eleanor looked away from him, but it did not free her mind of his strong image. She should be glad he looked indifferent; they must keep their secret. In public their gazes must never be possessive as if they were bound lovers claiming each other.

She realized with alarm that her pulse quickened, her breath shortened, and her knees turned to water. How dare he have this effect upon her! She was furious. She wanted to rake her nails down his dark, arrogant cheek. She wanted to slap that

detached, impersonal look from his face. A tiny flame of satisfaction burned inside for she had not been to the walled garden
during daylight hours. She would not give him the chance to
get her alone again.

She stood up to leave, but Henry was there, taking her arm,
saying "Eleanor, you have not met the new Earl of Leicester."

Her eyes widened in panic. "Henry, you forget . . . I cannot converse with any man except a brother."

"Oh, damn, why did you take that silly vow?" Still holding
her arm, he propelled her toward Simon de Montfort. "I was
going to introduce my sister Eleanor, but it goes against her
vows," he explained to Simon.

She gazed up at him wordlessly. His eyes were restless and
alive. His impact upon her was enormous. He had a magnetic
presence that was larger than life, qualities that marked him off
from other men. His skin stretched smooth and brown over
saber-sharp cheekbones. Suddenly his nostrils flared and for
one moment she saw the raw desire in his face. "Ille est tibi,"
he murmured in Latin. "This man is yours."

She glanced guiltily at Henry, her cheeks a dusky rose, then
she cast Simon de Montfort a challenging glance. She deliberately turned her back upon him and smiled up at her brother.
"Will you challenge the Earl of Leicester in the tournament,
Henry? I swear none but the king will have courage to challenge the great war lord." She knew de Montfort would have to
let the king win, and she wanted nothing more than to see him
humbled by a fall in the dirt.

"You are wrong, Eleanor. Every earl present has already
challenged him. You don't know men very well, I'm afraid. If
they were lucky enough to unseat Simon, they would cover
themselves with glory."

She shivered delicately. "You are right, Henry. I don't know
men very well, nor do I wish to. Good night," she said coolly.

The day of the tournament dawned glorious and fair. The
field was filled with horses, squires, and armor-bearers as England's nobles played out this deadly serious business of entertaining themselves. All of Windsor took on such a festive air; it
affected even the children and dogs as they chased each other in

giddy circles and the boys flew homemade banners in imitation of the great earls and barons.

The King's chamberlain was acting as field marshal of the joust, using half a dozen knights to keep track of the challenges. It was complicated because the code of chivalry forbade a man from challenging one of higher rank. Equal or lesser rank could be challenged; the king must issue his own challenge as must Richard of Cornwall, since he was the only duke present.

There were earls aplenty, however. Derby, Norfolk, Hereford, Surrey, Richmond, and Oxford all challenging Leicester. The barons, de Clare, de Lacy, de Braose, and de Munchensi, were pitted against each other and had issued challenges to the knights reputed for their fighting skills, such as Rickard de Burgh.

The queen's relatives and Henry's young brothers had taken an immediate dislike to each other for they instinctively realized they would have to vie for the same royal favors and posts. Those who had prepared the lists already dubbed them King's Men and Queen's Men.

The spectator stands had turned into a fashion parade for the ladies. The headdresses ranged from the spectacular to the ridiculous with steeples predominating. Their points were adorned with fluttering veils that could be detached and given as favors to the jousters.

The queen had chosen royal purple and cloth-of-gold. She always needed to emphasize that she was the queen and the most important lady in the land. Her ladies had all chosen bright colors that would show up vividly in the stands, and when Eleanor arrived she was glad she was the only female wearing white. Not only did she stand out, but she looked and felt refreshingly cool in the hot sunshine.

The attire of the men was more resplendent than that of the women. The loose, sleeveless surcoats and tabards that covered their armor were emblazoned with brilliantly embroidered crests and devices, their helmets adorned by dyed plumes. Even the horses had silk trappings covering their protective leather armor.

Henry wore his favorite green, encrusted with gold and jewels; his half brothers wore green in flattering imitation of the king's colors. The English barons favored azure, mulberry, and forest green, whereas the Savoys of Provence had more flamboyant taste and wore dramatic black and silver or scarlet and gold.

Everyone was curious about Simon de Montfort and speculated about which device would adorn his wide back. He was entitled to wear either the heraldic device of Leicester or that of a warrior count of Montfort l'Amauri. However, when Simon rode onto the field he wore plain white damask with the red cross of a crusader upon his shield. He needed no gorgeous raiment to make him stand out from other men. His magnificent physique towered head and shoulders over every other man in England.

The color standards marked the length of the field, the royal herald sounded their fanfares, and the combatants rode out upon the field, each stopping before the stands to beg a favor from their chosen lady. Eleanor had not planned to give her veil to any contestant, but she did have a special prize up her trailing sleeve to present to de Montfort should he emerge champion of the day.

She watched the queen's smug face as her Savoy uncles thoroughly trounced the king's half brothers, but she felt a measure of satisfaction when her brother Richard in turn defeated the Savoys. She also noted with deep pride that Sir Rickard de Burgh won against the three barons who challenged him.

Simon de Montfort, however, unhorsed ten earls in a row and Eleanor was looking forward to watching him ride against the king. She knew it was the only time she would ever see him go down in defeat. Even though it would only be a gesture of chivalry, she would have the satisfaction of seeing him fall in the dust.

Finally the long-awaited joust arrived. The king and the Earl of Leicester rode out onto the field together. The crowd cheered wildly as the two men raised their lances in acknowledgment and rode toward the stands to salute the queen and the ladies of the court. Simon de Montfort gallantly tipped his lance toward the queen, asking for her favor. With a seductive smile she took one of her royal purple scarves edged in gold and draped it on the tip of his lance. Eleanor was secretly amused, for when de

Montfort went down, the purple scarf would lie in the dust. Eleanor rose, detached her own head veil, which was fine-spun as a spider's web, and offered it to her brother, King Henry. The two men affixed the scarves to their scabbard rings and wheeled away to opposite ends of the field.

Henry went carefully over the lessons instilled in him by William Marshal, who had been the champion of his day. He heartily wished that de Montfort would not take a deliberate fall, but accepted the fact that chivalry dictated that he not unseat the King of England.

Simon de Montfort had a decision to make. He was supremely confident of his abilities and would not feel the slightest humiliation in going down before the king, but he wanted to show Eleanor that if she chose, she was not bound by custom or vows or what was expected of her. She was free to choose for herself, as was every man and woman on earth. She would need courage to defy the king, the council, and the church, and he wanted to show her that he had enough courage for both of them.

His decision made, he lowered the visor of his helmet and couched his lance beneath his powerful arm. The field marshal lowered his mace and the two men rode full tilt, veering neither to left nor right. A hush had fallen over the spectators for even though the joust was for pleasure, great risks were involved. The thunder of the hooves was the only sound that could be heard until the two men clashed. Simon's lance hit its intended mark with his full weight behind it, and Henry lay sprawled in the field.

The crowd gasped at the champion's audacity. He wheeled his destrier about, jumped from the saddle, and aided the king to his feet. Henry good-naturedly threw his arm about Simon, laughing, and said, "Damn, for a minute there I thought I had you."

Simon took off his helmet and grinned. "You didn't stand a chance; my reach is twice yours."

For some reason Henry felt good. Actually it was humiliating when men let him win only because he was king. This man had treated him as if he had been a worthy opponent, and the joust had been scrupulously fair rather than contrived.

When the crowd saw that the king was untroubled by the outcome, they roared their approval and cheered both men wildly. The Earl of Leicester raised the queen's scarf on high, and she became so flushed at his championing her over the king, she turned almost the shade of her gown.

Eleanor sat very still. Simon de Montfort made his own rules. She knew she must conceal the wicked feelings he aroused in her. If the world knew, it would brand her a wanton harlot. Moreover, she must never let this arrogant nobleman know the effect he had upon her. He was insufferable now. What on earth would be the measure of his conceit if he knew his mere presence sent her heart fluttering like a bride's?

Henry held out her scarf which was no longer white. "Sorry, Maggot." He grinned sheepishly and she knew he would never be anything more than a boy. When the jousting was finished and the champions came forward to receive their prizes at the hands of the queen and her maids of honor, the crowds left the spectator stands and gathered on the field in a milling circle, eager to catch every word exchanged.

The champion of the day was, of course, the Earl of Leicester. He came forward and knelt before the queen. Even kneeling his eyes were almost on a level with hers. She presented him with a golden chalice encrusted with gemstones and as she raised her lips to bestow a kiss upon him, he could not mistake the invitation writ plain in her eyes. His experience with women told him the only sin they never forgave was *not* wanting to make love to them. His eyes lingered on her face, complimenting her beauty with a single look as only a Frenchman could, then he rose amid the cheers of the crowd.

Eleanor's eyes had never left Simon de Montfort. His plain white surcoat with its simple red cross was unsullied, almost as clean as before he had jousted. She wished she belonged to this man, but knew it could never be more than a wish. He had shown her he was above convention, above the law of chivalry, above other men. So that his head did not grow apace with his conceit, she raised her hand and beckoned to him coolly.

He saw her gesture immediately for he was acutely aware of her every breath. When he came before her, he knelt as he had done before the queen. The crowd eagerly watched the two figures garbed in white, their black hair curling about their shoulders, one petite in the extreme, the other immense.

She did not let even a glimmer of amusement into her eyes as she reached into her sleeve, then held out her hands to offer him the reward. She gave it with solemnity, and he reached out his damnably attractive hands to receive it. For a moment he was appalled. What obscenity had she placed upon his palms? He looked at her in disbelief, then looked back down at the foul objects. Suddenly he knew what they were and amusement filled his black eyes. She had been conspicuously absent from the walled garden for days, but now he knew she had been there for what she had just presented him with were two owl pellets that contained such delicacies as mice skulls, teeth, bones, and fins from the pond's fish, which the young owls had pilfered. Owls devoured their prey whole, then each day presented a pellet containing the undigested parts.

"I shall cherish them and think of you whenever I look at them," he said gravely, tucking them beneath his surcoat.

The curious onlookers had not seen the objects but assumed the princess had presented the champion with gold medallions or perhaps jewels.

Simon de Montfort was elated. Eleanor was quite capable of playful tricks providing they were kept absolutely private. He could think of quite a few playful tricks he'd like to share with her—and would, the next time they were alone.

24

The celebrating went on long into the night. Simon looked about the hall in vain. He knew she would not come and be part of this boisterous merrymaking, and not because she did not like fun. He guessed she was capable of more mischief than any woman in the room. She did not come because she was contemptuous of the queen and her court.

The Provençals looked down their arrogant noses at the natives and even Henry's half brothers wrinkled their noses at anything English, from the climate to the food. As Simon drained his third tankard of ale, he in his turn became contemptuous of them. England was his chosen country and he thought it the finest land in the world. Her climate was temperate, her generous earth produced bountiful harvests of grains and fruits. Each and every county luxuriated in abundant fields, verdant meadows, wide plains, fertile pastures, milky herds, and strong horseflesh. Her rising streams, majestic rivers, and watercourses teemed with fish and fowl. Fruitful groves and forests covered the hills and the kingdom's chestnut woods abounded in game. England's yeomen farmers were the salt of the earth. Her peasants were plump, her children red-cheeked and happy, and the ale was unbelievable. He was the Earl of

Leicester and this England belonged to him. All he needed was a countess, and he knew exactly where to find her.

He went over the garden wall silently, his eyes slowly becoming accustomed to the darkness and the shadows. The corners of his mouth lifted with delight. If she wished to elude him, she had made a tactical error by not changing from her white gown. Stealthily he managed to get quite close before she sensed his presence.

She lifted her head like a doe in a forest glade when it scented danger. When she saw him she fled, lifting her trailing skirts in an effort to elude him, but he closed on her almost instantly and lifted her against his heart.

"Kathe," he whispered, his lips against her silken tresses.

"No, no," she cried, not bothering to keep her voice low for every inhabitant of Windsor tonight from the king down to the lowliest pot-boy was in the great hall at the tournament banquet. The entire Middle and Upper Wards were deserted.

"Yes, yes," he insisted. "There is that between us which cannot be denied. *I* know it, but more important, *you* know it."

"It is impossible," she cried, struggling like a wildcat.

He held her firmly. "I showed you today that nothing is impossible. In my heart I know you were meant for me. The inevitability of it all is so tangible I can taste it," he said fiercely.

"It would cause a scandal from one end of the realm to the other," she cried.

He chuckled. "What could they do? Stone you like Jezebel?" He pinioned her flailing arms to her body and fused his mouth to hers hungrily. His flesh reacted instantly, swelling, filling, aching for her. The kiss lasted a lifetime. For Eleanor it was like slow torture. Her mind and her body were at war with themselves. Her blood sang with delicious excitement, but her mind protested vehemently at her wicked behavior. Her innocence had primed her for a headlong descent into abandonment. Though she protested wildly she felt that whatever he did to her she had somehow agreed to.

The kiss grew in intensity. Mouth fused to mouth, body melded into body until it was no longer necessary to pinion her arms. His firm mouth separated her soft lips and at last he was able to enter her delicious mouth with his tongue. The taste of her drove him mad.

She moaned softly, loving it and hating it. When at last he released her mouth for a moment she breathed, "You make me feel like Jezebel; you make me feel wicked as sin. You are so strong, de Montfort, you know you can force me to your will."

"Nay," he denied, "you are too tiny for a man my size to force. I'd have to woo you and play with you for an hour before I could make love to you. Let me be your secret lover, Kathe . . . I'll devote my life to bringing you pleasure."

"You promise me pleasure but not happiness?" she questioned breathlessly.

"No one can promise happiness to another, however much he may wish it," he said softly.

"And no man can measure the torment he may cause a woman," she accused.

"No pain is unbearable," he said, "save that of regret. You torment me when you hold me at arm's length and deny me. Put me out of my misery, Kathe." His burning mouth trailed a fiery path down her throat and his arms tightened about her.

"Please don't! When you press me to your heart I want to . . ." She caught the words back guiltily.

"You consume me," he whispered savagely, and his hands closed over the mounds of her breasts.

The swift intake of her breath told him exactly what effect he had on her. Eleanor had to fight him and herself both. The feel of his magnificent hands upon her was like an aphrodisiac. She knew if there had been light enough for her to see the dragons, to see those irresistible hands as well as feel them, she would have been lost, lost.

"Let me go, de Montfort," she said, desperately summoning her anger.

He removed his hands from her. "How ironic that after winning every joust today, I should lose the final one—the only joust that means anything to me."

She wanted to cry with frustration. If only he would leave her alone, she could fight these disturbingly compelling feelings he aroused in her, but what chance did she have against him when he constantly wooed her? Her mouth felt bee-stung from his demanding kisses and her senses were filled with the male taste and scent of him.

He was so attuned to her, he knew she felt a pang of regret that he had set her free, so he again enfolded her into his embrace and brought her against his hard, muscled chest. His mouth touched her soft lips gently, playing, warming, rousing until her arms crept about his neck.

In her mind Eleanor wanted to pull away from his touch. She shook her head until her hair formed a wild, tangled mass against her white shoulders. He lifted great handfuls of it to his face, breathing in its fragrance, feeling its silky texture, even tasting it in his desire to experience everything about her. His strong hands encircled her waist and he pulled her to his body until she rested against his hips. She could feel his hard, pulsing manhood against her secret part and she was suddenly filled with abandon. Like a fierce black cat she fastened her mouth to his and her sharp white teeth bit down hard into his lower lip.

He swore a foul oath and put his hand to his mouth. It came away bloodied, and when he looked up she was gone. He heard the key turn in the heavy wooden door to the garden as he stood there gazing into the darkness. The fragrance of her lingering perfume filled his brain. Far off a flash of lightning was followed by a low rumble of thunder, and raindrops pattered on the leaves of the copper beech trees. He lifted his face to meet the downpour. Perhaps it would cool his blood. Someday, he promised himself, they would stand naked in the rain while it washed over them, then slowly he would make love to her.

Back in her tower, Eleanor was in a turmoil. He must never guess how he made her feel, and just as important, no one else must ever guess. She paced about the chamber restless as a tigress. She could not get away from him. He invaded her private garden by day and by night. If she kept to her chamber, he had shown her he was perfectly capable of climbing the tower and stretching himself upon her bed. She would have to put distance between them. Once she had removed herself, his eye would fall upon some other female who would welcome his impatient lust. God knows, there were enough smitten females at court, starting with the queen herself, from what Eleanor had seen.

She pictured Odiham, the lovely little estate William had deeded to her. She smiled sadly as she remembered the terrible scene when William had discovered her brother Richard in bed with Isabella. That had happened two years ago, or was it three? It was still as fresh in her mind as if it had happened yesterday. Odiham was only twenty miles away, she could be there before lunch. A warning sounded in her mind. If she considered twenty miles a morning's ride, what would Simon de Montfort consider it? An hour's full gallop. She would be no safer from him at Odiham than she was at Windsor. Less safe perhaps, away from the eyes and ears of the court and the church.

She made her decision in a moment. She would go to Wales. Oh, how happy she had been there with William in that beautiful, wild land, before she had lured him to her bed and to his death. She would tell no one where she was going, and yet she knew she could not simply disappear. She would have to put Henry's mind at rest about her absence. She would need the services of Rickard de Burgh and a small troop of his men for escort.

It did not take Eleanor's quicksilver mind long to come up with a plan. She would tell the king and those in her service that she was going to Odiham for a time, and in truth she would go there, but from there she would make preparations for the journey into Wales. She would not go to Pembroke, there were far too many mountains to traverse, and the snowstorms in Wales came in early autumn. She would go to Chepstowe in the beautiful border country across the River Severn.

She decided to take only her serving woman Bette, for both Odiham and the much larger Chepstowe had their own staff. She told Henry of her extended visit to Odiham and pleased, he did exactly as she thought and urged her to take Rickard de Burgh and a few of his men for escort. After swearing Bette to secrecy, the two women spent a whole day packing the warm things they would need for the colder climate.

Eleanor was both surprised and relieved when she saw de Burgh was taking a dozen strong men along for a journey of only twenty miles. Had he read her mind? Did he somehow know that Wales was her destination? One never knew with

Rickard de Burgh and his strange powers. When de Burgh saw the baggage he couldn't believe his eyes. He was determined not to be hindered by a wagon, however, and instead used half a dozen pack horses.

On the ride to Odiham he approached her about his own plans for the future.

"My lady, may I assume that you have no plans to enter the convent of St. Bride's?"

She smiled at him. "Spoiled princesses make poor nuns, I warrant. Were you waiting until I was safely in the convent before you returned to Ireland, Sir Rickard?"

He flushed. "Aye, I suppose I was, though I'd a thousand times rather have seen you wed again," he added quickly.

"I took vows to remain the Countess of Pembroke for the rest of my life," she said quietly.

He hesitated to speak his mind, but there were no secrets between them. He had been the one to free her from her husband's dead body. "My lady, in my opinion those vows should never have been taken seriously by the bishops. You were far too young and far too distraught at the time to know what you were doing."

Her lashes swept down to her cheeks. She had had the same irreverent thoughts lately, wicked though they were. She changed the subject slightly. "So, will you return to Ireland?"

"Nay." He shook his head. "But once I see you safely settled at Odiham, I thought I would ride into Wales to see to the de Burgh castles."

She lifted her dark lashes and her sapphire eyes widened. Had he read her thoughts? She knew he had the gift of second sight. "I might as well confess to you I'm only going to Odiham as a diversionary tactic, then I'm going to Chepstowe."

"Then I shall see you safely to Chepstowe before I go on to see how Hubert fares."

"Oh, Rickard, I was so immersed in my own troubles, I spared no thought for your poor uncle."

De Burgh could not bring himself to tell her how base her brother Henry had been to his old favorite. What good would it do to tell her he had ordered Hubert dragged from sanctuary and shackled to the dungeon walls? Then when the bishops had raised a hue and cry, he had returned him to sanctuary without food or water. Rickard de Burgh changed the subject. He raised an eyebrow. "Who necessitates your using diversionary tactics, my lady?"

Her laughter floated out upon the crisp autumn air. "You are the one with the second sight."

It was good to hear her laugh, but the thought that she must flee to Wales to avoid unwanted advances greatly disturbed him. The leering face of Peter of Savoy flashed into his mind. "If one of those damned Savoys has the temerity to pursue you, lady, I will consider it my duty to kill him."

"The vows I took at least protected me from those wretched Savoys," she assured him with a smile. "I simply have a great need to see Wales again and want none of the court following me."

Eleanor knew Rickard de Burgh would and could protect her from any man, save the one who was uppermost in her mind.

When they arrived at Odiham the entire household was thrown into panic. None in authority had been there for so long, they had grown lax. The steward, however, immediately obeyed de Burgh's orders for he remembered that William Marshal had appointed the knight castellan whenever the Countess of Pembroke was in residence.

Eleanor was amazed to see the familiar red head of her old maid Brenda.

"What in the world are you doing here?" Eleanor demanded.

"Please let me explain, my lady," Brenda said. "I ran away from Windsor because I was afraid. Someone tried to kill me!"

Eleanor eyed her with suspicion. She did not believe her tale for a moment. Likely she had run off with some man. Brenda continued, trying her utmost to be convincing. "I had nowhere to go, my lady. I ran to Durham House in London, but one of the Marshals came and his servants threw me out. I found my way here knowing it belonged to you. I feared the Marshals would swallow up everything that belonged to the earl."

"And so they will if I let them," Eleanor replied with spirit. "If I allow you to remain, you will have to take orders from

Bette here. She is a trustworthy woman whom I rely upon completely."

Brenda bobbed a curtsy and one to Bette for good measure. "May I prepare you a bath, Lady Eleanor?" she asked quickly, hoping she would be able to remove her things from one of the pretty guest rooms before the Countess of Pembroke discovered she had told the gullible steward she was lady-in-waiting rather than servant.

As Bette was unpacking the things Eleanor would need, she said, "That's a saucy wench, if ever I saw one."

Eleanor laughed, remembering. " 'Tis my own fault, Bette. When I was nine years old I chose her for her sauciness. She was maid to one of the Marshal cousins and I deliberately stole her." Bette helped her out of her riding dress and petticoats. "After my bath, I'll go down to the kitchens to ensure we'll get a decent meal tonight. If you feel up to it, I'd like to start for Wales in the morning."

Bette was a large-boned woman who sat a horse almost as well as a man. "I feel up to it and I'm happy to see you so vigorous, Lady Eleanor. The ride has put the roses back in your cheeks. This change of scenery will be like a tonic for you, mark my words." Bette cast her an anxious glance. This was a lovely manor house, but she hoped it would not stir too many poignant memories for the princess. Not just as she was beginning to recover from her tragic ordeal.

After Eleanor finished in the kitchen, she wandered over the house and garden reliving the past. Though the memories were bittersweet, the manor house did not have William's indelible stamp upon it. In fact, she imagined he had scarcely ever visited the place before he had given it to her, for his holdings were too vast and his duties to the crown too heavy.

After supper that night Eleanor gathered the entire household together, including the gardeners and the grooms. They thought they were in for a tongue-lashing and came reluctantly, but before she had finished speaking, she had won their hearts. She stood before them gowned in turquoise velvet, which accentuated her vivid loveliness. "I want you to know that I love Odiham and that in the future I shall probably spend a lot of my time here. The Earl of Pembroke had vast holdings, but at the present time my affairs are a tangled mass of assets and debts instead of a proper dower. The Marshals, it seems, have not been pressed to give me any estates endowed from William. Odiham, however, was a direct gift from my late husband and I have the deed firmly in my possession. I pledge, therefore, that none of you will lose your place here. Yet I do think that Odiham could be run more efficiently. I should like to see every room turned out and cleaned from top to bottom. I should also like to see the weeds cut and bulbs planted for the spring. Sadly, Odiham has about it an air of neglect, and I am just as guilty as you for that neglect. In a month's time I shall return. We could even have the Christmas festivities here, if you make Odiham the warm and welcoming manor that it could be."

She had noticed at supper that Rickard seemed embarrassed by Brenda's attention. The knight was scrupulously polite to the redheaded wench, but Eleanor could see he was trying to keep her at arm's length. She decided to speak to him about it.

"Sir Rickard, you don't seem eager for Brenda's attention. Would you prefer it if she did not accompany us on the journey into Wales?"

De Burgh looked so relieved, Eleanor laughed aloud.

Slightly shamefaced, he too laughed. "Indiscretions from my past rising up to haunt me, I'm afraid," he said apologetically.

"Why don't you tell her it was your twin Mick she knew intimately?"

He almost choked on his ale, wondering just how much she had guessed.

Before Eleanor retired for the night, she took Brenda aside for a frank talk. "As I understand it, you have no wish to return to Windsor?"

Eleanor saw a look of real fear come into the girl's face. "No, no, Lady Eleanor, please let me stay here. When you come in future you won't need to bring your other woman, I will do everything for you. You always liked the way I dressed your hair, and I would just love to take care of your beautiful wardrobe."

"That may be true, but I must know you are reliable, Brenda. I cannot have you disappearing whenever I turn my back. Also I must know that I can count upon your discretion."

"You can, my lady, I swear it. You may tell me anything. Wild horses would not drag it from me," she vowed.

"I hope not. I am leaving for Chepstowe on the Welsh border tomorrow. It is a secret. If anyone comes here to inquire of my whereabouts, you will tell them I have returned to Windsor. Is that understood?"

"Yes, my lady," promised Brenda, thankful she was not to accompany her mistress into that heathen land. Rick de Burgh had turned all monkish since their last encounter, and she much preferred the attentions of Odiham's menservants.

25

Simon de Montfort haunted the gardens for three days and nights. He was starving for a glimpse of Eleanor and had to spend endless hours training the fighting men with sword and shield or on horseback in the tiltyard to rid his body of lust.

When he was with her he felt every inch a man, able to overcome her every objection. She was so small and feminine he could easily master her. His strong hands could bind her to his side or release her, bending her to his will. His powerful body dominated their encounters, showing her plainly his male appetites and desires that she aroused in him. But when they were apart his personal vulnerability crept up upon him, whispering in his ear that perhaps he would never be able to take the place in Eleanor's heart that was still firmly held by William Marshal.

Simon was a man who had never before doubted himself in any capacity, least of all when it came to engaging the affections of a woman. But, he admitted to himself with many a wistful sigh, this woman was different. He was all lusty flesh and blood. How could he compete with an idealized memory? He must find a way to banish the ghost of William Marshal for he would never endure being relegated to second place in his beloved's heart.

Queen Eleanor often watched Simon de Montfort from her windows. She had never seen such a superb body on a man and daydreamed of what he would be like in bed. In the dining hall at night she saw that the Savoys and the other Queen's Men avoided him. The Lusignans, or King's Men, seemed to hate him also. She decided with amusement that they were all jealous of the magnificently endowed male, who put them all in the shade.

De Montfort usually dined with the knights and the men-at-arms. These men, by contrast, seemed to hold him in such high esteem they almost worshipped him. For amusement one evening she called him up to the dais table. "My lord, pray join the king and me. 'Tis unfitting that the Earl of Leicester sup with lesser men night after night."

He bowed his acceptance graciously, but glanced at the petty nobles from Provence and Lusignan and said, "Their lack of title does not make them lesser men, your Grace."

"How odd for a nobleman to champion the common man." She smiled, patting the seat beside her.

Simon sat down, stretching his long legs beneath the table, and expounded upon his beliefs. "The common man is what makes a country strong. The common men of England will make her great. I believe, as your husband's grandfather believed, that the common man should have a say in the government of his country."

Henry overheard him, of course. "God's foot, Simon, I have enough trouble with my barons and nobles having too much to say about everything. Deliver me from a system where every man-jack has a say in things."

The queen laughed flirtatiously and touched Simon's arm. "What about women in this fantasy world of yours?"

"Who knows?" He grinned. "Perhaps someday, even women will have a say in government."

"Would you allow your wife to have a say in things?" the queen asked playfully.

"Ah, there my theory falls apart, I'm afraid. My wife would

have to know her woman's place and keep it. There could only be one head of my household."

"Bravo!" cried the king. "She usually teases that handsome young devil Rick de Burgh, but now he's escorted my sister to her manor house of Odiham, she's decided to plague you to death," he said indulgently.

Simon bestowed a brilliant grin upon the queen. How fortunate that her roving eye had selected him to join her tonight. So, Eleanor had bolted. A woman ran away so that a man would pursue her. He bent toward the king and said, "Sire, I think it time I saw to my estates in Leicester and Coventry. Your permission, Sire, to leave Windsor for a time."

"Of course." Henry waved his hand. "Just so you return to us quickly."

The queen pouted and Simon's lying eyes told her how attractive he found her. Her thigh brushed his beneath the cover of the tablecloth, and Simon decided to put a stop to her playful games. With a soulful look from his magnetic black eyes, he covered her hand and squeezed it ardently. He felt the vulgar rings she displayed and squeezed her fingers together unmercifully. He saw her go white and pretended not to notice. She gasped aloud, but it was not from pain. She had just learned a most erotic secret. The man beside her was no gentle giant. He was capable of being deliberately brutal. Waves of heat and ice washed over her as his massive hand imprisoned hers. What would it be like to be imprisoned between his thighs? The contrast between this superb male animal and her husband was almost unendurable. If she left the hall now, would he follow?

At last he released the cruel grip upon her hand and she rose to leave, but his great boot was clamped upon the fragile material of her train and a sickening tearing sound confirmed her worst fears. Simon de Montfort was on his feet, abjectly apologizing. "Your Majesty, please forgive my clumsiness. I forget my strength and my size. I am unfit to dine with a queen, I fear. I am much more suited to the company of the common man."

She was ready to scream with frustration. They had attracted far too much attention to themselves to arrange a rendezvous tonight. Now it would have to wait until he returned to court.

As her eyes ran down the length of his powerful torso, she shuddered. He was well worth waiting for.

Though the hour was advanced, he rode to Odiham, arriving at midnight. When he led his black stallion into the stables, he saw neither Eleanor's horse nor Rickard de Burgh's destrier, which puzzled him somewhat. The high pile of fresh horse manure outside the building told him the stables had recently accommodated at least twenty more horses than were there presently. The stableboys were asleep and he did not wish his arrival to cause a stir of any sort, so he wrapped his cloak about him and bedded down in the straw.

Brenda had worked her way through all the men who were employed inside Odiham Manor, now she was working her way through the stables. She knew Turner, the head groom, was about to fall into her hands if only from curiosity of what the other grooms had told him. Suddenly she came upon a sight that made her blink with disbelief. A man, nay a god, lay stretched upon the straw sleeping. The impact of his magnificent physique hit her like a thunderbolt. She wanted to be tumbled by him into that straw more than she had ever wanted anything in her life. She measured him with her eyes and guessed his length to be over six-and-a-half feet. God's blood, how long must his manroot be? She decided to find out. She knelt down in the straw and reached out an itchy palm to touch his man's center. Simon de Montfort had the keen hearing of a warrior even in his sleep. At the first rustle of the hay his black eyes shot open and he sat up, swiftly reaching for his dagger.

Brenda's lips parted in a little round O. "Who are you?" she asked huskily.

"I came from Windsor with a message for the Countess of Pembroke."

His voice was so deep her bones felt like they were melting. She licked her lips. "She's not here," she said absently, her mind on other things. Her eyes deliberately lowered to his groin in hopes that she had aroused him.

Simon watched her closely. Her bold thoughts were so blatant they were etched upon her saucy face. "Where is she?" he demanded, preparing to rise.

A veil came down over her eyes before she replied, "She has returned to Windsor."

In a flash he knelt before her, his powerful hands seized her shoulders, and he brought his face level with hers. "Why do you lie, wench?"

She groaned at his touch. The smell of the hay and his leathers acted as a powerful stimulant to her senses, and she slid her hand between his muscular thighs and tried to cup him. He overflowed her hand and she tumbled head over heels in lust with him. He was what she had been searching for her entire life.

Simon de Montfort had never met a woman whose need was so great. He would not have been a man if he hadn't been flattered by her blatant desire for him. Most women threw him subtle glances and hints; this one reached out for what she wanted and took it.

With ungentle hands he pulled her gown down from her shoulders, letting it fall about her waist, then he filled his palms with her generous breasts. His mouth took hers swiftly, savagely, and as he thrust his tongue in deeply, he turned and lowered her to the hay, pinning her beneath his body. Brenda was stunned as she felt herself climax. It so seldom happened even when a man had been inside her for an age that she thought she must be dreaming.

"Where is the Countess of Pembroke?" he demanded.

"I know, I really do know." She gasped. "Come to my chamber and I will tell you."

Simon de Montfort was many things, but a fool was not one of them. There was no way on God's earth he would be foolish enough to fuck the maid of the woman he wished to make his mistress. "You will tell me now," he said grimly, his hands circling her throat.

Brenda's face went ashen. "Did Winchester send you?" she cried fearfully. He had seen a look like that on an animal that knew it was trapped. He tucked Winchester's name away in his memory for future reference. "Where is Eleanor?" he repeated for the last time.

"She has gone to Chepstowe in Wales," she whispered fearfully.

Simon flashed a smile and swung the girl to her feet. As she gaped up at him, he pulled her gown back up to her shoulders to cover her breasts. "Thank you, *chérie*," he said gallantly, his eyes brimful of humor.

"Who are you?" she asked again in wonder, as she realized he had not been sent to murder her.

"I am a man in a hurry," he said with a wink.

Rickard de Burgh set as fast a pace as he dared as he and his dozen fighting men escorted the two women toward the Welsh border. The weather had turned bitter cold, and he wanted to get the countess safely settled before the first snowstorms of autumn made the land impassable.

His men were hardbitten enough to crawl through the Welsh mountain ranges, taking shelter in caves if they had to, but anyone who had never experienced the ice, snow, and winds of that heathen land would never have believed her beautiful green valleys and majestic vistas could be so deadly treacherous.

It took three days to travel eighty miles. De Burgh heaved a sigh of relief once they were west of the River Severn for a light coating of snow now covered the land as far as the eye could see and heavy, pewter-colored clouds hung low over the mountaintops in the distance.

Chepstowe was like a small universe. It was completely self-sufficient with its Welsh guard, its armory and smithy. It had its own brewhouse and gristmill and was surrounded by out-farms and villages fully stocked for the winter months. As Bette dismounted in the bailey she thought her knees would never touch again, so long astride had she been. She marveled that Eleanor ran laughing into the warm, welcoming hall, hailing the familiar Marshal servants in their native tongue.

Eleanor issued her orders with the regal air of a princess born. Extra fires were lighted, cooks dashed about preparing the spits, servitors rushed down to the castle cellars to fetch up ale and wine as Eleanor showed her men where to deposit the heavy trunks they carried in from the backs of the packhorses. Eleanor told Rickard de Burgh, "Don't banish your men to the knights' quarters. You may all dine here tonight. We'll be a merry company holed up by our blazing fires."

He looked down at her observing the marked change in the last weeks. The pale, quiet wraith had disappeared, forever he hoped. She had been replaced by a dark, sparkling creature of verve and challenge.

A Welsh harper sang sad laments and stirring ballads until well after dark. Eleanor mingled freely with the company, joining in the men's laughter as they lounged about the floor dicing. Rickard de Burgh arose to stand beside her at the great fireplace. Out from under the watchful eye of the royal court and clergy, she felt free and unrestrained. She made up her mind that in future she would have her own court. She would take back some Welsh harpers and minstrels. She would enjoy the company of whomever she pleased whether it be man or woman. Her vows of perpetual widowhood would not prevent her from enjoying friendships, she decided.

She looked at her friend Rickard now as she sipped her wine reflectively. "Can I not tempt you to stay awhile at Chepstowe? When I was last here with William we rode out into the mountains, explored caves, flew our hawks, and the hunting hereabouts makes Windsor Forest seem tame and unexciting."

Rickard de Burgh thanked her for her generous invitation but shook his head. "The snowstorms are on their way even though it is only September. We must press on." He indicated his men who lounged before the fires. "They will grow soft with idleness."

About ten o'clock the blizzard began. The wind raged like a vicious, mad thing, tearing apart everything that wasn't fastened down. The snow swirled blindingly as the temperature plummeted to freezing. Chepstowe Castle was such a well-built fortress that those within were ignorant of the blizzard's devastation. Those waking in the night heard the wind howl through the chinks in the shutters, but turned over, thankful of their snug beds and warm fires.

Simon de Montfort reached the banks of the Severn River as the blizzard hit. He was forced to take shelter and ask hospitality at Berkeley Castle. The following day the river could not be crossed, and he was forced to go so far north before he could bridge the waters, then all the way back south, that he lost almost two days.

Rickard de Burgh and his men had departed as soon as the calm descended after the blizzard. His experiences in Wales had taught him there was much worse to come and they had better forge ahead through the daylight hours.

When Eleanor awoke after the blizzard, a calm had descended upon the land. A thick white blanket had fallen, making everything look still and picturesque. The sun shone brilliantly upon the crystals of snow, making the entire landscape look both enchanted and inviting.

In her newfound freedom Eleanor felt she had been a prisoner long enough. Her confinement had set up such a desire to enjoy life and nature to the full that she grew more restless with each hour. Finally in the early afternoon she could tolerate it no longer. She pulled on high boots beneath a velvet riding dress and took up her sable-lined cloak.

"Bette, find my warm riding gloves, I've decided to fly one of the falcons for an hour."

"God's nightgown, you're not going out in the snow, surely, my lady?"

Eleanor laughed. "Of course I am. It's exhilarating! I love the snow."

Bette looked worried. "The Black Mountains are treacherous in winter."

Eleanor laughed again. "Those are just the foothills, they're not the Black Mountains proper. I remember William had a hunting lodge in the hills. I took refuge there once from a downpour and stayed all night. It was most comfortable."

"All the same, Lady Eleanor, I don't think you should venture far. It looks lovely now in the sunshine, but dark will fall early this afternoon."

"Please don't nag me, Bette. I feel I've missed so much, I'll never catch up. It will put roses in my cheeks."

Bette got up from her knees before the trunk. "Here's your fur hat. Promise me you'll wear it. I don't want you with an earache all night."

Eleanor giggled. "I never had an earache in my life."

As the groom saddled her horse for her he asked in Welsh, "Where are you going, lady?"

She mounted with a flourish and bent toward him in a conspiratorial fashion. "Wherever I wish, for the rest of my life!"

The falcon fastened its talons into her embroidered glove and tested its wings. She held it at arm's length and looked it straight in the eye. "Today we are birds of a feather—let us risk all!"

The icy mountain air was heady as wine. She stood in the stirrups to cast the falcon, and as she watched it soar into the sunshine she was giddy with exhilaration. The snow was fetlock deep as she cantered off in the direction the hawk had taken, but in places it deepened where the wind had piled it into drifts, so Eleanor avoided these smooth, white, innocent-looking mounds and kept to open ground as much as possible. As she rode west lifting her face to the sun she did not notice the threatening, bruise-colored clouds sweeping in from the east.

The falcon flew ever farther and higher into the hills. It had twice returned obediently with its prey, and Eleanor was preoccupied with its soaring beauty. The next time it returned she intended to head back to Chepstowe whose warm fires and secure walls beckoned temptingly. Yet the falcon flew to the top of a majestic Douglas fir and would not be coaxed down.

Eleanor noticed how much the wind had picked up; it swirled the snow madly about her. Was it another snowstorm, or was it simply the wind blowing yesterday's snow? She decided she could not wait for the obstinate falcon and hoped it would follow her back to the castle.

The wind had obliterated her horse's tracks; indeed it seemed to have altered the whole perspective of the landscape. Heavy gusts swirled the blinding snow, and Eleanor realized it was again coming down thick and fast, for it had now obliterated the sun. She began to shiver as a finger of fear touched her spine, telling her she did not know in which direction to ride. She continued to shiver as the icy cold crept up her legs from her feet.

She told herself not to panic. Somewhere in these hills was the small hunting lodge. She gave her horse its head and whispered encouragement, hoping its instinct would lead it to shelter. She clung to its mane, bending low over its neck as it laboured slowly through the heavy drifts.

She knew she was on high ground because the wind howled unmercifully, whipping the snow from jagged boulders and piling it high on ledges and in crevices. Suddenly a crack like a whip rent the air, terrifying her horse. As the wind brought down the gigantic Welsh fir, the frightened animal surged forward. Eleanor was thrown from the saddle. Her body was cushioned by the snow, but her head came down against a jagged rock so forcefully it might have killed her had she not been wearing the fur hat. The tree trunk came down to trap her body against the rocks as she lay unconscious and blood ran freely from her lacerated scalp into the pristine snow.

26

Bette's apprehension grew with every hour. Lady Eleanor should have returned long ago, she told herself as she stood glued to the high tower window. The snow fell so thickly she could no longer see into the courtyard, so with determination she threw on her cloak and hurried to the stables.

The stocky, dark Welsh grooms stared at her when she spoke to them in English. They knew what was troubling the woman for they were uneasy themselves, but they knew she did not understand their language. Finally the steward was brought to interpret. Bette's worst fears were confirmed when she learned that Lady Eleanor had gone hawking alone without a groom to attend her. Frantically she told the steward they must go and look for her, organize a search party, *do something,* but they told her bluntly if they went out before the storm subsided, they would lose both men and horses.

"She will have taken shelter," the steward told her over and over until she thought she would scream from frustration. Finally she ordered them to saddle her a horse, thinking them less than real men when the Countess of Pembroke was in peril. She had no idea of the deep-seated resentment the Welsh felt for the English. They would not try to save an English life by sacrific-

ing Welsh lives, unless they were forced by a strong master to
do so.

Bette got no farther than the castle walls before she realized
her quest was an impossibility. The wind-driven snow made
visibility impossible. Her horse floundered in the deep drifts,
and she had no idea in which direction Lady Eleanor had gone.
After an hour of freezing futility she reluctantly returned to
Chepstowe. She was distraught and spent the entire night alter-
nately pacing and kneeling in prayer.

When Simon de Montfort rode his weary stallion into Chepstowe's bailey, he had never before been so glad of reaching his
destination. He dismounted and led the animal inside the stables where he immediately fed and watered him, then removed
the heavy saddle and rubbed him down thoroughly.

The dark, stocky men in the stables stared at him openly
because of his size. They knew Englishmen and Normans were
taller than Welshmen, but here was a giant. Only when he had
seen to his horse did he venture into Chepstowe's hall, hoping
he had not missed the noon meal.

Bette recognized the Earl of Leicester immediately. She had
never spoken to him, but she had watched him defeat everyone
at the tournament earlier that month. She rushed forward now
seeing a glimmer of hope in his timely arrival.

"My lord earl," she cried, dipping low in respect, "Lady
Eleanor rode out yesterday afternoon and never returned. I beg
you order the men to form a search party. They refuse to venture out until the storm has passed."

Simon set his saddlebags on the floor and ran his hand
through his wet hair. "Eleanor's been gone twenty-four hours?"
he asked in disbelief. "Where did she go? Did de Burgh accompany her?"

Bette shook her head. "Sir Rickard and his men rode deeper
into Wales. After the first snowstorm the sun came out and she
went off for an hour's hawking . . . alone."

"Splendor of God, she needs her backside warming," he said
angrily. "I've never encountered weather like this in my life."
He strode to the fire and held out his hands to the blaze.

"It seemed so calm and serene yesterday. She told me not to
nag her, that it would put roses in her cheeks."

"A blizzard like this is more likely to put lilies on her chest!"

Bette closed her eyes. "May God keep her safe. She said something about a hunting lodge in the hills. Mary and Joseph," she said, crossing herself, "I hope she has taken shelter there."

Simon glared at the servants in the hall. "Where is the steward?" he demanded.

An older man came forward fearful that the huge, black-eyed man would fell him.

"Bring me food," he ordered. "Anything will do so long as it is hot. Fetch wine, or stronger brew if you have it. I'll give you five minutes while I change into dry clothes."

"You'll go out after her?" Bette cried with relief.

"Aye," he said grimly, "but I won't be responsible for my actions once I lay hands on her."

Bette's face was wreathed with smiles. Lord God, if the Earl of Leicester could find her, Bette would hold her down while he applied his belt. As Simon returned to the fire, clad in dry clothes pulled from his saddlebags, the steward accompanied by two servitors brought hot food and a potent liquor the Welsh brewed.

Simon drained the cup, feeling the fiery fingers of the potent brew creep along his veins and spread warmth throughout his wide chest. He took the trencher from the servitor and wolfed down the hot food where he stood. Between mouthfuls he ordered, "Fill me a flask with some of this devil's water, it might come in handy if I get frozen to the bone." The steward hovered and Simon beckoned him again.

"Chepstowe must have kennels. Do you have brachet hounds that hunt by scent?"

The steward nodded uncertainly.

"Get me a pair now," de Montfort instructed. He turned to Bette. "Get me something she has worn so the dogs can get her scent."

Bette flew upstairs to Eleanor's bedchamber. She picked up a bedrobe, then realized it would be too big if he wanted to carry it with him. She snatched up a pair of silken hose that Eleanor had exchanged for woolen stockings before she went for her foolish ride.

Simon de Montfort's eyebrows rose slightly as Bette pressed the intimate apparel into his gloved hand. Before he emerged into the bailey he could not resist pressing the hose to his face to inhale her delicate fragrance. He carried his saddlebags back out to the stable and packed a measure of fodder for his horse. As he resaddled his black stallion, he murmured his apologies, more to assure himself than the animal. "Sorry, Nomad, old man, we're off again. I think the storm abates somewhat." He led the horse outside and took the leashed dogs from the young kennel master, then offered a stocking to each lean dog until both began to bay and strain on the leash. He freed them and tucked the hose inside his leather doublet.

He mounted swiftly, Nomad's hooves striking sparks against the ice-covered flagstones of the bailey, and surged after the brachet hounds. As he rode higher into the hills, the swirling snow was blinding, but he told himself the wind had slackened and the worst of it was over. It was slow going for the massive horse, and after three hours his sides were heaving noticeably.

At first the dogs had been frenzied and eager, sometimes tunneling beneath the snow, sometimes picking up the trail of a rabbit or fox, but always circling back. De Montfort dismounted in a somewhat sheltered copse where the snow lay heavy upon the branches but not so deep on the ground. He rested his horse and gave him a couple of handfuls of oats. The feeling had left his own feet long ago, and he stomped his boots to restore his circulation.

He was extremely worried, but doggedly pushed his fear to the back of his mind as he took out the fiery liquor for a large swallow. He observed the hounds keenly. They were trying to climb up an ice-covered, rocky ledge, but they slid back each time. It proved too high when they tried jumping, and they fell back and rolled over in the snow.

Simon hoped that at last they were onto something, either Eleanor or her horse. He remounted and rode a long way looking for an opening in the ridge of jagged rock. Finally he found one and urged his destrier into the gap. The snow came up to Nomad's underbelly as he labored upward. Then Simon heard the unmistakable howl of a wolf pack.

He was already cold, but the sound almost froze his heart.

Nomad was now in the snowdrift up to his shoulders and though he struggled valiantly, he could clearly go no farther. The wolf pack was in sight now and Simon counted four. The hounds were almost mad with fearful excitement. They were torn between fleeing the wolves and fearing the whip that had been liberally used in their training.

Simon knew if the hounds deserted, the wolves would attack his horse, which was neatly trapped in the snow. Making his decision instantly, he slid from the saddle and threw his saddlebags into the snow. He was up to his own chest in the stuff, but he helped to turn Nomad so that he could struggle back down through his own tracks. Then he slapped the horse's hindquarters sharply and broke into a relieved sweat as he saw the black stallion head back the way they had come.

Simon had his knife in his palm although he knew wolves would not attack a man if there was lesser prey about. He watched the pair of brachet hounds lose their courage and flee with their tails between their legs; the wolves picked up speed as they began to hunt in earnest. He didn't think the wolves had had a meal recently and hope for Eleanor's safety rose one small notch.

With his saddlebags slung about his neck, he clawed his way through the snow. When he came up against jagged ledges of rock, he inched up them by using his fingers and toes and by the skin of his teeth. His leather boots, breeches, and doublet were good protection against the cold and the wind, but eventually even these became saturated and he knew he was losing his body heat.

Defeat, however, was not in de Montfort's nature. He set his mind and doubled his efforts. He came into a vast clearing just as the last of the afternoon light was fading from the sky and saw a low-timbered structure he hoped was the hunting lodge. No smoke came from its chimney, however, so if Eleanor was there she was without a fire.

Inch by inch, foot by foot, yard by yard, he made his way toward the small building. At last he reached the door. He had to force it open, then he fell to his knees inside the room, his hopes dashed as his eyes scanned the dimness within and he knew no human had set foot inside in at least a year. His first priority was a fire. After he had warmed himself he would renew his search.

At the rear of the lodge was a three-sided lean-to that should have held logs but did not. He was relieved, however, to find an ax. Suddenly he heard the unmistakable nicker of a horse, and his heart leapt in his breast as he saw Eleanor's mount with its reins entangled in the branches of a massive fallen fir. He struggled through the deep snow murmuring encouraging words to the animal. The moment he freed its reins it had sense enough to seek shelter in the lean-to.

De Montfort raised his ax to chop a heavy limb from the fir. As he heaved it back, he saw Eleanor's limp body tucked beneath the crevice of a rock. She was so pale he feared she was dead. His very heart trembled as he stooped to gather her body in his arms. Her body was not yet stiff! Blood of God, though, it was icy cold and lifeless. He ran with her back to the cabin and placed her inert form upon the bed.

His heart constricted at the tiny mound she made upon the huge bed. He felt for her pulse. Finding none, he dipped his ear to her mouth. His own heartbeat thundered inside his eardrum, but finally he discerned a shallow breath.

That she still lived was all he needed to know. He was a good hunter and could keep them fed all winter if necessary, but she needed sustenance and warming immediately and could not wait for a good fire to be built. He took the flask of liquor from his doublet and tipped it up to her lips. She gasped and choked as a little dribbled down her throat, but her eyelids fluttered closed almost immediately and she was again still as death.

He feared she had injuries but they would have to wait until he'd revived her. She had been outside for over thirty hours without food or water, and it was a miracle that she was still alive. Only the cover of the thick fir needles heavily blanketed with snow had kept her from dying from exposure.

Without hesitation he took his knife and nicked the vein in his forearm, then he placed it against her lips and clenched his fist open and closed so that his warm blood trickled into her mouth. His anxious eyes watched her swallow painfully. He'd learned this trick to save wounded men who had lost nearly all their lifeblood. It was a quick restorative until they could receive other sustenance.

Gradually her eyes opened and closed more frequently and her breathing seemed less shallow. He knew his next task was to warm her. First he removed her boots and vigorously rubbed her small feet. Then he stripped her naked and threw her sodden clothes toward the hearth where they would dry once he'd had time to build a fire. He took up the flask of liquor, took a quick swallow then poured a few drops of it onto her belly, thighs, and breasts. With long, smooth strokes he rubbed warmth back into her frozen body. A brandy rubdown was the most stimulating remedy known for restoring vigor to a lifeless body.

His mind was detached as he noted how exquisitely she was formed. At the moment there was no room in his brain for thoughts of lust. As his powerful hands circled her breasts and belly, massaging in a steady rhythm, Eleanor opened her eyes beneath her heavy black lashes and murmured. He did not catch what she said, but it sounded very much like "Sim." He turned her over and after pouring more of the fiery liquid onto her back and buttocks, he set to work stroking heavily down her back and down her long, slim legs. He gave up thanks that nothing seemed broken. When he examined her scalp laceration he saw that it was superficial, though it had probably bled profusely until the cold snow had congealed the blood.

Soon he could tell by the feel of her skin that her body temperature was becoming normal, and he pulled back the covers of the bed and slipped her beneath them. She was conscious now but very drowsy. He looked quickly about the lodge, noting another chamber with a bed and a large kitchen room with larder, cupboards, and a big stone hearth complete with oven, spits, and cooking utensils. The cupboards were bare save for dried herbs, candles, pots for the fire, and linens for the beds. The room was furnished by a long trestle table and chairs cut from logs.

De Montfort knew he must stay in his wet clothes until he had built a fire, cut enough wood to last them through the night, and provided them with food. He took a woolen blanket from the cupboard, picked up his saddlebags, and went out into the lean-to. He gave Eleanor's mare the last of the oats, took off her saddle and bridle, and secured the blanket over her back and withers.

He cut a fir limb into short lengths, returned inside and carefully lit a fire, then hurried back out to cut logs before the branches and needles burned themselves to ash. At first the fire smoked vilely and sputtered as the melting ice ran off the branches, but with patience, using bark and bough, then thicker logs, he built a fire that would last and throw off heat.

When he returned to the bed to check on his patient, he noticed the blue circle had left her mouth. He reached out a finger to trace the curve of her cheek, and she sighed softly as her lashes lifted over her deep sapphire eyes, then closed again in exhaustion.

In the lean-to he painstakingly fashioned snares and plodded off to conceal them in the snow, away from the lodge. He then took up the ax and chopped wood until it was almost dark. Thinking to make a bow and arrows for hunting on the morrow, he cut a dozen long, straight branches, then he retraced his footsteps and methodically checked the six traps he had made. They were all exactly as he'd left them, save one that had snared a hare, still struggling. He mercifully dispatched it with his knife and bore it back to the cabin.

His wet leathers had rubbed his skin raw in many places and all he could think of was stripping the wet, stiff clothing from his freezing body. Yet still he took the time to fill a cooking pot with snow, put in a handful of pine nuts he'd gathered, then skin the hare and spit it over the fire.

Finally he sat down to remove his heavy boots and shrug out of his doublet. He spread it beside Eleanor's clothes to dry, then took off the heavy wool tunic he wore beneath his leather jack. The delicious aroma of roasting meat spiraled about the room, and Eleanor stirred at last and struggled up on her pillows.

He was beside her in two strides, his brows drawn together in anxiety.

She gathered her defiance. "Your brows are even blacker than usual," she breathed.

His inner relief was so great he felt giddy, but he concealed it from her and spoke harshly. "I should take my belt to you, you reckless little bitch!"

Her eyes followed his attractive hands as he undid his belt. He was already naked to the waist and suddenly she was filled with alarm. "Please, de Montfort," she begged, "don't remove all your clothes."

His eyes softened at her plea. "Kathe, I have no choice," he said softly. "My leathers are so wet they are plastered to my skin. But I promise you I won't be entirely naked."

She looked somewhat reassured at his words, but as he removed the soaked garment she stared in curious disbelief. He had not lied to her, he was not naked, but the thing he wore was worse than being nude. He wore a black leather sheath over his shaft, held in place by a strap about his narrow hips. He was such a large man he needed penile protection in battle or when he was twelve hours in the saddle.

Eleanor felt strange as she gazed at the magnificent giant with the dragons upon his forearms and his long shaft encased in black leather. Her blood seemed to rush up to crimson her cheeks, then drain away too quickly. The room swam before her and she fell back in a faint.

"Kathe." He was beside her in a moment, cradling her against his chest, stroking her tangled black curls with his infinitely tender hands. Her lids opened lazily and she heard his deep voice caressing her with his words. "You will have to get used to me, my darling, you will be seeing me without clothes every night for the rest of your life."

"You dream, de Montfort." She gasped low, as if she could not summon another ounce of strength.

"Food," he said, moving her up against her pillows. He removed the hare from the spit and carved it with his knife, then he brought the carving board to the bed and held it up to her nose to tempt her. Indeed its aroma was delicious, the meat soft and juicy, the skin brown and crisp.

"I cannot lift a finger," she whispered helplessly.

He grinned. "You never need to lift a finger for the rest of your life; you have me." He selected a choice morsel and proceeded to feed her. Eleanor had never tasted anything quite so heavenly. The hare had a strong, gamy flavor as if it had been feeding upon cedar boughs.

As he lifted the meat to her lips, she watched his hands as if she were in a trance. His hands are beautiful, sensual, disturbing, she thought. Then her memory caught the thread of something they had done to her earlier. It eluded her for a moment, then she caught the memory and held it. His hands had massaged her from head to foot, back and front, above and below. Her eyes sought his and his look almost devoured her. She could not help herself. Her tongue came out and licked his fingers. He was staring at her mouth. His eyes were like black velvet. Then his mouth was on hers, not fiercely demanding, just tasting her, savoring her, celebrating her.

"De Montfort, eat," she said with a gasp, "please eat."

Simon wasn't even hungry.

"I swear you are a sorcerer," she said angrily.

"Perhaps, but I did not cast the first spell. That first day in the forest I thought you were a wood sprite."

She closed her eyes remembering. She had flown at him with nails and fists, then stoned him and still he pursued her. When she opened her eyes she saw that he was staring at her nipples where the sheet had slipped. His mouth watered for a taste of her. Since he usually took what he desired, he dipped his head and ran his tongue across the pink crest of her breast. His mouth scalded her and she moaned in her throat. He whispered huskily, "You taste like brandywine."

When she did not reply he drew back and looked down at her. Her eyes were closed again, her breathing shallow, but he suspected she was feigning unconsciousness to avoid him. He lifted her chin with gentle fingers to observe her at very close range. When her lashes lifted, her look of pure outrage pierced him and he knew without doubt she had been pretending.

"You are a brute to take advantage of me." She turned her face from him, knowing he would read her response there. At all costs she must keep secret now and forever the effect Simon had on her when he touched her.

"Splendor of God, I'm not going to eat you!" He flung from the bed, poured two cups of the pine-nut tea he had boiled, and returned to her. He knew he must be firm with her. She would probably reject his offering as a way of rejecting him, but he knew he must get the hot drink into her. When she made no move to sip the steaming liquid, he goaded her. "God's death, you are weaker than a kitten. You cannot even hold a cup." Immediately she made an effort to take it from him.

"I admit it is poor fare I've offered you tonight, but tomorrow I pledge to do better." He drew a log chair to her bedside and sat down to fashion a bow and notch arrows with his knife.

Eleanor watched his hands, almost mesmerized. "How did you learn I had fled to Wales? I thought I had covered my tracks," she said resentfully.

"Your red-haired maid was most reluctant to tell me, but I managed to force the information from her."

"At knifepoint?" She sneered.

He smiled lazily. "I have other weapons," he drawled suggestively.

"Oh!" she said, burrying her nose in her cup. Why was she annoyed that he had had dealings with Brenda? Deep down she knew exactly why. The wench was far too saucy and attractive for any man to resist. "Why didn't the men of my castle come to my rescue?" she asked bitterly.

He looked at her and gave her the truth. "It was a blizzard. They would not risk their necks for a spoiled female, English."

"You did," she pointed out.

He spread his hands. "I am in love."

"You think of nothing but your prong," she spat.

Her language shocked him, but he was glad she was strong enough to try to antagonize him. "As usual you are audacious."

"Audacity appeals to you," she returned.

"True, I do lust after you, but 'tis no itch an evening's play would satisfy."

"I'll never marry again!" she declared.

He merely grinned. "I'd advise you to wait for a proposal before you reject me."

"Oh!" She gasped. "Take this vile concoction away before I throw it across the room."

"If you are able to do that, it has strengthened you considerably. Perhaps you are even strong enough for more than verbal games."

She flung her hand toward the other chamber. "Go to bed."

"The mere thought of you has a way of coming between a man and his sleep," he said, towering above her.

"To lowest hell with you," she spat.

"A strong palm applied to the bottom corrects a sharp tongue," he said, snatching at her blanket.

She shrank from him, but his hands tenderly tucked her covers about her more closely. Then with a fingertip he traced her eyebrow, cheekbone, and kiss-swollen mouth to commit them to everlasting memory. He looked deeply into her eyes and saw the defiance and anger, but she could not hide that which told him he had marked her as his woman.

When he knew she slept, he stretched himself on the floor before the fire. De Montfort had probably slept on the ground more often than he had slept in a bed, so it was no hardship to him. In the last hour before dawn, he heard the frightened scream of her horse. In one fluid movement he palmed his knife and threw open the door. The wolf pack was back and closing in on the mare. They fell back when they saw the man, but one, more bold than the rest, rushed forward to leap upon the mare's back. Simon leapt at the same time. With one powerful arm he pried back the wolf's head and buried his knife in its throat. Eleanor staggered to the door swathed in a blanket. She screamed as she saw the wolf and a naked Simon roll over and thrash in the snow, then for a space of time they both lay still, until at last the man disentangled himself from the body of the animal and came inside.

Eleanor swayed on her feet. "You must be freezing," she whispered, but she could see a sheen of perspiration covering his dark throat and chest.

"You should be abed" was all he said as he lifted her and padded across the room. "They know I've killed the dominant male, they won't be back," he said before he returned to the fire.

She did not doze for a long time. She watched the firelight play upon the superbly muscled flanks of the colossus. What chance did she have against him? All things were merely a challenge to this magnificent warrior. He must have a weakness somewhere. She would find it and turn it into a wound! She buried her face in her pillow as she tried to deny the desire he had awakened. She had too few weapons to use upon him, only her quick mind and her sharp tongue, but a tongue could be a deadly weapon if you discovered where a man was tender.

At last she slept again. Only then did he trust himself to draw near the bed to gaze down upon her. "Sleep well," he murmured, "for once you're mine, I'll never let you sleep again."

27

Eleanor awoke early when sunlight came through the windows of the lodge, yet Simon had already shot and plucked a pheasant and had it simmering on the hearth with some delicious-smelling herbs.

She struggled up in the bed and saw with relief that he was dressed. He came to her immediately with hot broth, and her belly gurgled loudly at the mere thought of its tempting aroma and taste. "I'm sorry I slept so long, we should be on our way back to Chepstowe."

"Not today," he said. "The sun is warming up; we are in for a great thaw. By tomorrow all traces of the blizzard will be melted away. By tomorrow your strength should be back to normal," he added.

"I'd rather go today. Bette must be frantic about me, and it is unseemly for us to be alone here like this."

"The decision is mine," he said quietly.

"Why so?" she challenged.

"Because I am the man, you the woman." She saw his face carved in stone, the low tone of his voice ominous. "It will be ever thus," he warned her.

She lowered her thick lashes over her defiant eyes. She was

determined to have her own way, but realized she would have to go about it in a subtle manner, for there was a hidden devil in each of them that set off sparks whenever they were together. She needed two things at the moment to strengthen her position: food and clothes. Daintily she picked up the bowl of stew and cup of broth he had brought to her and slowly devoured every drop. The man was a sorcerer, a warlock.

Making her voice sweetly deceptive, she said, "May I at least get dressed, my lord earl?"

For a moment she saw the raw need in his eyes, then they softened and he said, "I've heated water so you may bathe. Your clothes are dry. You may be private while I chop wood enough to last us until tomorrow." He put on his heavy leather doublet and picked up the axe.

The first thing she did was help herself to another bowl of stew. Amazingly she had never felt better in her life. She bathed quickly, gingerly washing the shallow wound on her head, and was pleased that it neither hurt much nor bled. She gathered up her clothes and saw that something had fallen from de Montfort's doublet. It was her silk stockings. What in the world was he doing with such intimate articles? She'd make sure he did not get his damned hands on them again, she thought as she sat on the bed and drew the stockings up her legs. She took the garters from her wool hose and slipped them up past her knees. She was admiring her legs when she thought she heard him returning. Hastily she pulled on her gown and stuffed her wool stockings and undergarments beneath her pillow.

He threw down a stack of logs in the lean-to but did not enter the cabin. She watched from the window as he felled a young oak and methodically swung the ax until it was cut into uniform lengths. He was so untiring, perhaps he did not need sleep. He was extraordinary in every other way, so why should that surprise her? She gazed out over the landscape. The sun was brilliant, reflecting off the snow. The wind had dropped considerably. The icicles had all melted from the roof and the snow had turned soggy from the warmer air.

He was right, it would all be gone by tomorrow, but she had no intention of spending another night under the same roof as the devastating Earl of Leicester. A shiver ran over her as she remembered how he'd looked, naked save for the black leather that sheathed his manhood. She felt powerless against the intense sexuality of the powerful man. "I'll not love again," she said aloud. "It hurts—it ends in loss. I want no more losses!"

She moved restlessly to the kitchen and made herself some herb tea. No one had ever wanted her for herself . . . until Simon, her traitorous mind added. How ironic life was. The only one who had ever really wanted her could not have her. She had not even thanked him for saving her life, for saving her horse. And she would not thank him either. She'd be damned if she'd be beholden to him, grateful to him. She would be a thankless bitch, so he might as well leave her alone . . . but she knew he would not.

Eleanor heard him at the door and lay down atop the bed to pretend sleep. She lay still and forced herself to breathe very slowly. She heard him tend the fire and knew his clothes must again be soaked through from the melting snow. Any minute now he would strip them off again.

She peeped through her lashes after a while and saw his naked back and buttocks as he knelt at the hearth to spit a brace of game birds for roasting. Then he stretched his enormous length before the fire in a prone position, his dark head resting upon his folded arms.

Eleanor forced herself to lie still waiting for him to drowse. She reasoned he had had little sleep in the night and had expended a lot of energy on very little food. When she heard his breathing slow to an even, steady rhythm, she cautiously got off the bed. When he obviously did not hear her rustling about, she picked up her cloak and went through the door, opening and closing it as softly as she could. Immediately putting her hands upon her mare's muzzle to keep her from whickering, she whispered, "Softly, softly, my beauty."

She struggled with the saddle and realized she had used up most of her strength. She walked away from the lodge, leading her mare through the deep wet snow. Already her boots and the bottom half of her gown and cloak were soaking wet. She leaned weakly against the warmth of the horse, wondering how she would summon the strength to put her foot in the stirrup and throw her other leg across.

Suddenly she heard the door of the cabin thrown open. Simon's naked body filled its frame. In a panic she tried to mount. Breathlessly she pulled herself into the saddle. As she straightened she looked into a hard, dark face, rigid with anger.

He grabbed the bridle and jerked her from the saddle. She kicked out at him and screamed, but it was a wasted effort to think she could pit herself against his strength. He managed woman and horse, one in each hand, until they were back inside the lean-to. His grim silence alarmed her. She feared his fury was so great he did not trust himself to speak. Finally he did. "Get inside," he ordered, low.

"No! I'm leaving! I'm going back to Chepstowe now. Look at yourself!" she cried, and swept her hand to indicate his naked body, tattooed with dragons, his weapon encased in its black leather sheath.

His voice came like the crack of a whip. "Do not speak again until I give you leave. Do you understand me?" She knew his anger and worry combined to make him capable of violence. His ruthless black eyes told her clearly he was ready to beat her.

She stood mute, unable to disobey him.

He unsaddled the mare, fastened her securely, then covered her again with the warm blanket. Then he threw open the door, roughly pushed Eleanor inside, and kicked the door shut behind them.

Her wet cloak slid from her shoulders and lay where it fell. She was shivering from cold and fear, afraid to speak. He dragged her before the fire. "Remove your boots!" he ordered. With shaking hands she bent and did what he commanded. He picked them up in one hand and violently threw them across the room. She jumped as they crashed against the wall.

He stooped to lift the hem of her sodden gown. She half raised her hand thinking to prevent him, but the fierce warning that flashed from his black eyes made her abandon any resistance. He lifted the gown above her thighs to reveal silk-clad legs and no other undergarment, no barrier to keep him from her. The firelight played over her bared thighs and the black curls between them.

Stunned, he lifted her skirts higher. Blazing anger turned instantly into blazing passion. "Christ, English." He groaned. His fingers raked through the tight curls. As she shivered he pulled off her wet gown and carried her to the bed.

"No!" she cried.

"Not a bloody word!" he ordered. He pulled back the covers of the warm bed and jerked his head in a wordless command. Slowly she slipped inside and Simon followed her. He pulled her hard against him, his arms molding her body to his. He held her there imprisoned until gradually her body warmed and her shivering ceased. Her heart hammered and as she lay with her cheek pressed against his chest, she heard the slow, strong thud of his heartbeat.

For one terrifying moment she feared the exertion of struggling with her and carrying her through the snow while he had been stark naked would prove too much for him and he would die. Then she realized that was completely irrational. It was a ghostly finger of fear from her past.

She began to giggle nervously. His lips brushed her temple. "Kathe . . . what?" Her name was a caress.

"Oh, Sim," she whispered, "I am ridiculous . . . I thought I had overtaxed you."

Now that they were warm, he lifted the covers back so he could see her body. She held her breath as she watched his hands skim down her curves and his long fingers sought between her legs. He stroked her there gently, watching her face intently, and held her firmly when she tried to pull away.

Her face showed surprise and clearly told him the sensations he evoked were new to her. With the pads of his fingertips he stroked, then circled the tiny bud of her womanhood. At last he saw the dawning of pleasure. She parted her thighs a little and he knew that she was beginning to trust his touch. He knew his size, his swarthy looks, and his temper must be extremely intimidating, yet she stood up to him on every occasion. Her own pride and temper matched his, yet he would not have her any other way. All he had to do now was teach her to match his passion. Think of the sons he would get on her. He warned himself to go slowly.

Eleanor thought, He is ruthless, but do I want a gentle man? She wanted to arch her mound of Venus into his hand. His strong fingers sent threads of hot pleasure to her woman's core, blotting out everything save the unique sensations.

A look of great surprise suddenly came into her face and her soft lips parted. He was aware he had awakened something only he could satisfy. Then she gave in to the sensual arousal and arched high into his hand, crying "Sim, Sim!"

He looked down at her in wonder. "Have you never done this for yourself?"

She shook her head and hid her face against his shoulder. He brought her palm to his mouth and his tongue traced the love line in it. She became aware of the scent of the man who held her—leather, horse, male flesh. She felt his breath upon her skin and knew she wanted this man more than she had ever wanted anything in her life. The thought shook her and frightened her, because she had surrendered herself to her need for him.

A voice within asked, "Who are we hurting?" A louder voice said, "The scandal will rock England." The first voice asked, "Who will know?" The louder voice replied, "None must ever know."

Simon's excitement sent the blood beating in his throat and in his engorged shaft. He schooled his ardor, banking the fires of his raging desire as carefully as he had banked the fire on the hearth. She was not yet strong enough for him to make love to her. When they came together it would be no pale, tame imitation of love. It would be a fight to the finish between them— winner take all. It would be cataclysmic. "Look at me, love," he coaxed.

Shyly she lifted her face from his shoulder and lifted her lashes.

"There is no shame in what I just did to you."

"My vow," she whispered.

"We broke no vows . . . yet," He changed the subject. "I want you to rest. Store up all your strength for the journey back to Chepstowe. We will leave at dawn. Your mare had no fodder today, but she will manage well until tomorrow. She will still be able to carry you down the mountain if I lead her."

"You cannot walk all that way through such heavy drifts."

"By then most of the snow will have gone. The temperature has risen steadily all day."

"Have it your way," she said, glad to leave the decision to him.

"I intend to," he murmured, grinning down at her. "I think you would rest better if I left the bed."

She nodded her head, then bit her lip. "When we are back at Chepstowe, you must keep this secret. Please promise, Simon."

He slipped from the bed. "Close your eyes and stop worrying." She sighed and did as he commanded, not noticing that he had not promised a thing. At dawn he awakened her and brought her dried clothing to the bed. He picked up her shift and slipped it over her head. Her cheeks were pink with indignation. "I can assure you, de Montfort, I don't need you to dress me. I feel perfectly recovered, sir."

He hid a smile. She was back to defying him and that was good. With a straight face he said, "I just want to make sure you put on your undergarments today. To think of you naked beneath your gown drives me insane. I could not be responsible for my actions unless these hands pull on your woolen hose."

She slapped his hand away, knowing if he put those damnably attractive hands upon her, she was the one who would not be responsible. He carefully rolled the wolf pelt and snow-hare skin and attached them to the saddle. She wondered when he'd had time to clean and scrape them so they could cure and felt a pang of guilt as she realized he'd done it while she slept.

Outside it was a beautiful autumn day. If she had not lived through the nightmare of the early blizzard, she would not have believed it had happened. The ground was exceedingly soggy but only the merest traces of snow lay beneath the thick trees. Meltwater ran in rivulets down the mountain path where he led her, and it seemed that at every turn they startled wildlife that had ventured from their lairs and burrows to feed before the next heavy snow blanketed the land.

Flights of swans and herons were leaving for their winter

feeding grounds and the earl remarked, "The hunting will be excellent for the next few days."

She remembered how much William had loved to hunt in Wales and how he'd insisted she hunt at his side. "Mayhap I will join you tomorrow," she said, like a true-born member of royalty bestowing her favors.

He grimaced. "Women are not much use in the hunt."

She flared. "Damn your eyes, de Montfort, you think women are only of use in bed!"

He gave her a level look. "Very few actually, unless they have been schooled by a connoisseur."

"Oh!" she cried. Her mare misstepped and she bade him, "Watch where we are going. I swear you are the poorest lackey I've ever had."

No woman had ever spoken to him so before. "Lackey?" He raised a lazy brow. Her insolence matched her pride. He knew he would rather have a fiery woman to subdue than one who obeyed his every command, but this was going to be his woman, his wife, and he intended to start out as he meant to carry on. This exquisite creature had been called the King's Precious Jewel all her life, and he intended to give her a little taste of what it would be like if she were insolent to him.

"I am afraid we overestimated the stamina of your little mare, Eleanor. You will have to walk if you don't want to lame her."

She swiftly examined his features to see if this was a deliberate taunt. He called her Eleanor whenever he was annoyed with her. When she saw no teasing light in his eyes, she was immediately contrite for burdening her mare. He made no offer to lift her down, for he knew she would use such an opportunity to disdain his help.

She slid from the saddle and sank ankle-deep in mud. His long strides urged the horse to keep up with him, but Eleanor had to struggle and very shortly the hem of her gown and cloak were bedraggled with mud and the slush splashed up her legs to soak and befoul her stockings. She almost called out to him to ease the pace, but just then her foot slipped upon the slate rock and she sprawled headlong into the mire. She picked herself up quickly before his eyes could sweep over her with amusement, but she was too late.

"Hunting with you would be a slice of heaven," he said blandly, and moved off again.

She trudged on uncomplaining until at last the massive stronghold of Chepstowe loomed ahead. She bit her lip. He'd succeeded in shredding her pride before his, but she could not bear to walk into Chepstowe like a subdued captive. "De Montfort, do not make me walk in."

He turned and bestowed a look of admiration upon her. Then he carried her to the mare and lifted her into the saddle. By way of explanation he said quietly, "If you attempt to control me, Eleanor, you will be in for a battle royale."

She lifted her pretty chin. "I'll fight, if only for my amusement. I'll test my mettle and sharpen my skills upon you."

28

♛

When the men of Chepstowe's garrison and the stable-men and grooms saw the tall Earl of Leicester leading the countess into the bailey, they could not hide their admiration for his courage in completing what he had set out to do. Here was a man indeed. In their eyes his worth went up a hundred-fold. His destrier had returned two days since with the hounds, one of them wounded. They had thought never to see him again.

The heavy front door opened and Bette rushed out, crying "God be praised. I'd given you up for dead after all this time."

Eleanor waved her hand as if her woman was making a mountain from a molehill. "I was perfectly all right. De Mont-fort found me at the hunting lodge, where I told you I would shelter if the blizzard returned."

Simon did not contradict her, but he followed Bette out to the kitchens where she went to order a meal be prepared. He held his hands out to the blazing fire and said, "Cosset her a little. She's had a hard time of it."

They went their separate ways to bathe, change, and eat. Then Eleanor rested and Simon tended the horses and talked with the men of Chepstowe. They tested his ability with the longbow, and when he proved his skill were delighted when he organized a hunt for the morrow. He ate the evening meal with the Welshmen then joined Eleanor and Bette in the hall where the women sat before the roaring fire listening to a minstrel. He pulled up a chair and stretched his long legs to the flames, content to watch the firelight flicker over Eleanor's beautiful features.

They began to banter with each other, striking sparks in verbal challenge. Bette soon realized there was sexual tension between the couple and excused herself to brew Eleanor some herb tea.

"Surely your palate prefers something stronger than tea," he challenged.

"I am unused to wine," she said repressively.

"Order us some, or are you afraid it will put fire and passion in your blood?"

"Your demeanor is ever assertive and swaggering. You speak as if you expect to be obeyed," she pointed out.

"I do," he asserted.

"In any case, I have always had fire and passion in my blood without wine. You forget I am a Plantagenet."

"If I forget, you will remind me, Princess," he said, slanting a mocking black brow.

"You can convey lust with the lift of an eyebrow," she accused.

"I intend to lift more than an eyebrow," he said with a leer.

"You are disgusting," she said, glancing about to see if the servants overheard.

"You put a man's mind on bed," he told her.

"Hush! Have you no discretion? Your tongue will brand me wanton with such loose talk."

Her words inflamed him. He stood to tower over her, not knowing if he could keep his hands from her. "My tongue *will* brand you. It will scald you when I make love to you," he promised. Blood of God, the fire was snaking through his loins.

With alarm she saw a servitor approach with wine, and Bette was returning with her tea. "How dare you stand so close to me?" she hissed.

"I dare anything, English. Do you want me to carry you up

to bed? Have a care, lady, lest I brand you my woman before the whole of Chepstowe."

She was breathing deeply to calm herself as she took the herb tea Bette handed her.

The last thing he wanted at this moment was to fight with her. She was ravishing and he wanted her desperately. She saw him reach for her and in desperation she deliberately let the steaming tea slip from her hands. He didn't even flinch as the scalding liquid splashed over his hand and thigh, but she saw the need in his eyes turn to rage and it filled her with satisfaction.

"I came all the way to Wales to avoid you, my lord," she said, not caring that Bette heard. "Now you are forcing me to retire to bed to avoid you."

"Rest assured, lady, that if I willed it, I would share your bed"—his eyes flicked over Bette—"as I've shared it twice before." It was his turn to feel satisfaction.

Eleanor fled the hall. Later Bette kept a wise silence as Eleanor paced about her chamber, calling de Montfort twelve different kinds of villain. "He has a bronze fist inside a velvet glove. He needs to exert control over even the primal forces around him," she muttered as she remembered his triumph over the wolf and the blizzard. "He enjoys command so much, he would like to control the universe. Well, he won't control me. I won't buckle under to his lechery. The wretched man will not leave me alone. He pursued me to Odiham, then he pursued me all the way to Chepstowe. He's like a thorn in my side, ever pricking me to remind me of his presence."

"Hush, my lady. Do not fret so. There are only my eyes to see, and you know my lips are sealed."

"Thank you, Bette. I wish I could rid myself of the brute."

But in the morning when she discovered the Earl of Leicester had gone off hunting for the day and taken the entire garrison of Chepstowe with him, she was livid.

"This is damnable, beyond all!" she cried. "He knew I wished to join the hunt. I hate being cooped up when the herons are on the wing and the roe deer are running."

Bette rolled her eyes. How could she call herself cooped up when she had not been back from the dangerous wild mountains a full day? "I don't think the earl's intent was cruel, my lady. I think it was kind. He told me you had had a hard time of it. He left you at the castle today so you could rest and regain your full strength."

Eleanor knew a restlessness she could not explain. She talked to the Welsh women of Chepstowe who showed an open curiosity about her beautiful clothes, and she admired the cloth they wove, especially the scarlet wool they made into skirts and warm capes. She inspected the kitchens, watching the baking and cooking of the strange dishes and tasting everything that went into them. She talked with the steward and the scribes, and they showed her the books William had collected from different parts of Wales. She spoke to the minstrel and asked him if he would come back to Windsor with her to be part of her court.

When the first shadows of the afternoon began to gather, she retired to her chamber to bathe and choose a gown for the evening meal. There was no mistaking the sounds of a returned hunt. Horses, dogs, and men tended to be noisy whenever they were grouped together, and whether the men were French, English, or Welsh they shouted, they laughed, and they cursed.

The hall was busy when she came down the stairs dressed in the striking deep-blue velvet with her sapphires blazing about her throat. Every male eye admired her beauty, every man of Chepstowe envied de Montfort for whatever was between him and their countess, yet none would have wanted her for his woman. There was too much fire in her, too much passion. Eleanor Plantagenet was too willful, too beautiful, too extravagantly expensive for their tastes.

As Simon watched her descend the stairs, he knew he wanted her exactly as she was. She looked down at the powerful man. He had a masterful stance. His strong presence marked him as a leader. She thought, He does not really want me to buckle under to his will, he just wants a challenge.

She held up her hands for silence. "I have no doubt the hunt was successful, so I would like all of you to dine in the hall tonight. We will celebrate."

On cue the servitors hurried in to set up the trestle tables, throw logs onto the fires, and hand the men leather horns filled with October ale.

Simon's eyes kindled as he smelled the delicious roasting meats. "Thank you for the warm welcome."

With exquisite sarcasm she said, "We are playing our roles to perfection. The lord and master returns with his bounty; the subservient woman stays behind tending the kitchens."

His eyes swept down her body taking in the velvet and sapphires. "You make a magnificent chatelaine."

Her eyes blazed. "I would have much preferred to go hunting."

His black eyes held hers. "I don't believe it is the hunt you enjoy. Even now you recoil from the blood on my clothes. I shall go and change immediately. I believe you love being astride a good horse with the wind whipping your cheeks and hair. I believe you are a nature lover, enjoying the seasons to the full, watching birds take flight rather than watching them fall to the hunter. That is why you are such a poor falconer."

"A poor falconer?" She gasped.

He shrugged. "You always manage to let your bird of prey escape into freedom." When she opened her mouth for a scathing retort, he held out his hand. "A truce, Eleanor. Tomorrow promises to be a glorious autumn day. Will you ride out with me?"

She stood on the third step from the bottom of the staircase, their eyes on a level. He was actually asking her rather than telling her. Finally she placed her hand in his and said, "It would be my pleasure, sir."

He raised her hand to his mouth and playfully bit her fingers. She snatched her hand back immediately. He threw back his head to laugh and exposed white teeth and a powerful corded neck.

When he joined her at the table he was garbed in black, his linen immaculate. No trace of leather or horse clung to him, only the clean, fresh smell of his shaving soap. In spite of herself she enjoyed watching him eat. He had a true man's appetite, large and healthy. He began with fish, followed by a brace of partridge, then helped himself to a platter of succulent venison. His eyes told her how attractive he found her. "You look as fashionable as if you were attending a royal banquet rather than a plain meal with your people. These Welshmen have never before beheld the likes of you."

"Some of their clothing is quite beautiful. I admit to lusting for one of their scarlet wool cloaks."

"The color would suit you to perfection. So rich, so proud, so bold, so incautious. 'Tis the color of blood."

"Then it should suit you better than I, sir. As a war lord your whole life has been blood. You revere battle and bloodshed. It is your passion. It is what makes you so vibrantly alive. If you had been born in Rome, you would have been a gladiator."

He stared at her in disbelief, then he said quietly, "Eleanor, if you believe that, you do not understand anything about me. War is hell. Battle is a living nightmare." He hesitated, wondering if he should reveal the horrific details or keep her in ignorance. He decided she was woman enough to hear the truth.

"The smells are obscene—the hot, metallic scent of blood, the discharged excrement, the smell of vomit caused by panic. But the smells are as nothing compared to the sounds. The deafening crash of weapons, the thunk of arrows sinking into flesh, the sobs of the frightened, the moans of the maimed, the screams of the berserk sicken your very soul. Worse than the smells and the sounds are the pain and discomfort. Your own sweat runs into your eyes to blind you. Death attracts clouds of flies, which stick to your skin and feed on your wounds. Your garments, wet with sweat and blood, rub your skin raw. After a few hours the weight of your weapons is bearable only because your mind is numb with exhaustion as your feet slide in brains and guts from dawn to dark."

Her eyes had widened, her nostrils flared.

"You've heard the word 'bloodlust'—do you know what it means? A good leader of men must not allow them the spoils of war. He must control them so they do not rape women until they die or cut off their breasts or use a head for a football."

Her face had gone white, her hand had gone to her throat.

"Eleanor, that is why there is nowhere in this world I would rather be than with you. You are the one who will bring joy to my life. You will be my salvation."

"Are you trying to tell me you are a warrior who does not believe in war?"

His features were as hard as granite. "Sometimes war is a necessary evil. But if a land is ruled firmly by a strong hand, if the laws are just and fair for peasant as well as noble, then the realm prospers and there is no need for dissension."

"What if that realm is attacked by another who covets such prosperity?"

"That is precisely when it becomes a necessary evil. But every man is willing to take up arms to protect what is his, and it usually ends in a quick victory."

She knew he spoke of countries and wars in the abstract, yet his words pointed up exactly what was wrong with England. King Henry was weak and feckless. He ignored the laws of the Great Charter and squandered fortunes on his favorites. There was always dissent in the land and the barons refused to fight for their king and country.

"The strong leaders are gone and your brother is listening to false council that could destroy the realm. Already the Irish shout 'Too many kings in England' when they speak of Henry's and his wife's relatives."

Eleanor pushed back her chair. "I think I shall retire now, my lord. You have given me much food for thought."

He sighed dramatically. "What good is a woman with her mind on politics when mine is on bed?"

She almost slapped him, then suddenly her laughter rang out as she realized he was teasing the life out of her.

29

The next day she could not help but be pleased when he showed great impatience to be off on their promised ride. He knocked on her chamber door before she had finished her breakfast. "Slug-a-bed, the daylight will be spent before you are ready to ride." A scarlet wool cloak was slung across his shoulders and he held out another for her.

She was thrilled. "Oh, Simon, how lovely, thank you!" She snatched it up, threw it on, and twirled about for him to admire her.

"You look sinful," he said, winking at Bette.

She dug her fists into her hips and swaggered toward him, looking him up and down. "Splendor of God, de Montfort, have you any idea what you look like . . . six-and-a-half feet wrapped in a scarlet cape, topped by that wild hair, blacker than hell?"

"Please don't tell me I look like the devil." He grinned.

"No," she said studying him. "No, you look like a king . . . or a rebel, I cannot decide which." A shiver passed over her. Her words sounded prophetic, and she knew he was capable of being both.

While she pinned back her hair and pulled on her gloves, he

slapped impatiently at his boots with his heavy, short whip. The warm chamber seemed to cage him and she understood exactly how he felt, for she too needed an outlet for her energy.

"Ready!" she cried. As he led the way, the scarlet cloak swung to his heels, his spurs jingled, and his wide shoulders filled the entire doorway.

At the stables he took the liberty of lifting her into her saddle. He parted her cloak and his strong hands encircled her tiny waist. Her nipples ruched and she knew it was not from the cold but from his touch. When he mounted his black stallion he stood in the stirrups, and she knew he was going to give her a run for her money.

It was a glorious day. The colors of autumn were brilliant, all red, russet, and golden. The day had a prophetic air about it from the very beginning. Eleanor decided that if their time together was enjoyable and ended happily, she would tell him kindly but firmly and irrevocably there could never be anything between them but friendship.

The air was crisp and clear like rare wine as they galloped away from the castle. Within minutes they were submerged in a land that was untamed, untouched. Eleanor had always thought she was observant, but Simon's eye was so keen he saw things she would have missed. He flung up his arm to point out curly-horned Welsh rams high on a mountain ledge. She was amazed that he could differentiate birds in flight. He knew a hawk from a merlin, a falcon from a kite. They rode out from a wooded area into a clearing so fast it startled a roebuck with a full set of antlers. It poised majestically before leaping away. For the thrill of the chase they rode after it, their scarlet cloaks billowing like red sails in a seawind.

The path forked and they chose the high road up a steep mountain slope. Higher and higher they climbed until they touched the misty clouds. At the summit they poised side by side to look down in wonder. Before them was the vista of a valley, so hidden and secluded it seemed as if man had never set foot there since the dawn of creation. They laughed into each other's face and he saw the droplets from the cloud-drenched atmosphere clinging to her beautiful eyelashes like diamonds.

He heard it before she did. It sounded like a low, far-off

rumble of thunder. Then he pointed a brown finger down into the valley below and she saw something that truly took her breath away. It was a large herd of wild Welsh ponies. The leader had brought his mares and yearlings down from the mountains into the shelter of the valley before the next snowstorm. The scene was otherworldly in its primitive beauty, a sight to make your throat ache. To even glimpse them was a rare privilege, but they both had the urge to join the herd and become a part of it.

Together they bent low over their horses and urged them forward. It seemed like they were almost flying down the side of the mountain, then miraculously they were thundering along the valley's floor, flank by flank with the herd of shaggy wild ponies. Simon took a rope from his saddle and, keeping pace with the herd, managed to lasso a black mare. It fought and reared and kicked wildly, but Simon was out of his saddle in a flash, digging in his heels to bring the thickset animal to a stop. All Simon had to do was lift a brow in Eleanor's direction. Without words he questioned if she was daring enough to ride the untamed creature.

Eleanor needed no urging. In an instant she had dismounted and was allowing Simon to boost her onto the black pony's broad back. She grasped a handful of rope and a handful of mane and was off on the ride of a lifetime. Simon, again astride his destrier, galloped alongside her, grinning like a madman, assuring her he was there to help if need be. She was able to take only quick glances at him, but they were enough to tell her he rode like a centaur, that fabulous monster which was half man, half horse. Horse and man alike were enormous and powerful especially beside the ponies, but he had a fluid, natural grace that showed he was completely at home in the saddle.

Eleanor knew she couldn't stop the mare, but she also knew she had placed her life and her safety in Simon's hands and that he would be responsible for her. Finally he rode up close beside her and took the rope from her hands. The dragons upon his forearms bulged as his unbelievable strength slowed the black mare and finally brought her to a halt.

"Do you want to keep her?" he called.

"No! I want her to be free forever," she cried breathlessly.

With a quick flip he removed the rope and held up his strong arms to her. "Jump!" he ordered. She sprang from the mare's bare back into his waiting arms. The impact sent them sprawling to the ground, and he rolled over and over with her to cushion her landing. Eleanor lay on the hard ground with Simon de Montfort astride her. Never in her whole life had she felt so invigorated. He laughed down at her, knowing exactly how excited the experience had made her. She gazed up into his black, magnetic eyes with sheer wonder. He had seized the moment and made it happen for her. She somehow, some way wanted to do the same for him.

"Sim, Sim," she cried passionately. "To hellfire with the whole world! Be my secret lover."

He kissed her hard and swift, then they were back in their saddles, racing each other to see who could reach Chepstowe first. He allowed her to pull ahead for the sheer pleasure of watching her look back over her shoulder to see if he followed. They raced over the drawbridge, blind to the squawking fowl and gaping sentry. They rode into the stables and tossed their reins to an available groom, then, handclasped, they ran toward the castle. Before they went into the great hall they tried to compose their features and move more slowly and sedately. They walked across the hall to the stairs, she trying to be casual, he trying to be nonchalant, but their desire surrounded them, dizzying their heads, curling tightly, hotly about their vitals so that none seeing them could have been ignorant of what was about to happen between them.

They could not keep secret a second longer the hot desire that at last blazed up between them. No man or woman who saw their eyes meet, their fingers cling, could doubt that they were bound lovers about to claim each other.

At last, at last they were alone together in her bedchamber, the door secured against the world. She strained to him in her need, now that all barriers had been set aside, but Simon knew better than to take her in haste. "Softly, my love. Softly, slowly, come to me, bend to me, yield to me." His head dipped to place his lips against her throat and her head fell back allowing his mouth full rein.

His hands parted the scarlet cloak and he cupped her breasts until he could feel her nipples harden against his palms. Then he slid his hands over her tiny waist and down to curve about her round bottom as he pressed her against the demand of his groin. His fingers worked swiftly to undo the fastenings of her gown and slide it from her body, all the while watching her exquisite features for a sign of denial. When none came, he gently removed her undergarments and stockings, yet still she wore the scarlet cape to cloak her nudity.

She met his black eyes with a soft smile as his hands stripped her garments for their love play. Her breasts were ripe and thrust the cloak open to reveal the inside, swelling curves above the pale belly and inward curve of her waist. The cloak hung closed again over her long, slim legs, but her slightest movement parted the scarlet cloth to reveal the mass of black, silken curls between her legs.

His long-starved passion flared high as he gazed down at the small exquisite beauty. Again she knew a need for haste and reached inside his scarlet cloak to hurry his undressing. She had discarded all her reserve. This man was fully worth any risk. She felt devoured by his black eyes and realized that she desperately wanted him to think her lovely and to desire her at all times.

He aided her hands to remove his garments while at the same time he retained the scarlet cloak. His eyes saw how wantonly her breasts thrust from her cloak, almost touching his chest. "Kathe." He whispered the caress as he again reached inside the cloak to stroke and fondle the satin skin that had been denied him for so long. An urge to ravish her immediately flooded over him, but he checked it with his iron willpower. He parted his cloak and took her inside against the long, hard length of his body.

She gasped in disbelief as she felt the evidence of his arousal pressed between their bodies like a weapon molded from marble. He saw the flicker of fear in her eyes that he had known would be there when she learned his full size. He knew also that her fear was justified. Her only experience with intercourse had ended in death. He must overcome this fear, obliterate it completely, and in its stead produce a longing for him to make love to her over and over.

Added to this was the simple fact of his great size. While she was small and perfect in the extreme, his shaft was longer and thicker than that of other men. He was on the horns of a dilemma. Would it be better to make love to her while she seemed eager and willing and get the pain behind them—be cruel to be kind? He thought not. He must teach her how her body could give her pleasure and how his body could increase that pleasure a thousandfold and bring her fulfillment. "Kathe, sweetest love, let me hold you." He put his arm beneath her knees and swung her up into his arms, then carried her to a massive chair before the fire. He unfastened the ties of her scarlet cloak, and it fell to the floor with a whisper.

"My precious jewel, your breasts are absolutely perfect." He brushed the inside curves with the back of his fingers as if they were made of delicate porcelain, then he bent his lips to brush a kiss upon the tiny, budding crowns. With an effort he forced his attention away from the more intimate parts of her body, and his fingers threaded through her shining black curls. He took a strand of his own hair and blended it with hers. "See how exactly the color matches? You cannot tell where mine stops and yours begins when they are joined. Darling, when I make love to you it will be that way. Our bodies will become one."

She lifted her lashes to shyly look at their bodies. His seemed split in half by his scarlet cloak, half concealed, half revealed. Her bottom rested upon the thigh that was covered, her breast pressed against the side of his chest that was concealed by the material. In stark contrast, the other half of his chest was an immense slab of muscle covered by black hair and his naked thigh rose from the cloak, thick as a tree trunk and more solid than rock. "Sweet, sweet, explore me," he urged. "I want you to lose your fear."

Her hand moved to lift the scarlet cloth from his male center and her breath caught at her own boldness. Today he wore no black leather sheath to keep her eyes from seeing every detail of his manroot. It lay along his thigh, but the moment her glance fell upon it, it had a life of its own. It awoke and stretched like a great beast. Her eyes widened as she saw it rise up slowly, strongly, filling with blood. The shaft lengthened and thick-

ened, the head burst forth from its protective cowl in all its
blood-crimsoned glory.

In that moment he reminded her of his black stallion; both
were superb male animals.

"My little love, there is nothing to fear. I will be gentle and
playful. I won't take you like a stallion takes a mare."

Her eyes widened. Could he read her every thought? She
trembled slightly. "I once saw an Arabian stud force a small
filly. When he covered her, he bit her neck savagely and
screamed." She paused. "Yet ever after the mare followed him
faithfully."

"Someday, I promise you that you will want to make love
savagely, but this is not for now." He brushed his lips against
her temple. "However, if you feel like screaming or biting feel
free to do so. There are dozens of things I want to teach you
before you are ready for rough love."

"Sim, I'm ready for the first lesson," she teased, her eyes
sparkling with the excitement of doing something forbidden
and secret.

"The first lesson is the kiss. Like snowflakes, there are no two
kisses alike. Each is unique. The different kinds of kisses are
infinite." He lifted her hand to his lips and placed a kiss upon
each finger, then he opened her palm, placed a kiss inside, and
folded her fingers upon it to capture and hold it.

She smiled at the pretty gesture. Just then a beam from the
late-afternoon sun reflected through a windowpane, making a
rainbow arch across her bare breast. He covered it with his
hand and then of course the rainbow appeared to be on him.
"I'd best hasten with the kissing, we only have 'til dawn."

She laughed up into his black eyes and slipped her arms
about his neck, for didn't the sun still shine?

They exchanged over a thousand kisses. He began with tiny,
quick kisses to her temples, eyelids, nose, and finally the corners of her mouth. His lips kissed her hair, traced along her
cheekbone to her ear, then down against her throat. She could
not wait for his lips to touch hers, then when they did she could
not wait for the kisses to lengthen.

For a whole hour they lost themselves in the bliss of slow,
melting kisses. Never once did he try to part her lips with his

tongue and force it into her soft exciting mouth. Simon knew that love talk brought a woman to her rapture more quickly than silence, so he held his lips against her throat and murmured, "You have the most wondrous hair I have ever seen, and all men who lay eyes upon it must ache to caress it and play with it like this. Oh, love, you enthrall me. Your image is before me day and night. Your loveliness haunts me. I have an unquenchable thirst for you. When I see you across a room, I have to draw close to you, and then when I am close to you, I have an uncontrollable desire to touch you. I want to touch you all over. Here and here." He cupped her breast in his hand and caressed its pink tip gently with his thumb. "Your skin feels like creamy, smooth velvet in my calloused, rough hands."

"Oh, Sim, you have the most thrilling hands of any man alive. They are so sinfully attractive I fell in love with them months ago." She lifted one to her lips to kiss, but it was not enough for her. She suddenly lost all self-control. One by one she took each finger into her mouth and sucked upon it.

His shaft jumped at the exquisite sensations her sucking aroused, and she felt it seeking against her soft belly. Impatiently she unfastened his scarlet cloak and pushed it aside so she could touch every muscle upon the broad expanse of chest. "Please, Sim," she begged.

He placed his lips upon hers and murmured, "Little innocent. You think you are ready, but you are not." With the tip of his tongue he traced the outline of her lips, then when she parted hers in a sigh he allowed the tip of his tongue to slip into her mouth. He went deeper, caressing her tongue with his, tasting the nectar of her honey-drenched mouth. Her fragrance made his senses reel. His mouth became more demanding, then suddenly she began to kiss him back. Their kisses went on and on, fierce kisses, wanton kisses, sensual kisses, erotic kisses, until finally their lips felt bee-stung, swollen with love. Yet still they needed more.

She began to move against him restlessly until his large, warm hand reached between her legs to stroke and play among the silken curls. "Mmmm." She sighed, arching into his beloved hand as he teased the tiny folds with one strong finger. Very gently he allowed his finger to enter her and to rapidly stroke in and out. "Does that feel nice, darling? Do you want more?"

"Mmmm, yes please." She breathed raggedly.

When he could feel her begin to get slippery, though she was still impossibly tight and small, he slipped his finger from her delicious sheath and licked off her sweetness.

"Sim," she protested.

He whispered, "Don't move, I'll be right back." Her arousal was progressing as he had fervently hoped, yet still he knew there was a great deal of pain ahead of her if he did not take steps to deaden it a little. He poured a large goblet of wine and returned to the chair. He scooped her onto his lap, carefully positioning her so that his erect arousal rested in the hot cleft between her legs. Then he lifted the goblet to her lips and urged, "There is nothing like dragonsblood to make you relax enough to let down the last barrier."

She drank deeply and felt the effect immediately. It was as if the wine turned to fire as it ran along her veins, igniting tiny flames that heated her entire body with magic, liquid heat. Again she raised the goblet to her lips and again quaffed deeply for the pure pleasure of feeling her blood rush into her cheeks, her throat, her breasts, her belly, and her loins.

Simon dipped his head to take a mouthful, then he kissed her deeply so they both tasted the rich sweetness that flavored their mouths. When his tongue thrust inside she moaned with need and moved in a way that made her hot cleft rub up and down his long shaft. Her head fell back, her throat and breasts arched with her sensual movements. She was arousing herself to such heights that she began to kiss him wildly.

Her lips and tongue traced his throat, his collarbone, then she began to bite his shoulders, leaving tiny, crescent-shaped marks with her teeth.

He whispered, "I know a secret."

"Wh-what?" she said with a gasp between a kiss and a bite.

"Wine makes you amorous," he said with unconcealed joy.

"Not wine . . . dragonsblood, and you my dragon." She gasped, clutching his wide shoulders and trying to impale herself upon his weapon.

He swept her into his arms and stood up from the chair.

"Finish it," he directed, and held the goblet to her lips. She drained the cup then looked boldly into his black, magnetic eyes. She was learning the power of a woman's sexuality. With triumph she knew all he could think of was bed. Physically he was probably the most powerful man in the country, perhaps the world, and tonight she had more power than he. She could control him. She could make him do anything she desired.

Deliberately she wrapped her legs about his back. His hands went beneath her bottom cheeks to steady her, not to support her slight weight, for that rested wholly upon his rigid, pulsing erection. He walked with deliberate slowness across the room to the massive bed. Each step slid his shaft forward then backward along her cleft, which was now creamy with moisture.

Her nails dug into his shoulders as she tried to prevent herself from screaming with excitement. Just as they reached the bed her anticipation became so frenzied, a scream gathered in her throat, but Simon quickly covered her mouth with his and took it into himself.

He rolled onto the bed clasping her to his heart. There was absolutely no way he was going to lie on top of her this first time. The difference in their size might make her feel suffocated, trapped, and he knew that she had lain helplessly imprisoned beneath William Marshal's body.

"Kathe, my own darling, I am going to let you be in control this first time." His flexed arms held her high above him. She looked down at the impossibly wide shoulders that took up most of the big bed. She gazed with dismay at the raw, male virility spread out beneath her and felt totally inadequate. "I-I don't know what you mean."

Her black, silken hair had tumbled onto his chest as he lay sprawled and powerfully lithe below her. "I mean I will let you set the pace. I will let you make love to me."

She gazed down at his dark face. He looked hungry as a wolf, ready to devour her. "I don't know how."

He reached out a gentle finger and touched the curls between her legs. Her need was so great that she sucked in her breath and bit her lip. "I am so erect at the moment you will be able to position yourself above me and take at least the tip inside of you. Kneel above me. Put your knees on either side of my hips and gently lower yourself. Take your time, sweetest. Only do what makes you feel wonderful. When you are on top you can take as much of me or as little of me as you wish."

She held her breath and raised herself so that her sheath was directly above the tip of his phallus. Then she began to move down upon him. Her movements were slow and delicate. To her utter amazement her lover's enormous weapon began to bury itself inside her. She knew she would never experience anything more magnificent than the fullness she felt when Simon de Montfort was inside her body. "I did it," she whispered.

"You took about half of me," he said huskily.

"Is that all?" she cried in dismay.

"That is more than I ever dreamed possible for the first time, my little love. How I've burned to touch you inside."

She took a deep breath and then another, and then she allowed herself to relax her rigid muscles. When she did so he slid in deeper, and they both moaned at the unbelievable pleasure they gave each other. "Dear Christ, don't let me die of pleasure," Simon prayed.

Slowly, delicately she began to move upon him. Though he had an iron control, it did him no good at this very special moment. He too began to move. She rode him faster and harder, and he held her breasts cupped in his strong palms so they would not bounce until they became sore. Finally she arched backward and released a cry of shattering bliss into the still, dark air. He allowed himself the final rapture of letting his hot seed spurt up inside of her, then he gathered her close in a tender embrace while he experienced every last pulsation of her exquisite woman's center.

When at last they lay still with only their heartbeats intermingling, he poured out his love to her. "I have never felt this way in my life before. I love you so deeply from the bottom of my heart and the depth of my soul that you have made me feel immortal. You have given me this night and you have bound me eternally. I pledge my love to you now and forevermore. Kathe, you consume me, waking or sleeping. Now that I've tasted your exotic flavor, it will plague my every waking hour, every moment of my dreams. Never tell me you are regretful that we are lovers!"

He was amazed at the enormity of the love he felt for her. If it was the last thing he ever did, he would make her love him in return. Nothing would stand in his way. The love she had known before his would pale into insignificance and be blotted out to nothing more than a faint, forgotten reminiscence. The all-consuming love they would share could be experienced only once in a lifetime.

Strangely she was not guilt-ridden over what they had done, but she was frightened by the sense of perfection and rightness, the feeling of contentment that filled her heart, her mind, her very senses when she lay naked in this man's arms.

"You were made for love, made for a man like me. I will never regret that I forced you to become a woman rather than a chaste widow." He pushed up the pillows behind them and drew her up against him. Darkness had begun to fall and the shadows in the room did not allow him to see her as he wished to. He rose and lit the candles. "We will share a loving cup," he said, and refilled their goblet. They drank the wine as lovers have since the dawn of time, sipping from the same place on the rim, then shared lingering kisses with the taste of the dragons-blood rich upon their tongues.

His eyes, black with passion, devoured her. Then his fingers followed, touching her everywhere, tracing intricate patterns upon her silken flesh. His body was an open invitation to her curiosity, and her fingertips caressed his small, hard nipples, the crisp black pelt covering his chest, the line about his hips where his torso stopped being tanned from the sun. She was gathering courage to examine his maleness, but was not quite ready. Her eyes swept down his muscled thighs and legs, noting how the black hair covered the front, but not the inside of his thighs. Then she realized it was long hours gripping his saddle that made them almost hairless. He was more male than any man had a right to be, she thought, dismay mingled with awe and admiration. Her eyes at last could not resist exploring his sex. She saw a thick forest of black fur with what looked like a felled tree lying semihard along one thigh. Nestled beneath were two tight, hard spheres, as large as swan's eggs. The candleglow reflected upon the head of his manroot and she saw a pearly drop fall upon his thigh. Her finger flashed out to touch it and examine its texture. A rosy blush followed at her own boldness.

Sim laughed deep in his throat, boyishly delighted that she was unfamiliar with such things. She drew back from him and knelt upon the bed to gaze at him. She would never get enough of looking at him. He made other men suffer mightily by comparison. She was so absorbed in him she had no idea of the fetching picture she made with her wildly disheveled hair falling to her waist, her pink nipples impudently peeping through the black silk tresses. Her mouth was love-swollen and tempting as sin to the man who sprawled before her with night-black eyes.

He was so masterful and had a delicious way of enforcing his will that let others think they were having their own way. She decided to test her power over him. At that moment Simon was thinking if a man married for love, his woman could lead him about by his member.

"Sim, if I gave you an order, would you obey me?"

When she called him Sim, it raised goosebumps on his skin. "If I gave you an order, would you obey me?" he parried.

Her chin went up stubbornly. "I asked first."

He could not resist teasing her. "Well, let me see. If you ordered me to make love to you again, I would not obey you, but if you ordered me to leave your bed now, I would obey you."

She was so taken aback by his answer she forgot what order she had had in mind. "Why wouldn't you make love to me again?" she asked fearfully.

"Once is enough tonight. If I took you again and lost control, you wouldn't be able to walk tomorrow."

"Oh," she said, disappointed, "but why would you leave my bed?"

He jumped up and grabbed her. "To show you what we look like together in the mirror," he teased. He swung her high into the air and sat her upon his wide shoulders. She screamed and clung to his hair, thinking she would fall, but as he walked across the chamber to the mirror she forgot about falling. All she could think of was that his tempting hands were holding her legs and that her woman's center was rubbing against the back of his neck. He stopped in front of the mirror. "See, you are riding me again," he teased as she gazed at the unbelievable reflection they made.

"Let me down, you great ox." She laughed.

He flexed his neck muscles to tease her, then said, "Damn you, wench, it's just one order after another with you." He went down upon his knees so that she could dismount, but even then her toes were barely able to touch the carpet. He bent his head until she could climb off him, then he slipped an arm about her waist from behind and held her before him in front of the mirror. Her head only reached to his rib cage and she began to giggle at their disparity. Then wickedly she rubbed her bum against his groin and was thrilled that she had the power to make him grow against her.

Still laughing she asked, "And what was your order for me, my lord earl?"

"Marry me."

The laughter fled from her face. "Oh, Lord God, Simon, don't say that, please. We are to be secret lovers, no more."

He said lightly, "I will only ask you once a night." He could see that his words had shaken her.

She begged, "Pour us some more wine."

He shook his head. "No more dragonsblood for you, my darling, it will make you insatiable."

She twisted in his arms until her pelvis pressed against him. "Too late," she whispered as she went up on her tiptoes to lift herself onto his jutting erection. Simon carried her back to the bed and stood her upon its edge. Then he started at the top of her head and traced kisses down the length of her body. When he reached her mound of Venus, his hands went behind her bottom cheeks and he forced her forward to his mouth. At first his lips touched her as softly as a moth's wing. Then as his tongue thrust into her, learning the mystery of her treasured folds, she cried out in ecstasy and threaded her fingers through his long, black hair to hold him at her center. She thought wildly, His tongue is violating me as surely as if he were raping me. But she loved it, knew too she loved him. His mouth drew all her sweetness and all her strength from her, shaking her with a sensation that frightened her even as she surrendered to it.

Later, curled together in the big bed, she realized he had changed her life forever. Her body was still vibrating to his touch, and she realized how close she had come to missing out on experiencing the mysteries of true womanhood. He had commanded that she join him in the ancient act of worship of man for woman. She felt so safe and secure locked in his arms, entwined in the bed. She felt invincible, for now she had all his great strength to add to her own. In her innocence she thought she had conquered him.

Simon came up from the dark depths of sleep, dreading what she was saying. This woman he had marked for his own was no longer in her rightful place, locked in the curve of his arm. She was clothed in a bedgown, shaking his shoulder with frenzied hands. "De Montfort, begone! 'Tis almost dawn!"

The last stub of the candle flared and guttered as he sat bolt upright with his hands upon his knees. He looked into her face as the candle momentarily flared and reflected in her dark-blue eyes, making them look like cold, glittering jewels. She was almost distraught. "Devil take you, Frenchman, make haste to your own chamber!"

"I see my precious Kathe has evaporated with the mists of dawn and Princess Eleanor has returned with a vengeance." He threw back the bedcovers and planted his feet firmly on the floor.

A great wave of relief washed over her and she quickly averted her eyes from his nakedness.

"You fear your dragon has some mortal hold upon you," he stated knowingly. He snatched up his clothes and wrapped the scarlet cloak about his nakedness. That was her undoing.

She flew to his arms and begged, "Forgive me, Simon . . . this is the way it must be."

His mouth came down upon hers and his tongue plundered her mouth. The kiss was abandoned and ravenous. "Tonight!" he stated. "I'll have you or die." He had not closed the door before she threw herself in the warm hollow he had left in the bed to cry out her heart.

Before Simon could gain his own chamber he passed a worried Bette standing with a candle in her hand.

"Pretend ignorance," he murmured before he entered his lonely chamber. He stood at the window to watch the sun rise, but his eyes saw only the maddening creature he had just left. He knew she would be his wife. He knew as surely as if the book had been written and they were just acting it out, one page at a time.

Absently his fingers touched his chest where she had left tiny crescent teeth marks. His stark look eased and a curve came to his mouth. He had tried for a light note and he felt sure he had succeeded. It had been a playful interlude and he had allowed none of the dark fires of passion to consume them. He had been afraid that their first sexual encounter would intimidate and threaten her so that she would be unresponsive. He smiled, remembering, then he quivered. Lord God, if she had been this aroused the first time, what would the second encounter be like, or the tenth?

30

They did not see each other until early evening. Eleanor had fallen asleep exhausted and slept until early afternoon, then she fought a wine headache for the next two hours.

Simon had spent the day with the Welsh bowmen of Chepstowe and thought they would make a damn fine company of fighting men. Suddenly they came face to face in the great hall. No servant was close enough to overhear.

"My lord, I will retire early, my head aches."

"Good," he said with a wicked leer.

"No, no! You deliberately misunderstand. I cannot receive you tonight," she informed him imperiously.

Without another word he took hold of her by her tiny waist, set her aside out of his path, and strode from the hall. She stamped her foot in frustration as she watched his broad back disappear through the doorway.

At dinnertime she was ready for him, her words carefully chosen to keep him from her bower, but she dined alone. He had chosen to keep the company of the Welsh knights in their quarter. Eleanor was irritated, mostly with herself for being disappointed at not seeing him. After supper she bade her minstrel sing to her, but she was restless as a tigress and finally asked for wine. When the bard changed from a sad lament to a love song, she lost all patience. She drained the cup and went up to bed.

Simon was waiting for her in her chamber. "How dare you come when I expressly forbade you?" she hissed, but her throat filled with heartbeats at the sight of him.

"Never use that tone with me again, English." His face was dark, swarthy, carved in stone. He drew close and towered above her. God, how she wanted him, and he knew full well he had awakened something only he could satisfy. His façade of lust and danger did not scare her off. She was ready to handle the depth of his passions even though she would never give him the commitment he desired. He wanted her to wife, yet he knew he would never gain her consent. Her vows of perpetual widowhood were sacred to her. Forevermore she wished to be known as the Countess of Pembroke. As he had suspected all along, her mind was too strong to control, but he knew he could enslave her senses and her body. He intended to make her crave him like a drug. Simon had every intention of emulating Henry II. He would impregnate her and effect a *fait accompli.* He knew the way to enslave her was to concentrate on her body's pleasure, never his own.

His hand moved to the neckline of her gown and she braced herself, thinking he would tear it to the hem, but he reached out a gentle finger and traced the swell of her breast. "I want you beneath me tonight. Open to me in the bed."

"Sim." Her arms slipped up toward his neck possessively and she leaned into him sensuously, no longer denying the desire that blazed up between them. Her hands moved down to his chest, his shoulders, and she wished she was tall enough to touch the silk of his hair at the back of his neck. Again as if he read her mind he lifted her against him. As they fused their hungry mouths together her fingers threaded through his long, black hair and she held his head captive so that he could ravish her mouth.

His fingers were so maddeningly slow as they worked the fastenings of her gown—his beautiful fingers that made her body sing. It seemed an eternity before they were both naked, then Simon put her arms back about his neck, hungry for the clinging to begin.

"Warm me," she begged raggedly.

He was concerned immediately. "Why didn't you tell me you were cold, little one? I'll build up the fire."

She almost cried, because she could not wait, but remembered she had vowed to keep secret forever the effect he had on her when he touched her. As he knelt naked to repair the fire, her eyes licked over him like blue flames.

"I am never cold," he explained, "but from now on we will always have a good fire in our chamber so you may walk about nude." She watched the fireplay dance over his body and drew close to feel the warmth of the flames and the heat of her lover's powerful body. She rubbed her mons against him, wanting him to touch her there. Her body craved it and she did not care if it was right or wrong.

When he stood and reached out his hand to caress between her legs, she thanked God he could read her mind and gauge her needs so accurately. He dipped his head and his warm lips closed on her throbbing nipple. He teased and licked it, tonguing it playfully before his hot mouth began to draw upon it in earnest.

Instinctively she pushed her breast against his hot, loving mouth, and he sucked hard, loving the feel and taste of her silken flesh. Blindly she reached out a hand to cup his maleness, and he felt her slippery, satin center between her legs respond erotically to his fingers. She spread her legs wide apart and leaned into his hand, yielding to the questing fingers, begging him to enter her with any part of his body. He too leaned into her hand, loving the feel of her delicate fingers as they cupped, stroked, and fondled him until his erection jerked and bucked from the teasing. "Let's go to bed," he said with a husky gasp.

"Carry me as you did before," she begged.

His hands slipped over her pretty hips and he lifted her onto his shaft. She went wild, covering his throat, then his face with kisses, finally plunging her tongue into his mouth until his took over. Now it was her turn to suck and draw, and he knew she was aroused to such a pitch she would let him do anything to her. He lay her upon the bed and stood gazing down at her, wondering if he dared mount her and bury himself to the hilt.

She almost sobbed from wanting. "Sim, please, please," she begged. Her writhings made him feel primitive, savage, yet he knew he must not be brutal with her.

"Kathe, darling, listen . . . look at it, feel its size." He took her hand in his and guided it to his erection. "My cock is overlarge, darling. More than anything in the world I want you to be able to take me, all of me." His hands spread her silken hair across the pillows, then his fingertips manipulated her rose-tipped nipples until she was sobbing with need.

Her fingers seemed to have the ancient knowledge of Eve as they tried to lure him to impale her. Very deliberately he took one of her hands, which was curled about his shaft, and, holding it firmly, he laid it between her own legs. He took one of her fingers and whispered huskily, "I want you to know exactly how small and tight you are inside."

"Sim, no, I couldn't." She gasped, shocked at the idea of doing such an intimate thing to herself.

"Shh, darling, let me help you. Let me guide your finger." Her fingertip slipped inside her but she was fearful to push it deeper. Simon lay down beside her and gathered her close, then firmly he forced her finger all the way up inside her body. With one hand upon his enormous male organ, the other inside her own small sheath, she realized that if he had impaled her as she had longed for him to do, he would have torn her brutally.

"Oh, Sim, 'tis an impossibility," she cried.

"Nay, love, not impossible. But now you see why I need to arouse you to your limits." She made a move to withdraw her finger, but he held it in place firmly. "Just a moment longer, darling. You said you were ready for lessons, so let me instruct you." He moved his mouth to within a centimeter of hers and murmured, "When I kiss you and caress you, your body slowly begins to open for me." His lips touched hers and she felt a tiny flutter inside. Then his demanding tongue plunged into her mouth to taste her and her sugared walls expanded and contracted upon her finger. Gently he withdrew her finger and took it to his mouth. He stood up and moved away from the bed.

She cried out, "Don't leave me," and he murmured, "Dragonsblood, sweetheart." He was back instantly, urging her to quaff deeply. "The wine will heighten your desire, lower your inhibitions, and relax all the delicious little muscles up inside your love passage."

"Oh, Sim, I want to be able to satisfy you. Your male appetite must be enormous. I want to be able to blot out any other woman from your thoughts. Teach me everything, all the love tricks. Teach me forbidden things. I want to be everything to you . . . lover, mistress, whore."

"Wife," his brain screamed silently, "wife!"

He held the cup to her lips, until it was half drained, then he dipped his fingers into the goblet and began to anoint her silken skin with the sweet red wine. He brushed her shoulders, breasts, belly, thighs, and finally her pretty mons. Then with the deep erotic sensuality that was part of his nature he licked her body from her throat down to her tiny navel, then from her knees up to her tiny slit.

She lay before him in a silken, wanton sprawl, writhing and arching and thrashing her head from side to side. He knew she was ready. He towered above her on his knees, positioned her legs so that they were spread wide, then moved between them. Slowly, slowly he began to slide himself inside her. He moved smoothly, firmly, opening, expanding, stretching, filling her with his thick, long rod.

Her eyes widened with the sheer, unbelievable enormity and power of his maleness. And still he was not seated to the hilt as the smooth, marble-headed lance thrust home. His strong hands had begun to force her body closer to his, and while she could still feel him moving up she felt her chalice moving down to receive him. She was so aroused that the moment his tip touched the vault of her love chamber she began to climax. For a split second she closed upon him so tightly he cried out in pleasure-pain, then his seed burst from him in scalding spurts. In that moment nothing else in the entire world mattered to her but the feel of him inside her. When Simon de Montfort made love it was like a raging storm, and she felt as if she had been struck by lightning. Then she spun away into darkness.

For a moment he was horror-struck at what he had done, but

she came blinking back to consciousness in a few moments, sighing and clinging sweetly as if she would never have enough of him. "Kathe, beloved, I want you to sleep, rest . . . I know I exhaust you."

She curled upon his broad chest, her cheek pressed against his heart. The heavy, strong, sure beat of it lulled her to sleep. He had never felt so protective in his life. If any dared even try to take this woman from him, they would regret it with their last breath. If any dared to slander this woman for giving him her love, he would take a terrible revenge.

They savored each and every moment of the night's dark hours, but before dawn broke Simon arose and left her. He knew it would please her that she did not have to beg and entreat him to seek his own chamber.

The steward of Chepstowe approached the Countess of Pembroke after breakfast with a list of disputes that had arisen in the two years since Eleanor was last in residence. "I know the marshal allowed you to sit with him when he held court to settle disputes. These matters are only minor, my lady, but they have dragged on so long. . . ."

"Say no more. I should have attended to these things the moment I arrived. I will hold a court today. I will need a good interpreter and a scribe."

The steward departed then returned to the hall immediately. "My lady, your captain, Sir Rickard de Burgh, just rode into the bailey."

"Fetch him some warm food. If he spent the night in the Black Mountains, he will be near frozen."

De Burgh's spurs rang against the slate floor of the hall as Eleanor poured him ale and moved toward the chairs in front of the great fire. "Sir Rickard, I thought you would winter with Hubert. Is aught amiss? I hope you were not worried about me."

He gratefully took the warmed ale she held out and undid his hauberk. As always Eleanor was startled at the young man's beauty. "Amiss?" he repeated. "Everything and nothing," he said enigmatically, "and yes, I was worried for you. I had one of my dreams that you lay in the snow near death, but my own eyes tell me you have never looked healthier or happier."

"Nevertheless your dream was a true one. I behaved foolishly, but fortunately I was rescued. This Wales is such a paradox. Who, seeing the weather today, would believe the blizzard we had last week?"

"Before next week there will be another upon us," said Rickard. "I would prefer to escort you back to England before that happens, since I must return there myself."

"A mission for Hubert?" she asked shrewdly.

He veiled his eyes and said noncommittally, "I am only a messenger. I have missives from Hubert for the war lord."

"Simon?" she asked, blushing deeply.

"De Montfort, yes," confirmed the knight, sensing something in the very air.

Eleanor stood up quickly and busied her hands rearranging the pewter goblets which ornamented the mantel. Dear God, how did one go about hiding a liaison? Her mind flashed about like quicksilver. Then she turned with a cool smile upon her lips. "The Earl of Leicester is here, Rickard. He too had business in Wales and asked hospitality of Chepstowe. But perhaps your visions have already told you as much."

Both raised their heads as the unmistakable sound of horses clattered into the bailey.

Eleanor said, "I thought we were well off the beaten track, but if I am not mistaken we have yet more visitors."

Half a dozen horses came to a halt at the sight of Simon de Montfort's unmistakable form. The young captain of horse had been training under the war lord only a fortnight back. He saluted him smartly. "Sir, my lord earl, I had no idea you were in Wales."

Simon frowned. Had the king learned of Eleanor's destination and sent for her? He probed, "Riding hell-for-leather, your business must be urgent."

"Yes, sir. We have been sent to ready Chepstowe for its new owner. The king has given it to his brother, William de Lusignan."

Simon was stunned. In that moment he knew an urge to take the idiot king and pull him from his throne by the scruff of his neck. "The Countess of Pembroke is in residence. I do not envy you your job of evicting her."

The young captain swallowed hard. He had always heard rumors of the streak of madness in the Plantagenets. In this moment he believed it. He told his men to stable the horses and reluctantly went with the Earl of Leicester to face the royal princess. They found her sipping ale with Sir Rickard de Burgh.

Simon was surprised to see him, but he saw immediately that Eleanor must have informed de Burgh of his presence. The two men liked and trusted each other and greeted each other warmly.

Eleanor was horrified. She felt she wore a scarlet letter in the center of her forehead proclaiming her a whore. For Rickard de Burgh to find her here with de Montfort had been embarrassing, but at least he was a loyal friend and she could trust his discretion. One of the king's soldiers was another matter entirely, and she knew from the clatter of horses she had heard that he was not alone.

The captain went down upon one knee before her. The men in the room did not strike him as being irregular in any way. He knew Sir Rickard had been William Marshal's man and he simply thought Princess Eleanor was being guarded by Simon de Montfort because he was the strongest warrior in the realm. He trembled at the task before him. "Your Highness, please forgive this intrusion, but I am under orders from the king."

Eleanor's hand went to her throat. Dear God, surely Henry did not suspect what she had been up to.

"You have been absent from court and cannot know of the royal wedding."

"Royal wedding?" Eleanor repeated blankly.

"The king's brother . . . your brother, William de Lusignan, was given the heiress Joan Marshal in marriage."

Eleanor almost laughed aloud at the incongruous mating of the effeminate William and the haughty, wealthy Marshal niece, then her eyes narrowed. "I shall never acknowledge de Lusignan as my brother, Captain. Tell me what this has to do with me, pray?"

The young soldier swallowed hard and his voice came out

shrilly. "The king has given them Chepstowe as a wedding present."

She stared at him in disbelief. Then she threw her ale into the fire and swept all the goblets from the mantelshelf. She did not trust herself to speak. Her eyes swept over the three men present with loathing as if they were her enemies. All men were vile; she wished every last one an early grave. She departed the room as if their mere presence could contaminate her.

The young soldier rose to his feet and looked helplessly up at Simon de Montfort, whose face was like stone. "S-sir, I did not dare to disclose the king had also given them Pembroke."

"That is impossible. Eleanor is Countess of Pembroke," de Montfort stated.

The young soldier looked miserable. He was dizzy with relief when Sir Rickard de Burgh told him he should find room for himself and his men in the knights' quarters.

When they were alone Simon exploded. "He is the sorriest fucking excuse for a king England has ever known!"

"He's a puppet. There are too many kings in England. Peter des Roches, the Bishop of Winchester, is the power who merely lets Henry have all the glory. Then there are the Savoys whose greed is only exceeded by their numbers."

Simon nodded grimly. "Just when the queen's relatives had decided to divide up England for themselves, along come the king's with an insatiable thirst for land and titles." He shook his head. "The barons must be seething. Why do they not act?"

"Because they have no leader. Also because the king can be vicious. He stripped my uncle Hubert de Burgh of every groat. Even when the bishops made him return Hubert to sanctuary, Henry ordered that no food or water be allowed in. That he could inflict these cruelties is bad enough, but that he could inflict them upon a man who had been like a father to him shows exactly how venal he can be. I know Winchester poisoned William Marshal though I have no proof, but even if I found proof, Henry is too weak-livered to do aught about it."

Simon lifted his head ceilingward, thinking of the woman upstairs. "She loves Henry, even though he has taken this away from her, but if she knew he was connected to the marshal's death, she would hate him forever."

"Aye, I know she loves him, and so I spared her most of what he did to Hubert. I worry for her future," said Sir Rickard, low.

Simon de Montfort searched the knight's face for long minutes, then said, "Cease worrying. She is mine."

Rickard de Burgh was both relieved and alarmed. He could wish no stronger man to be her protector, yet he did not envy them the insurmountable opposition they would encounter on every side. He would not be presumptuous enough to offer the earl advice. Instead he handed him the missive from Hubert de Burgh.

Simon scanned the parchment, then deliberately put it into the fire. Rickard spoke quickly, thinking he rejected Hubert's offer. "He knows you are the only man strong enough and honest enough for the task. He also knows it will take time, but if you help him so that he is reinstated, he pledges to put all his wealth and all his power behind you." Rickard opened his hands in a last-ditch appeal. "I know it is difficult to choose sides."

Simon de Montfort looked him squarely in the face. "It is not difficult for me. I am ever on the side of justice."

31

A large party set out from Chepstowe to Windsor that early winter morn, for not only did Eleanor and Bette have de Burgh men and de Montfort men for escort, they also had the thirty Welsh fighting men of Chepstowe.

When the garrison had learned their overlord would be a hated foreigner, William de Lusignan, they sought out Simon, whom they had grown to respect, and asked him to take them into his service. He had explained that since they had pledged to the Earl and Countess of Pembroke, they would technically have to stay in Eleanor's service, but in actuality he would make them his men.

Then at the last minute, half the household staff had begged Eleanor to take them with her. She felt a small measure of triumph that when the usurper came, he would find the place almost deserted.

Simon grinned down at her as the cavalcade moved off toward the English border. "This will teach Sweet William not to piss in the tall weeds with the big dogs."

They arrived at Odiham just at nightfall. The small estate was near bursting at the seams to accommodate them all. Eleanor sent a silent prayer of thanks to William Marshal that he had given the deed to Odiham into her hand. This was one place they could never take from her.

In the small hours of the night when she thought they would be safe from prying eyes, she lay in Simon's arms begging him not to ride straight to the king and challenge him on her behalf. "Sim, please, if you champion me, our secret will be revealed. If you love me, let me fight my own battle with Henry."

He brushed his lips against her temple. When she called him Sim he could deny her nothing. Finally, reluctantly, he said, "I will take the Welsh fighting men to Leicester. What the hell will you do with all the servants you've attracted?"

"Leave most of them here, I suppose; I have all the Marshal servants from Durham House at Windsor."

"I don't suppose it ever entered your head, but where is the money coming from to support all these people?"

She moved playfully against him. "You always bring money into it." She bit his earlobe. "You haven't even asked me to marry you today."

"That's because I cannot bloody-well afford you," he whispered fiercely.

Suddenly she realized this would be their last night together if Simon was off to Leicester. How could she bear it? Now that they were at Odiham, they could not be as blatant as they had been in Wales, and she had forbidden him to come to her until two in the morning. He had come at one, making certain none save Bette knew of the secret affair. By four or five he would be gone, and she knew it would be like the sun going out of her life.

Simon de Montfort made her feel beautiful. She had been known as the King's Precious Jewel all her life, but now for the first time she actually felt like a precious jewel. She felt cherished. Now as he enfolded her in his embrace and brought her against his hard-muscled length, her lips parted in a low, wordless moan. His hot mouth nuzzled her throat and she thrilled to it, knowing any minute now it would come seeking her own mouth. She was breathless with anticipation, knowing it would begin softly, then it would tease, then it would grow hungry. She would open to him, let him feast upon her ardently, passionately until his needs became savage and demanding.

She reveled in her chosen role as woman when Simon de Montfort was the man. She was all sweet submission; he was all dominant conqueror. His lips traced molten paths downward and she quivered uncontrollably because she knew his goal. He tempted her to join him, to match him in abandon. Her response was so rich, so generous, it was more than he had ever dared hope in his wildest dreams.

Once she came up from the depths of sleep, feeling panic because she thought he had left her, but then she felt the powerful, hard body entwined with hers and she felt like purring. She was sorry she had disturbed him, but within seconds she was deliriously happy. He bathed her with his love until she was sated with contentment.

The next time she awoke he was gone. She wept bittersweet tears. The separation that stretched before her was insurmountable, yet what they had shared was so beautiful, it was incomparable.

She took three days to rest from her journey, but after that she became restless as a vixen in heat. Her anger at what Henry had done to her had no outlet. It festered and grew until she knew she must ride to Windsor and have it out with him.

When at last she faced her brother, she savaged him with her temper as she had when they were younger, but she was totally unprepared for his reaction. This was a new Henry, an older, wiser, and far more devious Henry, though she did not realize it.

"Ah, little cockroach, you are beautiful when you are angry, and I am so pleased to have you back I don't care what you say to me."

"Don't you dare patronize me! How dare you give that little queer *my* Welsh holdings?"

"Eleanor love, you do not know what it has been like for me. My domestic situation is a nightmare. Unless I give in to the queen over every little thing, she puts me through sheer hell. William is our brother, Eleanor. It is our duty to honor him with castles and land, but the Queen's Men are so jealous of our brother I had to effectively remove him from England. That's why I gave him Chepstowe and Pembroke. You will never venture into Wales, so I thought I would put it to good use."

She wanted to shout at the top of her lungs that she had just returned from Wales, but managed to keep her secret. "You cannot make him Earl of Pembroke, Henry," she raved.

"No, no. He shall never have the title, but your Marshal holdings are so vast and young Joan is legal heiress to some of them, you know, even though you don't like to admit it."

"If they are so bloody vast, how come there are not enough Marshal estates for me to have one?"

"They are vast, Eleanor; they cover a sixth of Ireland alone."

"What the hell good to me are lands in Ireland unless you will allow me the revenue from them?" she argued.

"I should have realized you would need money. My coffers are almost empty as usual so I cannot give you anything exorbitant. I'll tell you what, I will give you four hundred crowns a year in exchange for the Irish holdings."

She opened her mouth to refuse. She thought the revenues were worth at least double that, but there was no guarantee she would ever see a penny of them. Thinking how she needed money for her vast number of household servants, she reluctantly agreed to the pension.

"Eleanor, I love you. I swear to you on our father's grave if you ever need a favor from me I will grant it. Here, take my sapphire ring; you know how I prize it. It will be a pledge to you for the future."

"Oh, Henry, I swear you are the most exasperating brother a sister ever had. Give me the four hundred crowns today and I will say no more about it, for now. But you owe me, and I will hold you to it!"

"Sweet, I cannot give it to you today. Tomorrow I will demand the money from Parliament. It would help if you stayed here at Windsor and faced them with me."

Eleanor was torn. She wanted to return to Odiham to await Simon de Montfort. It might be possible to continue their liaison there, where her secret had to be guarded only from her own people. If she remained at Windsor it would be impossible, for the very walls had ears and eyes to say nothing of the fact that the place crawled with her enemies as well as bishops and clergy. She reluctantly agreed and thought to make short shrift of the King's council. However, it took over a week to assemble them, and the things she heard as she sat at her brother's side in the great council chamber alarmed her.

It was obvious they disliked their king. They disapproved of his every request and were hostile to Eleanor.

"You do naught but demand money, money, money from this Parliament. Your debts are so great now they are almost insurmountable. Last month alone you gave your brother William de Lusignan the richest heiress in England. Through her he received Pembroke in Wales and Wexford in Ireland. As if that were not enough, you gave him five hundred pounds a year pension and the castle of Goderich."

Eleanor's mouth fell open and she fixed Henry with a cold stare.

"Guy de Lusignan has returned home with his saddlebags filled with gold, and your half brother Aymer has been given so many rich churches he has appointed a steward to collect his incomes. Now you have asked that he be appointed Bishop of Durham, but we hope the church will refuse him. He is only an acolyte and is far too young and ignorant to be a bishop."

"Damn it, you forget I am the king!" Henry shouted in full rage. "This is my sister, Princess Eleanor Plantagenet! If you refuse to grant her this pension I shall appoint a new council!" he threatened.

"We will grant Eleanor the pension, but you must adhere to the provisions of the Great Charter. You must stop going into debt for foreign relatives and you must appoint responsible men to the posts of justiciar, treasurer, and chancellor."

Back in her tower in the Upper Ward, Eleanor was shaken at the open hatred the council had shown toward the king. He had finally promised to adhere to everything they asked, but once they were alone he had laughed and told her he was giving young Aymer the churches of Abingdon and Wearmouth and by hook or by crook would see him appointed Bishop of Durham. Obviously his preference had been transferred to his young brothers; no longer did he give all the plums to his wife's uncles.

Her longing for Simon grew each day. At night in her lonely bed, the hours were interminable. Every time she closed her eyelids, his powerful physique stood before her. His scent lingered in her nostrils, his touch was remembered by her very skin, and she knew she was starving for the strong security of his arms. The vast bed was so cold and lonely she hated the nights with a vengeance. Her very insides ached with the need to have him fill her with his long, thick manroot. She moaned softly, remembering his shaft deep within her, and hugged her breasts to still their ache. They had become so sensitive lately the fabric of her underclothes made her want to scream. She sent for wine to make her sleep, but its effect upon her was devastating. Her blood grew so hot she was in a fever to have her secret lover put out the fires that raged in her body.

When Simon de Montfort had not returned in a whole month, she was so angry she wanted only to strike out at him. Well, when he did manage to drag himself back to Windsor, she decided to show him that she did not need him.

The queen's birthday came at the end of October and was to be celebrated on All Hallow's Eve. Eleanor was surprised to receive a special invitation from the queen to attend the banquet and was immediately on her guard. She gave her sister-in-law an exquisite enameled girdle mainly from pride. She wanted her gift to be lovelier than any other, and at the same time she wanted to display her faultless taste.

When the queen unwrapped the magnificent jeweled and enameled girdle, she made much of the expensive present in front of Henry and said, "Ah, the little nun must have the seat of honor next to me."

The queen was dressed in glittering gold upon this birthday occasion, and Eleanor wondered how she could stand the damned color. She must have a score of dresses fashioned from the same cloth-of-gold, with only their ornamentation differing slightly. It was as if she had a compulsion to let everyone know she was the queen.

For the first time the queen appeared to be friendly toward her husband's sister and seemed to treat her graciously before the assembly. Actually the gossip with which she regaled Eleanor was all lewd and off-color, and Eleanor was at first secretly amused that she thought to shock the "little nun."

The queen began by telling Eleanor of all the bastards Thomas of Savoy had produced as well as the eleven legitimate children he had, and now his son Peter of Savoy was following in his footsteps sowing his own crop of bastards. From there she went on to tell Eleanor some of the obscene things Eleanor's father, King John, had done over the years, not leaving out the fact that her mother had been a whore from the age of fourteen.

Eleanor started to become uncomfortable as the queen continued. " 'Tis no wonder such a voluptuary spawned children with such peculiar sex lives."

"Peculiar?" repeated Eleanor, her color high.

"Well, take her son William de Lusignan. I pity poor Joan Marshal. Anyone can see he prefers to bed with men. And even Henry here likes to pretend he's my little dog. Just loves me to throw things across the bedchamber so he can retrieve them. Then he sits up and begs my favors."

"If he is the dog, then you must be the bitch," Eleanor said sweetly.

The queen laughed, but her eyes were anything but amused as she narrowed them dangerously. "Speaking of bitches, Isabella Marshal was your brother Richard's whore long before she got rid of her husband and forced Richard to marry her."

Eleanor for once was speechless for the queen was deliberately twisting things. It had been Richard who had done the pursuing in that relationship. Eleanor was on the verge of jumping to her feet and slapping the queen in the face when she said something that hurt Eleanor so deeply she was frozen to the spot.

"And then there is you, the real scandal of the family. Your insatiable sexual demands upon William Marshal were so excessive he actually died 'on the job.' "

Eleanor's throat closed and a great lump developed that threatened to choke her. Tears sprang to her eyes to blind her and a great roar came into her ears to pierce her very brain. Through a watery blur Eleanor saw Simon de Montfort enter the hall and walk a direct path toward her. Now she was really in a panic. Her mind screamed to him, No! No! No! She dashed the tears from her eyes and saw that he was not looking at her, but at the queen. He knelt before the woman in glittering gold, presented her with a birthday gift, and passed on down the hall.

Thank you, Simon, for not looking at me . . . thank you, Simon, for keeping our shameful secret . . . thank you, my darling love, for returning to me, her heart whispered.

"I should like to cause a scandal myself with that one," said the queen in a low, excited voice. "Did you notice how he paid court to me with those black eyes of his? He is waiting only for me to give him a signal." The queen shivered with desire. "He is desperately seeking an heiress because he needs money so badly. The European widows he woos are said to be so old and ugly he can only bear to fuck them in the dàrk."

Eleanor did not remember leaving the great hall; did not remember making her way from the Lower Ward in the chilly winter night through the Middle Ward and on into the silent Upper Ward. She became aware of her surroundings only when she realized she was sitting in her walled garden.

Her bare arms and shoulders were very cold. The night wind rustled the leaves about her feet and her nostrils picked up their pungent but pleasant fragrance. The stars hung like brilliant jewels in the dark sky, and she wondered briefly why there was no moon to shine its pale light upon her misery.

She did not see or hear him, yet she sensed his presence. "Kathe." The word stole to her softly. It was an endearment, a caress, a pledge of love. She was torn asunder. She wanted him, she needed him, she loved him, but she knew she could and would not have him under any circumstances.

"Do not touch me." It was a cry from the heart. The leaves rustled to give her warning. "Come no closer." It was a cry from the soul.

He was the man, she merely the woman. He would make the decisions. "You are freezing," he said as he pulled her hard against him and enfolded her within his cloak, next to his heart.

She cried out in pain and he was all tender concern. He knew his strong hands were capable of brutality, but he could have sworn he had not handled her too roughly. "What, love? Where did I hurt you?"

She drew in her breath upon a ragged sigh. "My breasts . . . they are so tender I want to scream."

Simon de Montfort's heart did a cartwheel. If he guessed

correctly he had bound this woman to him forever. His seed had planted his babe in her.

"De Montfort, you say you love me, yet I have just learned that you have been searching for a wealthy widow on the continent."

He allowed her to pull from his arms. He removed his heavy cloak and wrapped it about her before he spoke. "The king proposed a couple of names because I was in debt. A marriage of convenience is a common enough practice, but I am the most relieved man on the face of the earth that nothing came of these proposals. Anyway, it was before I ever met you, Eleanor. I am not in the habit of explaining myself to a woman, but in your case I have made an exception," he said quietly.

She was so still and silent.

"On my honor as a knight I swear to you there is no need for you to be jealous."

Yes, she thought, jealousy is devastating me, jealousy is consuming me, jealousy is killing me! By sheer willpower she stopped herself from swaying toward him. The unbelievably wild emotions he stirred in her were too devastating. The passion, the jealousy, the insatiable appetite were taking her dangerously close to Plantagenet madness.

She was covered with guilt remembering that William had never inspired such a passion in her. But that love had been a pure love, a safe love, sweet and steadfast. She decided that was the only kind of love for her . . . harmless, shielding, without risk. She must stop this headlong dash to abandon with Simon de Montfort. He would lead her directly into scandal. His very nature made him risk all. He had just gifted her with a month of misery. She would end it now before he brought her a lifetime of misery.

"Jealous?" she said in a tone of incredulity. "My dear Earl of Leicester, my feelings and emotions are not involved in this in any way. When my husband died I built an iron carapace around myself, and such as you cannot pierce it. My reputation is so precious to me I cannot jeopardize it by a sordid little affair with you. Apparently there has been gossip of my sexual excesses and I am ashamed to admit that the gossip is true; they simply have the wrong man. The things I have done in bed with you are immoral. Thank God I have finally come to my senses. It is finished."

Suddenly the moon floated out from behind a cloud to illuminate the lovers. Simon thought her more beautiful than he had ever seen her, but in this moment she was inviolate. As she gazed up into his face, her heart was breaking into a million tiny pieces.

"Then all there is left to say is good-bye," he said quietly, taking her small hand and placing a gold bangle upon her wrist. A single tear fell upon his hand before she turned and left him forever.

Simon lifted his hand to his lips to savor the salt tear. He knew before many months she would cry a river of tears, and he cursed himself for being the cause.

Alone in her chamber, she clasped the gold bangle to her heart, thankful that she had some small but very real token to cherish from her beloved Sim. She took it from her wrist to examine it more closely. It was pure Welsh gold. Her eyes fell upon a date inscribed inside. For a moment she was puzzled, then a pink blush suffused her throat. It was the day they had first made love.

32

The Countess of Pembroke withdrew her personal court to her private estate of Odiham. She managed to fill the winter days with elaborate plans for Christmas and the New Year. Her nights, however, were endless. It was exactly like being bereaved once again. No, it was worse. She was totally honest with herself for the first time in years.

William Marshal had been a fine man, but she could clearly see now that he had been a father figure to her. He had educated her and she had excelled to win his approval. Her love for him had been very real, but it was almost the love a daughter gave to a devoted parent. When he died she had taken the full blame upon herself. She had struggled beneath a mountain of guilt and had thought to expiate her sins by devoting her life to the church.

It had taken the magnificent Simon de Montfort to make her realize she was not cut out to be a nun. She did not regret one moment of her interlude with Simon. If she had only met him before she had married England's marshal, things could have been different. They were a perfect match for each other. Both were made up of equal parts of pride and passion.

Her night hungers for him never ceased, but as each day melted into the next she began to feel very virtuous that she had been able to deny herself happiness and live the chaste life she had vowed.

The Earl of Leicester was busy from dawn until well past dusk. He was training an army that grew larger every day, but not from allegiance to the king. Simon de Montfort drew men like a lodestone. He was a natural leader who was admired and looked up to. All men knew there were more underdogs in the world than top dogs, and Simon's name came to be synonymous with justice. On his journeys to his own lands he became great friends with the Archdeacon of Leicester and the Bishop of Lincoln. They in turn introduced him to the learned scholar Adam Marsh and Walter, the Bishop of Worcester, who talked among themselves that here at last was a leader with every noble quality, who believed in justice and the rights of the common man.

Simon missed Eleanor totally, completely, painfully, but he was a patient man who was playing a waiting game. He was heartsore that she had seemingly withdrawn her love. There were times during the lonely nights when his vulnerability rose up to defeat him. She seemed to have turned away from him, back to William Marshal. He could have challenged and vanquished any other man, but competing with a ghost made him heartsick.

Resolutely he pushed away the negative thoughts. The outcome was certain. She would have to turn to him whether she loved him or not, and he would take her any way he could get her.

Eleanor's maid Brenda was delighted by the changes at Odiham. There had been an infusion of new people to the household both from Durham House in London and Chepstowe in Wales. Now that Eleanor was in residence, the dining hall was a merry place with minstrels and music and laughter and an abundance of choice dishes to sample at every meal.

Bette was helping Eleanor chose a gown for dinner when an innocent remark she made sent Eleanor down a path of thought from which there was no return.

"I can't get into that green gown, Bette. In fact, all my dresses and shifts seem to have shrunken. Who on earth has been doing my laundry?"

Bette's busy hands sorted through the wardrobe to find a loose-fitting garment for her mistress, making a mental note to check up on the laundress. Her mind was on the Christmas festivities now that it was the first day of December, and Bette said absently, "I hope I don't get my menses on Christmas day. It seems like every holy day festival that comes along is spoiled for me by the curse."

For some inexplicable reason Eleanor lied to her woman. "Bette, I'm feeling tired tonight. I don't think I'll go down to dinner."

"I'll fetch you a tray, love," said Bette.

"No, no, I'm gaining far too much weight. I'll just have some of this fruit," she said, pointing to a silver dish overflowing with late-autumn pears and nuts. After Bette left, Eleanor spoke out loud to herself. "You've made such a pig of yourself lately, you look like the fat woman at the fair!"

A voice from within called her a liar. *That is not true. Since you said good-bye to Simon you have hardly eaten a thing.*

Aloud she said, "Only this morning I had ham and eggs and wheaten cakes."

The voice mocked, and she promptly vomited!

She removed her clothes and stepped before her mirror. Her stomach protruded to an alarming degree. Her breasts, which had always been round, pert, and upthrusting, could only be described as voluptuous. Her ears were pounding and a growing fear was threatening to consume her. She stared into the mirror and the face that looked back at her was full and positively blooming.

She snatched up her underclothes and searched them frantically for the tiniest trace of blood. Her mind flashed about helter-skelter trying to pin down when she had last had her menses. With growing horror she realized it had been before she had gone to Wales. Her fingers nervously twisted her gold bangle and the date inscribed inside it burned into her brain. September! This was December. She immediately denied to herself that she was four months gone with child.

Eleanor spent the next week willing herself to menstruate. She checked every half hour for the telltale signs of blood. Denial disappeared quickly and was replaced by conviction that she was indeed carrying a bastard. Her very first thought was suicide. Her second was abortion. Her third was running away, disappearing for good. She was so emotionally distraught she became dysfunctional and did nothing, nothing but sit and stare into space.

Before she realized it, Christmas was upon her. The king and queen and their respective courts had gone to Winchester to celebrate, as had become the custom. Odiham would get no visitors, thank God, which suited Eleanor, yet she was in a panic that Simon de Montfort would not let the holiday go by without trying to see her. As she frantically pushed her problem away and tried to make a festive occasion for her overflowing household, she began to panic that Simon de Montfort *would* let Christmas go by without trying to see her.

A score of times she almost confided in Bette, then changed her mind. A dozen times she decided to take Brenda into her confidence and a dozen times she stopped herself. On New Year's Eve she found herself sitting alone except for ghosts from the past that rose up to haunt her. She called up a scene from Ireland that was so vivid it could have happened yesterday. She heard the terrible voice of the Bishop of Ferns cursing her and William. "The almighty Marshal family will end! In one generation the name shall be destroyed. You will never share in the Lord's benediction to increase and multiply." Then she heard her answer ringing clearly, "I swear by Almighty God that before I am twenty I will have a houseful of children."

She took a goblet of watered wine. She had said so many prayers in the last three weeks that had not been answered that she felt hopeless. She knew it must be close to midnight. If only she could hold back the hands of time. If only she could stay in the old year forever, like a butterfly frozen in amber. The dawning of the new year frightened her beyond her darkest nightmare. How would she ever face it?

She lifted the goblet to her lips and thought cynically, When we sip from the cup of knowledge, we lose our faith. Then she drank more and her thoughts swirled about her. Suddenly a calm descended and she finally acknowledged, When we drain the cup to the dregs, the face of the cosmic God gazes up at us from the empty cup. She must face the truth. She must share her guilty secret with Simon de Montfort.

She heard the bells begin to ring out the old year and ring in the new. She threw open her tower door that led onto a little balcony. The tall figure of Simon de Montfort was ascending the pentice, the outside staircase leading to her tower. She gasped. Was he the devil? Had she conjured him?

His arms reached out to enfold her on that fateful New Year's of 1239. She clung to him desperately and his very size brought her a feeling of security. She whispered, "Simon, I . . ." but her voice failed her. She tried again. "Simon, I-I am with child."

The sound of the bells receded and the silence about them was heavy. Had he heard her? she wondered wildly. If he had, he was not about to make it easy for her. She trembled against him and finally he spoke.

"And so, Eleanor?"

"Simon, I am a princess of England, I cannot have a bastard," she whispered raggedly.

"And so, Eleanor?" he repeated.

"Simon, you will have to marry me!"

He swung her up into his powerful arms. "My God, I thought you'd never ask me."

He carried her through the balcony door and locked it. He sat down in a carved chair before the fire, and she sat propped upon his knees like a child.

"I don't know why I said that, you know it is impossible," she said frantically.

"Nothing is impossible, my Kathe," he soothed.

"Anyone in the royal family needs the consent of the council before they wed. They will never give it. Henry fought with them for years to give me consent to wed William Marshal, and there was no impediment then. The church is an even greater stumbling block than the council. Holy vows cannot be disregarded or recinded," she said, her voice choking.

His strong hands curved about her shoulders and he shook her to make her listen to reason. "When we tell them you are with child, they will be forced to make an exception."

She looked at him with horrified eyes. "De Montfort, swear

to me you will not reveal my shameful secret. I will kill myself if it gets out!"

He shook his head in disbelief. "Embarrassment to you is more horrifying than premature burial."

She clutched his doublet frantically. "Swear you will keep my secret."

He covered her hands tenderly. "It is *our* secret, my love. You may be willing to allow your child to be a bastard, but I am not. It is imperative that we marry, Eleanor."

"Then it will have to be a total and absolute secret," she insisted vehemently.

Simon sighed. "I will go to the king and explain we are in love and wish to marry."

"No, no, no," she begged.

"Eleanor, stop it!" he ordered firmly. "The whole thing can be secret, but if I wed you without the king's knowledge I can be imprisoned and beheaded for treason."

"Henry would never allow that to happen to you, Simon. He is your friend . . . he is my friend, my flesh and blood."

He could not bring himself to assassinate her brother's character, but he could not help saying "You do not think him a friend when he gives away your property."

"He is allowing me four hundred crowns a year for Ireland."

Simon was appalled. By Christ, it was time someone took control of Eleanor Plantagenet's affairs—overtime!

Her lips trembled as she said nervously, "I will go to Henry and ask him to let me wed secretly. Then you must take me away, Simon . . . to Leicester or somewhere. Please let the baby be a secret between just you and me?"

"I would prefer to go to Henry myself," he said firmly.

"Please, please, Sim, let me do it my way? I will never ask you for anything again."

He kissed the crown of her head and smiled wryly to himself. He knew the little minx would ask him for something before five minutes went by. "Eleanor, you may do it your way or any way, so long as you do it. Don't be afraid. What happened to the courageous woman who rode with the wild ponies?"

She burst into tears, for that was the day she had thrown

caution to the wind and allowed Simon to make love to her, to make a baby in her.

He carried her to the bed and undressed her with firm hands. "You should be abed. My own precious love, what is between you and me can never be torn asunder. You are my world and I want to be yours. The marriage ceremony is merely a legality so that our children will be legitimate and inherit my lands and titles and so that you will be the legal Countess of Leicester."

He was naked now, and slipped into the bed to enfold her in his massive arms. She clung to him desperately as if she was drowning. "I pledge that with me at your side you need never fear anything. I will give you all my love, my understanding, my strength, my friendship, my courage, my castles, my name, and all my protection. But tonight, more than anything else in the world, you need to be held."

"We should not be here like this," she whispered against the sable fur of his chest.

"No power on earth could keep us apart tonight. You need my strength; lean on me. Talk and I will listen. I'll banish the darklings and the fears." His beautiful hands brushed the silken tangles of hair from her lovely face, and he stroked her back until he soothed and lulled her to relax in his arms. They did not sleep, they simply lay entwined, their secret child surrounded by two heartbeats that mingled into one. They curled their bodies together, kissing. Their language of love was wordless murmurs. Their hands and lips pledged promises to each other that bound them eternally.

As always, before dawn they grew desperate because of the approaching separation. He gathered her up and lifted her on top of his long, hard body. His eyes were black and bottomless and he whispered raggedly, "I need the feel of your breasts spilling into my hands."

His words and his irresistible touch brought her a wave of raw, molten pleasure. He suckled her fiercely and his fingers caressed her thighs, moving ever higher until they tangled in her wild silk. He found her swollen, damp and aching for him, yet he drew out her arousal to its limit, knowing her desire must be at its peak before he could fill her without pain.

His mouth sought hers and he kissed her as a woman has

seldom been kissed before. His lips, his mouth, and his tongue became the center of her universe. What began tenderly, sweetly, ended in fierce, hungry domination. Then with the aid of his fingers he opened her little by little, going ever deeper until he arrived at his final destination. He rested inside her until she relaxed enough to move on to the erotic dance of love. Her body was becoming so luscious he wanted her with an animal hunger that lured him to take her savagely, violently, yet inexplicably at the same time he wanted to love her tenderly and beg for her sweet, clinging kisses. He groaned. "My delight . . . my torment!"

Their bodies burst into scorching flames and his tongue began to plunge and withdraw in sensual imitation of his long, hard shaft. She pressed his hard buttocks, wanting more, wanting everything he had to give, and he shoved forcefully into her, burying himself as deeply as he could go. His hands sought hers and with fingers entwined they reached explosive, earth-shattering bliss.

When their bruised lips parted, he did not stop kissing her, but allowed his mouth to move down to feast upon her throat and swelling breasts. Her cries were hauntingly beautiful as she gave her body up to her dark lover's smoldering lips.

They could not hold back the dawning of the new year. Eleanor dreaded what lay ahead. Simon embraced it. He needed life-and-death challenges. He relished the feel of the brief, immediate passion of the struggle. He left the bed and moved across the room to stand perfectly still before the window. Eleanor stopped breathing. He was a naked god framed in the pale light of the dawn. Finally he dressed. "Promise me you will speak to Henry."

"I will, I will," she vowed fervently, "only you must give me time to choose the perfect moment. Promise me you will do nothing until I send you word?"

He looked at her in the bed: so small, so afraid, so exquisite. "I promise I will do naught that will hurt you. That is all I can promise." He swallowed his impatience and told himself he would give her some time. How much time he did not know.

33

The king and queen and their silly, fun-loving courtiers did not return from Winchester until the middle of January had gone by. Each day after that Eleanor told herself she must return to Windsor to speak with Henry, but there always seemed to be something to keep her at Odiham. Finally she gathered her courage and returned to her old rooms in the King John Tower. She intended to speak with Henry each day, but there always seemed a plausible reason why she could not.

Matilda Marshal Bigod and her husband, the Earl of Norfolk, descended to protest Henry's giving Chepstowe to William de Lusignan. They insisted that if he got Pembroke, then they should have Chepstowe. Then the queen's youngest uncle Boniface arrived and the queen was pressing Henry to make him the new Archbishop of Canterbury. That he was totally unsuited, grasping and violent, did not bother the king for his own half brother Aymer wanted to become Bishop of Durham and Henry himself went to bully the poor monks into making the appointment.

By now Eleanor was almost five months into her pregnancy and she went abroad only after dusk, concealed in a flowing cloak. While the king was off in Durham she went to compline service in the chapel to pray for courage. She was thankful the place was deserted save for the young priest. The Provençals seldom attended church and never compline, the last service of the day.

As she knelt she became aware of an enormous dark shadow that came and knelt beside her. Fear was etched upon her lovely face and he tried for a light note. He whispered, "I am an incurable romantic."

"I will work diligently on a cure," she whispered repressively.

"I doubt if I would respond to treatment."

"You respond . . . most pointedly."

"That response is for you alone."

She turned to reply but the shadow had withdrawn. She prayed for the strength to carry her guilty burden. She asked St. Jude to give her the courage to speak with Henry the moment he returned, and she asked the apostle and martyr to stay by her side while she gained her brother's help.

Simon de Montfort never relied on anyone, man or saint, save himself. He was appalled that no lands or castles had been settled on Eleanor and that it looked as if she would receive no dower rights whatsoever. He decided to do something about it. The moment the king returned from Durham, he asked him for a private meeting.

The Earl of Leicester was almost as important to the king as the Bishop of Winchester. The two great military leaders of his reign, Hubert de Burgh and William Marshal, were now lost to him. Simon de Montfort filled the gap they left, and Henry would have done almost anything to keep him happy and firmly on his side. Leicester was his only bastion against France, Scotland, Wales, Ireland, and his own English barons.

Henry truly liked Simon de Montfort, and he clapped him on the back and said, "Simon, you should have come to Winchester with us for Christmas. We had so much fun. Winchester always shows us such a lavish time."

"Sire, I am too deep in debt to indulge in a lavish Christmas."

"I know, I know, Simon, and all on my behalf. The council controls the purse strings. I submitted your expenses for the army, but you know how it is. My barons and nobles are expected to shoulder the burden of the debts."

"I can hardly do that off Leicester. It had been run into the ground and squeezed of every groat before I got it back from the late Earl of Chester."

"Yes, I must find you a decent holding. Can't have my best military leader going about like a beggar. You should have come to me sooner and reminded me, Simon. Although I admit there has been a bloody long lineup lately for land and castles. But hellfire, if you don't ask, you don't get in this world."

Henry consulted an enormous map that showed every fief and castle belonging to the crown. "Let me see now," he said, scratching his head, not really knowing what would satisfy the war lord.

"Kenilworth," said Simon.

"Eh? Kenilworth, did you say?" Henry asked in astonishment.

"It's south of Leicester. I go by it to reach my own lands."

"I know where Kenilworth is, for Christ's sake, it is the jewel of England! Kenilworth isn't just a castle—it is a total feudal state."

"Sire, I have asked a certain lady to marry me. I propose you make Kenilworth the hereditary seat of the Earl of Leicester."

A grin spread across Henry's face. "Simon, you dog, you have found your heiress. Who is she?"

"The lady has not yet given her formal consent. When she does so, you will be the first to know the lady's name."

"Ah, I begin to see why you covet Kenilworth. But, Simon, it is such a wealthy estate, I hate to let it go out of my hands." Henry sighed. "I will think on it. Give me a few days."

Simon bowed and left the king to his deliberations. Henry wanted to keep Kenilworth in Plantagenet hands, and yet he knew it would be safer in de Montfort's hands than any but his own. The castle and outbuildings, manors and hunting grounds covered over twenty miles, then there were the towns attached to it. It was situated on the rich, rolling hills and valleys that bordered the River Avon, and was an impregnable fortress whose only entrance was a portcullis at the end of an earthen

causeway whose outer ward was so vast it became a small city
when war threatened.

The last week of January was upon Eleanor and she dare not
let the days slip into February without doing something. February would be her sixth month of pregnancy, and she would
soon be unable to conceal it.

She chose a loose tunic with a flowing underdress in Henry's
favorite green, slipped the sapphire ring he had given her into
her pocket, and sought him out at an early hour. The habits of
childhood were hard to break. They had been brought up to
rise with the sun, and Eleanor knew that the queen and the
Provençals were habitually late risers.

She found him watching some knights practicing in the tiltyard and listened patiently while he extolled the virtues of Simon de Montfort, who was keeping his fighting men in top
physical condition. A light snow had fallen on the ground and
Henry scooped up a handful, pressed it into a snowball, and
aimed at one of the arched windows, laughing uproariously
when it hit its mark and a worried face appeared at the window
to see which youth was playing pranks.

Eleanor solemnly held out his sapphire ring to him. He
raised an eyebrow to look at her quizzically. "Henry, what I
am about to ask of you will shock you terribly."

"Eleanor, I gave you my pledge, so the answer is yes." He
said it lightheartedly, as if it were in his power to grant her
anything in the world.

She shook her head to caution him. "Wait, wait, Henry, until
you know what it is I ask. I want to marry again . . . my
happiness depends upon it. I know it is impossible after swearing a vow of chastity, but perhaps . . . perhaps if it were kept
secret?"

"My little cockroach, you have fallen in love!" Henry
laughed.

Eleanor began to panic. My God, could he not treat anything
seriously?

"We will get around the vows . . . I am an expert at it," he
said, laughing, "providing, of course, I approve of your
choice."

"What do you mean, you are an expert?" she asked.

"Every time I want something from Parliament or my damned council they insist I repledge myself to the conditions of the Magna Carta. They write up some stupid paper that I must sign. I make the bloody promise, then I do exactly as I please. Now tell me who it is you fancy."

Her eyes were liquid with apprehension as she looked up at him and whispered the name. He looked down at her in amazement, then his face broke into a dazzling smile. "Bones of God, if that doesn't beat all! I have wanted him in my pocket since the beginning. I have cudgeled my brains how to make him totally committed to the Plantagenet cause, and here you are offering him to me on a silver platter."

She searched his face, amazed that her words had brought joy rather than the anger she had expected.

Henry laughed with delight as his brain began its devious plotting. "We will have a secret ceremony in the chapel in the middle of the night, then the two of you must leave immediately. Once it is a *fait accompli* there isn't anything they can do about it. I have been waiting for an opportunity to put one over on my bloody council and this is it! Eleanor, I am the King of England, and I give you my royal consent."

"Henry, I beg you not to tell the queen," she implored.

"Ha! Might as well stand atop the Tower of London and shout it to the mob. I shall tell no one, not even the priest until one minute before he is to say the words over you. Speak to no one," he cautioned. "Two o'clock in the chapel vestry. I will speak with the Earl of Leicester."

Eleanor did exactly as her brother Henry bade her. She did not even breathe a word to Bette, lest the secret be revealed. The winter day seemed endless. She was restless as a cat. She could not eat, she could not rest. Though there was a good fire in her chamber, she could not even seem to get warm. She did not dare to pack anything, and in any case her mind would not let her plan beyond the actual secret ceremony that must be performed to keep her from the shame of bearing a bastard.

Damn Simon de Montfort to hellfire. It was all his fault. He had pursued her relentlessly, seduced her shamefully, and like a little wanton she had responded to his enticements. Like a ripe peach hanging upon a sun-drenched wall she had fallen into his damnably attractive hands.

The winter darkness drew in early and the hours crawled toward midnight. She retired at ten o'clock but instead of going to bed, she opened wide her wardrobe to select her garments. She donned lacy stockings, then drew on woolen chausses over them for she knew the chapel floor would be icy as a crypt in the middle of the night. She chose soft leather boots that came halfway up her legs since she knew she would be riding somewhere after the ceremony. Her gown would be velvet, but she was undecided upon the color to choose. It was a wedding, but white was only for a chaste bride and she was anything but. In any case she would need to choose a color that would blend into the darkness of the night. Her hand fell unerringly upon a deep jade-green riding dress. She would have to leave the back unfastened beneath her cloak, but she knew the shade flattered her vivid dark coloring and she needed to look beautiful to bolster her courage.

She laid the scarlet woolen cloak from Wales across the foot of her bed, then she did the same thing with her sable cloak. She was shivering uncontrollably and decided when it was time to leave she would wear one over the other. Even though there would be very few eyes to see her, she did not want her pregnancy to be detected by anyone. Somehow the idea of two cloaks draped over her made her feel more secure.

As the hour grew nigh suddenly time seemed to speed up and she wished she could slow it down. She gulped a cup of wine, took her courage in both hands, and cautiously made her way through the freezing night to the king's private chapel. There was no movement, no sound, just dead stillness and silence about the place. Her heart beat rapidly and her knees turned to water. Something had gone wrong with the plans and no one was there save her. Why, why had she been foolish enough to put her trust in men? They were all so selfish and vile. She closed her eyes, feeling her courage ebb away and wondered what she should do. Suddenly a tall figure appeared at her side, the chapel door opened silently, and a strong hand guided her inside. Henry's familiar face swam before her eyes as he spoke

low with his priest, and then she raised her eyes to the face of
the man whose powerful arm supported her back.

He was the darkest man she had ever seen, and the tallest.
He wore black, which added a sinister quality. Already the
priest was intoning Latin phrases and she noticed how much
Henry's left eyelid drooped tonight. She did nothing but make
her response, then when a document was produced for her signature, Bette stepped forward from the shadows to witness it.
Eleanor opened her mouth in surprise. She had left her serving
woman asleep. The king and de Montfort spoke with Bette as if
Eleanor were not even present. "Take her back to bed now. At
daybreak pack and depart for Odiham as usual."

Like a puppet she allowed Bette to lead her away, glad that
all responsibility had been taken from her for once. She allowed
her serving woman to remove her cloaks and put her to bed. It
was all so much like a dark dream. So, she was being sent to
Odiham. She had had some vague notion that her new husband
would carry her far away, perhaps to Leicester, where they
would be able to live together secretly. But it seemed that nothing would change. She would live at Odiham alone, where de
Montfort would ride secretly at his convenience. The mumbled
words of the priest had been a mere formality.

She closed her eyes wearily, emotionally drained. She placed
her hands protectively upon her swollen abdomen and tumbled
into darkness. When she opened her eyes she saw that everything was packed in readiness for Odiham and Bette was urging
her to rise and break her fast so they could be upon the road.
As she swept aside the covers and rose from the bed, she
blushed shamefully when she realized how obvious her pregnancy must be.

Bette firmly pressed her lips together and said, "There is no
shame in bearing the great Earl of Leicester an heir, especially
when you are the Countess of Leicester."

Eleanor's finger went to her lips. "Don't call me that while
we are still at Windsor," she begged.

"I'm not daft. I shall call you Countess of Pembroke as everyone else does."

Eleanor wore exactly the same things she had worn to the
chapel. She was starting to feel a little better. Her energy was

returning as she felt an urgency to be gone from this place. It was almost like leaving a prison. She had been captive here for longer than she cared to remember.

The air was cold and clear and crisp and as she sat her horse with her sable fur wrapped snugly about her, she realized today was February, the start of a new month—the start of a new life. Before her household cavalcade had traveled two miles out into the countryside from Windsor, they were met by what looked like an army. Ah, God, they have come to arrest me, she thought. Then she realized that the giant in charge of the armed men was Simon de Montfort.

His spirits were high as was his blood. He had no need for hat or cloak. "Good morning, Countess. There has been a last-minute change of plans. We ride north." He dismounted and came to her side. His voice was low and intimate as he worshipped her with his eyes. "Are you feeling well?"

"Yes, thank you," she replied, and suddenly it was true.

"We will be in the saddle for two days," he told her. "I shall take you up before me." He held up his powerful arms. She looked down at his hands and she was lost. She came down to him all shyness and sable, and in that moment he felt invincible as a god. He had seized the moment and made it happen. For today at least he had vanquished the enemy.

Snuggled against his broad chest, high up on his great destrier, the world seemed a safer place. "Where are we bound?" she asked.

"Home," he answered with conviction.

She knew the need for secrecy and did not press him, save to ask "Will there be room for this vast company?"

He threw back his head and laughed. The columns of his neck stood out and his strong white teeth flashed. Surely this boyish rogue could not be the same darkly forbidding man she had wed in the night?

"I have sent Rickard de Burgh to fetch all your people from Odiham and still the place will be half empty," he promised.

Eleanor thought it sounded like heaven, but it could turn out to be hell, she thought with a slight shiver. His black eyes laughed down at her and suddenly she didn't care which it was, so long as Sim was there with her.

She clung to him all day, sometimes listening to his deep voice reassuring her, sometimes closing her eyes and resting against him. But in the late afternoon before full dusk descended, his fingers traced the faint shadows along her cheekbones and he knew he must find an inn. Miraculously they had traveled as far as Oxford. Simon bade his men to find their own shelter and be on the road again by six.

He skirted the town itself and rode into an inn yard at the village of Woodstock. Oxford had become the seat of all learning since the religious order of Franciscans settled there to teach and to serve. The great cultural center drew the noblest men of the realm, and Simon felt that either himself or the king's sister might be recognized if they stayed there.

In the small chamber beneath the rafters Simon insisted upon undressing her and putting her to bed. Then when the serving wench staggered up the stairs with a tray laden with hearty country fare, he carried the food to the bed and fed her with his fingers.

"Will you feed me with your fingers every night, husband?" she purred.

"Nay," he teased, "you are fat as a piglet now." They kissed between mouthfuls. Simon firmly decided that she needed her rest and her strength, and he would make no demands upon her this night. When he undressed, however, and she saw that he wore the black leather sheath to protect his shaft from the saddle, she seduced him into making love to her.

At the end of the next day they arrived at Kenilworth just as the sun was setting. It reflected golden in the River Avon and touched every window, turret, and tower with a welcoming, shining brightness. The walls were crenellated and the outer wall was broken by five towers. They rode over an earthen causeway to a two-story gatehouse and through a portcullis.

Eleanor looked up at her new husband. "This isn't Leicester," she said, a note of uncertainty and longing in her voice.

"No," said Simon, cantering into the outer ward, "this is Kenilworth."

"Oh, 'tis like a world of its own," she breathed with admiration. The stone walls of the inner ward were over twenty feet thick with built-in rooms for guards and soldiers. "Whoever owns this Kenilworth?" she asked.

The Earl of Leicester swung from his destrier and lifted her to the ground. She looked like a tiny doll against the vast structure whose main floor rose eighty-seven feet into the air. "You do, Eleanor," he said quietly.

Her eyes were wide. "What do you mean?"

He reached into his doublet and pulled out a crackling parchment she had rested against on the two-day ride. The light was fading quickly, but she read that King Henry III had deeded Kenilworth to Simon de Montfort for faithful duty to England and the crown. He towered over her. Then he reached out a finger beneath her chin and lifted up her face. "I shall probably never be able to give you jewels nor sable furs as costly as these, but this day I give you Kenilworth. I shall make it impregnable so you will be forever safe."

She was astounded. "You are a magic man, a wizard!"

He enfolded her in his arms before the assembly and kissed her upon the mouth. Then he grinned. "Hocus-pocus, fish bones choke us."

Eleanor's silvery laughter floated out upon the chill evening air, and he thought it the loveliest sound he had ever heard.

The next weeks were honest and truly the happiest of her life. Her days were filled to overflowing from dawn 'til dusk. Her household was a large one, a blend of her people from Windsor, London's Durham House, Odiham, and the servants and men-at-arms from Chepstowe in Wales. All had to integrate with the staff who had worked at Kenilworth all their lives.

Eleanor and Simon chose the large impregnable Caesar Tower for their private domain. From its high windows they could see all of Kenilworth with its double ramparts and deep, wide moat. There were so many tenants at Kenilworth, it had its own mill to grind their grain. It had its own courts of justice where prices were regulated, disputes settled, and crimes tried. It had its own prison and gallows, and a small town known as Banbury had grown up around Kenilworth's brewery. It had its own armory and chapel and a small order of Franciscan brothers who were beginning to compile a library.

Her nights were like Paradise. High in the Caesar Tower the lovers were at last private enough to say and do all the things they had only dreamed about. Immediately Simon had had built an enormous bed, twice the usual size to accommodate his giant frame. Eleanor at last had a purpose in life and became such an efficient chatelaine it amazed everyone. She checked the kitchens for cleanliness, the salt meat for maggots, and the flour for weevils. She took stock of her food supplies and herbs and directed her servants to do the laundry, change the rushes, replenish the rushlights, mold tallow and scented wax candles, and made sure someone checked the drains and the well water.

She directed her maids to visit the sick and her seamstresses to sew russet or green garments for the smiths, grooms, cooks, bakers, and washerwomen. She appointed a steward, studied languages with a chaplain, and began a household journal, signing each page Eleanor, Countess of Leicester. Each day she placed her hand upon the earth and whispered, "Mine!"

34

Eleanor stood in the Caesar Tower gazing from a high window early one morning toward the end of February. Early signs of spring were everywhere, and on this clear morning she could see the beautiful hills of West Anglia beyond the river.

Simon lay naked upon the bed, watching her every move beneath lazy eyelids. He rose and came to stand behind her, his powerful hands cupping her shoulders. "Take a good look at everything. It will never look the same again after today."

Her brows drew together apprehensively. "What do you mean?"

"I'm going to flood a hundred acres of meadowland. From now on Kenilworth will sit in the center of a mere."

"A mere is a lake, isn't it? How will we get in and out?"

"Same as always, over the earthen causeway and through the portcullis, which will stand high above the water. But it will be the only way to approach Kenilworth. It will make it completely impregnable. We have worked long and hard on the plan. I will divert the water from the River Avon, then dam it back up. The mere will be deep enough for us to have boats and a little barge for you."

She turned in his arms so that her cheek was pressed against the sable pelt of his naked chest. "Sim, I don't want February to end. It has been the most wonderful month of my life."

He wanted to assure her that March would be even better, but he could not bring himself to lie to her. He had done his very best to keep out the world, but he was a realist and he knew that before much longer, their secret wedding would be secret no longer. He had called the tune and he was ready to pay the piper, but he knew that Eleanor would also have to pay and he prayed that she would be strong enough. In the beginning he had set out to enslave her, to make her crave his caresses, but he had become ensnared in the plot and become so enraptured by her that the captor had become the captive. His hands denuded her of her nightrail and he dipped his head to run a sensual tongue along her throat. Simon's nude body pressed against hers always sent the desire snaking through her limbs and belly. She stood on tiptoe to slide her arms up about his neck, and her fingers entwined in his long black hair.

His thick muscled arm went beneath her bare knees as he swept her high and carried her to the bed. He cautioned himself to be gentle in his lovemaking and promised himself that shortly he would abstain totally until after their child was born. Pregnancy had made her absolutely bloom. Her breasts, belly, and thighs were lush, inviting his hands and his lips. He lay her back in the bed and spread her dark hair across the pillows, then he knelt before her and opened her knees so that he had an unimpeded view of the cleft between her legs, crowned by tight, black silk ringlets. His eyes were black with passion and she watched his face become taut and hungry with his great need. As his mouth moved closer to her secret center, she wanted him to devour her. His thumbs caressed her cleft, opening her slightly, and just before he covered her with his hot mouth, he whispered, "It looks exactly like a rosebud."

He loved to do this to her. She was so small and exquisitely made, and he knew it aroused her to madness. After he loved her this way, it was always easier to penetrate her with his great manroot. She lay sprawled before him with all her senses heightened. He licked delicately at the rosebud until she gasped and arched into his mouth with her first climax, crying "Sim,

Sim." He lifted his head and hung above her, watching every tiny expression of pleasure.

When she could breathe again she looked beneath heavy lids at his swollen cock and whispered, "I have such an urge to love you with my mouth, but you are too long."

"Sweet, sweet, you don't have to put your mouth over all of it, just the head," he explained intensely.

"Come closer," she whispered.

He arched above her so that his erection brushed her cheek. She caressed him with her small hands, and her tongue darted out to taste the salt of him. Then her lips covered him and held him inside her soft mouth where she felt him pulse and throb. She ran her tongue beneath the ledge and molded it to the heart-shaped tip.

"No more, love," he cried raggedly, then he scooped her up into his lap and lay on his side behind her. He raised one of her pretty thighs and entered from behind. The feelings and sensations were totally new from this angle, and as she built to an unbelievably hard climax she clutched handfuls of bedclothes in the throes of her passion.

"Sim!" She moaned. "All your thrusts press forward to the front where I love it, oh, oh, ohmigod, Sim." No sooner had she taken her enjoyment to the full than Simon's hot seed erupted into her, and she cried out anew at the pleasure he brought her.

Later in the day she stood at the windows of the high tower and watched in wonder as her Kenilworth was transformed forever. The jewel of England rose up from its silvery setting. The crenellated, double-walled castle with its five towers now sat in a lake that covered over a hundred acres.

Rickard de Burgh had had another vision and had ridden back to the capital to await the coming storm.

Simon invited his friend Robert, Bishop of Lincoln, to Kenilworth for a week. He was the head of the largest and most important diocese in England. Simon wanted to tell him of his secret marriage to Eleanor before the story leaked out. Realizing Eleanor would be frantic if she knew he intended to reveal their secret to someone high in the church, he kept his mouth shut about the child.

Robert was both philosophical and practical. "I will support you in this," he said firmly, his shrewd eyes hooded. "You will need all the support you can gather. In the years I have known you, you have risen to be the highest lord in this part of England. You have always tempered your punishments of the citizens by being a pattern of mercy and forgiveness rather than a master of cruelty. Justice is a passion with you, and you care about the common man." The Bishop of Lincoln was far-seeing. He knew a born leader when he saw one.

Simon de Montfort, Earl of Leicester, had such strength not only in body and character but in numbers. More fighting men were drawn to him every day, and now that he occupied Kenilworth he was almost invincible. This household already held more people than the king's court and was capable of holding hundreds more at a pinch.

When the queen laughed up her sleeve that she had rid the court of Eleanor Plantagenet, Henry could not resist imparting the knowledge that he had aided his little sister in a secret marriage. Upon learning that her enemy had married the magnificent war lord, the queen almost ran mad with envy. She swore she would be revenged for what she took as a personal injury. She had formed an infatuation for the devastatingly handsome warrior and considered him a Queen's Man.

She denounced Eleanor from one end of Windsor to the other, and within hours the council of fifteen were incensed with the king for orchestrating the royal princess's marriage without their consent.

The council's reaction paled in comparison to that of the church. The church men collectively were horrified by Eleanor's breach of her vow of chastity. The Archbishop of Canterbury immediately declared the marriage invalid, and Rickard de Burgh rode full gallop to Kenilworth to confirm the bad news.

Simon de Montfort paced about the great hall, which could seat three hundred. Each end boasted massive, walk-in fireplaces, and the high ceilings were beamed and raftered. It was intolerable to him that his marriage had been declared invalid. When Eleanor found out she would be devastated that in the eyes of the church and perhaps even the rest of England, they were living in sin and their child would be a bastard.

Sir Rickard said, "I regret, my friend, that I must hit you with more bad news, but you must know what you are up against."

Simon nodded grimly. "Forewarned is forearmed."

"The barons on the council are threatening to get the other barons to join them in an uprising against the king. They have appealed to the king's brother, Richard of Cornwall, to lead them."

Simon raised his head like a stag who suddenly scents danger. "Blood of God . . . that a simple marriage should bring the country to the brink of civil war."

"No royal marriage is a simple marriage," Sir Rickard said quietly.

"I understand the objection of the church because of the broken vows, but what is the barons' objection to me?" As soon as he asked the question he knew the answer; de Burgh's reply confirmed it for him.

"They are sick and tired of the king acting without authority. They are sick and tired of the king's foreign favorites and relatives taking England's castles and titles and heiresses. The king and queen have no children, no heir, and so if Eleanor is allowed to wed they want a royal husband for her in case she is the only Plantagenet to bear a child and an heir to the throne."

Simon de Montfort had never sat and brooded upon a problem in his life. He was a man of action who made his decisions both swiftly and firmly. "I will seek advice from Robert, the Bishop of Lincoln, then I will go to Richard and ask him to let me speak with the barons face to face." He grimaced at his old friend. "First, however, I must face someone more formidable than all the bishops and barons combined."

He found her before the fire, relaxing in a warm bath. He hesitated for long moments, hating to disturb her tranquility. She was the loveliest sight he'd ever seen with her damp, black curls pinned up atop her head, falling down in tendrils of disarray, the fireshine splashing over her body.

"Kathe," he said softly. She was immediately alerted. He called her that only in moments when he felt unbearable tenderness for her.

"Whatever is it?" she asked, her hand going to her throat.

"Something to upset you, I am afraid."

She stood up in alarm. "Our secret has become known."

He nodded yes, then, after taking up a large towel to wrap about her, he lifted her from the water and sat her in his lap before the fire. "The barons are on the brink of an uprising against Henry because of our marriage."

"You must go to his aid. You have trained most of his army, and you have so many fighting men of your own."

He chose his words carefully. "My men feel a loyalty for me that I do not believe they feel for Henry. The barons are rallying to your brother Richard. To fight would mean civil war. I will go to Richard and speak with the barons myself." He did not tell her their marriage had been declared null and void; she would learn that soon enough.

"I will go to Henry," she said decisively. "He will need my loyalty."

"Splendor of God, you will do no such thing! Kenilworth is your haven, your sanctuary. You will remain safely here."

A look of stubborn defiance came into her face.

"I forbid you to leave." The tone told her that she must not disobey him. He was such a big, powerful man that it took all her courage to defy him, and when she sat naked upon his knees it was an impossibility. "It is very commendable to be loyal to your brother, but your first loyalty is to yourself and this child you carry. Have you so little faith in me you think I cannot put all to rights?"

She felt a rush of shame. Wasn't he her magic man, her wizard? She touched his face tenderly, blinked back her tears and whispered, "Hocus-pocus, fish bones choke us."

"Put some clothes on, you're driving me mad." When she learned they'd been living in sin for over a month, she probably would not appreciate his trying to make love to her. "I am leaving today, Eleanor."

"When will you return?" she questioned anxiously.

"I shall be back when I am back, and not before. It will ever be so, my love. When I leave to do a job, I won't return until I have accomplished it."

She came to him in her shift and he opened his arms to her. "Sim, promise me you will take care."

His hot hungry mouth swallowed her words before he forced himself from their chamber high in the Caesar Tower.

Robert, Bishop of Lincoln, had already heard the news by the time Simon arrived. They sat together now drinking wine in a small laboratory the learned bishop used for his scientific experiments. "I will do all in my power and write letters to the king and to the Archbishop of Canterbury telling them I support you in this marriage. However, there is a higher authority than the Archbishop of Canterbury, you know."

Simon de Montfort's face set in rigid lines. "You mean the Pope. You know damned well I am against the Pope's interference in English matters. I have fought against the Pope all my life. He would not even listen to me."

Robert held out his hands in a conciliatory gesture. "You are behind the time. We have a new Pope in Rome called Gregory IX. Simon, I'll let you in on a church secret. It is only a matter of a bribe. Let the papal court decide if her vow was binding. It will effectively cut off every objection in England."

"Since I came to you for advice, I should have enough good sense to take it."

"You will need three things: money, money, and money. I will give you five hundred crowns, and I know a couple of good citizens of Leicester who will be glad to match my donation. I will start fund raising while you go to Richard and speak with the barons. You must beg, borrow, and steal enough for a quick trip to Rome and a dispensation."

Rickard de Burgh accompanied Simon on his journey south. His uncle, Hubert de Burgh, had commanded all the castles and men of the Cinque Ports. Now they gave their loyalty to Richard of Cornwall because of what the king had done to Hubert.

Simon decided he needed the backing of the men of the Cinque Ports as well as the barons and knew he could get it if he could persuade Richard of Cornwall to approve the marriage. Simon and Richard's meeting was more of a confrontation.

"Do you realize that by marrying my sister you have flaunted the authority of the church and the council? The barons are ready to arm because Henry has thrown yet another plum to a hated foreigner. Why the hellfire did you commit such a reckless act?" demanded Eleanor's brother, who always before had been on friendly terms with Simon.

"Because she was six months pregnant," said Simon, cutting straight to the heart of the matter. With the six words he effectively wiped out Richard's disapproval and opposition. The two men glared at each other savagely. Richard could not moralize to Simon for he himself had fathered a child on Isabella Marshal while she was still married to Gloucester.

"I am prepared to bribe you if it is the only way," Simon said bluntly.

"Splendor of God," Richard exclaimed, then the hint of a smile showed in his face. "Well, for better or worse we are brothers, and I don't mind admitting I would rather have you than that pack of jackals my mother has foisted upon me." Richard poured them ale. "I too am to be a father. That means both Eleanor and I have beaten Henry to the punch." An amusing thought caught Richard's imagination and he slapped his thigh. "If we have sons, let's call them both Henry, just to rub salt in the wound as good brothers should."

Richard of Cornwall accompanied Simon de Montfort and Rickard de Burgh to all the main ports, starting with Dover. The men of the Cinque Ports only had to see Simon de Montfort, Earl of Leicester, to realize they would need this outstanding warrior and leader of men on their side if an enemy ever threatened England. Before he departed Simon promised them he would work to get Hubert de Burgh pardoned and his castles and titles restored. That convinced them he was interested in justice, something the crown did not even pay lip service to these days.

Then Richard of Cornwall called the barons together and Simon spent a week talking with them. Most of England's noble families were represented. Before Simon de Montfort had spent three days with them, they recognized him to be a man of rare ability with keen political insight. There was a dearth of leaders in England, and they saw he was a man with a lofty purpose and a resolute mind. Here was no foreign Provençal or Savoyard, but an Anglo-Norman like themselves who would give his all to this England that he had adopted and clearly loved.

He pointed out to them the genius of the old English institutions established by the late, great Henry II, and each baron realized that here was a man cut from the same cloth.

Simon was impatient to get back to Leicester to get on with the business of borrowing money for Rome, but before he took leave Richard returned his bribe of five hundred crowns. He handed over the money, saying "When my sister's happiness depends upon it, how can I think of profit?"

When Simon returned to Kenilworth, the only opposition remaining to his marriage came from the church. He had traveled so far, so fast that his horse was exhausted, yet Simon himself was not even tired. His spirits were buoyed by what he had accomplished. Now he was keyed up to face the Pope and the papal court to overcome the great remaining obstacle.

35

As he neared home Simon realized that Eleanor must know by now of the terrible scandal she had caused and that, by edict of the Archbishop of Canterbury, they were no longer married. It was close to the end of March and she was in her seventh month.

Word of approaching riders spread quickly at Kenilworth. Eleanor was in the buttery where everything was kept cool, from wine to cheese, when she heard that mounted men were upon the causeway. She rushed to the high Caesar Tower to see if it was Simon de Montfort. She was blazing with anger at him and angry at herself. She should never have let him pursue her, never have succumbed to his charm and his physical magnetism. Sparks had ignited between them from their first encounter. What had begun badly had ended badly. Now the price she would pay would be horrendous.

He had made her pregnant, talked her into a secret marriage that had been invalidated immediately, then he had deserted her for a month. By the time Simon climbed the stone steps to the Caesar Tower she was ready to draw her knife, but when his tall, broad figure filled the doorway, blocking out the world, she rushed into his arms, blinded by tears, clinging to him, straining to him, for his strength, his protection, and his love.

She did not want the tears to spoil her face, but to Simon she was always beautiful. He picked her up gently and cradled her with infinite tenderness. He lowered her to the bed and lay down beside her to comfort and hold her. "Try not to be so upset, my own sweetheart. I have accomplished much. The barons and the men of the Cinque Ports will support me."

She recoiled from him. "Against Henry?"

He held his patience. "Eleanor, you cannot have it both ways. Either the barons and all their armies are against us and Henry alone supports us, or it is the other way about. Your brother Richard supports us. He and Isabella are having a child," he said to divert her thoughts.

" 'Tis easy for them, they have a valid marriage!" she cried, struggling up from the bed.

His powerful arm held her at his side. "It was not always so, Eleanor, as you well know. Compose yourself; it is bad for the child when you are angry and upset." He smoothed back her wild tangle of black curls and kissed her temple.

She looked into his dark eyes and saw the tiny reflection of herself there. I am a part of him, she thought, just as he is a part of me. She slid her arms about him possessively. His smooth, full lips molded to hers, and his powerful hands slid down her body to mold her to the great, hard length of him. His hands massaged her back until she relaxed against him. Until she felt his magic touch she had no idea how tense she had been. They curled their bodies together, touching, kissing, tasting, trying to get enough but unable to.

As he fondled her, she quickly lost all semblance of resistance to him. "Sim," she whispered, "I don't give a damn if they keep us from being legally married! I'll live with you in sin. Kenilworth will be our world."

"Kathe, my darling love, I pledge to do everything in my power to get the church to recognize our marriage. Tomorrow I go to Rome to prove that your vow was not binding. I am determined to have the lawfulness of this marriage established."

"Oh, Sim, if only it could be so." The tears slipped down her cheeks and he kissed them away.

"Why do you cry, love?" he murmured.

"We only have 'til dawn. 'Tis ever the same with us. Promise me when you return you will never leave again," she demanded passionately.

"You know I cannot, sweet. I will promise to take you wherever I go . . . will that satisfy?"

An unbearable thought came to her. "Oh, Simon, you'll be gone when my time for the baby comes!"

He saw the fear in her eyes. "Nay, not if I can help it," he vowed. His resolution almost failed him. For the first time in his life he knew real, numbing fear. She was so very tiny he feared any child from his loins would be big enough to kill her. Splendor of God, he would have to move heaven and earth to get his marriage validated and return before the month of May was out.

He held her safe until she slept, then eased himself away from her in the great bed. He knew that almost everyone in Kenilworth was devoted to her, from Jack who supervised the bathhouse to Dobbe the shepherd. He communicated all his worries about childbirth to Bette and begged her to keep Eleanor safe for him. Then he left Kenilworth in the capable hands of Sir Rickard de Burgh.

He decided the fastest possible way was across the English Channel, then overland to Rome. He took six of his hardest-bitten knights with him because he knew the roads on the continent were thick with thieves, and he carried over five thousand marks.

In the Holy City there was protocol to be observed before he got an audience with the Pope. He used his time to set out everything on paper about Eleanor, Countess of Pembroke, who lost her husband the marshal at sixteen years of age. He told how she had been so grief-stricken she had sworn a vow of chastity and perpetual widowhood and asked for a dispensation so that his marriage to her could be declared valid. He had a scribe make copies for each member of the papal court, then was left to cool his heels.

After a week had gone by, he decided to take matters into his own hands. He visited the Pope's treasury clerk and spoke of money, a language the Vatican understood. "When I arrived I placed five thousand marks with a goldsmith as a donation to the Holy Church of Rome. Each day my men and I stay in Rome depletes the amount of gold on deposit. I have six knights and two squires, and the expense of stabling and feeding our horses alone is heavy. If you could find a way to expedite matters, the money I save on our food and lodging could find its way into your hands."

At the end of another week Simon de Montfort had his ruling, but not before promising another two thousand marks. To get the paper in his hand ruling in his favor he would have solemnly pledged another two million, let alone two thousand! He would take a page from Henry Plantagenet's book this one time and promise whatever it took.

Simon started the long trek home, arriving back at Kenilworth in record time. May in England was incomparable. It seemed as if the entire country was in bloom. As the earl rode from Dover, his love for England increased a thousandfold. The grass really was greener there, the hedgerows dotted with wildflowers, the meadows neatly bordered by stone walls. Every hill was covered with sheep and lambs, every valley held milky herds, and field after field sprouted from spring planting.

There was much wrong with England, of course, all of it stemming from the crown. The country was almost split in half. The greed of the Provençals and Savoyards, which the king did nothing to discourage, sowed seeds of discontent among the Anglo-Norman barons so that the king had no English adherents. Disloyalty and disaster loomed.

In spite of all this, deep in his heart and soul Simon de Montfort had an overwhelming sense of homecoming. His hungry eyes swept Kenilworth possessively from the distance, and as he neared the causeway he smiled with satisfaction to see that waterfowl had nested upon his newly created mere. Inside his chest a knot of excitement that he'd held in check for so long suddenly exploded. Anticipation of seeing her, touching her, then watching her face as he gave her his news filled his imagination and set his pulses racing.

Eleanor had despaired that he would ever return with good

news. As March ended and April began, her patience and faith wore thin. When April galloped into May she began to panic that her child would be born illegitimate. When hope deserted her she was willing to settle for Simon's return before she gave birth, but even that was dwindling rapidly.

She had kept herself busy, of course. Kenilworth did not run itself. She had directed the spring planting and then she had tackled the books. It was very involved. Parchments listed acreages, livestock, produce, and revenues. The books told what taxes had been paid and what were still owed. There were long lists of debts and expenses. Another book listed the names of Kenilworth's villeins, the land worked, which days they worked for Kenilworth and which for themselves. It listed the rents, the crops, and the profits.

She had taken it upon herself to order land cleared and planted and the wood sold for a profit. She had also gone into debt to increase the livestock. Eleanor had fought off labor for three days. Her pains almost cut her in half, but by sheer dint of will her mind had stopped them after two hours, only to have them start again in the middle of each night. Ironically it was not the hours when she was on her feet at her busiest that labor threatened, but when her body was still and at rest.

At times she cursed and vilified Simon de Montfort, cataloging every offense, every fault, swearing she would never, ever allow him access to her bed again. He was the author of all her trouble and pain, and she would make sure that he never, ever put her in this position again. She had learned her lesson. She had committed a sinful crime and she was receiving her punishment.

Eleanor knew she must keep active. Unfortunately, she could not walk far. Then she decided she would get a mount saddled and ride among the outbuildings. Bette forbade her to leave the Caesar Tower, but she flared, "Who do you think you are, my mother?"

Eleanor was spoiling for a fight by the time she reached the stables and ordered a groom to saddle a horse for her. A young knight stepped forward in alarm. "I would not advise a ride, my lady."

"Why not?" she demanded, bristling.

Her condition was obvious and surely he need not point it out to her. "The Earl of Leicester . . ."

She cut him off. "A pox on the Earl of Leicester!"

Simon de Montfort dismounted and in three strides swept his wife into his arms.

"Faugh! You stink of horsesweat and leather," she protested.

"And you stink of fire and brimstone, my reckless little bitch!"

"Put me down, you ugly great giant! Your natural demeanor is assertive. You speak as if you expect to be obeyed always. I give you back your own words, de Montfort. If you attempt to control me, you are in for a battle royale."

"I am taking you upstairs to whelp," he said crudely.

She clenched her fists and began to pummel him, but a contraction stiffened her body and turned her words into a scream. Simon started to run. He took the stairs two at a time, calling out for Bette as he entered the tower. He lowered his wife carefully to the bed and left her to her women.

He spent a good deal of the next ten hours on his knees in the chapel. "Dear God, now I have all I desire in the palm of my hand, do not snatch it away from me," he prayed fervently.

Eleanor experienced every emotion known to woman during those hours, from deepest despair through hysterics, rage, acceptance, and finally on to joy.

When Simon was allowed in to see her, she was utterly exhausted with her newborn son tucked against her breast. They both looked so tiny in the vast bed that he was overwhelmed. He sat down beside her and took hold of her hand. Finally he lifted it to his lips and reverently kissed each finger.

She whispered, "I could not hold it off any longer."

A great lump came into his throat. Blood of God, she had fought against the birth thinking shameful stigma attached to it. He said softly, "Eleanor, the papal court ruled in our favor." He took a crackling parchment from his doublet. "This is a dispensation that says there was no invalidity in the marriage I contracted with you."

"Oh, thank God and St. Jude!" she breathed. "In my own heart I knew that my vow was not binding."

"I am going to get the scribe to make a copy of this for the

Archbishop of Canterbury, so there's an end to it," he said firmly. "Now we can get on with our lives."

She looked down at her child with love-filled eyes. "I am going to call him Henry because he was the one who made it all possible," she said fervently.

Simon's mouth twisted wryly. He had pursued this woman against all odds, planted his seed until it had taken root, obtained Kenilworth for her, ridden across England to appease the Duke of Cornwall and the barons, begged and borrowed enough gold to go to Rome and bribe the Pope for a dispensation, but all her gratitude was reserved for the king.

"We will call this son Henry after his illustrious grandfather. We will call the next son Simon," he said, grinning.

She pulled her hand from his. "Oh, you brute, to speak of the next before I have recovered from this one. From now on I think I shall have my own chamber so I can avoid your attentions!"

The next months were to be among the happiest of their lives. Eleanor did anything but avoid Simon's attention. She was so proud to be slim again, she showed off her figure to him every chance she got.

Bette no longer hovered about her. Instead she had transferred her attentions to the baby. Eleanor chose two young sisters, Emma and Kate, to help Bette in the nursery, which left Eleanor free to take Kenilworth in hand and make some changes. She began in the kitchens by ordering 350 new utensils all made from shining copper. The kitchen, with its high-vaulted ceiling to reduce heat, smell, and smoke, was becoming a showpiece. Eleanor discovered an immense painting of an ox carcass with instructions on its proper carving and had it hung on the west wall.

The wine that came from Wiltshire was decidedly iron-flavored and Eleanor ordered that it be discontinued. In its stead she ordered expensive, imported wine be brought in. She ordered hens from Buckingham, eels from Bristol, and herrings from Yarmouth. The amount of food eaten daily grew steadily as Kenilworth expanded. Eleanor appointed a stewardess rather than a steward to keep a tally of kitchen supplies and expenditures and went over the accounts with her each month. Eleanor did not bat an eye that over 3,000 eggs were consumed in a week as well as 188 gallons of ale at a half pence per gallon, with 80 skins of Gascony wine.

Merchants, Franciscan brothers, scholars, artists, and mercenary soldiers all began to flock to Kenilworth. Eleanor began to compile a library with the works of Aristotle, Ptolemny, Thomas Aquinas, and Roger Bacon.

Whenever Simon noticed that something had been changed or something new had been acquired for Kenilworth and he questioned someone, he always got back the same answer. "The Countess of Pembroke ordered it." He would grit his teeth and correct them. "You mean the Countess of Leicester, I believe."

When de Montfort found the armory and guardrooms deserted one day, he was informed that Tuesday was now market day. The Countess of Pembroke had established it and it was thriving. The last straw came for Simon while he was holding a Court of Justice. His eyebrows rose a little when he saw Eleanor arrive gowned in an extravagant creation of green and gold, interwoven Syrian silk edged in sable. She sat quietly enough while he held court—until the last case. Apparently the brewer in Banbury had died, and there were two applicants for the position. One was the brewer's brother, which seemed right and proper to Simon since he did not have a son to fill his shoes, but the other claimant for the job was the brewer's widow. Simon heard them out and decided in the brother's favor, explaining to the woman that brewing was a job for a man.

Eleanor swept forward with her challenge. "Not so, my lord earl! This woman knows all there is to know about brewing ale. She has helped her husband for years and in fact has done all the brewing during her late husband's illness. His brother, on the other hand, has been a farmer all his life. Surely you will not discriminate against her because she is a woman, my lord? In my judgment I think we should have a breweress in Banbury."

Simon's anger was aroused. Why couldn't she have had a private word with him about this matter? Why did she find it necessary to try to overrule him in his own court? He almost made the wrong decision purely and simply to teach Eleanor a lesson. However, his sense of justice saved him. It was only logical to appoint a breweress since she had the requisite experience.

Simon de Montfort was looking for his wife within half an hour and was told the Countess of Pembroke was in the kitchens. It seemed to him this day that his household was overfull of women. He was forever tripping over cooks, bakers, washerwomen, maids, nannies, and stewardesses. He entered the kitchen, took one look at the excessive display of new copper utensils, and demanded, "Who the hell ordered all this?"

The head cook, a red-faced country woman, full of her own importance in the pecking order beamed. "The Countess of Pembroke, my lord."

Simon booted a stool across the kitchen, which sent a copper cauldren rolling after a pot-boy. "Christ Almighty," he exploded. "Once and for all time, she is the Countess of Leicester. The next person to call her Countess of Pembroke gets chucked in the bloody mere!" He looked about him in frustration at the gaggle of women. "All hens and no cocks . . . too many women in this household for my taste!" Simon strode toward Eleanor and with hands firmly planted upon her hips she met him halfway.

Simon's voice was dominant as it rang round the high-vaulted ceiling. His arm swept over the sea of burnished copper. "How much did this lot cost me?"

"I know not and I care less," Eleanor said, tossing her black curls impudently.

"You simply order whatever you fancy without a thought to cost?" he asked incredulously.

"Surely you do not expect me to haggle over pennies like a fishwife?" she demanded haughtily.

"Forgive me, *Princess,*" he replied sarcastically. "I thought you were the chatelaine of Kenilworth. Perhaps you had better wear your crown and have your pot-boy hold up your train to remind us all of who you are."

"Oh!" She gasped as his dart found its mark. "I am the chatelaine. Remove yourself from my kitchen. I do not interfere in your affairs."

Simon thumped the table and the kitchen staff became invisible. "Do not interfere? What the hell was that all about at the court I held this morning?"

"I remained inconspicuous at the back of the hall."

"Inconspicuous? In that gown?" he demanded.

"I don't understand what you are angry about," she spat.

"You never do when you are in the wrong, madame. This morning even before you interrupted my court and tried to make my decisions for me, everyone in the hall was watching your very expressive face to see whether you thought my judgments wise or stupid. I let you get away with this breweress business, but in future I will not tolerate your interference."

The tone of his voice warned her she had done and said enough, but heedlessly she railed, "May I inquire why you canceled my order of Gascony wines?"

He thought the answer to that ridiculous expenditure was obvious. He reached out his powerful hands to her waist and removed her from his path. Then he quit the kitchen. The very air in the room shuddered as he slammed the door.

36

Simon avoided her the rest of the day and did not climb the stairs to the Caesar Tower until after compline. This was usually the hour they set aside to enjoy their baby. All three of them rolled about the massive bed, laughing and playing, and then she would feed him. Simon would watch her face grow rapt with love and Eleanor would know her husband's hungry needs were greater than those of her son.

Tonight, however, Eleanor was not in their bedchamber. Simon, in no mood to tolerate womanish behavior, set out to find her. On the far side of the nursery was a chamber that Eleanor had decided to use for herself. She had furnished it with delicate small chairs and tables suitable only for use by a female. The bed was narrow and not designed to hold a couple.

Eleanor sat at a tiny desk making entries in her journal. Gone was the green and gold gown. In its stead she wore a finespun bedrobe of pale lavender sarcenet. Her beautiful hair had been brushed until it looked like a black cloud of smoke billowing about her shoulders.

Simon's mouth went dry at the sight of her. His anger was quickly dissipating and in its place arose a searing desire. His black magnetic eyes burned into hers as he spoke. "Since you seem disinclined to join me in our chamber, I decided to join you in yours."

She ran a provocative tongue over her lips. "I have to make some journal entries."

"I'll wait," he said implacably, and lowered himself into a delicate chair. An ominous crack was followed by a total collapse and splintering of the chair.

"Lud, I swear if you brought your destrier in here it would do less damage," she said, rising from the desk and affording him an unimpeded view of her body through the transparent gown.

"You are right," he acknowledged, feasting on her naked beauty, hinting at the violence he was barely holding in check. Since he had no alternative he sat upon the bed.

Eleanor was thoroughly enjoying herself. She reveled in the power her beauty exercised over him. Simon had shown her the hidden depths of her passion, and she intended to goad him until he took what he wanted so badly. Since she'd had the baby it was never painful when Simon made love to her. It was still a very tight fit, of course, because of his size, but now it was like a sheath fitting the sword for which it was designed. Now she did not need over an hour of arousal before they made love. She experienced instant arousal whenever she saw his hungry eyes linger on her breasts or her mouth. Sometimes she feared her needs would become greater than his, for often when he was gone from the castle she longed for the sight of him, the smell of him, the taste of him. Quite often even picking up one of his garments or even an object that his attractive hands had touched would arouse her, and she would begin to fantasize about the things he would do to her that night in the delicious privacy of the Caesar Tower. The thought of his hands or his mouth on the secret, intimate parts of her body made her pulses race and a low moan escape from her throat. Her silken undergarments rubbing against her ruched nipples or the swollen bud between her legs sometimes made her want to scream. She dare not take wine in the evenings anymore lest it make her so wanton she threw off all her clothes and spread her legs in abandoned invitation.

She lifted her chin defiantly and said, "I don't know what you are waiting for."

"I am waiting politely to take you to bed," he ground out.

"I'm not sleepy," she threw at him.

"I don't intend to sleep, I intend to fuck. I guarantee you will be sleepy when I am finished with you."

"If you think I'll let you make love to me tonight, think again, Frenchman."

"You are my wife and I am going to bed you now!" She had dared to come just a tiny bit too close, and his powerful arm snaked out to grab her.

Her throat filled with heartbeats. "I shall fight you!" she vowed passionately.

"Good. If it's rough you want, I recommend a Frenchman every time." He tore the flimsy gown from her and plunged a hand between her tempting thighs. His fingers found her hot, wet, and creamy with desire for him. She struggled for the pure pleasure of having him breach her defenses. He soon had her pinned beneath him, imprisoned exactly as she had longed to be. The anticipation of having him fill her made her want to scream with excitement.

Suddenly the small bed collapsed beneath them and Eleanor cried impatiently, "Oh, bugger!"

Simon ignored the collapsed bed. It mattered little what was beneath him save the feel of his wife's body, which told him plainly he was the only one who could satisfy what he alone had awakened. He intended to use the floor for his next bout of lovemaking. Then he would begin all over again in his chamber, which was where she would be from now on. It was his woman's place to be in his bed and from now on he would keep her in her woman's place.

From that day on she teased and tempted him, denied and refused him, flouted his authority and disobeyed his orders, but he knew he gave her exactly what she wanted every night behind the closed door of their chamber. He forbid her women access to the Caesar Tower after the hour of six at night. Each evening he lit a fire so that she could walk about naked for him, and sometimes he even fed her dragonsblood for the sensual pleasure of watching her lose all control.

He was always amazed that such a savage passion lurked just beneath the surface of one so tiny, so dainty, so young. There was never any question that he could satisfy her; the miracle of their mating was that she could satisfy him so deeply, and yet he always wanted more. He longed for all of her, body and soul, but there was always a small part of herself that belonged to her alone. Eleanor was her own woman, who made decisions no matter how much he showed her her woman's place, yet he knew he would not be consumed and enchanted by a simpering wench and thanked heaven for her.

Kenilworth was a hub of activity. Travelers came and went continually and brought all the news of the outside world to their doorstep. They learned that the king had dismissed the council and appointed a new one consisting entirely of the queen's relatives, who in turn were ruled by Winchester.

At last the queen was pregnant. Henry decided that England and the barons would pay through the nose for this heir they had demanded of him. Rumor was rife that the king was about to impose a tallage on the barons amounting to one-third of all their wealth. His new council had already agreed to such a measure, but the common council of England was demanding that a parliament be called. The barons began to arm themselves secretly.

Simon de Montfort wanted to protect Henry from the destruction that his false counselors were preparing. When he arrived in London he was appalled at the angry tone of the common man in the street. The queen was openly reviled and hated, and she dare not go into the streets for fear of the mob. The only safe way any member of the royal household could travel was by barge down the River Thames. There was now even an outcry against the Jews because they financed Henry's insatiable demands for money, which in the end the country must pay back with high interest.

Henry welcomed Simon, but he was hated by the queen's uncles, the Savoys, and by Henry's half brothers, who now ironically were also Simon's half brothers by marriage.

The queen flaunted her long-awaited pregnancy, even wearing gowns that exaggerated her swollen shape. The heir to the throne monopolized every conversation, and the queen acted as if she was the first woman ever to give birth.

Simon de Montfort could not help comparing her self-aggrandizing behavior with that of his beloved wife. Poor Eleanor had hidden her pregnancy in fear for as long as she could, then she had worn flowing, loose garments to conceal her condition from all prying eyes. A growing anger took possession of him as he recalled she had given birth not even knowing if her child was legitimate.

He took special pleasure one evening in removing the smug look from the queen's face. She had just pointed out to a large court gathering that her child would be the first of a new generation of Plantagenets, the first grandchild of King John and the first great-grandchild of illustrious King Henry II. "You are mistaken, your Grace," Simon said blandly. "I believe Richard and Isabella have a well-kept secret who will be arriving any day. Your child won't be born until late June, I believe."

The queen turned an unbecoming shade of purple and almost choked. Clearly she had been so full of herself she had not known of her sister-in-law's expected child. Her tone was icy as she spoke loudly to all who cared to listen. "And you, sir. When will the little nun be providing you with an heir?"

"Ah, she has already done that, your Grace. By the time you and Henry are parents she will probably be carrying another son."

In that moment the queen decided to join Simon de Montfort's enemies, and together they would poison Henry's mind against him.

It was difficult for Simon to get Henry alone, but they spent one day together while Henry showed off the new additions he'd been building at the Tower and at Windsor. Simon knew his passion for architecture and let Henry exhaust the subject before he spoke to him of more serious affairs. "Your Grace, the barons will never agree to pay this tallage you are about to impose. You have been ill advised by your new council. I believe they urge you to arbitrary extremes."

Henry denied it hotly. "The old council bound and gagged me and kept me penniless. I have long anticipated the gratifications of personal rule."

Simon suspected he was more a puppet now than he had ever been. The demands for larger amounts of money were being instigated by the Queen's Men. "Sire, the barons are arming themselves secretly. If it comes to war you will have few adherents. If you reinstate Hubert de Burgh, you would immediately regain the support of the men of the Cinque Ports."

"That is a brilliant idea, Simon. Come back to Windsor, I need advisors like yourself."

"Henry, all you need do to hold this great country together is adhere to the provisions of the Great Charter. The men who hold high office must be Englishmen. Remember how smoothly things ran when your justiciar was Hubert de Burgh and William Marshal was head of the military?"

Henry nodded solemnly, remembering. Simon sighed. It was so easy to sway Henry; he was a boy in a man's body. Trouble was, the moment he listened to William of Valence or Winchester his mind would be changed again.

"Give Hubert a royal pardon. Confirm William Marshal's brother Richard as Marshal of England. If you are always without money, then your chancellor of the Exchequer is not doing his job. He is supposed to be a humble priest, but I know for a fact he holds at least three hundred church offices and collects fifteen thousand marks per year from them for himself, not for you."

"Is that so?" Henry asked in amazement.

Simon tried to hold his patience at the king's ignorance. "Why do you think the barons are so outraged? You propose to tax them, but not the greedy churchmen who are raping England."

Henry listened intently. "I'll take the matter up with Winchester. Fifteen thousand a year, you say?"

Simon groaned inwardly. Henry was fixated on the sum of money he'd mentioned but was blind to the fact that Winchester was worse than all of the others rolled together. Simon realized in that moment that the king had been reduced to a servant of the Winchester party.

The Earl of Leicester rode back to Kenilworth, taking with him two dozen knights and men-at-arms, some of them actual members of the king's own Welsh Guard. He had not recruited

them, in fact he had discouraged them since he could ill afford
more fighting men, but all they asked was space in the knights'
quarters and room at Kenilworth's board.

The weather turned hot and sticky on the ride home. They
bedded down in a hayfield at dusk and were entertained by a
display of sheet lightning that lit the sky for hours. No thunder-
storm came to clear the air, however, and the next day was
even hotter. By the time Kenilworth's crenellated towers were
in sight, Simon could think of nothing but removing his sweaty
clothes and visiting the bathhouse.

When he learned that his wife had taken one of the small
punts onto the mere to catch the afternoon breezes, he changed
his mind. He looked down eagerly from the Caesar Tower to
pinpoint her exact location and decided to swim out to the little
boat to try to surprise her. She had filled the punt with cushions
and lay back drowsing away the summer afternoon. In an effort
to keep cool, she wore only a white linen smock with nothing
beneath it.

The small boat had drifted beneath some weeping willows at
the edge of the mere, and she trailed her fingers in the water as
she closed her eyes drowsily. At the edge of the lake Simon
threw off his clothes and plunged into the cool water. He cut
smoothly across the mere to the spot where the weeping willows dipped to kiss the waters. As he neared the punt he tred
water quietly and positioned himself so she could not see him.
With finger and thumb he nipped lightly at her fingers that
trailed in the water.

"Oh." She gasped and withdrew her hand, thinking a fish
had bitten her. She looked about, but when she saw no ripples
of any kind, she lay back and closed her eyes. Simon took a
long reed and tickled her nose. She wafted what she imagined
to be an insect from her face with a mild "Oh, bugger!"

Simon, in a relentlessly playful mood, immediately moved
the reed to tickle her chin. "Oh, balls!" she muttered, and sat
up to do battle with the annoying creature. Simon braced two
strong arms on the side of the boat and raised himself up from
the water, laughing at her.

"Oh, you beast!" she cried. "I thought you were some great
sea serpent."

"And so I might have been," he said, grinning from ear to ear. "Who knows what lurks beneath the mere of Kenilworth?"

The pupils of her deep-blue eyes dilated at the sight of him, glistening with water, the dragons on his forearms coming to life as he braced his muscles. As he hoisted his entire length into the boat, she screamed again. "Blood of God, you are stark naked!"

"I was born this way," he teased, spreading his legs for balance and towering over her reclining figure.

"Simon, don't rock the boat! It isn't big enough for a sea monster your size."

He shook his thick, black mane and showered her with droplets.

"Simon! You are wetting me!"

"Such a fuss over a splosh of water. Come and play. Take off your clothes and join me for a swim."

She pretended outrage. "I cannot take off my clothes. Someone might see me from the castle."

"We are too far off for anyone to get a good look. Don't be a coward," he taunted.

"No, I don't swim very well. I'll just watch you," she suggested to divert him.

He alternated his great weight from one foot to the other and the boat began to rock precariously.

"Simon!" she cried. "You'll tip us over!"

He stopped rocking. "Well, if you won't play in the water, we'll play in the boat." He grinned wickedly, before stretching himself out beside her.

"Simon!" But his mouth covered hers, stopping any further protests, as his lips molded hers lustily and his hand lifted the white linen hem to caress a bare limb. "Eleanor de Montfort, you too are naked! No wonder you didn't want me to discover your naughty secret." His fingers began to tease and tickle her thighs and tangle in her silken curls.

"I'm too hot," she half protested.

"I know." He grinned. "That's just the way I like you." He removed the white linen gown without her putting up too great a struggle. The smell of the sun on his clean, dark skin aroused her, and his whispered words lured her along the path of sensual seduction. "Did you know there are exotic places in the world where dusky maidens run about bare under the sun? English sailors have been driven mad tasting one flower after another like bees drunk on nectar." His eyes roamed possessively over her. "No dusky maiden ever had such dainty ankles, slim calves, or soft, sweet thighs." She could feel his voice, warm, rich, and deep against her throat. It sent delicious shivers along the length of her spine. "I have traveled many lands and often sampled their womenhood, yet never have I seen such a vision of beauty as you my love. Your face is ever before me, sleeping or waking. I am so consumed by you, my Kathe, I am senseless before you, pleading for your slightest touch, your briefest glance. You haunt my dreams when I am gone from you, and I awaken empty and shaking from the deepest sleep. Though I am reputed to have greater strength than most men, one taste of you leaves me weak and mindless. I live and breathe for you alone; you are my earth, my sun. I want no other world but you."

Eleanor's eyes were soft and shining and the ache in her throat equaled the one in her breast and that in her belly. This man of hers was full of surprises. She knew his strength, knew his passion, but until now she had never known he had the soul of a poet. His magnetism wove a magic spell around her until she sighed and writhed beneath his questing hand. His lips played about her shell-like ear, sending a flood of shivers up and down her sun-warmed limbs. She forgot they lay outside, forgot they floated upon the mere, forgot their bed was a boat, their mattress soft cushions. Their bare limbs entangled, their black hair tossed wildly about them as he rolled with her until she was imprisoned beneath him.

"Now, my water sprite, my temptress, I've caught you. Will you love me until I am mindless? Will you let me drown in the deep-blue pools of your eyes? I am like a moth who returns again and again to your flame until I am destroyed."

Eleanor smiled her secret smile. "Moth indeed! You are like a great rutting stag who tosses me upon my back to take your pleasure. Or better yet, like a rampant stallion who won't be denied until you have mounted me and reduced me to a yielding, quivering female animal who longs to be mated."

"Nay, love, I am just a man with a man's lust, but it is tempered and mingled with a deep abiding love for you." His mouth took hers in a deep, consuming kiss, his tongue plunging and tasting as if he had been starving for her.

The fire inside her ran molten gold along every vein like burning rivers all rushing to her woman's center. She gasped against his fierce mouth. "Sim, take me, take me now." They did not even see the flash of lightning or the crash of thunder. The storm of passion they created deafened and blinded them to the elements. Their bodies were so heated, he felt scalded as he plunged within her. His sword of fire sheathed itself in her molten liquid until he cried out hoarsely to the storm gods. Their fused bodies smoldered, then like glowing coals burst into flame to consume them. Her climax was so sensual she almost spun away into darkness. He buried his face in her hair, savoring the fragrance, the taste, and the feel of her all in the same earth-shattering moment.

They seemed to awaken to the world about them at the same moment. Large cool splashes of rain were falling upon them from the heavens, and as they looked into each other's eyes they suddenly began to laugh. Eleanor became aware that their bodies were still joined. Each spasm of Simon's laughter caused a delicious friction deep within her that caused her to arch her back and thrust her mons until his semiarousal built and filled to its full, hard length again almost immediately. She wrapped her legs high about his broad back to keep the great treasure within her secret cave and they laughed harder, unable to control their mirth or the raw sexuality they aroused in each other. The boat rocked wildly as if it had caught their reckless, abandoned mood and would join them in their tempestuous love play. Her need grew so intense she was laughing and crying, the raindrops mingling with her tears. Simon's needs were warring within him until all pretense at gentleness was washed away, replaced wholly by savage hunger. His movements became so violent the little boat decided it had had enough and tipped the coupling lovers beneath the waters.

It was enough to cool their ardor temporarily. Eleanor came up gasping and Simon reached out to aid her, remembering her admission that she did not swim well. Only when his strong arms clasped her and she felt safe and secure clinging to his powerful torso did she trust herself to speak. "You beast, you did it on purpose," she accused.

"Me?" he asked incredulously, unable to keep the laughter from his voice as the silken cushions bobbed all about them. "It was the gyrations of your pretty bottom that landed us in the drink."

"How can you say such a thing?" she demanded as she pulled a fistful of his wet, black hair. "Anyone who is six-and-a-half-feet long shouldn't even be in a little boat like mine."

He threatened to duck her beneath the water again and she squealed with alarm. "The only way to settle whose fault it was is to ask them at the castle . . . someone will have been watching us," he teased.

"You brute!" She gasped, unable to keep from blushing. "Simon, my gown!" she suddenly cried in alarm. "Oh, no. It's gone. I'm naked! I'll have to stay out here until after dark, until everyone's gone to bed."

"Darling, I intend to finish in our chamber what we began in the boat and I am in no mood to wait more than a few minutes," he informed her. He immediately stroked out strongly for the causeway that led to the drawbridge and carried her with him, kicking and protesting all the way. He teased her unmercifully. "It's all right, sweetheart, I'll be naked too. Half of them will be looking at me."

"Simon, stop, I'll die of embarrassment and shame."

"Where's the shame? We're married, aren't we? We have a paper from the bloody Pope telling the world our lovemaking is lawful!"

Her blushes had spread all the way down to her saucy breasts by the time he deposited her on the bank of the mere. With a wicked grin he reached down for the clothes he had discarded earlier. He wrapped his shirt about her and slipped into his pants, then he took her hand and literally had to pull her along over the drawbridge and under the portcullis. "My legs are bare," she whispered furiously.

"Then you take the pants and I'll take the shirt," he offered, grinning.

"Simon!"

"Oh, stop fussing. It covers your titties and your pretty bum, much to the sorrow of the guards up on the wall."

She glanced up in horror, but the men of Kenilworth all seemed to be gazing into the distance with faces like stone. Simon took pity on her and led the way to the pentice, which wound about the outside of the massive Caesar Tower, rather than taking her through the castle. She heaved a sigh of relief when they had climbed halfway without encountering too many gaping faces. She turned to address him over her shoulder. "You really are a barbarian. You come home from court without even a gift for me . . . all I get is a dirty shirt," she scolded, tossing her damp curls.

With a firm hand he snatched the shirt from her. "If it offends you, I'll have it back." He laughed wickedly.

She screeched and flew up the rest of the stairs, but before she reached the privacy of their bedchamber she heard him shout graphically exactly what gift he was going to give her.

37

The momentous news arrived at Kenilworth that King Henry III and Queen Eleanor had produced a son and heir, born on the twentieth day of June in the year of our Lord 1239. He was to be named Edward, and the christening and the queen's churching were to be celebrated with all pomp and ceremony.

It was hoped that the people of London would set aside their hatreds and predjudices for the royal court now that they had a royal prince who had been born on English soil. Londoners were known to be fickle and nothing diverted the mob like a celebration, which was always an excuse to eat, drink and be merry, to overspend and overindulge. In doing so perhaps they would overlook their monarchs' shortcomings.

Henry's arrogance had grown apace with that of the Provençals and Savoyards. He personally inspected the gifts for the newborn prince as they began to arrive from all over the country. If he thought the gift inferior, he refused to accept it and returned it to its owner suggesting something more costly and lavish. Even the court jester said, "God has given us this child, but the king sells him to us!"

For the baby prince Simon de Montfort bought a breeding

pair of miniature horses that had been bred in Coventry. He had never seen the breed before and he knew the king had a passion for animals to show off in his zoo. Without consulting her husband, Eleanor had ordered a beaten silver christening chalice adorned by her favorite blue sapphires. Since her brother had a passion for anything green, she ordered the Litchfield silversmith mount uncut emeralds upon the foot of the chalice.

Sir Rickard de Burgh had been chosen to carry the gifts to court by both the earl and countess, unknown to each other of course. Suddenly the household staff became invisible. The tempestuous months of the Leicesters' marriage had trained them to recognize when a storm was about to rage. The cook threw her wooden spoon down in disgust as she heard Simon raise his voice and thump the table. She had labored hours over the meal and knew when de Montfort's temper was aroused he always found fault with the meat. The serving wenches changed their aprons and caps because when the countess was annoyed she was overcritical of their cleanliness.

"Splendor of God, Eleanor, your extravagance is beyond the beyond. Why do you always take the initiative without consulting my wishes or the state of Kenilworth's coffers?" he demanded.

"Why do you always choose mealtime to vent your temper . . . and must you wear that leather tunic to the table? 'Tis more fitting for the stable."

"Ah, the Countess of Leicester has vanished and we have the pleasure of Princess Eleanor Katherine Plantagenet tonight."

There was a hidden devil in each of them that set off sparks. She turned her back upon him. "You are mistaken. You will have the pleasure of neither of us." She began to march from the hall.

"Come back here," thundered Simon. "Did you hear me? I told you to come back, madame!"

She ignored him totally. He strode after her, not caring a whit that half the room was filled with his knights and the other half with those who sat below the salt—priests, merchants, squires, troubadors, and ladies without rank.

She had gained the stairs and when she reached the fourth

step she turned and faced him on eye level. "I do not take orders kindly, Frenchman."

His dark eyes swept over her angrily, then opened wide as he took in the low-cut gown that exposed over half of her breasts. "Who is this unseemly display for, pray?"

"This is one of the new gowns I'm having fitted for court, if you must know. I cannot go to London looking like a country milkmaid."

"What in Christ's name put the idea into your head that you are going to London?" he bellowed.

"We received an engraved, formal invitation today to attend the christening and the queen's churching at the Abbey. Of course we are going to London!"

"I am always stunned at the convenient way you forget I am the master here at Kenilworth. I shall make the decision of whether or not we go to London."

"Dream on, Frenchman!" she said impudently.

"Seek your room . . . *now*!"

She had been doing exactly that when he had waylaid her; now perversely it was the last thing she wanted to do. However, she knew she had goaded him too far. She tossed her curls and stamped her foot defiantly, but she did as he bade her. She heard her son's lusty cry before Bette carried him in to her. Her woman spoke to her with the familiarity of one whose position was secure. "You may not be hungry, but the prince of Kenilworth here is demanding his dinner." Eleanor took him into her arms, adoration replacing the anger on her face. She took inordinate pride in her son's size and beauty. "He is his father's son . . . he thinks he rules heaven and earth, but tonight he's in for the shock of his life." She turned to the young nursemaid who trailed after Bette and the baby with an armful of clean breachclouts.

"Emma, fetch some fresh milk from the stillroom. We are going to start weaning him."

Bette said doubtfully, "Do you think that's wise? So long as you're feeding him you cannot get pregnant again."

"That is an old wives' tale," Eleanor scoffed. "I am going to London in August, so I must start to wean him." Eleanor gave

Bette an amused glance. "I see all your disapproval has vanished now that you think you will have him to yourself soon."

Bette said anxiously, "You won't take him to London, will you?"

Eleanor laughed. "Splendor of God, I would not dare suggest taking him from the stronghold of Kenilworth. Simon would run mad. However, *I* am another matter entirely." She smiled her secret smile. She would persuade her husband to let her have her own way . . . she always did.

As soon as Simon had eaten, he saw Sir Rickard off on his journey to London. He was to stop the night at Coventry to pick up the miniature horses. At the last minute Simon relented and had Eleanor's silver chalice packed carefully and gave it into de Burgh's hands for safekeeping. When he came into the family quarters of the Caesar Tower, he saw four women pitting their wits against one very determined baby. From the looks of things, the baby was winning.

Simon relieved the women of their burden and jerked his head in the direction of the door. Bette and her young assistants departed in haste; they had no desire to stand in the line of fire between the master and mistress of Kenilworth. In Simon's secure arms the baby quietened immediately, but his face was still a fiery red from temper.

"I was trying to wean him," Eleanor said defensively.

"I know what you were trying to do, I'm not blind," Simon said quietly. His black eyes took in the new green silk gown with its fashionable but impractical trailing sleeves. It was edged in sable, which had no doubt been imported from Siberia and sold to her by a merchant at an exorbitant cost. He sighed inwardly. It made her look infinitely lovely. She was all woman and he would have her no other way. "Feed him," Simon directed quietly.

She opened her mouth to protest, saw the determination harden in her husband's face, and changed her mind.

"You may take off the pretty gown first, but then you must feed him. Tomorrow will be soon enough to start his lessons." Simon averted his eyes from her to make it easier for her to disrobe. He gave his son his little finger to suckle for a few minutes. "I'll have a word with one of the shepherd's wives. She fashions little teats to suckle the motherless lambs."

Wearing only her shift, Eleanor sat on the bed and held out her arms for her son. Grudgingly she said, "Thank you for being reasonable for once."

"I am always reasonable," he asserted as he came to the bed and laid the child in her arms.

"Not so! 'Tis unreasonable to ask me to return the christening cup to the silversmith of Litchfield."

He said quietly, "De Burgh is on his way to London with the cup."

She lifted her lashes to assess her husband's face. "Well, I'll be damned."

"One of these days you may very well be. You are guilty of being a disobedient wife every day of your life," he pointed out.

Her child's sucking calmed her. Blood of God, she would miss this as much as her son would. She saw Simon remove his doublet and her flesh responded with goosebumps that soon he would be naked in the bed with her. She pulled her nipple from the babe's mouth and changed arms so he could suckle on the other breast. "Simon, I am not disobedient, I simply take the initiative to do things on my own."

"I see no difference. I am used to being in command. There is only one way to run things whether it is a castle or an entire army. One person gives the orders and everyone else obeys."

"I see," she said, stiffening.

"Not yet you don't, Eleanor, but you will," he promised. "Take him to Bette, then come straight back to bed," he ordered.

She rose from the bed and took her son to his nursemaid. She did not, however, return to her husband's bed. He waited a full quarter of an hour, assuring himself that surely he was the most reasonable man alive. He knew her so well, he knew exactly where to find her. She had retired to what she thought of as "her" room, "her" bed.

He threw open the chamber door and strode in naked. He did not trust himself to speak, but jerked his thumb in the direction of their bedchamber. When he watched her face set in stubborn lines, he whipped back the covers and pulled her from the bed most ungently. Then he cupped her shoulders with his massive hands and shook her like a rag doll.

She screamed in fear. Surely he wouldn't be deliberately brutal to her? He gave her a violent shove toward the door. When he saw her dig in her heels to deliberately defy him, he reached down and gave her a resounding slap across her arse. The thin material of her shift did nothing to protect her from the stinging pain his large palm inflicted and she felt so miserably sorry for herself, tears sprang to her eyes, but she was motivated to flee to their chamber. He crashed the door closed and they stood glaring at each other for long moments. Eleanor did not dare speak first.

Finally Simon said, "I was not angry that you took the initiative to order a gift for Prince Edward. I have come to recognize that you are an independent woman and I quite like it. I couldn't bear a simpering, useless wench. What angered me was the cost. Your extravagance is beyond anything I have ever known. You are aware how deeply in debt I am. I still owe the Pope money for the dispensation. I mortgaged all of Leicester to pay for your brother's stupid war games on the continent. Everything I inherited from Chester was debt-ridden. Kenilworth is the only holding that pays for itself. If this fief is managed well and its profits husbanded rather than squandered, both we and all our people will be reasonably well off and can live comfortably. Eleanor, I am not unreasonable. I overlook your extravagance in regard to your clothes. I know a woman needs pretty things, especially a princess of the realm, but I bloody well draw the line at sending your idiot brother silver cups dripping emeralds!"

She opened her mouth to protest, but his words drowned out hers. "If you think Prince Edward will ever own that cup, you are deluding yourself. Henry will hock it the minute he gets his hands on it and laugh at us for being fools enough to send it."

"How dare you malign and blacken my brother's character to me?" She gasped.

"He needs no help from me to mar his character, he's capable of doing it himself. I'm afraid I have always protected you from his character flaws, but God Almighty they are obvious enough for a blindman to see."

"Well, I admit one Plantagenet failing stands out—our poor choice of marriage partners!"

Simon could not resist the barb. "Yes, I always thought it extremely eccentric you insisted on marrying a man in his forties when you were nine years old."

"Oh, you brute. I wish I were still married to him!"

"Women!" Simon snorted in disgust. "Women don't know what the hell they want, except they all want to be seduced." He snatched her into his arms ruthlessly, yet in truth she did not want a gentle man. His towering anger changed to towering desire. His kiss was abandoned and ravenous as his lips and tongue plundered her mouth.

Desire was snaking through her, yet she protested, "You'll not seduce me!"

"I'll have you or die," he ground out. "I'll have you right here, right now."

She felt powerless against the intense sexuality of the man. Effortlessly he lifted her high in the air, until her thighs were on a level with his mouth, then he lowered her slowly, inch by delicious inch, allowing his hungry mouth to taste her and feed on her soft flesh. When her mons touched his lips he entered her with his tongue. She moaned deeply in her throat, wishing to be suspended there forever, but relentlessly he slid her body past his wicked mouth, which tongued her belly and navel and sucked hard upon each sensitive, milky nipple. He did not allow her feet to touch the carpet but spread her legs and wrapped them about his waist. As his mouth fastened upon hers she could feel his long erection reaching all the way through to her bottom, then sliding up along the cleft between her bum cheeks, and she realized for the first time how many sensitive nerve endings she possessed in that very private area.

She thrust her tongue into his mouth and heard his deep, masculine groan. "Take me to London, Sim," she whispered.

"That's a whore's trick," he said hoarsely, "using sex to get what you want."

She outlined his lips with the tip of her tongue. "How dare you brag of your use of whores while making love to me," she said, biting his neck passionately.

"You are smaller and hotter than any whore," he confided.

"You do everything in your power to prolong our mating. A whore uses tricks to get it over with quickly."

"Such as?" she coaxed, thrusting her breasts at him so that her swollen nipples brushed across his lips.

His hands separated her bottom cheeks and he placed a fingertip upon her sphincter. "If a man is taking too long they'll slip in their finger to make him ejaculate."

She whispered, "Take me to bed. You make me feel like a whore when you take me standing up." Simon was only too happy to oblige. Anger turned to lust had a heightened quality about it that aroused lovers to fever pitch. He knew his back would bear deep scratches from her nails and that his neck and shoulders would be covered with teeth marks from her biting, but it was worth it to know he could bring her to the peak of rapture.

The beast within him crouched above her, then leapt upon her fiercely. He incited her to such wildness that she screamed with excitement as he filled her with his pulsing manhood. Almost immediately she began to climax. She knew he was not yet ready to spend, so she looked directly into his eyes as their hearts beat against each other. Then she deliberately slipped a finger into the shallow cleft of his buttocks.

A cry rose up in his throat as he ejaculated inside her, unable to hold himself in check. She held him clasped to her tightly to experience the pleasure of his shudder. "Sapphire-eyed witch," he whispered, too spent to be angry with her.

"Black-eyed devil," she whispered back, more contented than she'd felt in ages.

When the missive arrived proclaiming Simon de Montfort one of nine godfathers to the new prince, Eleanor was elated. She still had not been able to cajole a promise from her husband to take her to London, but now that he was being honored there could be no refusing.

Simon still had doubts. He felt uneasy that all eight of the other godfathers named were his enemies. He wished he could converse with Rickard de Burgh. Not that he put credence in the knight's visions, he was far too practical and down-to-earth for such nonsense, but the young knight was sensitive to the mood of the court and was adept at sniffing out intrigue.

Finally, grudgingly, he gave Eleanor permission to write to her brother Henry accepting the invitation. When King Henry's personal reply arrived at Kenilworth, he told them that the Bishop of Winchester had graciously put his London town house at Simon and Eleanor's disposal for the duration of their stay.

Brenda was styling Eleanor's hair in a new fashion, braiding it into a crown, when Simon said, "I don't think we should stay at Winchester House. It sticks in my craw to accept anything from him."

Brenda dropped the brush in alarm and, excusing herself, fled from the chamber.

"Now see what you've done," accused Eleanor. "The servants know when you are about to create a scene and flee in fear."

"That one afraid?" Simon said in disbelief. "She eats men alive."

"There is no need to be lewd," she said repressively, pinning up her long braids.

"Me, lewd? I abhor lewdness," he said innocently.

She brought the subject back to London. "I much prefer a town house close by the abbey to staying at Windsor with the queen and her tribe."

"Then I'll ask our friend Robert, Bishop of Lincoln, if we can share his town house."

"What in the world do you have against the Bishop of Winchester? He is the most generous, hospitable man in the world. I remember the Christmases of my childhood were always spent in the ancient capital of Winchester. He footed the bill for everything."

Simon knew he could not vilify Winchester without heaping shit upon Henry's head and the moment he did that, she would fly at him in defense of her brother. Simon shrugged and remembered the Bible: "Even a fool is considered wise when he does not speak."

The days seemed to speed up as they raced toward August as there was much to do before they departed Kenilworth. Eleanor spent painstaking hours with her steward, showing him her method of bookkeeping. She ordered all the supplies in advance for the weeks they would be away and wrote out lists of instructions for all, from the chaplains to the washerwomen. She appointed a Franciscan, Brother Vincent, to be in charge of compiling the library she had begun and spent days going over instructions with Bette, Emma, and Kate regarding her baby son's feeding, clothing, bedtime, and fresh-air outings.

She was going over the entries in her personal journal, which was for her eyes alone, when suddenly her eyes came to rest upon a date two months before. She scanned the pages frantically for another entry since then and when she found none, she angrily slammed the journal closed. "I'll kill him!" she fumed. "He has done it apurpose!" The possibility was strong that she was breeding again, and she felt the blush turn her cheeks pink.

She looked down from the Caesar Tower and saw him in the bailey. God rot the lusty Frenchman, why did he have to flaunt his great virility at her expense? Suddenly she saw that he conversed with her red-haired maid, Brenda. The girl was touching his chest in a most appealing manner, looking so small and helpless next to the towering giant. She saw Simon put his arm about the girl and take her inside the weapons room. So! Not content to plant his seed in his wife's belly, he was planting a crop of bastards by fucking the maids!

Simon had never seen the saucy wench Brenda reduced to tears before.

"My lord, I beg of you, do not make me go to Winchester's town house."

Simon had so many things to do before he left Kenilworth that he was annoyed with the maid. Surely this was Eleanor's territory. Why was she bothering him with her silly whims? As he gave his full attention to her, however, he realized how distressed she was, and his conscience pricked him that he always championed the common man but could not give a woman the time of day. "I recall you spoke the name Winchester to me once before," Simon said, remembering that this was the girl who had run away and hidden herself once for over a year. Here was a puzzle indeed, and there was a piece missing.

"You had better unburden your secrets to me if you want me to protect you."

Simon's black eyes were so shrewd, Brenda feared he might already know everything. There were few men she would ever trust, but Simon de Montfort was an exception. She choked back a sob and whispered, "It all began when I made my confession to the bishop. He used me to get information about William Marshal. A new squire was taken into the household, but he was Winchester's man. The night the marshal died, the squire tried to push me off the roof of Westminster. He fell to his death."

Simon's eyes were like black obsidian. "You have conveniently skipped over the nub of the matter. Why did he have instructions to silence you?"

Whatever she said would implicate her in the poisoning. De Montfort could kill her with one blow, and yet, and yet, if the Marshal had lived this man could never have had Eleanor. The words came slowly. "I knew he had a powder to put in the marshal's food and drink."

Simon's fists clenched into balls of iron. This little whore had been involved in a successful plot to murder one of England's finest men. He tried to focus his anger where it belonged, on Winchester and on the weak king for allowing evil men to control England's destiny. This little slut was only a pawn. He experienced Eleanor's pain. How long she had carried her guilt because William died in bed with her. "I will tell the countess to choose another maid for London. If you remain at Kenilworth you need not fear. No one connected with Winchester will ever be admitted here." Unless they come in chains, he added silently.

Strangely enough, the knowledge he had gained about Winchester whetted his appetite to have dealings with the bishop. The unease about lodging at Winchester's town house vanished. Simon de Montfort relished challenge. He was whistling when he climbed the stairs of the Caesar Tower, but the tune died on his lips when he saw that his beautiful wife had been sharpening her claws all afternoon. Here was another sort of challenge. He would tease her into a loving mood. He winked at her. "When you want me to make love to you, you always wear that sexy red gown. But do you mind if we eat first? I'm starving."

Her chin went up and her eyes flashed. "If you think I'd let you touch me after you have been with her—"

"Her? Who?" Simon asked, puzzled. Then he knew she had spied him talking to Brenda. A great whoop of laughter rolled about the room. "By God, you are jealous."

"Jealous?" she cried. "Jealous of a cheeky-faced wench who spreads her legs for every man in Kenilworth? I am not in the least jealous, but next time your prick swells don't take her into the weapons room where all the castle may know of your lechery."

Amusement danced in his eyes. "You silly child, she asked to be excused from going to London. I told her you would choose another maid. So you see, you guessed the wrong one if you were trying to discover my latest whore!"

Eleanor felt so relieved, her knees buckled. Simon hadn't finished with her yet, however. His eyes ran over her with speculation. "You know, next time you are trying to lure me to bed, don't wear that red gown, it makes you look fat."

Eleanor burst into tears. He was immediately contrite. "Sweetheart, whatever is amiss?"

"I think I'm breeding again. How could you, just when I am going to London?"

Her news filled him with joy. He picked her up and swung her about. Laughing down into her woebegone face, he whooped. "You are afraid everyone will know you've been fucking with me again."

She blushed and hid her hot cheeks against his shoulder. "Sim, we have only been wed six months and I am already swelling with your second son. I swear you have done it on purpose."

"Me?" he teased. "You are responsible for this one. Remember the night you slipped your finger into my—"

"Sim!" she cried. "Stop!"

He kissed her heartily. "Why aren't you happy? Are my sons not beautiful enough for you?"

"Oh, yes," she replied softly, her heart skipping a beat at the mere thought of her fine baby in the adjoining chamber.

"And you only said you *think* you are breeding," he reminded her as he handed her a cup of warm spiced wine. He gathered her onto his knee and watched her sip prettily. Then he put his lips to her ear and whispered, "Finish the dragonsblood. I want to take you to bed and make a *surety* of it."

38

Simon gave last-minute instructions to the captain of the guard at Kenilworth. Though it was impregnable, he wanted no laxity in his absence. Guards must still walk the walls twenty-four hours a day. He conversed with the master-of-arms of the weapons room, ordering him to see that the arms and armor were always kept clean and sharp and a strict tally maintained. His knights and squires were so rigidly trained they needed no reminders of their duties, and Simon had no doubt that by example the newcomers would behave accordingly.

The grooms had curried all the horses and the stableboys had cleaned and washed every stall so that Simon could inspect them before he left. The wagons were gathered in the bailey to transport the servants they were taking to London. The baggage was stacked in the courtyard ready to be loaded, and the knights and squires who were to ride with Simon and Eleanor were assembling at the portcullis gate.

Eleanor, looking most fetching in a sapphire-blue riding dress with little gray kid gloves and boots, hailed Simon and his squire. "Darling, these two crates hold my personal things. Would you be good enough to put them on one of the wagons for me where they will be safest?"

Simon thought she had never looked prettier. His squire blushed to the roots of his hair as he quickly dismounted to do her bidding. She pointed to the crate and gave him a dazzling smile as he hoisted it in strong arms and headed for the wagons.

Simon dismounted more slowly. Honey wouldn't melt in her mouth when she wanted something, and he knew he would always be her willing slave. He leered after her as she reentered the castle, then bent to his task. A frown came between his eyes. Splendor of God, the crate was heavy. He struggled with it, but it took him a minute or two to lift it chest high. How in the name of God had his squire managed so easily? He carried the crate for about fifty yards and was forced to set it down to rest. He actually flushed as he imagined his knights were observing his difficulty. What could Eleanor possibly own that was heavier than lead? He knelt and unfastened the crate. It was filled with boulders! She was playing a dangerous game, wanting to see him ridiculed and humiliated in front of his squire and his knights. It was a game, in fact, that two could play.

He had given in to her demands that he take her to London, and this was the thanks he got. He eyed his knights suspiciously. Someone must have helped her in her devious little plot. He laughed to himself. God's death, it could have been any one of them. She was an expert at twisting a man about her little finger. He was the prime example. He tipped the boulders behind the horse trough and piled the empty crate on the cart.

Eleanor now had her own guards who always rode at her side, and the four young knights came out of the stables leading her mare. In a few minutes she stepped out into the courtyard, wiping a last tear away as she waved good-bye to Bette and the baby. Simon took her mare's bridle from the knight who held it and fastened it just outside the stable doors. He smiled down into his wife's eyes as he effortlessly lifted her into the saddle. However, at that precise moment his foot slipped and he grabbed at her skirts to save himself. Down tumbled Eleanor right into the fresh pile of horse manure that the stableboys had just gathered.

"Oh," she cried, outraged. "You did it on purpose!"

His eyes gleamed with amusement. "I knew you would say that. You are becoming so predictable, my princess. We will wait while you change your clothes, if you hurry."

"I will never forgive you!" she blazed.

He grinned. "You will be laughing about it before the day is out. When I discovered the crate of boulders I felt just as you do. Now, however, I find it quite amusing."

Eleanor felt the excitement rising within her as the towers and spires of London came into view. However, once they had ridden through the gates of the city proper, she saw it through different eyes. The streets were filthy and oh so narrow. The houses looked like rows of rotten teeth. Its citizens were ignorant and uncouth and the whole place stank. How could it have changed so quickly? she wondered. Then she realized it had always been as it now was. The change was in herself. Kenilworth was like a city, but it was clean and orderly and its inhabitants were civilized and mannerly.

She was greatly surprised that Simon de Montfort, Earl of Leicester, was recognized everywhere. Men hailed him familiarly, women threw him kisses, and children ran alongside his horse, begging pennies. As they slowly made their way past the Hoop and Grapes Inn at Aldgate, the landlord rushed out with pints of ale for everyone wearing the distinctive de Montfort badge upon his shoulder. When Eleanor reached for one to clear the dust from her throat, a loud cheer went up. She smiled her pleasure and drank to the health of everyone watching.

Winchester House was a luxurious place indeed. Its immaculate cobbled courtyard, spotless flagstoned kitchen, luxurious salon, and carpeted bedchambers pointed out to all eyes that no expense had been spared on its upkeep. Winchester's personal servants were not in residence, only a skeleton staff for security, and so the Leicesters' servants took over immediately. Before the sun set they had every crate unpacked, the countess's personal linen on all the beds, and her favorite dishes upon the table.

Robert, Bishop of Lincoln, accepted Simon's invitation to dine with them, since his town house was only across the street. It always amused Eleanor that Lincoln looked nothing like a man of the cloth. He was tall and powerfully muscled, and she reasoned that was likely why Simon and Robert enjoyed each other's company. She played at keeping her woman's place, and by keeping her mouth closed and her ears open she learned much.

The two men spoke in very unflattering terms about both of her brothers. She was surprised to learn that Richard would not be in London for the queen's churching or the prince's christening. According to the bishop, Richard's god was money. He was likened to King Midas, everything he touched turned to gold, and she learned that it was apparently common knowledge that he was so avaricious and tight-fisted, he still had the first crown he'd ever made. At the moment he had no interest in England. As the Count of Poitou he lived entirely on the continent and was now busy currying favor to be elected King of the Romans. Rumors abounded that he was planning a Crusade because the Holy Land and the territories surrounding it was where the real wealth, riches, and treasures of the world could be found.

She was on the point of hotly defending Richard when Simon said, "The money you so generously donated to me for my trip to Rome went straight into Richard's pocket. You tore the veil from my eyes the day you told me the church was based on a system of bribery, but it's a bit of a bastard when you are obliged to grease your brother-in-law's palm. Especially when he took control of Marshal lands that should have rightfully gone to my wife. It must have plagued hell out of his conscience, because he finally gave the money back."

Eleanor was startled. Simon had never mentioned these things to her, although she did recall him saying he had always protected her from her brothers' character flaws. She'd presumed he'd been alluding to Henry, of course. When the men's conversation switched to the king. Eleanor thought, more than a little shocked, They are both guilty of treason.

"I have it on the best authority that Henry has been negotiating to have the crown of Sicily conferred upon his infant son's head."

Eleanor could keep quiet no longer. Her sister Isabella was married to Emperor Frederick of Germany who was also King of Sicily. "Negotiating with Frederick because he has no heir of his own?" she asked.

Robert coughed rather delicately for such a big man. "No, my dear. Negotiating with the Pope," the bishop answered.

Eleanor was perplexed. She looked from Robert to Simon. "Frederick is King of Sicily. What does the crown have to do with the Pope?"

"Consensus is that Henry may have agreed to finance a papal war," the Bishop of Lincoln said solemnly.

Eleanor recoiled. Either her brother was dabbling in vile, sickening intrigue or these men were malignant gossipmongers. Both alternatives were abhorrent to her.

Simon laughed and Eleanor heard bitterness in it. "Henry never financed anything in his life. He'll squeeze the Jews and the barons dry."

Just at that moment Rickard de Burgh arrived, and Eleanor was never so relieved to see anyone in her life. He was such a gentle, perfect knight that he would not sit and listen to them malign their monarch. Eleanor rose from the table. She would order the minstrels to bring their lutes. How had she allowed the conversation at her table to sink to such a low level? She rushed from the dining hall so quickly a wave of dizziness swept over her and she put out a hand to steady herself. Then she went cold as she heard Sir Rickard's voice.

"Winchester has set a trap for you. I hoped you would remain at Kenilworth out of their reach."

"I suspected as much when we received the generous offer of Winchester House," Simon said quietly.

"Your enemies have poisoned the king against you. Henry went straight to Winchester with your suggestions of restoring power to Hubert and making Richard Marshal the justiciar. Richard Marshal was sent to Ireland and murdered. Winchester is terrified of your growing power in England. Now that you are here in London, I believe he will get the king to exile you."

Eleanor was on the point of rushing back to the men to tell them they were fools and liars. Henry was her dearest brother, her friend. How could Simon listen to such lies? Simon knew better than any man alive how the king had arranged for their secret marriage in his own chapel. Henry would allow no man to poison his mind about Simon de Montfort.

"How was Henry persuaded against me?" Simon asked quietly.

Eleanor held her breath so she could hear the answer to the question she herself asked.

"Winchester simply pointed out to Henry that you patterned yourself upon Henry II. 'Tis no secret you uphold the cause of English liberty as he did and are constantly calling attention to the genius of the laws he passed. Winchester accused you of ambition for the throne. Pointed out how you purposely got a royal princess with child so that you could marry into the Plantagenet line."

Eleanor's hand went to her throat. No denial issued forth from Simon de Montfort's lips. Eleanor climbed slowly to the bedchamber and stood at the window with unseeing eyes. The tale of Henry II and Eleanor of Aquitaine came flooding back to her. Henry, a mere count, had been so ambitious that he snatched the crown of England for himself. He needed a royal mate so he deliberately impregnated the King of France's queen, which enabled her to get a dispensation for a divorce and marry Henry.

How blind she had been! The circumstances were so similiar she could not believe she had never before thought of them. Simon de Montfort had always been so sure of himself. He had pursued her relentlessly. He had not chosen her for love. He had chosen her for ambition! Her hand went protectively to her belly. She was just the vessel he had used to attain his goal.

She must go to Henry at once. No, it was dark; London was unsafe. She would not be permitted to leave the house tonight. Tomorrow . . . she would go in the morning. No, the queen's churching was to take place in the morning. She would have to wait until she was inside the abbey before she sought out the protection of the king. She undressed and crept into bed. She would feign sleep tonight to buy her time until tomorrow.

When she rose she kept her maids in attendance so she would not be alone with de Montfort. The clothes she had brought to London for the festive occasion personified her innate good taste. She knew the court would be awash in cloth-of-gold, royal purple, and Henry's inevitable green. She had had her husband's new clothes coordinated with her own, keeping in mind his very masculine dislike for ostentation and "peacocking" in bright colors. For the christening of the prince where Simon was one of nine godfathers she had chosen deep, rich wine with matching cloak, its only ornamentation a ruby clasp. She would wear rose trimmed with silver. Today, for the queen's churching, her gown was pale peach silk, while her husband's garments were deep amber.

When he entered the chamber she busied herself putting her jet-black curls into place, her eyes not daring to meet his. He thought the pale peach made her look like an exotic flower, and he stood entranced. Before her maids and his own squire he said, "You are the most exotic, breathstopping creature I have ever known." He dipped his head to kiss her. She managed to turn her face so that his lips found only her cheek.

"We must hurry. If we want a seat in the abbey we must be there two hours before the king and queen arrive. Remember they are in residence at Westminster and will walk in a procession from there to the abbey."

"Yes, I know. The streets will be crowded. I know how much you dislike orders, Eleanor, but it is my express wish that you remain with your mounted guards until I lift you from the saddle. I don't want you in jeopardy."

She lowered her lashes and meekly acquiesced to his order. He looked at her askance, most suspicious of her demeanor. Then later, as she rode toward Westminster flanked by her guard, she could see the tall figure of the Earl of Leicester ahead of her. Mounted or standing he towered above his fellow men. She heard the cheers of the crowd but today, instead of pleasing her, it made her shiver. Many times she had heard him say "You can become whatever you behold." Was his ambition of such magnitude it encompassed the crown of England?

She was glad she had chosen a light silk. The day was hot, almost sultry, and was sure to end with a storm. She wished she had never come to London. She wished she was home at Kenilworth with her baby and her ignorance. Ignorance was indeed bliss. She dreaded the thought of arriving at the abbey. How could she choose between loyalty to a husband and loyalty to a brother and king?

Outside the church the crowds were heavy and the horses were skittish. She saw her husband dismount and hand his reins to his squire, then the crowds parted for him as he strode toward his wife. He raised his arms to her, and she lowered her lashes and allowed him to lift her to his side. Now she could see nothing. She was so small her head reached to most people's shoulders. Suddenly she raised her eyes in alarm. Something was wrong. She heard her husband raise his voice and his tone was deadly. She glimpsed his face. It was carved in stone, black-browed, black-visaged. Then she realized what was happening. The royal guards at the abbey door blocked their entrance, refusing to admit them on orders of the king. *On orders of the king!* Henry must be mad, she thought. Insanity does not run in my family, it gallops!

The insult to a man like Simon de Montfort was catastrophic. Surely they knew his pride and his temper were unmatched. He grasped his wife's arm in a steellike vise and propelled her back to their horse guards. His eyes were like black fire. "Eleanor, you will remain here with your guard," he commanded, then he vaulted into the saddle of his destrier and scattered the crowd.

He stalked down the halls of Westminster so purposefully his silver spurs struck sparks upon the marble floor. With deadly accuracy he aimed for the long throne room. The Welsh guards on the outer door fell back automatically to allow access to the inner sanctum when they saw the war lord stride up. Running behind, trying to catch up to him, came Princess Eleanor Plantagenet. He was through one set of doors before he sensed someone following him. He turned furiously and when he saw her he raged, "Christ's blood, don't you know your life is in jeopardy?" He shoved her roughly behind the door to conceal her, then stalked down the long chamber.

All seemed to be confusion as the procession of courtiers tried to establish a pecking order. King's Men always took precedence over Queen's Men, except perhaps today for the event of the queen's churching. The archbishops and bishops were all in line behind the old, failing Archbishop of Canterbury, but the king's half brothers were arguing the toss with Thomas of Savoy's brood of arrogant offspring, while a large-bosomed wet nurse kept the heir to the throne quiet.

One by one the assembly fell silent as Simon de Montfort swept down the room resembling the angel of death. He challenged Henry directly, but he could not utter the word "Sire" to save his soul. "Why do you forbid my presence in Westminster Abbey?"

The Bishop of Winchester stepped forward to answer the challenge. "You have been excommunicated," he said with a sneer.

"By whom?" roared de Montfort.

"By me," Winchester thundered.

"On what charge?" demanded Simon, keeping a rigid control over his sword arm.

"That you seduced the Princess Eleanor and extorted consent for the marriage." Winchester's face was smug. He lowered his voice slightly and said with relish, "Remember, de Montfort, there are two groups of people—the pitiful and the pitiless!"

Simon knew a murderous urge to cleave him into two pieces. His eyes swung to Henry and he pointed his finger. "You arranged our wedding yourself in your private chapel."

"Liar!" cried the king, courageous as a lion with his den surrounding him.

Eleanor had heard enough. "Henry!" she cried, and all eyes swung to the beautiful young woman in vibrant peach. She was more regal than any other in the room as she came to stand beside her husband. For the first time in her life she admitted to herself what Henry was. His lack of backbone sickened her. "I was ever your greatest champion . . . *You have betrayed me.*"

"Adulteress!" shrieked the queen.

Eleanor knew she must get Simon out of there before he drew his weapon and there was murder done. Simon tasted fear on his tongue . . . fear for his beloved wife who meant more to him than life. Her temper was so passionate she would end up in the Tower before the day was done. They clasped hands and withdrew in unison.

Outside Westminster Palace de Montfort's men quickly surrounded the earl and countess, and they galloped through the city at full speed to Winchester House. When they arrived they found their entire household had been turned out into the courtyard and the doors barred against them. Rickard de Burgh was there and had a hurried word with Simon. "There are soldiers at all the city's gates waiting to arrest you. You are charged with unlawful seduction, my lady is charged with adultery," he said bluntly.

Eleanor was already giving orders to the servants to ready the wagons. "We are returning to Kenilworth immediately," she announced.

Simon took her hand and looked down into her eyes which were so like deep, blue sapphires. "Nay, love, 'tis too late for Kenilworth. Warrants are out for our arrest. I won't ever see you in the Tower and they'll never take me alive. We'll take ship across the Channel."

"But my baby . . ." she cried in alarm.

"Will be safe at Kenilworth," he insisted.

"No, no, noooo," she wailed, but he had already swung her up into his powerful arms.

"Damnit, cast out your fear. In this life you get what you are afraid of!" He directed de Burgh, "Place the servants with the Bishop of Lincoln across the road, he will get them safely home."

They went downriver to Tower Wharfe where they took ship for the continent with only the clothes on their backs.

39

Eleanor swung gently in a hammock that had been strung between two laburnum trees. Her hand shaded her eyes as she looked out across the sparkling Adriatic Sea. She lived luxuriously, her every whim catered to by an abundance of servants. At a glance her world appeared perfect, yet she was pensive, almost melancholy. She missed her son unbearably.

They had sailed to Bordeaux where Simon learned that not only were Richard and Isabella in Italy, but Eleanor's sister Isabella who had married the Emperor of Germany was residing there as well. They went overland from Bordeaux to Italy, where they were welcomed with open arms. It was a happy family reunion for the Plantagenet brother and sisters. Eleanor and Isabella had not seen each other since they were children, and they reminisced for days, recalling incidents that brought both smiles and tears to their faces.

Eleanor was shocked at how matronly her sister looked though she was only one year older. She had to keep reminding herself that her brother-in-law was not only Emperor of Germany but was also the ruler of southern Italy and Sicily. He insisted that she and Simon take up residence in a great echoing stone palace overlooking the sea at Brindisi. In return Simon de

Montfort willingly went off to northern Italy with Frederick to help him besiege the city of Brescia, leaving Eleanor to idle away her days with the two Isabellas.

Over and over Eleanor chided herself for being discontented. Here the sun always shone, the azure sea was ever warm, flowers bloomed in profusion while the sea breezes wafted their fragrance to perfume the air. Yet Eleanor was irritated by the excess. Too much food, fruit, good wine; too many servants, poetry and idleness. It was all very well for Simon. He was off doing what he did best, but she was left with too many empty hours on her hands—hours, days, and weeks in which she had nothing to do but think.

Her brother Richard and Isabella's child was a boy named Henry of Almaine, and she delighted in helping Isabella care for him, in spite of the servants' disapproval that royal ladies should so occupy themselves. She divulged that she was again with child and was amazed that they should envy her so much. She was homesick and longed for her baby son left behind at Kenilworth. She penned endless letters to Bette even though she could not read. The Franciscan brothers read them to Bette, Kate, and Emma and wrote replies back to the Countess of Leicester answering all her questions and reassuring her that, yes indeed, baby Henry was thriving in spite of his parents' forced exile.

During her first weeks she could not shake off her feelings of betrayal. Henry, no doubt at Winchester's instigation, had charged her with adultery. Surely none would ever believe she had carried on a sexual relationship with Simon de Montfort while William Marshal had been alive? In truth she had been a sixteen-year-old virgin, not an adulteress. Henry had falsely laid shame upon a sister who had been a lifetime favorite. Worse, if she was found guilty, her children would be branded bastards.

In London she had chosen exile with her husband, closing her eyes to the fact that things might never be the same between them again. Now in her long idle hours the relentless thoughts crept up upon her stealthily, insidiously, demanding that she reexamine and reevaluate their relationship.

She longed to keep the knowledge buried deep within her

heart and consciousness that he had married her because of ambition. But her thoughts were insistent, springing unbidden from her subconscious, forcing their ugly way to the surface so that there was no way she could ignore them any longer. Down through history men had used women as pawns to further their ambitions, but when she thought of Simon doing these things her throat tightened upon her unshed tears and her lips trembled uncontrollably. He had come into her life at a time when she had been so vulnerable, so lonely. His strength and love, his warmth and protection had attracted her, lured her. She had opened to him like a flower opens to the sun. That it had all been a carefully calculated seduction on his part made her feel as if a knife was twisting in her breast and her vitals. Her heart felt bruised and it ached with the poignancy of her newfound knowledge.

In her heart she always thought the name Eleanor had cursed her. How ironic that she had been named after her grandmother, Eleanor of Aquitaine, then suffered the same fate of having an ambitious, powerful man impregnate her to gain a royal wife. No one had ever wanted her for herself. She was valuable because of who she was, a Plantagenet princess, daughter and sister of Kings of England. Pressure had been brought to bear upon the Marshal of England to go through a marriage ceremony with her, then even greater pressure had been brought to bear upon him before he had taken her to live with him. Her dark thoughts skipped over the consummation.

When Simon de Montfort pursued her so relentlessly, she had innocently, foolishly allowed herself to believe he had fallen in love with her and desired her for herself. Now all her illusions were shattered. A tiny sob escaped her and she bit down upon her lip to stop it from quivering. She pressed the back of her hand against her mouth until she regained a small measure of control. A tiny flame of anger came to her rescue. To lowest hell with romance; she could and would survive without it. Love was a silly game for girls. From now on she would fulfill the roles of woman, wife, and mother without perpetuating this myth of love. She and Simon were well matched at least, more suited to each other than many other men and women. It would be up to her to see that they had a good marriage. However, she could not help sighing and wishing and longing for what might have been.

Her quiet introspection was shattered with the return of her husband and his men. What was it in him that inspired such loyalty? Not a few of his knights and men-at-arms had followed him from Kenilworth, and the ranks swelled every day. She wondered if Frederick and her brother Richard knew how foolish it was to let de Montfort have command of their soldiers and retainers, for she knew with a certainty that when the Earl of Leicester moved on, over half their knights and men-at-arms would defect to Simon.

As the clatter and mayhem of mounted men assaulted her ears, she realized she was weak with relief. She had purposefully pushed to the back of her head any thought of danger to her war lord, but now she realized fear for his safety had been her companion day and night.

She remained where she was, but it was one of the hardest things she'd ever had to do. She wanted to run to him, to pay homage to the returning, conquering hero. She wanted him to open his arms to her and sweep her up to his powerful chest and see the hungry need in his magnetic, black eyes. However, she had resolved to be cool and distant, at least on the surface. It would take all her control to keep her real feelings hidden. She reasoned that in every relationship one partner probably loved more deeply than the other, but as she watched him approach her along the terrace that led to the garden, she realized it was pure hell to be the one who loved most.

Her heart turned over in her breast and her throat filled with heartbeats as he came closer. She hadn't remembered him being such a colossus, and he was bronzed mahogany from his weeks under the blazing sun. Then he engulfed her. His male scent of leather and horse was like an aphrodisiac. His deep voice sent shivers running up and down her spine. His breath on her skin was so pleasurable it aroused her senses. His mouth so ravenously demanding, it drew all her strength so that she was frightened by her passionate response to him. From somewhere she found the strength to draw away and smile coolly.

Simon masked the hurt he felt. He had imagined this moment of reunion for weeks, living and reliving it over and over.

She was even lovelier than he'd remembered, and now that he'd touched her, the feel and taste of her made him dizzy. But she was keeping that private part of herself from him, the essence that was Eleanor which he craved. She was still angry with him. He knew it wasn't for one single reason but many—the exile, the rift with Henry, the new baby she carried. His eyes traveled over her possessively and she felt shy as a bride. How would she bear the sexual tension that would build between them during the afternoon hours, through dinner, and on through the evening until bedtime?

She did not need to be concerned, for within the hour Frederick and her sister and Richard and Isabella descended upon them. Richard's Crusade dominated the conversation. The men sequestered themselves, but the two Isabellas seemed to know every detail of the plans that the men were discussing in private.

Eleanor smiled to herself as she realized she held the lowest rank in the room. Her sister Isabella was an empress, her sister-in-law was a duchess, while she was a mere countess. The women's talk of the Crusade centered upon the riches of the East: the silks, the jewels, the exquisite palaces with their indoor and outdoor bathing pools, the servants, slaves, and handmaidens.

Eleanor felt there was a gulf between herself and her sisters. She loved them, yet she could never be like them. She observed them and listened to their chatter, but she could not comprehend their materialistic attitude. Both were already so rich they need never concern themselves over money either for themselves or for any children they might have. She glanced about the lavish room. They already had more palaces than they could occupy, filled with more servants than they'd ever need. Even this stone palace on the edge of the sea had a household staff of over fifty women. Some were fair-skinned Germans while others were olive-skinned Italians. Suddenly Eleanor became aware that her sister was looking at her with pitying eyes, and she realized she had missed most of what had been said.

"It must be hell to be married to a man who is handsome as a god. Frederick has his pick of women, of course, but even he knows it is because of his power, so his peccadillos don't dis-

turb me overmuch. De Montfort's women must all fall in love
with him. I really don't know how you bear it, Eleanor."

Eleanor said the first thing that came into her head. "De
Montfort has no women."

Her sister laughed. "Eleanor, you cannot be that naive.
Though he only returned today I warrant he has already selected half a dozen of your prettier maids to receive his attentions."

Eleanor laughed incredulously. "You had better be wrong. I
take his fidelity for granted as I am sure Isabella does with our
brother Richard."

Isabella flushed darkly and Eleanor immediately realized
that Richard was unfaithful to her. Damn all men to lowest
hell! She would take him to task on the matter.

"Joan of Flanders is an intimate friend of mine," Eleanor's
sister said confidentially.

"Joan of Flanders?" Eleanor repeated innocently.

"You know," Isabella said, lowering her voice intimately,
"Simon's first wife."

"You are mistaken, Bella, I am Simon's first wife."

"Not according to Joan!" Her sister giggled.

Eleanor glanced at her sister-in-law and saw that she was
aware of what her sister alluded to, even though she herself was
in the dark. Isabella Marshal thought Eleanor had had enough
heartache in her life so she tried to downplay Simon's involve-
ment. "It all happened so long ago when he became Earl of
Leicester and was so deeply in debt. I believe he offered for
Joan but she owned so much land that the King of France
forbade the union. That's all there was to it, I'm sure."

"Oh, no, no, Isabella, you don't know the half of it," insisted
Eleanor's sister, warming to the delicious subject. "Joan of
Flanders is the richest widow on the entire continent. Simon de
Montfort swept her off her feet. His suit was completely successful. She fell madly in love with him. They were wedded and
bedded, according to Joan. The legal contracts had all been
drawn up—de Montfort was to have control of everything: her
castles, her land, her fortune. Highest stud fee ever paid!" Isabella laughed. "When Louis heard, he immediately sent a military escort to take her to Paris to explain herself. She told me

she burned the marriage certificate and the contracts to destroy evidence that might get her incarcerated, but she regrets her loss to this day. She is still madly in love with him."

Eleanor wanted to scream. Something was building inside of her that needed venting. If she could have taken a knife and slashed open every silken cushion in the room, then saddled her mare and ridden through the pounding surf of the ocean she might feel better, but all she could do was murmer inanities and smile or they would know her heart was bleeding.

When the servants announced dinner, the women joined the men in the airy dining salon, but now that the veil had been lifted from Eleanor's eyes she saw the inviting glances of the female servitors and she watched the men's responses to those invitations. How attentive the serving women were, especially toward Simon de Montfort, Earl of Leicester. His physical magnificence lured them to hover about him like pretty moths about a candleflame.

Eleanor could eat nothing. Lately she had developed a craving for dark, ripe olives but she knew if she put one in her mouth tonight, it would choke her. She sipped her wine instead of eating, then, realizing what a foolish thing she did, she diluted the contents of her Venetian goblet with rosewater.

Simon was acutely aware of Eleanor's strange mood. His eyes returned to her again and again, though Frederick and Richard dominated the conversation in an effort to convince him to join their Crusade. Finally he said to his wife, "You have eaten nothing, Eleanor, are you unwell?"

"I never felt better," she bristled, controlling the urge to pull the Damask cloth from the table and smash all the dishes.

The concern did not leave his eyes as he murmured, "Perhaps your stomach is a little delicate just now."

She flared, "I wondered how long it would be before you announced your virility!" All eyes swung to her and she knew the devil that dwelled within was looking to escape this night. Richard seemed highly amused at his little sister's outburst, but Frederick seemed unaware of the undercurrents and relentlessly pursued the topic of the Crusade.

Simon threw his wife a warning glance to curb her sharp tongue then gave his attention to Frederick. "One of the things that has stopped me from committing myself is money. However, I have just negotiated the sale of the forest of Lincoln to the Hospitallers."

Eleanor was speechless. How did he dare pledge himself to this damned Crusade without consulting her? Obviously her feelings and her wishes meant less than nothing!

When the table had been cleared, thick, sweet Turkish coffee was served out on the stone balcony. Eleanor was damned if she was going to be part of this family circle any longer. Rude or not she said curtly, "I shall leave you in the capable hands of your host. You must all please excuse me."

The bedchamber was large with great arched windows to let in the breezes from the sea, but tonight Eleanor's blood was high and she found the night hot and oppressive. She bathed and donned an Egyptian cotton nightgown, finespun as a spider's web. It covered only one shoulder in Grecian fashion and the hem was embroidered with gold thread in a Greek key pattern. The marble floor felt deliciously cool against the soles of her feet, and she leaned her cheek against one of the slim marble pillars that decorated the long, airy chamber. When de Montfort joined her she would be an ice maiden. She would not speak to him, she would freeze him with a glance. The Mediterranean climate might be hot and sultry, but he would find his bed cold this night. She was determined to totally and completely ignore him.

As the long moments stretched out to an hour, her emotions were in turmoil. Where the hell was he? How could she ignore him if he wasn't even there?

The guests departed shortly after Eleanor retired, then Simon returned to the stone balcony that afforded such a lovely view of the sea. It was a moonlit night, very conducive to romantic fantasies, and he wished his love would come down so they could walk on the beach. Or perhaps he could even tease her with some water play like they had enjoyed in their mere at Kenilworth. The water beckoned him and he decided not to resist.

He stood in the dark and removed his clothes, then he fastened back his hair with a leather thong and walked slowly to the water's edge. He knew she would see him from their chamber above if she was looking from the arched windows. If her need was as great as his, she would join him.

Eleanor did see him, but not until he emerged from his swim. As he stood poised upon the beach looking straight up to her windows, the moonlight glistened upon his powerful, wet body. He was Neptune, the ancient sea god rising naked from the waves. Her eyes clung to the bare length of his bronzed body, unable to look away. His torso turned in the moonlight until he was fully facing her, then as he raised his head she knew he was aware of her at the window. She went weak. His body looked sculpted from marble and she'd explored every plane and hollow, every muscle and sinew. His deep chest covered with sable-black hair was covered by moonlit drops of water. The thick pelt on his chest narrowed to a thin line that ran straight down over his hard, flat belly then became thick and dense at his groin.

The muscles in her thighs and belly contracted as she tore her eyes away from his virile maleness, and she almost choked on her jealousy. At last he moved and she saw his step was purposeful and determined. By the time he entered their chamber the ice in her veins had turned into pure molten lava.

He stepped into the room and stood mesmerized at the loveliness before him. "I wish you had joined me. This climate invigorates me. I have so much energy . . . sexual energy . . ."

"I wish you'd drowned!" she spat.

Simon's blood kindled. She wanted a fight. He knew from experience when she was in this mood her passion knew no bounds. He'd have to subdue her, of course, but their verbal dueling was like taunting foreplay that lifted them both to such a pitch they became almost insatiable and it would take a full night of ravishment before their appetite for each other was slaked. His shaft went rigid with anticipation, reaching all the way to his navel. It looked exactly like a battering ram.

"You whoremonger!" she spat angrily. She was exactly like a sleek and savage cat, spitting at him, and he knew she'd claw him before she was done with him, but before he was done with her he'd have her purring and filled with cream.

"Does this whore have a name or are you just accusing me in general?" he taunted.

The name almost choked her. "You *married* Joan of Flanders. I was your second choice, Frenchman!"

"So that is what you were gossiping about all night." He was furious with those two jealous bitches for telling her and furious with himself for not telling her at the outset.

"Gossip or truth?" she blazed hotly.

"It was before us." He said the statement in a final tone as if that was the end of the matter and stepped toward her.

"Don't touch me." She gasped. "Don't you dare to touch me."

"Eleanor, you are my wife. I haven't seen you for weeks. I cannot make love to you without touching you, and be assured I do intend to make love to you." He took another step.

"You act as if everything were the same," she flared, *"but it is not!* We fled from England to avoid imprisonment and charges. The charge of adultery against me was false, but the charge of seduction against you was not! I was blind not to see that you seduced and impregnated me exactly as my grandfather did to my namesake, Eleanor of Aquitaine. I have only just realized it was for ambition, not love," she said bitterly.

"I love you," Simon thundered, "and I am certain you love me."

"I did love you, Simon, but after what I heard tonight about Joan of Flanders, my love is dead."

"Don't kill love—you will regret it for the rest of your life!" His large hands encircled her waist and he pulled her against the hard, naked length of him. Her hand came up and slapped him squarely in the face. She pulled slightly away from him and then she was slammed against the hard wall of his chest, his fingers digging into her shoulders. His mouth descended upon hers, branding it with his ownership, teaching her anew his great power. Her nails came up and recklessly she raked his cheeks bloody.

With a savage curse he tore the leather thong from his tied-back hair, intending to secure her wrists behind her so that she was lashed to the marble column. A picture flashed into his mind of a man his size needing to bind a woman to have his

way with her, and it effectively stopped him. If he could not
subdue her with his powers of seduction, he did not deserve to
receive her passion. He flung away the leather thong, then
slowly, deliberately he lifted her furious face in his hands and
helped himself to her vulnerable mouth. It was achingly sweet,
and his delving tongue forced entry and thrust within her. As
she twisted against such intimacy he thrust ever more forcefully, stroking deeply in the primitive passion of man against
woman. Her body writhed against his muscular torso, but he
held her face immobile for his relentless invasion. The fire of his
passion scorched her breasts, thighs, and mouth, but soon he
knew he would ignite her with the flame of her own passion.
She was not afraid of him and his heart soared because it was
so. He did not want a woman he could intimidate, but one who
matched him in courage, in daring, in fury, and in passion. She
refused to close her eyes and surrender to the tempting pleasures whose hot flame licked at her so seductively. She watched
his eyes dilate with need as he pushed her Grecian nightrail
from her shoulder. It slipped down to reveal both breasts,
which thrust forward so provocatively because he held her
wrists behind the pillar with one of his big hands. His lips
teased them to ruching arousal in seconds, and she prayed that
they would hold his interest so that he would not lower his
dangerous mouth to her most private and most vulerable center, which he called her rosebud. She knew he was a conquering
predator wise in the ways of woman. If his mouth reached its
goal she knew she would be lost to her need for him.

Fight! she commanded herself, but her treacherous body
wanted to receive him in hot abandon. He lifted the hem of the
filmy gown to bare her to the navel. When his tongue parted
her it found the liquid fire. She tried not to arch into him, but
he simply took her bottom in his hands and lifted her mons so
that his tongue could stroke her more intimately.

Triumphantly he heard her tiny moan, watched her eyes
close in ecstasy, then with total male assurance he exulted as
her arms came up about his neck. "Sim, Sim," she cried.

If she could not deny her passion and her need, she would
make sure his needs brought him to the edge of begging along-
-side hers. She only used his Gaelic name when she was in the

throes of love, and it raised gooseflesh on his dark skin. With her arms raised so her fingers threaded through his damp black hair, he felt the whisper of her nightgown fall to her ankles. Then she went high on tiptoe and raised herself so that she straddled his manroot, levering it downward so that her cleft lay along its topside. As his tongue again slipped into her mouth she used her own tongue to duel with his, then darted inside to tease and arouse him further. She intended to taunt him and plague him until she owned his very soul.

He cupped her pretty bum as he took her to their bed, and she traced the outline of his ear with the tip of her tongue and whispered, "Sim, let me be on top." Her suggestive request sent a thrill into his loins, and she felt the throbbing evidence of his male power pulse against her. She held her breath as their bodies parted long enough for him to stretch his great length upon the bed, then lithely, seductively she straddled him. He was surprised that she had mounted him the opposite way, with her back toward him.

Eleanor smiled wickedly; this way his long, hard male muscle was vulnerable to any erotic whim she chose. She bent to drop a kiss upon the crown of its head and heard his ragged voice whisper, "Kathe, Kathe!"

Then she stroked the inside of his thighs knowing full well that though he was a man he was sensitive in many places. When she cupped his testes and her delicate fingers traced the outline of each large sphere, she heard his masculine groans of pleasure and felt his damnably attractive hands come up to stroke her creamy back, sending a knife-sharp thrill through her whole body. She took his shaft between her palms and rolled it, gently at first, then she increased the speed and intensity of her manipulations.

His voice rasped harshly, "Darling, stop . . . I'll spill myself." She did stop but before she slid about to face him she trailed her fingertips up and down the insides of his thighs one more time. She smiled down into his eyes. "Nay, I'll decide when you spill yourself." Then slowly, inch by deliberate inch she allowed him to enter her, anointing him with her liquid fire. She had used him expertly with lips and fingers until he was reckless and urgent. He could not remain still inside her but bucked and thrust wildly in an effort to bring to a climax the exquisite torture.

She locked her muscles upon him, trapping and holding immobile his male weapon deep within the honeyed walls of her tight sheath. He thought he would burst. Then she began to flex upon him and he knew he'd never experienced anything so sinfully pleasurable before. He built and built until the blood pounded in his ears and he felt it all the way to the soles of his feet. Suddenly she lifted herself so that only the head of his shaft remained inside her, then she plunged down and cried, "Now, Sim, now!"

His body obeyed her command and with a deep masculine cry he ejaculated, filling her with cream. When he spiraled back down to earth she was waiting for him. "Now will you admit that I am your equal in all things, Simon de Montfort?"

"Sweetest love, you are far above me. I put you upon a pedestal long before you were even mine and I have worshipped at your feet ever since."

His words were so disarming, she wanted to believe them with all her heart. "Oh, Sim, did you love Joan of Flanders?" she cried.

He gathered her into his arms and cradled her against the wide planes of his chest. "My own sweet love, she is old and plain-faced. I was never more relieved in my entire life than when Louis stepped in to prevent the marriage."

She was laughing and crying at the same time. He kissed the teardrops from her face and whispered, "Lord, you were so angry with me tonight."

"How could you decide to go on Crusade without consulting me?" she demanded.

"I haven't decided, I am only on the verge, but what is my alternative?" he asked quietly.

She considered for a moment, trying to put herself in his shoes. "Well, if you do go, I'm coming with you. I won't stay here."

"It's lovely here," he protested.

"Oh, Simon, it is lovely here. I'm pampered and indulged and feel wicked not to appreciate it more, only . . ."

"Only Italy isn't England, Brindisi isn't Kenilworth, the sea isn't our mere."

"Oh, Simon, you do understand!" she cried.

His lips brushed the tiny tendrils that curled about her temples. "Of course I understand, I feel exactly the same."

She lifted her mouth to his and was shocked at the sensual response she aroused.

"If we are equals I think it is now *my* turn to make love to *you*."

"Beast! I cannot lift a finger," she protested.

"That's a relief," he teased, and she knew to just exactly what he referred.

· 40

Simon de Montfort received the disquieting news that his brother Amauri, who had gone on Crusade the previous year, had been taken prisoner by the Sultan of Egypt. He immediately joined Frederick and Richard's Crusade, and together with his wife, they set sail for Acre. At first Eleanor had great fears about going halfway around the world to live and fight among barbarians. Simon laughed at her ignorance. "In the first place, it isn't halfway around the world, love. Come and look at this map." With one great arm about her protectively, he pointed to the parchment with a finger of his other hand. "Here is Brindisi, right on the heel of the boot of Italy. We are almost on the edge of the Mediterranean Sea. We simply sail to the far end of the Mediterranean, and there's Acre and Jerusalem and Palestine. We'll be there in a few short days. Look, here is the River Jordan, which empties into the Dead Sea. Everything on this side of the river is lush and fertile. The Syrian desert doesn't begin until the far side of the Jordan. There is a vast English and European settlement in the city of Jerusalem. It is crawling with barons and knights, and hardly a one of them is as civilized or educated as a Saracen knight. To our shame they can all read and write."

She had been thinking of her condition, even though her pregnancy was in its early months. Who knew how long they would remain in the Holy Land? "We won't have to live in a mud hut or a tent, will we?" she asked, only half jesting.

"The residences of the simplest baron or knight will dazzle your eyes. The floors are exquisitely patterned with mosaic tile. They have gardens with bathing pools and fountains. Why do you think such great numbers never returned to Germany or France or England? Our drafty castles and dearth of sunshine leave something to be desired."

Sailing the Mediterranean was one of the most pleasurable experiences Eleanor had ever enjoyed. The sun and the brilliant blue sky reflected across the sea, which night and day remained as calm as a millpond. The breeze was always like a warm caress and the sea teemed with dolphins and iridescent flying fish. The nights were conducive to romance for the large moon seemed to hang on the edge of the sea and the stars were like diamonds scattered over black velvet.

Eleanor heaved a sigh of relief when they sailed into the harbor at Acre and she saw for herself how civilized it appeared. Acre was a square city surrounded by a double wall with a deep, wide moat between. It was a most secure city, open only to its enclosed port. Both within and without the city were orchards and poplar trees as far as the eye could see.

Frederick, who was known in the East as the Holy Roman Emperor, was received with much pomp and ceremony, as was Richard, the King of England's brother. The Order of the Knights Templars had grown into a vast and wealthy organization and had made their headquarters in Acre. They had built a massive fortress called Castle Pilgrim on high land jutting into the Mediterranean. Here they were housed in one of the finest buildings Christendom had to offer.

Fetes and sumptuous dinner invitations began immediately. The moment that word reached the city of Jerusalem that the war lord, Simon de Montfort, Earl of Leicester, had traveled to the East, delegations representing barons, knights, and citizens arrived in Acre begging his services.

Eleanor hid her tears and fears and bid farewell to her fierce giant. Though his surcoat bore the plain white cross of the crusader, he stood out from other men as a supreme leader. She knew it would not take him long to cover himself with distinction for he had never lost a brush with the enemy and had never besieged a castle or a city in vain.

Simon led the fighting while Frederick promised to negotiate with the Sultan of Egypt for the release of Amauri. At one time the Holy Roman Emperor had had a truce with the sultan, but it had been broken over a year past and was what had prompted Frederick and Richard to plan the Crusade.

Although Eleanor dearly loved her brother Richard, he had character flaws that offended her. He left with Simon but returned to Acre almost immediately. When she questioned him, he excused his lack of support on the fighting front by telling her he was acting as liaison between the emperor and his crusaders. Eleanor was not a green girl any more and she realized Richard was there for the sole purpose of increasing his wealth. These days he made a better businessman than fighter. He dealt with wily Oriental traders and other nationalities. By the looks of some of the men with whom he did business, she would not be surprised if they were the enemy. Eleanor resented the fact that while Simon risked his life every day, Richard spent his time advancing no cause but his own. When she took him to task for it in her usual forthright manner, he had his answers ready.

"Fighting is what Simon does . . . it is his business, Eleanor. Crusades and wars cost money. I just happen to be talented in the art of making money, so I serve where I am the most useful."

She replied cynically, "Strange how your own purse is filled to overflowing at the same time. Oh, and by the way, while we are private I might as well tell you plainly that I am shocked at your faithlessness to Isabella. Your dalliance with the maids and serving women is the talk of Acre. Rumor also has it you sleep with native women and that you keep a slave girl."

He looked at her with pitying condescension. "Eleanor, surely you know women throw themselves at men in positions of power. It is expected of a man in my position, and I confess I have a weakness for beautiful women."

"You are disgusting. You don't even pay lip service to chastity. Do your marriage vows to Isabella mean nothing to you?"

"Vows, is it? I think it the height of hypocrisy for you to throw vows at me. What of your own?"

Eleanor's temper flared. "Damn you to hellfire, Richard. You know how long I was a widow before I lay with Simon."

"Ah yes, quite the little nun. Well, let me tell you men are made differently than women. One of the rewards that lures men to the East is a chance to have their own seraglio. De Montfort will be no exception. He'll have his own private harem once he has established himself here, if he doesn't have one already!"

She wanted to scream her denial, but inside she was unsure of her husband's fidelity. It was true that women threw themselves at powerful men; she had seen with her own eyes how the maids twittered about Simon, casting out their lures. Eleanor bit her lip and changed the subject. "Has Frederick done anything about Simon's brother yet?"

Richard shrugged. "Frederick is a realist. The Sultan of Egypt wants to renew the truce. Amauri de Montfort is of secondary import."

Eleanor was thunderstruck. "A truce? Simon will run mad! He risks his life each hour of every day gaining territory that Frederick will give back if a truce is signed!"

"It is no longer a case of 'if' the truce is signed, but 'when.' Negotiations have been underway for two weeks. It will just be a matter of how much gold Frederick can squeeze out of him and he'll sign on the dotted line. Of course that's where I come in. Tomorrow we leave for Jaffa, which is closer to Ascalon where the sultan maintains a summer palace."

Eleanor made her decision between one heartbeat and the next. She would go herself to negotiate the release of her husband's brother with this Sultan of Egypt. William Marshal had taught her how to negotiate. She had sat at his right hand at all his courts, and he had encouraged her to use her intelligence and her education. He had taught her how to be shrewd yet fair, and above all he had taught her to trust her own instincts. After all, she was royalty. She was a Plantagenet, the daughter and sister of kings. Since no else seemed to have the de Montfort interests foremost in their minds, she would have to take matters into her own hands.

Where there was a will, there was a way, and Eleanor found it the simplest thing in the world to persuade her brother-in-law Frederick to include her as a member of his party when he sailed to Jaffa.

With her face veiled and covered from nose to toes by a loose djellaba, she moved about unnoticed. She quickly learned that both male and female servants were amenable to bribes. She secured a room for herself in a quiet wing of the palatial house that had been set aside for the Emperor of the Holy Roman Empire and his scores of servants, which again was owned by the Templars.

Eleanor grew impatient as her plans to communicate with the sultan did not come to fruition. Frederick certainly did not bother to keep her informed of his dealings with Selim of Egypt, so it was most fortunate that her servants were a fountain of information.

It seemed that no mutually acceptable meeting ground could be agreed upon between the two venerable leaders. The emperor wanted the sultan to come to Jaffa, but of course he was far too shrewd to leave Egyptian territory and invited Frederick to accept his hospitality at his Byzantine palace in Ascalon. Frederick was much too fearful to set foot upon Egyptian territory, even though Ascalon was actually only on the border, and so it became an impasse.

Eleanor threw up her hands in exasperation, thinking men the most useless creatures in the world. It did not take the impulsive Countess of Leicester long to act on her own. A distance of less than thirty miles could be bridged easily, she decided. She dispatched a secret messenger to Ascalon with a letter to the sultan. She addressed it to His Supreme Highness, Selim, Sultan of Egypt. Its tone was imperious, from one royal personage to another. She set out her purpose plainly, to negotiate the release of Amauri de Montfort, and she signed it with a flourish, Eleanor Plantagenet, Princess Royal of England.

Within a week she had received her own invitation to enjoy the hospitality of the Sultan of Egypt at his Byzantine palace on the Mediterranean. Eleanor enjoyed the challenge of packing and arranging her journey in total secrecy. Frederick and Richard were too involved in their own affairs to inquire into Eleanor's whereabouts each day, and that was exactly the way she wanted it. God's blood, men were easy to gull!

Not quite so easy, however, was Simon de Montfort. He was a man of honor, yet being practical he was ever aware that other men were often less than honorable. Anyone who dismissed him as all brawn and no brains made the serious mistake of underestimating him. He knew every detail of Frederick's negotiations to renew the truce between Palestine and Egypt. He tried not to be too judgmental of Frederick, for his practical side told him they could never completely defeat the Sultan of Egypt. They could regain lost territory and conquer new, but they could not wipe out an enemy that succeeded by sheer force of numbers. If his knights wiped out a thousand today, tomorrow two thousand would replace them, and wholesale slaughter was abhorrent to Simon de Montfort.

He had also learned to depend on himself in this life and sent his own man to negotiate with the Sultan of Egypt for the release of Amauri. He had men in his pay at the Templars' headquarters to guard over his wife, and he knew almost immediately that Eleanor had sailed with the emperor's party to Jaffa. He was not unduly alarmed, for Jaffa was a hundred miles closer to his own position than Acre had been.

As Selim continued to politely but firmly avoid journeying to Jaffa, Frederick knew that a truce would never be signed unless someone gave in. He dispatched a courier for the war lord. Simon de Montfort would have to risk the journey to Ascalon to beard the lion in his den.

41

Eleanor stood outside the gates of the most sumptuous palace she had ever seen. It was heavily guarded and she was glad that she had brought a dozen servants with her. The palace guards certainly did not speak English, but her head man seemed to have no difficulty communicating and the gates were opened wide to admit them.

They were taken through both an outer and an inner courtyard before they entered the labyrinth that resembled a honeycomb with one chamber seemingly opening into another. Inside the marble halls of the palace it was relatively cool compared to the streets of Ascalon, where the fierce sun burned down without mercy. The tiled corridors had many archways that gave glimpses of the azure ocean, dotted with the colorful sails of ships.

Eleanor tried not to stare at the black-skinned guards who wore nothing but loincloths or the palace servants who wore white robes and headcloths. Two of her attendants walked ahead of her, the rest trailed behind, but when she missed the sound of footsteps behind her, she was shocked to find that her twelve servants had diminished to two. It was clear to her they had been spirited away. Though she became outraged and demanded an explanation instantly, she received only smiles and incomprehensible words.

Eleanor was led into a long, narrow room whose far end was open to a garden with a long, rectangular bathing pool. A tall, slim attendant in a white robe and turban approached her and spoke to her in heavily accented English. "My name is Fayid. I will provide whatever you desire." Fayid was black-skinned, and had a high singsong voice, but for the life of her Eleanor could not detect Fayid's gender. It looked and sounded like a woman and yet there was not one curve or indeed one extra ounce of flesh to cover Fayid's long bones.

"I *desire* to see Sultan Selim immediately," Eleanor said regally.

Fayid half smiled. "All things come at their appointed time, Princess. People from the West hurry their lives away."

"I am glad you realize who I am," Eleanor replied crisply. "I *desire* my attendants; tell me where they are."

"They have been accommodated as you have, Princess. This half of the palace is the women's quarters. Men are forbidden here."

"There are male guards on every door," Eleanor protested.

"They are no longer men, Princess, they are eunuchs." Fayid turned to the two female attendants. "This way, ladies."

"Just one moment," Eleanor demanded. "Where do you think you are taking my servants?"

Fayid spread long, slim hands. "I realize your customs differ from ours, Princess, but even you I think will not wish to share your bedchamber with your servants."

"I do not intend to sleep here!" Eleanor cried indignantly.

Fayid's hands spread wider and the gesture was accompanied by a slight shrug. "Then you will not see Sultan Selim, for he cannot see you until tomorrow."

"Why not?"

"He has many commitments, Princess. In the meantime my master invites you to enjoy the hospitality of his humble palace. You may rest or enjoy the bathing pool while I attend to refreshments." Fayid bowed and ushered Eleanor's attendants from the room.

Eleanor grasped one of her women by the sleeve. Lena was a

maid who had accompanied her from Brindisi. "Under no circumstances must you leave me alone here, Lena. When Fayid returns I shall demand that he . . . she ask Selim to make an effort to meet with me today. If it is impossible, I think we should leave and return tomorrow."

Fayid did not return, however, but many female attendants arrived. Some carried in large bowls of rosewater to keep the air cooled as it evaporated. Others brought towels, honey drinks, fruit, and something Eleanor had never before seen or even heard of. It resembled snow, flavored with fruit. She tasted it out of sheer curiosity and found its delicious icy texture was coolly refreshing in such a hot, dry climate. The female servitors could not speak her language, and Eleanor gave up trying to communicate for the moment as she helped herself to fruit and sweetmeats.

The pink marble floor was strewn with large cushions exquisitely embroidered in a black and gold Egyptian motif. Eleanor was not about to sit upon the floor and chose instead to rest upon a low divan that was enclosed by filmy pink hangings. She pushed the gauze aside impatiently and sat down to wait, tapping a slippered foot on the pink marble.

Time dragged its heels; each minute felt like an hour. Lena made herself comfortable on the floor among the cushions and was soon dozing in the heat. Eleanor reclined upon the divan, but when she felt her eyelids growing heavy she sat up, shook herself, and wandered out into the garden. It was a delightful oasis filled with exotic blooms, fig trees, and date palms all surrounding the pale-green marble bathing pool where lotuslike flowers floated and drifted with the perfumed breeze. The water was most inviting and Eleanor bent to trail her fingers in the cool depths, then sat down, removed her slippers and stockings, and let her feet dangle in the water.

She gazed up above her chamber at the palace walls, which were made of intricately patterned mosaic tiles. She thought it curious the walls were solid with no windows to let in the breeze, then she was thankful that no one could look down into the garden from above and see her. Her mind flew off to another garden, in another time, and the memories it evoked of Simon were so tangible she could feel his damnably attractive hands upon her breasts, his breath upon her throat, and the kisses that had left their imprint upon her lips forever. The pale-green water beckoned and her resistance melted in the warm afternoon.

Her gown, which had seemed so cool when she chose it this morning, was now far too tight and constricting. Her silk shift beneath it was sticking to her skin, and she fought a losing battle with herself until she finally succumbed and removed the offending garments. She slid naked into the cool green depths and closed her eyes in bliss. The water came just to her breasts and as she leaned back against the edge of the pool they bobbed up and down prettily, floating on the water's surface like two pale lotus blooms. The ends of her black curls dipped into the water and swirled about her naked shoulders. Eleanor closed her eyes and gave herself up to sheer physical pleasure.

Above her a pair of dark, intense eyes watched every gesture, every expression upon her lovely face. The mosaic tile wall with its grillwork pattern was designed to view the garden and pool without the observer being detected. Selim watched the beautiful female from above; the pale green water in no way impeded his vision of her naked form. He did not believe he had ever seen such a petite female in his life. The women in his harem, whether they were fair or dark, tended to voluptuous proportions. Some were even fat, but all were generously plump. This female was no bigger than one of his slave boys of ten or twelve years, yet with her slim legs and high round breasts her proportions seemed perfect and more than tempting. He had been aroused from the moment she lifted her skirt to remove her stockings. He imagined how tight her sheath would be, and his hand caressed his erection, noting with pleasure the length she had helped him achieve.

He was delighted with this turn of events. He had thought all the advantage was with Frederick, Holy Roman Emperor, and his horde of crusaders. He had assumed it would cost him dearly to renew the truce, but it was a price that must be paid for he was assailed on all sides by the Syrians, the Jews, and the mad Turks. If the crusaders would return home or at least be contained within the boundaries of Palestine, he could breathe easier. Now it seemed he would be able to use his hostage

Amauri de Montfort as a bargaining tool since the emperor was sending Simon de Montfort to renew the truce. His smile turned into a leer as he thought of the delectable princess who was fast in his lair. She was an unexpected gift, yet it was a common enough practice for men to offer their wives' bodies in exchange for favors rendered.

Eleanor reluctantly climbed from the pool and wrapped herself in a thirsty Turkish towel. She picked up her clothes and wrinkled her nose at the thought of putting them back on. She padded in bare feet back inside where the pink marble floor felt deliciously cool. She gasped with apprehension, for Lena was no longer in the chamber. She rushed to the door, unmindful of her déshabillé, and tried to fling it wide. Two fleshy black eunuchs stood in her path blocking her way. She was so angry she contemplated snatching one of their weapons and sticking it into a fat belly, but just as that moment the tall, slim Fayid glided into view carrying an armful of exotic silken garments.

"I am leaving at once," cried Eleanor. "Where is my maid?"

Fayid bowed. "As you will, Princess. However, Sultan Selim is awaiting you."

"Oh," said Eleanor, feeling as if she had been tugging on the end of a rope that had come unfastened. She backed into the room clutching the towel to her breasts and murmured, "I must get dressed."

Fayid spread the lovely silks upon the divan. "Perhaps you would wish to wear one of these, Princess."

Eleanor looked from the exotic garments to the small heap of clothing she had discarded earlier. Her chin went up. "Absolutely not! I refuse to dress as a heathen."

Fayid bowed her head. "It shall be as you wish, Princess."

"You can be very sure of that!" retorted Eleanor.

She took courage from the colors she had chosen that morning when she had carefully dressed for her meeting with the sultan. However, the brave green and white, the King of England's favorite colors, lay wrinkled. She disdained help from Fayid as she donned her shift and pulled on her stockings—garments that women of the East did not wear. Her underdress was pale leaf green, as finely spun as a veil. Over it she slid her dark-green silk tunic, decorated with small white swans wear-

ing golden crowns upon their proud, graceful heads. She
wished she had a golden crown for her own head at this moment as her hands tried to smooth out her long black tresses,
which were curling profusely from the pool.

She knew, however, that she had more important things to
concentrate upon. Her mind darted about like quicksilver re-
hearsing the things she would say to Selim. She knew she must
not act like a supplicant, appealing for him to release her husband's brother. She must not appear to be a weak female asking
the strong male for favors. She would deal with him as an
equal, as one royal personage to another. She would subtly hint
that she had great influence with the King of England and had
power to open up trade routes between the two countries. William Marshal had taught her that sometimes promises were
sufficient to achieve a goal and that those promises were not
necessarily carved in stone. The important thing to keep in
mind was to deal from a position of strength.

As Fayid led her along a myriad of corridors, Eleanor wondered how many people she would have to face. The Sultan of
Egypt most likely surrounded himself with ministers, advisors,
sycophants, and body servants, so Eleanor was surprised when
Fayid ushered her into an empty chamber save for one figure
who sat motionless upon a raised dais. Brilliant sunshine came
through a multicolored glass window behind him, making it
difficult to see the face of the man with whom she found herself
alone.

He sat not in a high-backed chair of state but upon an enormous backless throne. It looked as if it was made of solid gold.
The room was silent, echoing the whisper of her garments and
her quickened breathing. Then suddenly the figure stood up
and descended lithely from the dais. He was only about five-
and-a-half-feet tall with skin and eyes the color of old teak. He
wore cloth-of-gold pantaloons and a curious headpiece decorated by a coiled serpent. His entire body was devoid of hair,
Eleanor noticed, as her curious eyes swept up him, coming to
rest on his face. It was thin, his nose hooked, but he had beautiful teeth that flashed whitely in his dark face.

Eleanor extended her fingers for a handshake, but Selim captured her hand and held on to it. His eyes were so frankly

assessing she felt a blush stain her cheeks. Then, still holding her fingers, he walked around her in a wide circle as if he was appraising the fine points of a mare. Eleanor felt her blood rise, yet she knew she must maintain a cool and aloof demeanor to keep her dignity. "Allow me to introduce myself, Sultan Selim. I am Princess . . ."

"I know who you are," he interrupted. "Your name is Precious Jewel."

Eleanor was stunned. How on earth did this man know her father had called her his precious jewel? "No! That is not my name. I am Princess Eleanor Plantagenet," she stated firmly.

He smiled lazily. "To me you shall be Precious Jewel," he insisted, "my Precious Jewel."

"Nay, that is impossible, your Highness, I am a married woman." She wondered wildly if he had heard gossip about her. She had been accused of everything from killing her husband with her insatiable sexual demands, to adultery and producing a bastard. God, don't let me faint, she prayed, as she felt herself go dizzy and sway. Instantly his arms were about her. He lifted her and carried her to an alcove where a draped divan was partially hidden from the rest of the room.

"Put me down instantly; how dare you touch me!" she choked. "My letter told you plainly I am here to negotiate the release of Amauri de Montfort."

He laughed as he looked deeply into her eyes. "I cannot get over the way you look at me. Your eyes are like deep, blue Persian sapphires that blaze with fire. My other women dare not look me in the face. Their lashes are lowered when I give them permission to speak." He lowered her to the divan and she struggled to get up.

"Sir, I am a royal princess of England. I am your equal, nay, my rank is far superior to yours!"

Selim was genuinely amused at her words. "All women are inferior to men. Princesses are nothing unique to me. I have a princess in my harem. You will not be the first to come to my bed."

"This is preposterous," Eleanor said furiously. "I have no intention of coming to your bed, and how dare you insult me by comparing me to a princess from some tin-pot regime? I am a Plantagenet and you are treating me like a slave girl."

Selim studied her intently. "I thought you were here to negotiate."

"I am," she asserted.

"A woman has only one thing to offer," he said with a slightly perplexed frown. "I am willing to accept your offer in return for the hostage." Now that he had made all plain, he expected her to be pleased. She seemed anything but pleased.

"I came here to negotiate in good faith, sir. To offer to open up trade routes between our countries and you treat me like a houri."

"Such things are not within the sphere of women's capabilities. These things I will discuss with your husband this evening."

She was startled. "My husband is coming here?"

He chuckled. "Do not pretend ignorance, Precious Jewel. He has sent you as a gift to me, knowing that if you bring me pleasure it will smooth negotiations between us."

Eleanor for the first time felt real fear. She was far more afraid of Simon de Montfort than of Sultan Selim. "Ah no, you are mistaken. My husband would never share me with another man. I must be gone from here before he arrives. He is a war lord. He would not hesitate to kill you or kill me if I betrayed him!"

"Such passion delights me. You are so very dramatic, you sound as if you really believe what you say, but you forget I know all about you. He has already shared you with another man. The Marshal of England took you to wife when you were nine." He licked lips gone suddenly dry. By the moon and the stars, he wished he'd tasted her when she was nine. "Remove your garments for me, Precious Jewel. I would see your perfection now so I may savor the hours until nightfall when you will return to share my couch."

"You must be mad!" She ran toward the door, but Selim was after her in a flash. With ungentle hands he dragged her back and threw her upon the divan. "Just because I admire your passion and spirit does not mean I am prepared to suffer your insolence. When I give a woman an order, I get obedience."

Her chin went up in defiance and he launched himself upon her. He had a cruel strength in his hands, which he used to tear her garments from her body. Eleanor screamed and fought him wildly, but no one heard or heeded her cries for help. When she tried to bite him, he hit her so hard she blacked out for a moment, and as she came back to consciousness she shuddered with revulsion as she felt his hands run up and down the length of her naked body.

He grimaced at her reaction. "Tonight you will try an Egyptian prick for flavor; you will love it." He stood up from the couch with narrowed eyes. He did not want her fighting and biting. He wanted her tiny sheath hot for him. Fayid would know just what magic ingredients to add to the almond sweetmeats and honeyed drinks she would be served before she was brought to him.

Eleanor's clothes lay in shreds about her trembling body. She wondered if she should plead with him, tell him she was with child and beg him to let her go, but she knew in her heart it would make no difference to the evil swine. A woman meant only one thing to a man like the sultan—a warm body. If she did not comply she was less than nothing, without value whatsoever.

He went to the door and Fayid entered. The servant must have been waiting outside all the time. She held out a loose, white silk robe for Eleanor, who had no choice but to take it thankfully. Fayid was not at all surprised that the sultan had humbled the proud princess.

42

The hour when Selim's guest would arrive was fast approaching. As his slaves bathed and dressed him, the sultan discussed business with two aides and at the same time gave last-minute instructions regarding the dinner. He also changed the chamber assigned the war lord to one above his own, which overlooked the garden and pool where Precious Jewel was lodged.

Just then there was a knock on his chamber door. The captain of his guard informed him that his guest had arrived bearing many gifts. No less than twenty camels stood in the courtyard laden with large earthenware jars containing precious oils, rare spices from the Orient, forbidden golden wines, aromatic myrrh, and even gunpowder, an explosive mixture of sulfur, charcoal, and saltpeter.

It was much more than Selim had expected but he reasoned that since his wealth was legendary, the representative of the Holy Roman Empire brought tokens of great value to prove they could match or outdo him in all things. For two powers to negotiate they must appear to be equal in wealth, manpower, and determination. It was important not to lose face from the

outset. Selim gave orders that the hostage Amauri de Montfort
be present at the dinner.

Simon de Montfort dismissed the palace servants because he
had brought his own body servants with him. In actuality they
were his two battle squires, Guy and Rolf. They took no
chances. Knowing the proliferation of narcotic drugs in the
East, Rolf tasted the food and drink that had been provided
before he allowed his son Guy or his lord Simon to refresh
themselves.

The Earl of Leicester bathed and donned black silk for his
dinner with the Sultan of Egypt.

Eleanor found that she could not stop trembling. While she
was in Selim's presence she had fought the tears so long that
her throat felt constricted, and now when she thought the
floodgates would open, she found that she could not cry. Her
skin crawled as she remembered his touch. After pacing like a
caged pantheress for the best part of an hour, she finally could
bear it no longer. She walked rapidly into the garden to the
edge of the pool, threw off her white silk robe, and slid deep in
the water to cleanse her body of Selim's contamination.

As Simon gazed down from the latticed window, his eye was
caught by a movement far below in a garden. He stood transfixed as the unmistakable figure of his wife threw off a white
garment and began to disport herself in a bathing pool. His fists
clenched into iron balls. His fury almost choked him. He knew
he had never before known an anger so great in his entire life.
His informers had given him the information that she had gone
to the summer palace, that she had passed through the gates,
but that only her servants had left. He had been incensed at her
impulsive meddling in men's affairs. Would she never learn to
keep her woman's place?

Now, however, he was enraged. She had placed herself in
Selim's power, and he was obviously enjoying the fruit that
Simon owned and had assumed was his exclusively for all time.
His beloved Kathe whom he cherished above all things was
bathing naked as if she were in the privacy of their bedchamber
at Kenilworth.

Here was the woman he had pursued at all odds to make his
wife. The king had impugned the honor of Simon de Montfort

over this woman, and he even suffered exile because of her. Simon did not realize that it was jealousy that fanned the flame of his fury. He turned from the window and battled with himself for control. At least he now knew where the faithless little bitch was lodged.

A palace servant reentered the room to usher the three men to the room where they were to dine. When he came face to face with his host, Simon found that he could not unclench his fists. It took all his control not to smash the sultan in his beautiful white teeth. In his mind he knew he had to place his wife at one side while he focused upon Selim and the goals he must accomplish.

They sat cross-legged upon huge cushions before low tables inlaid with lapis lazuli. The gold medallion that hung upon a chain about Selim's neck was probably worth more than Simon would be able to accumulate in ten years.

Selim's sly eyes had been watching for what would pass between the de Montfort brothers as they sat at such close range, but the Earl of Leicester seemed totally indifferent to the presence of Amauri. Selim was amused to see the war lord's body servants who sat flanking him taste everything before their master did. If they suspected poison then they had no idea how desperately he wanted this truce. He veiled his eyes and forced himself to patience. He would not broach the subject until they had dined and enjoyed watching his dancing girls perform. He was impressed with the Earl of Leicester's courage in coming with only two attendants; he had expected him to bring at least a dozen guards.

The men in the room seemed mesmerized by the undulating rhythm of the gyrating females. Their finger cymbals clashed in time with the pounding of the blood in the men's veins. Their transparent skirts revealed their naked bodies while their yashmaks concealed their faces, which was most erotic. When the girls, one by one, walked upon their hands and their skirts fell about their heads, it confirmed what the men had suspected. They wore no undergarments whatsoever. Selim hid a smile as he leaned toward his guest. "I offer you one of my *precious jewels.* Feel free to chose."

Simon's eyes flicked over the women and came to rest upon

the tallest. Though her hair was golden, her skin was dusky. "Have that one remove her veil," ordered Simon. When he saw that the female had an attractive face, he nodded his head in acceptance. At a sign from the sultan, she slid to the floor beside the war lord.

Selim knew he must broach the subject of the truce for he knew instinctively that the giant before him would outwait him if it took the rest of eternity. "I offer the return of your brother Amauri without ransom. What do you offer if I renew the truce?" he asked smoothly.

Simon's deep laugh rolled about the room. "I offer nothing and in truth you offer nothing," he stated.

"You consider the life of your brother nothing?" Selim asked.

Simon looked squarely into Selim's eyes. "He is worth more to me dead than alive. He is a sovereign prince in southern France . . . I stand to inherit."

Selim drained the goblet of forbidden wine he had ordered served because his guest observed no taboos against alcohol. The negotiations inched forward as Selim realized de Montfort was determined to drive a hard bargain. Whatever he offered was refused out of hand, and the war lord made a counteroffer. When Selim offered camels, de Montfort shook his head and demanded Arabian horses. When Selim offered gemstones, Simon demanded gold. Simon had drugged Selim's wine and needed his signature on the truce documents that the emperor had drawn up before its effects were fully realized.

Simon's eyes flicked to an arched window to see if any light remained in the sky. When he saw that it was full dark, he knew his men would be slipping silently from the earthenware jars that concealed them. He pressed Selim for the first time. "Our terms are generous. We ask that you open trade routes that have been blocked by the Turks." When he produced the document bearing Frederick the Great's signature, Selim signed it immediately. Simon raised his goblet.

Selim signaled for more wine. "The accursed Turks are a scourge upon the land. Perhaps if we joined forces we could eradicate them." Selim fought a battle to keep his heavy eyelids from closing, but he was slowly losing that battle. Suddenly a bloodcurdling war cry filled the air and forty black-clad, knife-wielding Turks descended upon the diners. Selim's worst nightmare had become a reality; his summer palace would be destroyed by the mad Turks. He pitched forward into blackness.

It seemed that every honeycombed passage became filled with a panic of servants, slaves, scantily clad females, eunuchs, and palace guards. Hysterical screams and smoke spread through the halls of the palace as its inhabitants fled from the attackers' bloodlust.

Eleanor became aware of the pandemonium long before her chamber door crashed inward. The sound of her screams blended with others as a black-clad figure descended upon her and slung her across his shoulder. Smoke swirled in the door, but it did not hide the sight of the slumped bodies of the eunuchs who had been guarding it.

All was confusion; the din deafening. Acrid smoke caused her to choke and her eyes to sting painfully until tears streamed down her face. Through a blur she saw bodies and blood, yet no one seemed to be fighting back. The attack had taken all by surprise and uppermost in every mind, male or female, slave or guard, was the thought of fleeing.

The Turks' heads and faces were wrapped with black scarves so that only their wild and terrifying eyes were visible. Eleanor was passed from one to another until she was outside in the palace courtyard. A sudden explosion sent the iron gates of the palace crashing through the air and she heard herself half sob, half scream as a black-clad giant ran with her through the dust and smoke. Her captor handed her up to a man astride a destrier, and as he did so his black sleeves fell back to expose dragons tatooed upon his forearms. Her heart lurched as she realized who had rescued her. She swiveled her head to learn the identity of the man who now gripped her so tightly and stared into the eyes of her brother Richard. "By the beard of the Prophet, Cockroach, Simon will beat you to a jelly for the trouble you've caused him this night."

When Simon de Montfort was satisfied that the summer palace at Ascalon would never again be used by the Sultan of Egypt, he stalked back to the dining salon in search of Selim. Flanked by Guy and Rolf, Simon found the enemy he sought still slumped upon cushions in a drugged sleep. They carried him to his golden throne, stripped off his voluminous trousers, and laid him across that throne like a naked sacrifice upon an altar.

Simon de Montfort observed everything through the red haze of bloodlust. Very deliberately he pulled the chain from about Selim's neck and secured it tightly about the sultan's scrotum like a ligature. He intended to geld him for violating his wife. The operation was a simple enough procedure, which he'd performed on many war horses. All one had to do was slit the sac, then pop out the balls. Suddenly a mental picture of what he must look like came to the Earl of Leicester, and he felt a sickening distaste for the whole unsavory business. It was not his style to maim an unconscious man while his lieutenants held him trussed for the slaughter. He was near torn in half by his need to take revenge upon the swine who had dared to covet what was his, but he had hesitated and knew he would not go through with the abomination. His knife slit Selim's sac to leave his mark upon the man, but he did not geld him; he left him intact. With an obscene curse he sheathed his weapon and signed for his two squires to quit the place, but not before he slipped the gold medallion beneath his belt.

Safe once more in the rooms she occupied at the Templars' stronghold in Jaffa, Eleanor slowly recovered from her ordeal. She quaked inwardly whenever she contemplated the moment she would come face to face with her husband. Praise God that Simon had rescued her from the fate of sharing Selim's bed, but she knew he would be enraged over her interfering in what he called "men's affairs." He was the most renowned warrior of the age, and she could see his fierce black eyes and hear his deep voice demanding of her "Did you not have enough faith in me to renew the truce and effect the release of my own brother?"

She felt shame, remorse, and repentance. She must chose her words very carefully to make him understand her impulsive behavior. Damn this heat, she could bear it no longer; and damn Henry for the sniveling coward he was to let Winchester control him. She wanted to be in her own country, in her own home. She felt she could not bear to be separated longer from her first child and be forced to bear her second child in exile. With tender hands she cupped her belly and felt very sorry for herself.

Most nights she found that sleep eluded her. When Morpheus did claim her, her dreams were marred by such horrific nightmares she was apprehensive about going to bed. She knew what would cure her. She needed Simon in the bed beside her. She needed his strong arms to pull her down to him when she started up from a bad dream. She needed his big body to cover hers and blot out the world. She needed his long, thick manroot to fill the terrifying emptiness inside her.

Eleanor felt cold. Though the heat was stifling, a cold hand seemed to grip her heart. Her maids had informed her yesterday that Simon de Montfort had arrived with his brother Amauri. She had awaited him breathlessly, but he had not come to her. She reasoned that he would be closeted with Frederick for long hours, then when he did not come she told herself it was only natural that he would spend time with his brother, but when midnight came and went she knew that Simon would not come.

She felt haggard from lack of sleep when she dragged herself from her lonely bed the next day. She bathed, spent hours choosing her prettiest gown, then changed three times before she was satisfied with her appearance. She was just past the halfway point of her pregnancy and had begun to show. She decided to go down to the dining hall for the midmeal of the day. She would not be able to eat a thing, of course, but she would confront her husband who would be loathe to create a scene in front of the emperor, Richard, and Amauri.

The color of pale-yellow silk falling in soft folds about her tiny figure was most flattering to her sun-kissed skin and her cloud of black hair. Frederick came to greet her immediately. "You look as lovely and cool as an English spring, my lady. I swear you grow prettier every time I see you."

At the end of the hall she could see her brother talking with a large man who could only be Amauri de Montfort. Between the two men was a veiled woman. She caught her breath. Damn Richard to hellfire; he was even bringing his concubines to the dining hall now. She breathed a small sigh of relief that Simon had not yet arrived.

When she approached Amauri de Montfort he gallantly took her hand and brought it to his lips. He was obviously cut from the same cloth as her husband, though he was somewhat older and did not have Simon's devastating looks. His dark eyes held a teasing light as he said in heavily accented English, "You could only be the infamous Eleanor."

"Infamous indeed," said a hard, implacable voice behind her. She whirled about, and it was as if his face had been chiseled from stone. He towered above her, his black eyes boring down into hers. It took every ounce of willpower he possessed to keep himself from striking her. He knew that he could kill her with one blow. He stepped back from her, bowed curtly to the company at large, and rasped, "Excuse me." Then he turned on his heel and quit the hall.

Blood of God, he's made it plain to all he cannot bear the sight of me, thought Eleanor. Her cheeks were stained crimson. She swept her brother and the veiled female with a look of contempt. "How could you?" she demanded.

"She's not mine," he defended.

Eleanor drew her dignity about her like a cloak and walked from the room.

In the evening she tried to eat something, but she could not. She picked up a date, but the stickiness on her fingers made her shudder. Then she began to peel an orange, but its aroma was so strongly piquant, her nostrils pinched involuntarily and she knew her throat would do likewise. She poured herself a cup of wine and sipped it reflectively to calm her nerves. She felt like screaming. A storm was gathering about the de Montforts, and she knew she would not know a moment's calm until it had spent itself.

At last he came but Eleanor was on her third cup of wine and her mood was as dangerous as his. She took the initiative immediately. "I have never been so humiliated in my life! You did not have the decency to introduce me to your brother," she exclaimed.

"You dare speak of decency?" he demanded.

"Yes I dare. I have never acted indecently in my life," she asserted proudly.

"Cavorting naked in the sultan's pool is your idea of decency?" he thundered.

"I was washing away his loathsome touch!" she cried. The moment the words were out she could have bitten off her tongue. She knew she had just confirmed his suspicions that Selim had had access to her body. All day she had rehearsed the things she would say to him and she had decided to lie, to swear to him that the sultan had refused to see her. Now she had let the cat out of the bag and she could not backtrack.

"You will return to Brindisi until the child is born," he stated flatly, his voice devoid of emotion. "Frederick, Richard, and my brother will be on the same ship and will see you safe."

Her chin went up. "And why are you not returning to Brindisi since the Crusade is over?" she demanded.

"What gives you the right to expect explanations from me, madame?" he thundered.

"I am your wife," she cried, her eyes blazing.

"Too bad you didn't remember that little detail before you ran off to the Sultan of Egypt."

"I went as one royal personage to another thinking to negotiate the release of your brother," she explained defensively.

"Did you have so little faith in my abilities, madame?"

"Blood of God, you were off fighting, while Richard was busy making obscene amounts of money with his endless deals and Frederick was trying to negotiate a truce behind your back. I thought there was none to tend to de Montfort interests, so I took it upon myself."

He looked at her with disbelief. She was so very small and he noticed that the child she carried was beginning to show. "Sit down," he directed, "while I try to get something through to your female brain." His voice had gone quiet and she knew better than to disobey him. She sat down upon a divan and curled her feet beneath her.

"I am aware of the fact that you are a princess, but even if you were a queen or an empress I would still be master of my own house. While I live and breathe there is no need for you to take it upon yourself to look after the de Montfort interests."

Eleanor bit her lip as he laid down the law to her.

"Contrary to what you obviously think, I am nobody's fool. I made sure I was kept informed of every move Frederick made." Then he added, "And every move you made. I am a man, Eleanor, not a weathercock like your brother Henry: unsteady, unready, unreliable."

She stood up and placed her hand upon his chest. "Sim, please . . ."

He felt the heat of her touch seeping through his tunic and stepped away from her before he was lost. "Do not think to seduce me with pet names," he accused. She was crushed at his rejection. "There needs to be a great deal of sugar on the pill when someone else has licked it."

Her hurt turned to anger at his crude insinuation. "Get out. I hate you!"

He ignored her outburst, moved to the window, and looked out into the darkness with unseeing eyes. "The Knights Templars and the citizens of Jerusalem have asked the emperor to make me governor of Palestine."

Eleanor's heart sank. She wanted to beg him to reject the offer, but of course it would bring him the wealth he had never had.

"I am contemplating the offer, but rest assured, Eleanor, it will be *my* decision, not yours. Tomorrow you will pack your things for Brindisi. You may take all the servants back with you. There will be another female traveling with you."

Eleanor's mind was like quicksilver. "That veiled creature I saw in the hall? Richard swore she wasn't his. Don't tell me she belongs to your brother?" she said with a sneer.

Simon turned his head from the window to watch her reaction to his words. "She is mine. I chose her from Selim's harem, Eleanor."

For a moment she looked stricken as if he had mortally wounded her. Then she bared her teeth and hissed, "Do not call me Eleanor! It curses me as it did my grandmother! Is this the stage of my life where you imprison me and take a concubine like your great hero, Henry II?" She flew at him and scratched his face.

He stared at her as if she was mad. He loved and cherished her. He had given her his heart and his soul. A wide chasm had opened between them. "You are hysterical, madame; compose yourself."

43

Simon and Eleanor gave each other a wide berth until it was time for her to leave. He did not bid her a private farewell, but came aboard with the others and when he saw that she was comfortably accommodated, bade her a formal farewell in front of everyone.

On the voyage she glimpsed the golden-haired girl only once, but she did not even acknowledge her existence. Upon her arrival at Brindisi she retired quietly to the echoing stone palace by the sea, thankful to be back in a safe place where there were no Saracens, no Turks, and, praise heaven, no domineering husband to look at her with accusing eyes or dictate her every action.

Eleanor's attitude toward her sister and sister-in-law was now kinder and far more tolerant, yet inside she seethed that her faithless husband had placed her in their same pitiful position.

As her birthing time drew closer she told herself how much she hated Simon de Montfort. He was the author of all her troubles. She told herself fiercely that she never should have married him, and never would have married him if he had not taken complete advantage of her and gotten her with child. Her sister Isabella had taken it upon herself to furnish Simon's slave girl with a suite of rooms, and though the girl no longer wore veils and Eastern dress, everyone knew perfectly well who she was, and Eleanor felt deep shame.

As a result she became almost reclusive, feeling her pregnancy made her clumsy and unattractive. The last month she fell to weeping, at first only in private, then in front of her maids, finally in the presence of the two Isabellas, who were becoming increasingly worried about her. She suffered recurring bouts of false labor, and finally her sister put her to bed and made her stay there.

By the time Simon de Montfort returned to Brindisi, they feared for her life. Her beautiful eyes were purple-shadowed and in spite of her large belly, everywhere else she was thin as a rail and weighed almost nothing.

The war lord had never known terror in his life, but he became intimately acquainted with it when he crept into Eleanor's chamber and knelt beside the bed. When he gently took her hand he knew she was burning with fever.

Eleanor opened heavy lids. "Sim? Sim, is it truly you? I've seen you for days but it was only a vision."

His lips brushed her brow. He swallowed three times before his deep voice could get past the lump in his throat. "I'm here, love. I should never have sent you from me."

"I have made myself ill, hating you." She clung so tightly to his hand he wondered where her strength was coming from.

"Hush, love, don't try to talk, just rest. I will stay with you."

"Simon, I know now I don't hate you; I hate myself," she whispered fiercely.

He wondered if it was the ramblings of fever.

"Isabella wanted me to make my confession, but it isn't a damned priest I need, it's you. Will you hear me?" she begged.

Simon could not bear to see his beautiful, proud, passionate princess brought so low. He closed his eyes and prayed. She must have picked up some disease in the East, or perhaps her illness was due to complications of the child he had given her. Either way it was all his fault.

"Sim, guilt is eating me alive. Will you forgive me?" she whispered.

"Forgive you? My love, it is you who must forgive me." How basely he had treated her over the business of the Sultan of Egypt. As if it mattered what a wife did as long as you loved her.

"You were right. I never should have gone to the summer palace. He thought I had come to offer my body in exchange for Amauri. He was so ignorant and lacking in knowledge he thought a woman had nothing else to offer . . . had no other value."

"You are priceless," murmured Simon, his cheeks wet with tears.

"You must believe me when I tell you he did not defile me!"

"I believe you, Kathe," Simon said firmly. He lay down beside her and gathered her to him tenderly. Her eyes closed and she gave herself up to the total enveloping protection that was Simon de Montfort. He stiffened, his fear for her making him think she had drawn her last breath. Then he went weak with relief when he saw she was only sleeping. He watched over her as if he was a guardian angel, watching every breath, every flicker of an eyelash upon her shadowed cheek, every heartbeat of this woman who was everything to him.

After two hours of rest, Eleanor rose up screaming; she was in full, hard labor. The Earl of Leicester would rather have faced ten battlefields than watch his beloved precious jewel give birth. He knew it was the bravest thing he had ever seen. How humble it made him to see the courage and suffering a woman must endure to give her husband a son. When at last Eleanor smiled down upon the dark little head and murmured, "We'll call him Simon," the war lord was undone. His sobbing could be heard by all, and the women in the room exchanged glances that such a giant of a man should cry.

Over the course of the next few days as Eleanor regained her health, Simon spent much time at her bedside. Her eyes followed his tall figure about the room as if they were hungry for the very sight of him. The sun had bronzed him to a dark mahogany, and she knew by the reaction of the maids that he set every female heart aflutter. While he was far away Eleanor had not acknowledged the existence of the girl from the sultan's palace, she had not even asked her name. Now that he was here under the same roof, however, her presence rose up very real for Eleanor. Each time she tried to ask him, the words died in her throat.

He was bending over the cradle when she said, "I have not even asked what brought you back."

He straightened and adjusted the gauzy curtains about the cradle. He shrugged slightly as if he was talking to himself. "The truce was being upheld. It seemed a good time to return and settle a few things with Frederick." He looked at her and came to the bed. Then he sat down and took hold of her hand. "In truth, Eleanor, you and you alone brought me back. Things were not right between us when you left. I could settle to nothing. I knew your time was upon you and suddenly I knew that being governor of Palestine was less than nothing to me."

Eleanor closed her eyes and gave thanks. She had not realized until this moment how much she had resented her husband for even considering the lucrative post that had been offered him. She felt his fingertips trace across her cheekbones. Simon was relieved to see that the purple shadows had left her beautiful eyes. Even in that tender moment she could not gather her courage to ask him about the woman. She decided it was better not to know.

He gathered her in his arms and touched his lips to hers. Instantly a flame leapt between them and before he withdrew their tongues had mated over and over. She lay back against her pillows satisfied that he loved and adored her more than all the golden-haired women in the world. A tiny sigh escaped her. He still hadn't accepted her as an equal. Perhaps he never would. She decided to settle for what she had, at least for the present. Their time together would probably be short. She didn't have the courage to ask when he was returning to Palestine. She closed her eyes to rest, content for the moment.

As Simon walked quietly from the chamber, their thoughts were as one. Each wondered if they could spend the night in the other's arms.

In the late afternoon Eleanor came up out of a most restful sleep with a start. She knew something was wrong. Her eyes flew to the cradle, but a maid watched over her son attentively.

Then she heard the shouting and knew that's what had awakened her. Though she could make out no words, she knew it was her husband's voice. It had such a deep, rich timber she could never mistake it for another. He thundered on, shouting curses, and she heard the unmistakable crash of splintering furniture as it was booted across a room.

She grabbed a thin robe to cover her silk nightrail and on bare feet ran from her chamber to learn what terrible calamity had befallen. Like most large men, Simon de Montfort had a very even temper and it took a great deal to rouse him to a towering rage. Eleanor ran down the stone staircase to the front reception hall and found none other than her dear friend Sir Rickard de Burgh quaffing a great stirrup cup of cooled wine while Simon waved a parchment in the air as if it was a dreaded decree from hell.

"Rickard, whatever is amiss?" she cried.

Simon whirled about ready to transfer his anger upon any target. "What in the name of God are you doing out of bed?" he stormed. He stuffed the paper into his doublet and in two strides swept her up in his arms to carry her back to her chamber. He threw at de Burgh, "Not a word of this to Eleanor!"

"Simon, you must tell me," she insisted as he took the stairs two at a time.

He shoved her back into bed most ungently. "I won't have that feebleminded, useless imbecile upset you."

She knew he was not speaking of the gentle parfait knight below. It could only be the king who had riled his temper.

"Rickard has brought a message from Henry."

He looked amazed. "However did you know?"

"Hocus-pocus, fish bones choke us," she whispered.

"There is nothing whatsoever amusing in this, Eleanor," he said sternly. "You once told me insanity galloped in your family and Splendor of God, truer words were never uttered. The man has the unmitigated gall, the bare-faced temerity to appeal to me for help." He pulled out the letter and threw it across the bed. "He writes as if we parted the best of friends. We went into exile on threat of imprisonment. The charges against me were seduction and treason, and even if my pride allowed me to swallow those insults, I will never, ever forgive him for charg-

ing you with adultery and besmirching you forever. If he thinks
he can sweep all that away with the stroke of a pen, his brain
has addled like a rotten egg."

Eleanor became still; she almost stopped breathing. Here was
their chance to go home, if only she could make Simon amenable. She looked at him askance. God's bones, there was scant
chance of making Simon de Montfort amenable to anything. If
she had learned one lesson since she had been married, it was
that this man made his own decisions and ruled his own
destiny. She'd not get round him with women's wiles either. He
was wise to the ways of women, having had a vast experience of
them, damn him to hellfire, she thought.

He was in a dangerous mood and if she questioned him on
the whys and wherefores, he would accuse her of meddling in
men's affairs. She opened her mouth, thought better of it, and
closed it again. She would not manipulate him. He was too fine
a man for that.

He looked down at her in the bed. "Well? Have you nothing
to say? It's damned odd you are not telling me what to do."

"I have every faith in your ability to handle the King of
England, my lord," she said quietly.

"Well, it's about time!" he replied, but she could see that
some of the sting had gone from his tail.

The next day she spent the afternoon on the portico that
overlooked the azure sea. She knew Simon and Rickard were
discussing England's affairs openly, exchanging frank ideas,
and she wished with all her heart she could overhear them.
Every now and then one or the other would come out to see
how she was feeling. If only they would ask her opinion of what
they discussed. With Simon she kept a wise silence, but with
Rickard she knew she could speak what was in her mind and
her heart without offending. As he crinkled his eyes to look out
over the glittering sea, he said, "The climate is so favorable
here, I don't suppose you would ever willingly trade it for England's damp and drizzle."

"Rickard, I would do almost anything to return to Kenilworth," she said passionately.

"Anything?" he questioned.

"I said almost anything. The only thing I wouldn't do is ask

Simon to swallow past insults and bend his knee to Henry. That would be intolerable to a man with Simon's fiery pride."

Rickard de Burgh, ever faithful to Eleanor, did not repeat all that she said to de Montfort, even though he knew that her feelings lent a great deal of weight to the war lord's decisions. King Henry's was not the only letter he had brought to the Earl of Leicester. He had one from his uncle, Hubert de Burgh, who was still exiled in Wales. It pledged the support of all the men of the Cinque Ports if Simon was instrumental in obtaining the king's pardon for Hubert and restoring his vast holdings. Rickard also gave Simon a verbal pledge from his father in Ireland, Falcon de Burgh. He ruled a paletinate that stretched across Connaught from the River Shannon and was reputed to be able to muster five hundred men in a single night.

The last communication he brought was a surprise. It came from Roger Bigod, Earl of Norfolk and nephew of the late William Marshal. It stated bluntly that he knew William Marshal's brothers who had succeeded him as Marshal of England had each been murdered. Incriminating letters had been sent to Ireland urging Marshal opponents to accomplish their deaths. Though the letters bore the king's seal, he suspected the Winchester party. If Simon returned, Bigod would add his voice to bring about the downfall of Peter des Roches and his son, Peter des Rivaux. Bigod had ambitions to become England's next marshal and made no bones about it.

Eleanor was surprised to receive a letter from her mother, of all people, the first communication she had received since she was a child. She was not surprised, however, to learn that she corresponded because she wanted something. Suddenly all became clear. The questions she'd wished to ask Simon were answered.

Hugh de Lusignan, Count of La Marche, whom her mother had married before King John was cold in his grave, was in open conflict with Louis of France. Her mother had asked for her son Henry's support in an all-out war against France. Hugh de Lusignan was the highest Poitevin noble, and when Louis conferred the country of Poitou on his brother Alphonse, Isabella and Hugh had been outraged. She considered Poitou hers and often wore a crown. She had practically ordered her son, the King of England, to come to her aid. She pointed out that it was his duty to uphold their cause and gain back land for her sons, who were Henry's half brothers. In her letter to Eleanor she urged her to persuade Henry to help his brothers, who were, after all, Eleanor's brothers also.

It was now Eleanor's turn to fly into a rage, waving the crackling parchment in the air while she blistered her husband's ears with her fine opinion of her mother. "The thing that baffles and perplexes me is her great love for those three piss-poor excuses of sons she bore de Lusignan. She sure as hell never loved any of her Plantagenet children! Now she is trying to manipulate and exploit us to further the ambitions of her favorites. The mere thought that William de Lusignan is my half brother makes me want to puke!"

Simon frowned as he listened to her tirade. It was obvious she did not want him to return to England to aid Henry. "If only Henry had your common sense. Alas, his mother still dominates him to the point where he runs to do her bidding. He even extends the hand of friendship to me, whom he injured irrevocably."

"Well, you can tell him to go to hellfire and I shall tell my mother the same!"

"Softly, darling, softly." Simon took the letter from her and pulled her into his arms. "Don't waste all your passion and fire on them, give it to me."

"Oh, I wish I had a fireplace. I'd burn their damned letters."

He tipped up her chin and his eyes kindled with desire as he looked down into her lovely flushed face. "I fantasize about a fire. The first thing I'm going to do if we are ever again in a cold climate is light a blazing fire in our chamber. Then I'm going to pull you down on the rug and make love to you. I long to see the fireshine splashed across your body. I crave to nuzzle you in places the fire has heated. Nothing compares to making love to a woman before a fireplace."

He could feel the heat snaking through his loins, and he slipped his hands over her bottom cheeks to press her close so she could feel his hard desire for her.

"Mmmm, Simon, it sounds like heaven, but we aren't going home to Kenilworth," she swore.

To himself he said, Yes we are, sweeting. It is what you want most in the world. To her he said, "Come to bed, I intend to make love to you for a couple of hours."

"First, Simon, tell me what you replied to Henry?"

"Not a chance," he teased as his fingers unfastened her gown and slipped it from her shoulders. He decided to keep her in ignorance of his plans. She would misinterpret his intentions and now that the chasm between them had narrowed, he had no interest in widening it again.

"I won't yield to you until you tell me," she swore.

"Ha! Won't yield to me?" he said, sweeping his hands down her bare back until they came to rest beneath her bottom, then he lifted her up to him so that her face was on a level with his. "I wager it will take about three kisses to wear down your defenses."

In fact it took only one.

44

Keeping all secret from his wife, the Earl of Leicester agreed to return and recruit an army for Henry on condition that he be allowed to attend the king's council meetings and have a voice in government.

A phrase from Henry's letter had jumped from the pages. It repeated over and over again in Simon's mind and had probably been the deciding factor in his decision to return. Henry had begged him "for England's sake." Simon shook his head regretfully. England was being ruined by injustice. He knew he should have taken a stand long ago against what was happening "for England's sake." What had prevented him? He knew the answer in his heart as well as his head. Eleanor had prevented him.

Before he took action he was able to think things through to their conclusion. You could not topple a king from a throne without a civil war. Where would her loyalties lie? He knew if Henry was killed as a result of any action on Simon's part, Eleanor would hate him forever. Henry was weak. Eleanor had always been stronger; so strong that she had always taken Henry's part.

De Montfort knew himself well. He did nothing by halves.

The step he was about to take was irrevocable. Once he set his feet on the path of restoring justice to England there would be no stopping, no turning back until it was accomplished, whether it took a year or a lifetime. He did not doubt his own ability for a moment; he would do or die, but he did have doubts about Eleanor's priorities—Plantagenet or de Montfort? Which was she?

He had a deep, yearning need for her to trust him implicitly. He would decide their future, and she should love him enough to accept his decision whatever it was. Either one trusted totally or one did not. Either one loved totally or one did not! He took his resolve, knowing full well that if it so ended that he should rule England, it would prove to her beyond a shadow of a doubt that he had married her for ambition.

Only when he had readied his ships and his men did he even hint to her that the morrow would part them. She was taking a cool, leisurely sponge bath when he walked in on her and dismissed her women impatiently. It was obvious he was in a hurry, and she assumed he had something private to discuss.

"Simon, whatever is it that couldn't have waited until I finished?"

He came to the bath and towered over her. His eyes devoured her, leaving no doubt of what he wanted. The naked lust upon his face brought a blush to her cheeks. He undressed rapidly, flinging off his clothes with such purpose she thought he intended to join her in the water, but when he was naked he reached down two powerful arms and lifted her up to him. "I want you now, this minute," he demanded.

"My lord, your haste is unseemly," she protested as he crushed her wet breasts against the dark pelt of his chest.

"I like unseemly, it is so improper and indecent." His mouth was hot and demanding as it took hers savagely. Between burning kisses he said, "I also like unreserved, unresisting, unrestrained, unruly, and unthinkable."

Eleanor caught her breath as his hot mouth took her ruching nipple and her whole areola inside and his tongue curled about the peak, sending a streak of molten fire along every vein. His lovemaking had been so gentle since the baby, but clearly gentleness was the last thing on his mind tonight. He was making love as if it were the first time, or the last.

Her lips pressed against the strong column of his throat and traced a path to his ear. "Why hurry?" she purred.

"We only have 'til dawn," he said hoarsely, telling her that after one night of passion he would be gone the moment she closed her eyes in exhausted sleep. He had deliberately awakened her desire before he had told her he was planning to leave. Her woman's cleft was all slippery from the bath and he had already managed to slip the head of his huge shaft inside her and was urging her to wrap her legs about him so he could bury himself to the hilt.

She moved, forcing him out of her. "You leave at dawn? That means you have been preparing for days and said nothing to me!"

His hands pulled her thighs apart and he forced himself back into her. "I love to thrust up into you while we're standing." She loved it too and moved her hips so that she took him whole. She gasped at the sheer fullness of him. When she was able to speak again she said, "I have a hundred questions. Will you answer them?"

He thrust into her, hard. "No."

She withdrew her sheath. "Yes!"

His powerful hands cupped her bottom and pulled her downward so that he impaled her. "No questions. Just trust me."

Again she lifted her body so that he was all the way out of her. "No!" she cried.

He pulled her down and at the same time thrust up into her. "Yes!" His word was final. This was why she had been born. This was what her body had been made for. She could no longer speak or even think, she could only taste and smell and feel.

Between lovemaking when he cradled her in his arms and whispered love words that made her very bones melt, she tried to probe for information. He put his fingers to her lips to silence her questions. "Dearest love, once and for all time will you not trust me to do what is best, what is right?"

She sighed and kissed his fingertips, tasting herself upon them. She supposed that he was right. It was best that he return to being governor of Palestine so that their finances would no longer be a burden to them. De Montfort now had two sons to worry about, and she knew how extravagant she was. A smile curved her mouth as she remembered the hundreds of copper kitchen utensils she had ordered for Kenilworth.

He kissed the corners of her mouth. "Did a wicked thought just cross your mind?"

"My smile is one of guilt for all the things I buy myself," she confessed.

"Never feel guilty, my sweetheart. 'Tis good you buy the things you want, for the presents I buy you are few and far between," he said ruefully, fingering the gold bracelet with which he'd gifted her after the first time they had made love.

She blushed, remembering. "Splendor of God, Sim, when I first saw you naked with that black leather contraption sheathing your prick, it's a wonder I didn't expire."

He whispered, "So that's what tempted you to fornicate. I thought it was the exhilaration of the wild ponies."

"I confess it was a combination. You were so like a wild stallion—big, dark, powerful, savage. I knew I must experience you or regret it for the rest of my life."

After a moment's silence he asked softly, "Do you have any regrets, Eleanor?"

"Only one. I regret that it wasn't you I wed when I was nine. How different our lives might have been. No shameful scandals; no exile." She was thinking again and Simon had the cure for that. He lifted her over him and crushed her soft breasts against the hard muscles of his chest. She opened her thighs to his questing manroot and gave herself up to him.

"Ah, love, you trust your body to me so completely, will you not trust your life to me?" he beseeched.

"Sim, Sim, I trust, I yield to your will, your decisions, whatever they may be."

He kissed her deeply then. He heard her clearly promise him everything he had ever wanted from her, but he knew she was in the throes of sensuality, and he was jaded just enough to wonder if she would take back her promise in the cold light of day.

Her lips were love-swollen, her breasts ached from hardening and softening so many times, her rosebud tingled with unbearable sensitivity, yet as the night hours galloped toward morning she clung to him desperately.

"You will send for me as soon as may be? As soon as Simon is old enough to travel? I don't feel safe without you. I don't feel whole or alive without you." Was she debasing herself to tell him he meant more than life to her?

His lovemaking should have exhausted her hours ago, yet suddenly she knew a need to devour him. Her love-swollen lips moved down his body greedily seeking his male center, which never ever failed her. She bathed it with her tears then licked them off, feeling the onleaping as muscle turned to marble, filling her mouth with the full splendor of him.

"My love, my torment." He groaned, and she felt satisfied, not realizing that he had promised her nothing.

When Eleanor opened her eyes a faint half light could be discerned from the window. She was filled with the languor of too much lovemaking. She stretched, naked in the bed, and curved her body toward her lover. With a shock she realized he was gone. Already she yearned for him. Love madness filled her with the urge to run to him in the courtyard and fling herself naked into his arms. She longed to press her soft breasts and thighs into his rigid armor, which was not much harder than his magnificent body that lay beneath that armor.

She ran to the window and flung aside the curtain. She opened her mouth to cry his beloved name and then she saw her. She emitted a silent scream for there mounted upon a milk-white steed beside de Montfort was the golden-haired beauty Eleanor had forgotten. She saw him raise the hood of the girl's pale-blue cloak before they rode from the courtyard side by side. The hooves of his fighting men's warhorses pounded after him interminably until she feared her eardrums would burst.

They had spent the entire night in each other's arms. He had exhorted her to trust him and blindly she had pledged that trust. Now he had betrayed her! All the hours he had lain within her, he was planning his deception. For a few moments the sight of the woman blotted out all coherent thought, then slowly she perceived that something was odd. Surely if they were returning to Palestine they would sail from Brindisi, not travel overland.

She threw on a robe and with bare feet and hair flying she ran from her chamber and down the long flight of stone steps to the balustrade, then out to the courtyard. The last of the baggage train was rumbling through the gates. Wild-eyed she shouted to the driver to halt. "What is your destination?" she cried, suddenly knowing without being told.

The driver slowed, gave her a blissful grin and rejoiced, "We're going home!"

Eleanor staggered as if she had been struck. Its impact knocked her outside of herself so that she could see and hear and watch herself as if from a short distance away. The cry torn from her throat was like that of a wounded she-wolf. She thought of her cub and felt she had been abandoned by her mate. She saw herself run back to her chamber, heard herself swearing and raving and raining curses upon the head of de Montfort. She rent her robe to ribbons, then started upon the bed linen on which they had coupled. Finally she threw herself upon the floor to sob out her heart.

It must have been hours later when a cool, mocking voice asked, "Are you done?" It was her own voice. "Put your childish histrionics aside, Eleanor, and plot your revenge." When she dissected her feelings she knew she could have borne his going home without her if only he had shared the decision with her. He was no better than Selim had been, using a woman for only one purpose, negating her intelligence. She was honest enough to admit she could even have accepted that for now. In the near future she had intended to let him know that unless he treated her as his equal, their relationship would be a stormy affair. The thing that stuck in her craw was the blond slave girl. Eleanor knew she consumed him when they were together, that no other woman satisfied his needs as she did. She knew her power over him and did not fear his taking a casual whore to satisfy his body's needs. But the fact that he had taken the girl to England instead of her demanded retribution.

45

The king welcomed Simon back to the fold with the same rejoicing as the biblical father who killed the fatted calf. The barons had been adamant in their refusal to fight in Poitou, for as usual Henry was penniless and the barons knew he would try to squeeze them for the money for this war.

Henry knew de Montfort was his only chance and made it plain to the Savoys and his Lusignan brothers, who hated Simon, that they had better be cordial to the war lord who now sat with them in council. Simon convinced Henry that he never had any money because it was being mishandled.

Winchester and de Montfort had faced off in front of the king, and Simon had drawn steel threatening to rid England of those who sucked her dry. Henry had no choice but to order an investigation of the bishop. The king asked Peter des Roches for an accounting of all funds that passed through his hands in the multiple offices he held. Winchester knew this would be his downfall. Even if only a part of his machinations came to light, he would be accused of treason.

Winchester appealed desperately to the council. "Why do you allow this man's will to dominate? If I am investigated, who will be next?" he cried.

Simon de Montfort fixed every member of the council with his smoldering black eyes and gave them Winchester's own words. "There are two groups of people, the pitiful and the pitiless. I have no doubt to which group you belong." At long last he had decided that since Henry was a puppet king, from now on it would be Simon de Montfort who pulled the strings.

Accounting for monies was not Winchester's only worry. Rickard de Burgh had made a quick trip to Ireland and secured a copy of the incriminating letter ordering the latest marshal's demise. Realizing he could be blamed, and ever a coward, Henry pointed to the man who had use of his privy seal. By the time an order was signed for Winchester's arrest, he had fled the country, but his son Peter des Rivaux was seized and thrown into the Tower.

Simon de Montfort knew it was time to press for Hubert de Burgh's reinstatement. England's barons and citizens were outraged at the injustice done to the noble English leaders by the foreigners Henry had clasped to his bosom. Simon was loath to use blackmail and instead persuaded the king that if he pardoned Hubert, the fighting men of the Cinque Ports might be amenable to fighting in France.

Simon could not believe how much he had accomplished in such a short time. The elements hostile to Henry had turned to him for leadership. They seemed to revere his ability and soldierly gifts. Here was a man who was not afraid to stand up to the king. He was ever willing to take heavy risks in the name of justice, and more and more rallied about him. With seeming ease he had assumed the leadership.

Eleanor resolved to return to England within the month. She fed her lusty son Simon whenever he showed the least signs of hunger, outraging his nurses. She rode every morning and walked on the beach each afternoon until she was positively glowing with health. Without hesitation she asked her brother-in-law Frederick for a ship to transport her. She met with its captain and pored over maps and charts with him until she was satisfied he would sail the quickest route, taking her all the way up the Bristol Channel into the River Severn, only fifty short miles from her beloved Kenilworth.

Her days were overfull, but her nights provided long, lonely hours that she filled with plots of revenge. Her imagination worked overtime, picturing de Montfort and his slave girl. She swore that if she found the nameless creature at Kenilworth, she would kill her, then she would turn her knife upon de Montfort! Nay, better yet, she reasoned, since he had wed her only for ambition, for her royal Plantagenet connection, she would get her marriage set aside. Half of England believed her marriage was invalid anyway. She would have no trouble bending Henry to her will if she was determined enough. Had not de Montfort gifted her with Kenilworth? She smiled cruelly. If he set foot in the place she would have the guards turn him out. She would set the dogs upon him!

Eleanor whipped her thoughts to the boiling point so she could get through the unbearable dark hour from three to four in the morning when she often thought she would die if she did not soon feel his strong arms about her.

Grudgingly the barons and the lesser nobility committed to fighting in France, but they told de Montfort bluntly their allegiance was to him and not to Henry and the half brothers the wanton Queen Isabella had spawned. Most were reluctant to squander the lives of their knights and men-at-arms on French soil and offered only a token number. To make up for it however, they pledged money.

Tirelessly Simon visited every county, even traveling to Ireland and Wales to muster sufficient men and money for the king's latest cause. He had committed himself to Henry in exchange for a voice on the council and a position of leadership in the country. His staunch loyalty made him keep his end of the bargain since the king had kept his.

Roger Bigod was confirmed as the new Marshal of England and added his weight to Simon's efforts. In all the king spent over a hundred thousand crowns to outfit the army his mother had asked for, half of which had to be paid to buy mercenaries because the barons would not commit more than a fraction of their men.

Simon de Montfort warned Henry of France's might. He had spent over half his life fighting there and never underestimated

Louis of France. He gave the king his best advice, which was to postpone sailing until they had recruited more men. Henry, however, was adamant. He insisted they were only aiding his mother in Poitou. Her husband, the Count of La Marche, had united the provinces of the south and west and all the Gascony barons were committed to the rebellion. Henry insisted that England was not expected to win this war single-handed.

The campaign proved a disastrous failure. When Hugh La Marche found himself confronted by the superior French army, he became convinced it was a lost cause and began negotiating a peace treaty. King Henry found himself in the uncomfortable position of having to return home with absolutely nothing to show for the hundred thousand he had wasted. The wrath of the half brothers he had failed was nothing compared to the dangerous mood of the barons. They had had enough. A parliament was called for the following month and a rallying cry went up. "We already have an army, we already have a leader; let us utilize both!"

Simon de Montfort knew what lay ahead. He was determined to visit his beloved Kenilworth to arm and fortify it before the serious trouble began. He took with him twenty of his knights who were married and whose wives now resided at Kenilworth. They took only two days to cover the ground between London and the River Avon.

It was springtime and the beauty of the countryside made him wish fervently that Eleanor could see every hillside dotted with lambs, could smell the heavily laden hawthorne blossoms, could taste the salt of the seabreezes that swept inland up every valley, and could feel the raindrops of a fresh spring shower. He had a deep and abiding love for England and Englishmen. He felt good because he knew what he did was right. The short term might well be horrendous and he was glad that Eleanor was safely out of it, but in the long run he would be instrumental in restoring England to the English. He would bring justice and good government back to the people. He smiled to himself, knowing he had become almost fanatical in his devotion to the cause of better government.

In the late afternoon the Earl of Leicester and his men were silhouetted against the sky as they approached the causeway to Kenilworth. A great cry went up from the walls the moment the earl was recognized. As soon as Eleanor heard the clamor, the hair on the nape of her neck stood on end. The joyous cries could only be for one man, Simon de Montfort.

She had ridden out to inspect the spring planting and was wearing her scarlet woolen cloak from Wales. She took a firm grip upon her riding whip and ran as fast as she could toward Kenilworth's two-story gatehouse, her cloak and her hair flying about her wildly. She flew up the stairs of the gatehouse and breathlessly faced the guard on the portcullis. "Do not raise it!" she commanded.

" 'Tis himself, the war lord," the guard explained, his grin splitting his face.

"I know damn well who it is. Have I not eyes in my head? I forbid you to allow him entrance here!"

The guard gaped. "Lady . . . I dare not deny the master entry to his own castle."

She brandished her whip in his face. "I am master here . . . I, Eleanor Plantagenet!"

The riders had drawn rein and stood below looking up to the gatehouse. The earl's deep voice rang out. "Eleanor, Splendor of God, what are you doing here?" he demanded.

The breeze whipped her scarlet cloak and her black hair about her as if it wanted to play its part in this delicious confrontation. "Defending my castle against a traitorous, lecherous Frenchman!" she threw down at him.

Simon shaded his eyes to learn the identity of the man who worked the portcullis. "Jock, raise the grate, man, we've just ridden a hundred miles," he ordered impatiently.

As Jock's hands reached for the wheel, Eleanor lashed out with her whip. "You will obey my orders under penalty of death," she vowed.

As Simon glared up at her she stood proudly like a wild young animal, as unattainable as the moon. De Montfort swore an oath, which she heard clearly. His deep voice always aroused a queer little shiver in her. She focused all her will in her eyes as she looked down upon him. "Be gone from this place."

What madness possessed her? "This time—this time I really shall beat you, Eleanor," he threatened.

"Guards, to me!" she cried, summoning the soldiers who walked the crenellated outer walls of the ward. They came, not daring to disobey Eleanor Plantagenet. "Ready your longbows," she ordered. Again, yet more slowly, they obeyed and notched their arrows.

"Shoot!" she ordered. They looked down into the dark face of Simon de Montfort and did not dare to obey Eleanor Plantagenet.

Lord God, de Montfort thought, if that other Eleanor, her grandmother, so infuriated Henry II, 'tis no bloody wonder he imprisoned her.

Eleanor turned from the guards, determined to have her way. She ran to the guards of the inner ward and commanded, "Arrest those men, they refuse to obey me." As her guards rushed past her to the gatehouse, she went down to the hall. She passed a dripping haunch of venison that always stood roasting by the fire as a symbol of Kenilworth's hospitality. The people of the castle were gathering for the evening meal, and the tables were filling up both above and below the salt.

She walked proudly to the dais and sat down regally, keeping her eyes upon the entrance. Her blood was high, devils danced in her eyes, turning them a deep sapphire. She forced herself to breathe slowly to calm herself. She had seldom admitted defeat even when it stared her in the face. She had no doubt but that he would come. No castle had ever held out against him, so there was no chance his own would do so. But she would hold out against him. "My will is as strong as yours," she said aloud, and every head turned in her direction. She had bravery enough to flaunt every convention—he had taught her well.

There was safety in numbers. Simon would not dare lay hands upon her here in the great hall. He paused at the vaulted entrance as if for dramatic effect, filling the doorway. He came in his leathers, dusted and begrimed from the hard ride. He strode a direct path down the center of the hall and stood towering before her. Though she sat upon the raised dais, their eyes were on a level.

"Explain yourself, woman!" he ground out.

Her eyes traveled slowly and insolently up and down his huge frame. "I don't explain myself to any man, least of all you!" she said with contempt.

No one had ever dared speak to him in such an insulting manner before. He put one great hand upon the table and vaulted across it. She rose quickly to flee, but he had her by the shoulders and shook her like a rag doll. She knew she was driving him to violence, yet she could not prevent herself from retaliating. The moment his hands stopped shaking her, she pursed her lips and spat upon him.

For one moment his black eyes stared at her in disbelief, then he threw her over his shoulder like a sack of grain and carried her up to their bedchamber. He said not one word, and his grim silence told her she could expect the beating he had always promised. Struggling was futile with his cast-iron arm about her, so she cast about in her mind for words to throw at him that would wound and bring pain. As he ascended the stairs she fancied that her heart and his kept time with each other.

Simon's mind was also busy. This is what I get for loving her too much. When a man marries for love his woman thinks to lead him about by his member. His brain cast about for a reason for her behavior. It could only be because he had forced her brother Henry to his will. She had such a keen intelligence, she knew where it would all end, as did he, and blood was ever thicker than water. By the time he reached their great bed, he had already jumped to the conclusion that she had chosen sides between him and the king. The hurt in his heart demanded an outlet. His reasoning was on a much broader plain than hers. He did not realize that her motives were on a much more personal and intimate level.

He threw her across his knee, intending to administer half a dozen ringing slaps to her bottom, but after one slap, she screamed and he could not bear to mar her lovely flesh. He held her facedown while he hesitated about what punishment he should dole out. Though he was furious with her, he could not allow his violence to inflict pain upon her.

She wriggled angrily in his lap fully intending to bite him and sink her teeth into him, but his leathers prevented her. "Faugh! You stink of horse and sweat."

He ignored her insult. He shoved her roughly from his knee. "You will now explain to me why you closed the gates upon the lord and master of this demesne."

She threw up her chin, with tears glittering in her jeweled eyes, more defiant than ever. "Kenilworth is mine; every stone. You gave it to me."

"Aye, more fool me. You might own Kenilworth's stones and mortar, but I am lord and master of every man and woman who dwells here, down to the lowliest pot-boy," he ground out.

She drew herself up proudly. "You might be my lord, but you are not my master. In fact, you won't even be my lord much longer. I am going to ask Henry to declare my marriage invalid. The king and the Archbishop of Canterbury will take my part in this."

"You willful little bitch! I paid dearly for this marriage, and neither God nor the devil will take it from me. I bribed your brother, even bribed the bloody Pope, faced down a whole nation set against my having you, even endured exile for you. I coerced the king into giving me Kenilworth, then gifted you with the only thing I ever had of any great value. So rest assured, Eleanor, I consider you bought and paid for."

She wanted to feel her power over him. She knew a need to provoke his lust. She wanted him to take her then and there begrimed from his travels. She wanted to blot out forever his memory of other women. "I shall never share that bed with you again!" she taunted.

His eyes narrowed, his brows were blacker than she ever remembered. A feeling of panic assailed her. By now he should have swept her into his arms and branded her as his woman. "So be it!" he said coldly. "But know this, wench. You will adorn yourself as befits the Countess of Leicester and will dine with me in the hall before all our people. Your words to me will be sweeter than honey. Your lashes will be downcast to cover the challenging light in your eyes, and you will demonstrate before all that you know your woman's place." He picked up her riding whip and tucked it into his belt. Quietly he added, "I will have obedience from you, Eleanor."

"Dream on, Frenchman," she hissed, but she waited until he had departed to bathe. She was too impatient to summon her

tiring women. She decided she would astound him with her
beauty, which must be offset by an exquisite gown. Impatiently
she flung the garments about in her wardrobe until she drew
forth the one she wanted. It was made from material she had
brought from the East. When the light struck it one way it
glittered green, then when she moved and the light changed it
glowed a deep peacock blue. The neckline formed a vee low
enough to display her breasts, which thrust forward as impudently as they dared. She fastened a gold girdle about her waist,
crisscrossed it in the back, brought it to the front across her
hips, and fastened the tassels so they rested provocatively upon
her mons. It was a whore's trick she had picked up at court, but
an effective one for luring a man's eyes.

She opened her jewel case and took out the Persian sapphire
necklace William Marshal had given her. If it pricked de
Montfort's pride that he had given her no jewels, so much the
better. Instead of fastening the necklace about her throat, she
wore it on her forehead, anchoring the ends into her black
silken hair.

The moment she was dressed she left their bedchamber in the
Caesar Tower and awaited him in the nursery. There was no
way she was going to remain alone with him when he came to
dress after his bath. Her eyes upon his body would reveal to
him her weakness.

When he joined her in the nursery, his face was set so that it
was impossible for her to read his thoughts. How magnificent
she was and what sons she had given him, he thought with
satisfaction.

Her heart turned over in her breast when she saw again how
like his father her firstborn son was. He was talking a mile a
minute, and Kate just managed to scoop him from his mother's
arms before he grabbed the jewels that adorned her forehead.

"I see he has some of your grasping qualities," Simon said
mockingly.

A scathing reply sprang to her lips, but de Montfort's look
prevented her from uttering it. She swept her lashes to her
cheeks in mock subjugation and moved past him out of the
nursery. With quick steps she walked just ahead of him and
could feel his eyes riveted upon her pretty, undulating bottom.

For a man who usually dressed in black or some other somber shade, he looked unusually elegant tonight in a blue velvet doublet and hose. No lingering trace of horse or sweat remained; he smelled distinctly of sandalwood. Before they entered the hall he placed her hand upon his arm and she submitted meekly.

By now the room was filled to overflowing, and its occupants openly cheered the return of their lord. Eleanor bristled. No cheers had rung about the room when she had returned, but then de Montfort had the common touch, even knowing the names of the servitors. When they arrived at their places he courteously held her chair for her to be seated. With deliberation she stepped down upon his foot, making sure the high heel of her slipper came sharply down upon his soft suede boot. Her lashes fluttered up prettily. "Ah, forgive me, my lord," she breathed softly.

He pretended he had not felt a thing and took his place at her side. When the first few dishes were presented, he politely waited for her, then when she took nothing he helped himself. When the meat came and she made no move, he said, "You will eat."

She looked helplessly from the venison to the kid to the beef. "You will have to chose for me, my lord, the decision is too great for my *woman's* mind," she said sweetly.

Simon held his temper easily, recognizing the male/female game she was initiating. He piled her plate with a variety of succulent meat and watched as she picked up an elegant, two-pronged Italian fork and lifted a piece to her lovely pink mouth. "Tell me why the decision to return to England without my knowledge or permission was not too great for your woman's mind."

"You swine! I thought you'd returned to Palestine."

His hand shot out and squeezed hers painfully. "Softly, wench, I am warning you."

Her lashes swept to her cheeks and she said in a sweet whisper, "When I learned you had returned home to England, my lord, I thought my *woman's* place should be beside you . . . as a dutiful wife."

Simon held up his cup for ale. "Thank you, Thomas. Will you be good enough to serve the countess with wine?"

"Oh, thank you, my lord, you are too kind," she said prettily.

He drank off his ale quickly, then watched as Eleanor took a small sip of wine. Suddenly her goblet slipped through her fingers and its contents splashed across de Montfort's blue velvet. The dark-red wine looked for all the world like bloodstains. Simon's control slipped a notch.

"My dearest lord, do forgive me," she beseeched contritely. Her eyes flicked over the red stain. "I trust you were not wounded in the late disastrous war that you lost?" she inquired solicitously.

Simon gritted his teeth. "I pledged myself to the untrustworthy Plantagenets. I should have known better."

She smiled cruelly.

"The next war will see me on the other side," he vowed, and had the satisfaction of seeing the smile wiped from her face.

She took a deep breath and said sarcastically, yet in honeyed tones, "Ah, please, milord, do not involve me in decisions of import, it taxes my *woman's* brain too much." Her small hand came to rest upon his thigh. "My *woman's* place is in the kitchen."

"The bedchamber," he corrected lustfully.

The corners of her mouth went up in a secret smile of triumph, and she lifted her fork to her lips and provocatively nibbled a rare morsel of beef. "Ah, my dearest lord, I am indisposed tonight." She smiled apologetically. "My *woman's* time, you understand?"

He knew she deliberately goaded him. She played the game well, yet he was no slouch and decided that two could play. Though he did not need or want or had ever used a whore since he had been with Eleanor, he shrugged a huge, careless shoulder and lied, "I'll take another for a few days."

"Whoreson!" She jabbed the Italian fork down to impale the back of his hand. He shot up from the table, sending his chair flying. "That's it!" He did not trust himself to lay hands upon her. "Guard!" Two knights on duty in the hall came forward instantly, more than willing to do de Montfort's bidding. Each knew if she had been his wife she would have had the insolence beaten out of her years since. "You have always said the name Eleanor cursed you. You are wrong—it cursed me. We will try the same medicine that was used on your grandmother." He turned to his guards. "Imprison her in the North Tower. A week on bread and water should draw her sting."

Eleanor was aghast. This wasn't supposed to be his reaction. He was supposed to carry her from the hall to their oversized bed to play out the game of domination and submission to its natural conclusion. He must have his blond slave-whore close at hand. She would never forgive him for this humiliation.

46

Each day brought an earl or a baron to Kenilworth to show his support for Leicester. Gloucester came, then Bigod, the newly appointed Marshal and Earl of Norfolk. The next day brought de Lacy and the Earl of Lincoln, and close on their heels came the Bishop of Ely and John de Vescy of Alnwick Castle in Northumberland.

They laid their plans for the parliament they would attend and swore a pact to stand together in opposition to the king who had allowed his wife's relatives and his own half brothers to divy up England among themselves. At the end of the week Rickard de Burgh rode in with signed bonds from his uncle Hubert, John de Warenne, Earl of Surrey, and Roger de Leyburn, England's steward.

Simon and Rickard were walking in the courtyard as dusk descended. De Montfort's conscience was pricking him over the harsh treatment he had given his wife. Now he must confess his actions to de Burgh who was ever her champion.

Simon bit his lip. "Eleanor is here," he said tentatively.

De Burgh looked at him keenly, knowing he had not sent for her in the face of the trouble that was sure to come. "She came without your permission," said Rickard, knowing her so well.

"She's lodged up yonder in the North Tower under lock and key," Simon said grimly.

Rickard de Burgh stiffened. "You did not incarcerate her?" he asked with disbelief.

"By Christ, I'll tame her yet! She's got a maggot in her brain about dissolving the marriage."

Eleanor looked down upon the two men. A week in the tower had only hardened her resolve. She scribbled a note, wrapped it about a brass paperweight, and hurled it down into the courtyard. Simon bent to retrieve it, hope filling his heart that she was contrite. The words he read smote him between the eyes. She punned:

Send me Rickard de Burgh to warm my bed and I shall be content to remain here indefinitely. Seven days without sex makes one weak.

"Blood of God," de Montfort swore. He thrust the note at de Burgh. "Have you two been lovers?" he demanded. He felt as if a knife had been plunged into his heart.

"Nay, Simon, surely you do not need to ask such a thing," Rickard de Burgh said calmly. He shook his head and said half to himself, "I suppose a woman somehow knows when a man loves her."

Simon de Montfort had always known that Sir Rickard loved Eleanor. Her conquests were legion. Half the men in England lusted for her, and he admitted he was among their number. "Excuse me, friend, there is a matter that needs my attention." Simon had had the key to the North Tower about him for seven days in hope that she would yield. Suddenly he realized she would never yield, and that was why he worshipped her. He wanted no milk-and-water wench who would do his bidding without question. He needed a woman with the fire of passion in her blood. He valued her intelligence. 'Twas only a game of the sexes they played wherein he demanded she keep her woman's place.

He ran up the cold stone steps of the North Tower and turned the iron key in the lock. She stood ready to fly at him. He laughed. She was no bigger than a piss-ant. "For shame,

Eleanor, 'twas a scurvy thing to do to the lad when you know he loves you."

How dare he stand there laughing and chiding her after imprisoning her for a week! "You may have hysterics, de Montfort, but I am not amused," she spat.

He had learned more this week than she had. Putting her under lock and key had only hardened her resolve against him. He laughed triumphantly, relishing the thought of winning her over with his touch, his nearness. He reached out strong arms and took what he wanted. He lifted her off the floor. "I am the luckiest man alive. Your anger not only makes you beautiful, it arouses your passion." His arms tightened and he allowed her body to slide down his deliciously.

She had vowed to herself that this time she would make him beg and plead for her forgiveness, but damn him to hellfire, he was the great war lord, he would never beg. He would take what he wanted, whenever he wanted it. His bare-faced flattery about her passion was already having its effect upon her. He wanted a kiss, so he took one, turning it into the most blatant act of seduction with his demanding mouth and damnably attractive hands. Eleanor knew that at any moment he would melt her like molten lava, and her anger grew hotter because of his devastating effect upon her. Before he made love to her again she must have it out with him about the woman.

She pulled from his arms and ran away from him to put distance between them so she could think coherently. The bed loomed between them. "What about her?" she demanded angrily.

"Her?" he asked, at a total loss.

"Your fair-haired whore!"

Simon never used whores. In fact, he had never been unfaithful to her, even in thought. After Eleanor's explosive passion, any other would have been totally unsatisfactory. "Be plain with me, Eleanor. To whom do you refer?"

"Damn you, are there so many then?" Her eyes glittered with unshed tears.

"My little love, there are none," he swore.

"You lie! When you left me in Brindisi, with my own eyes I saw you ride out with the woman from Selim's harem."

Suddenly Simon threw back his head and his deep laughter rolled about the tower room. "Are you jealous? Is that what this has all been about, jealousy?"

"You need not look so inordinately pleased with yourself," she said through gritted teeth.

He took a step toward her and she retreated, refusing to let him come close. "I sent her to Brindisi because I learned that Italy was her home."

Eleanor's eyes flashed. "You expect me to believe that? Italian women have black hair!"

He was both amused and pleased that she felt so jealously possessive of him. "Not all, Eleanor. In northern Italy there are many fair-haired people. When you saw us leave Brindisi together I was escorting her home."

She went weak with relief, but she wasn't about to let him off the hook. She glanced about the inhospitable chamber. "I have taken a fancy to this North Tower. It overlooks the hills instead of the causeway. Mayhap I won't return to the Caesar Tower."

He was around the bed in a flash, scooping her up possessively. "You shall . . . and immediately."

"Put me down. Damn your eyes! What is it about big men that makes them want to carry women about? I have two legs."

"I know," he retorted with a leer. "I've seen them."

"If you think I will return to the Caesar Tower just so you can look at my legs, you can think again. For a man who is obsessed with justice for the common man, *and woman*," she emphasized, "you acted out of character to incarcerate me without a trial."

"I'll try you now," he offered, nipping her earlobe. "You would be the first to argue that there is nothing common about you." His hand was already beneath her skirt, sliding up her leg as if he owned every inch of her.

"Flattery will gain you naught," she said, squeezing her legs together to prevent him reaching his goal without resistance. "If you have come for a truce, I am willing to listen to your concessions. Mark me well—I don't set foot outside this chamber until I have your solemn promise I shall have my own way about everything."

"You *shall* have your own way. Since you don't want to set a foot outside this chamber, I shall make love to you here." His hands had already removed her stockings and garters.

Her protests would gain her absolutely naught, and because of it a deep thrill ran up her spine. His playfulness was infectious, and she was almost giddy with relief that the girl from Selim's harem was safely in Italy.

Simon had had a great deal of trouble keeping away from her for a whole week, knowing all he had to do was climb to the tower and unlock the door. Now he would make up for the abstinence she had forced upon him. He finished undressing her with impatient hands and lay her down upon the bed. He reached out to spread her mass of silken hair across the pillows, just exactly the way he loved to see her best.

"Since I am allowing you your own way about absolutely everything, you had better tell me exactly what it is you want, Kathe."

"Sim, Sim, you are a devil," she accused, laughing up at him, but if he thought her too shy to demand what she wanted, and in graphic terms, he was in for the shock of his life.

When he had acceded to all her demands, he made some of his own just to be scrupulously fair about their equality. She lay clinging to him in wonder. Their mating in this high North Tower had been cataclysmic, and she knew Simon agreed when he whispered, "Kenilworth has over a hundred chambers and I've decided to make love to you in every one of them, beginning tonight in our own Caesar Tower."

She slapped him. "You are insatiable. I intend to spend the rest of the evening with the children whom you have kept me from for a whole week." She sat up and reached for her gown.

He knelt behind her and dipped his head to touch his lips to the nape of her neck. He knew what he had to tell her would exasperate her beyond measure and kept his hands upon her to gentle her. "You'll have to hurry your time with the children tonight. Half the earls and barons of England are here at Kenilworth. If you will dine with me tonight, I promise it won't deteriorate into open warfare again."

"Oh, bugger! Why didn't you tell me?" she demanded, thumping him soundly. "What must they think of me as a chatelaine? Have you shown off the library; the books of Aristotle I acquired? Did the cooks use saffron in the rice? I pray to God you have not served them that iron-flavored domestic wine."

Simon lost no time carrying her to their own Caesar Tower now that he had diverted her. Suddenly she stopped her incessant questions and went very still. Her eyes widened as realization dawned. "Simon, what's going on? Why are they here?" Her voice had gone husky with apprehension.

He touched his lips to hers. "Don't worry your pretty head about such things."

"Simon, don't do this. Don't patronize me. I want to be your partner, not just your plaything."

He looked down at her lovely face. Their eyes met and held. Finally he nodded. "I will tell you all . . . in bed tonight." He set her feet to the rug. "Have the servants build us a fire up here. There are promises I made myself that I intend to keep."

She shuddered as a curl of desire spiraled from deep within her belly up to her breasts. As he left she heard him chuckle. "Jealous, begod!"

She stared at the doorway long after he had gone. He was the most physically magnificent man she had ever laid eyes upon. She was willing to bet that every female who had ever seen him had longed to know what it would feel like to be made love to by the war god. It was nothing so tame as jealousy she had experienced. It was like being consumed by the burning fires of hell.

She caught a glimpse of herself in the mirror and was appalled. She summoned her women and began issuing orders like a general, then she sent for the children so she could enjoy giving them their nightly bath before she took her own. The moment she was dressed she descended upon the kitchens and the buttery, giving her household clear and concise instructions about the food and wine. She spoke with the housekeeper in charge of linens to assure herself the guest chambers were plenished each day with fresh linens, candles, and refreshments. She ordered her Welsh minstrels to play at dinner and even selected the ballads that were to be sung. She sent half a dozen pages scurrying with messages: one to Jack at the bathhouse telling him to keep hot water available around the clock. She advised

Hicke the tailor that their guests might need his services for
small repairs to their wardrobes. She sent a note to the chapel
informing the priest that the doors must not be locked after
compline. She supposed Simon had spoken with the stable
grooms about keeping mounts ready for hunting, but just in
case she sent a squire with a reminder, then bade him go above
to the mews to tell the falconer his birds of prey must be put on
half rations to make them hungry for the kill. She stood absolutely still for a moment and counted off on her fingers the
items that she thought needed her attention, then just to be on
the safe side, she sent word to her breweress to double her
order for ale this week.

Seemingly without effort she managed to be in the dining hall
to greet each visiting noble as he arrived for dinner. She looked
deliciously feminine in pale peach velvet trimmed with delicate
swansdown. Eleanor knew the power of color. When she
wanted to steal the limelight from other women, she wore red
or another brilliant jewel tone; when she wanted to assert her
authority, she wore black or something equally dark. Tonight
she wished to make men's hearts melt; hence the pastel gown.

Simon de Montfort's heart filled with pride as he joined his
exquisite wife to greet their guests. She had a way of running
her eyes over a man's frame that made him feel all male. She
aroused the wish to protect her in a man, so that he envied de
Montfort his role. She dazzled each man with her smile, which
seemed for him alone, and her whispered inquiries about his
comfort and needs emphasized his importance in her eyes.

She moved graciously from group to group and if any there
were not in de Montfort's pocket when they entered the hall,
they were by the time they retired to bed.

It was late when they climbed to their impregnable Caesar
Tower. "Thank you. You have a magic touch. Until tonight the
hall was like bedlam. The beef was tough, the dogs slavered, the
men got drunk. Petty quarrels broke out so that no man could
agree with another."

She shrugged prettily, pleased with the praise. "It required
only my presence."

Simon's deft fingers unfastened her gown, then he quickly

disrobed and stretched his length upon the bed with his arms behind his head. She removed the gown, hung it in the wardrobe, then sat down in her filmy shift to brush her hair.

"Do that after. Why waste your energy when I'll soon have it in a tangle?" he said impatiently.

"After? Oh, you mean after our talk."

Simon groaned. She laid down her ivory brush and lifted her leg to slowly remove a garter.

"I am not a lap dog to receive my reward after I have done my mistress's bidding," he told her.

"Are you not?" she purred, lifting her leg higher seemingly to peel the stocking from it.

"Admit it, your need is almost as hot as mine," he said.

Hotter, she admitted to herself. That is why he must begin his talking before his loving or she was lost.

His eyes followed her hands as she removed the other stocking; then his mouth slackened as she lifted off her shift allowing her breasts to spill free. They bounced deliciously as she came to the bed, but once she turned down the sheet she danced away again and picked up the ivory brush. She walked to the fire and informed him, "I am listening." Playfully she began to brush the curls on the black, silk triangle between her legs.

His mind went blank. He had no idea what she wanted to hear. He licked dry lips. "Christ, stop that before I spill myself on the sheets."

She made a provocative moue with her lips. "You had better have more staying power than that if you intend to play with me."

He came up off the bed, lifted her off her feet, and sprawled with her before the fire. She scrambled to her knees, laughing, but before she could elude him, he came up behind her and enfolded her in his arms. He spread his knees and pulled her tight against his groin. She could feel his heavy testes resting against her bottom cheeks and feel his erection reaching halfway up her back. She rubbed against him teasingly, and he brought his palms up beneath her breasts to lift and thrust them forward toward the heat of the fire. "I like to warm your parts before I taste them." He held her there until her nipples almost burned his fingers, then he spread her thighs apart to heat her mons.

She moaned low in her throat. "Sim, Sim, you promised you'd talk to me." At this moment her rosebud was on fire and she knew she didn't want to talk.

"Kathe, I promise, I promise, only let me do this first. I swear my brain is empty, all the blood has gone to my cock."

"All right," she agreed, "just let me hold you to the fire for a minute." She groaned as her hand closed about his erection. She wanted to scream from excitement, then when he positioned her on the wolf pelt before the fire and plunged into her he felt like a red-hot poker and she did scream. He too cried out with passion as their scalding flesh melded together. They both lost control as their hot climaxes spurted and mingled. Her lashes fluttered to her cheeks and she felt herself drift off to Paradise.

Simon watched the fireshine dance across her beautiful body and knew this was the closest to heaven he'd ever get. He rested in her a long, magical time. When he finally withdrew he got no reaction from her, no usual murmur of protest. Had he slaked her? Was she pretending sleep? He sat up, but she lay on her back, sprawled in silken splendor, not moving an eyelash. He dipped his head to lick the pearly drops on the inside of her thighs and she cried, "Simon de Montfort, the things you do to me are too intimate. Is there nothing you won't try?"

"I wouldn't dream of doing this," he whispered, demonstrating totally immoral behavior.

She shrieked and he carried her to their oversized bed. He straddled her so that his long, hard shaft lay in the cleft between her breasts. She dipped her head to kiss its vermilion tip and giggled as it bucked and jerked each time her lips or tongue grazed across the smooth surface. "Simon, no more. Lie down beside me and hold me." He complied immediately. This quiet time after they had made love was precious to them. She lay with her cheek resting upon his heart and pressed her lips to the spot, feeling happier than she had since the first blissful night they had spent at Kenilworth.

Suddenly they became aware that they were not alone.

"I heard Mommy laughing," a small voice said.

"Ah, you want to join the fun," Simon said. "Come on, then, I know how tempting this big bed is."

Eleanor whispered, "Simon, I'm nude."

"Mmm." He pondered. "That is easily solved," he said, lifting off his son's nightshirt. "To sleep in this bed you have to be naked."

Henry giggled as Simon lifted him on the wide bed, and he slid down rapturously between his mother and father's naked bodies.

"Don't tickle me." He laughed.

"I won't," his father solemnly promised, "not unless you start it."

"Don't teach him to be uncivilized, Simon," Eleanor said.

Simon hooted. "Listen to who's talking! Let me tell you about the time your mother swam in the mere without any clothes on, in broad daylight," he added wickedly.

Just then they all heard the baby begin to cry. "That's Simon," their son informed them.

Eleanor looked helplessly at her husband. "Go on, get him too. Let's all be together."

Eleanor slipped into the nursery not bothering with a robe. Kate was just stirring sleepily. "It's all right, Kate, I'll take him." She climbed back into the warm bed and tucked the baby beside her.

"Let me have him," Simon said.

"No, you great brute, you'd roll on him in your sleep and smother him." She laughed.

"Before we are done, we'll fill this whole bed," Simon promised. He reached for her hand and their fingers entwined.

"Are you ready to talk to me?" Eleanor asked.

Simon sighed. "When a woman's mind is on politics, she makes a dull bed partner." He squeezed her hand, feeling more fortunate than any man had a right to feel. "I agreed to help Henry on condition I had a say in things from now on. I had been most remiss in my duty, darling. I had more than a suspicion that your husband William was murdered by Winchester, and of course he orchestrated our exile. Henry finally agreed to investigate him and he fled immediately."

"But William died in bed right after Richard and his sister

Isabella were wed. Do you mean he was poisoned?" She had often wondered.

"I'm afraid so, my sweet. His brothers have all suffered the same fate."

"How could Henry be so blind to such wickedness?" she cried.

"How indeed?" he said dryly. "You will be happy to learn that I was able to repay Rickard for his loyalty. I restored Hubert de Burgh to favor. Henry has pardoned him."

She squeezed his hand. "Your time has been well spent, it seems. I am so thankful you didn't have to fight in France. Thank God a truce was signed."

He could not bring himself to tell her there would be fighting ahead.

She laughed at an amusing thought. "I must say it seems an unlikely team. A spirited warhorse like you in double harness with Henry, sharing power."

An impossibility, Simon thought silently. She would learn soon enough he'd been appointed to lead the opposition to the crown. Let them have a few days of happiness together before she learned that lines were being drawn with Plantagenets on one side and de Montfort supporters on the other.

As Eleanor drifted off to sleep something nameless in the back of her mind nagged at her. She pushed it resolutely away to savor the precious moment here in the big bed with all her men. Her happiness was perfect. Her husband loved her above all things, and they were all together at Kenilworth where the outside world could never touch them.

47

It was not until days later when their guests had departed and Simon had left for the Hocktide Parliament that Eleanor realized he had never explained the presence of the barons. As she reflected, her common sense told her they had been there to hatch a plot. She had absently noticed that Simon had left Kenilworth heavily fortified. Now she suspected it was not done to give her peace of mind. He had fortified Kenilworth against an enemy, and pray who could that be other than the King of England?

The day was overcast and oppressive. Dark shadows loomed everywhere, especially in Eleanor's mind. She was filled with apprehension and she wished fervently that she had gone with Simon. If trouble arose between her brother and her husband, she was the only one who could smooth things over between them. She found she could settle to nothing, she was restless as a tigress.

Late in the day a steward rode in from de Montfort's holdings in Leicester. He was sorely distressed that the earl had departed.

"It is obvious there is a problem. You must confide it to me. The Earl of Leicester leaves me in charge whenever he is absent. I even sit and pass judgment in our own courts of law here in Kenilworth," said Eleanor.

The steward, red-faced from anger and embarrassment that he must give details of the sordid business to a lady, finally blurted out what had happened. "William of Valence, my lady, thinks he is above the law. He and his attendants stopped at Leicester after a day's hunting to demand refreshment. When they were given ale they deemed it an insult. They used unnecessary force to break into the cellars and break open the wine casks. They were drunk and out of control . . ." The steward's voice trailed off and he hesitated to tell the rest.

"The Savoys are hated by all, and with good reason. They are rapacious by nature. I know that William is a particular favorite of the king, but that does not give him license to commit abominations."

Suddenly the steward felt he was on firmer ground and poured out the appalling details. "When the servants tried to prevent destruction to the earl's property, fighting broke out and two of our people were killed. No remorse was shown. The looters went on to rape the maids and smash all the casks in the cellars with axes."

Eleanor's hand flew to her throat. When Simon learned of this he would want to kill William of Valence. Oh, God, why must there always be trouble?

The steward knew what he must do. "I shall have to take this news to my lord. I would be derelict in my duty if I did not."

Eleanor drew a deep breath. "I shall go with you." As soon as the words were out she knew she had been searching for a reason to join Simon, but why in the name of God did it have to be something that would cause more bad blood between her family and de Montfort?

When Eleanor rode into Oxford she couldn't believe her eyes. It was like an armed camp before a battle. The streets were patrolled by knights in chain mail, the inns overflowed with men-at-arms carrying longbows. Men were camped from Oxford Castle all the way out to Banbury Road.

In his blind arrogance, Henry had actually come to Parliament to ask for a tallage of one-third of all the belongings in the kingdom, but he gasped when he saw his barons sitting in Parliament in full armor. On one side was the king, his three half brothers, John Mansel, and the Savoys who were now leading peers. On the other side were the barons led by Simon de Montfort and Roger Bigod, the Marshal of England.

De Montfort wasted no time in making plain the barons' demands. They must have more than sworn promises that the king would break the moment he left Oxford. They were no longer willing to have their nation involved in madly expensive wars. The administration must be reformed from top to bottom. The offices of justiciar, treasurer, and chancellor must be filled by English nobles of integrity. The challenge was fierce as a swordthrust, and thus ended the first day of Parliament.

Eleanor had taken the precaution of riding with an escort to prevent Simon's wrath, but when he saw her arrive at the Beaumont Palace where he had made his headquarters, he could not hide the fact that he was furious. White-faced, he took her firmly by the arm and led her to his chamber where they could be private from all eyes if not all ears. "Splendor of God, Eleanor, for once in your lifetime could you not stay put where I left you?"

She took offense. "I love Kenilworth so much, do you think I would have troubled to leave it and journey all this way if it wasn't important? Damn you, I have only your interests at heart!"

A flicker of apprehension clouded his brow. "What has happened?"

"Your steward from Leicester came with terrible news. It seems William of Valence out with a hunting party stopped at Leicester. When he received no hospitality, hostility broke out and two of your people were killed."

"The little cocksucker sat in Parliament today sneering at the barons."

"Simon!" she reproved stiffly.

He looked to her with an apology upon his lips when a thought came to him. His eyes narrowed. "The steward came here to bring me this news, but why did you come, Eleanor?" he demanded. Before she could reply he said, "You have only my interests at heart, you claim, but we both know better than that, don't we, Eleanor? You feared for your brother, admit it!"

She angrily turned her back upon him. She went to the table and poured herself a drink from the jug. It was not wine, it was ale, and she pushed the goblet aside and turned back to him. "I-I just don't want trouble between you."

"Trouble? There will be more than trouble! You sure as hell didn't come to protect my interests. You know damn well I need no protection!" he roared. He was angry because she was the only one in the world who could make him feel defensive. Why in the name of God had she come to place herself smack in the middle of this conflict? Alone he was so resolute, so sure of purpose, but when she was close, his heart ruled his head and he was ever afraid of losing her. She had an elusive quality. He told himself that anyone who could be wholly owned was not worth wholly owning, but it didn't help.

How many times had he begged her to trust him? She was a Plantagenet and from a Plantagenet's view, was he not about to betray that trust? Everything was black and white so long as she was in a safe haven, looking to her babes, knowing nothing of the dirty business of politics. But when she was in the forefront, his thoughts turned an indecisive gray.

Eleanor's shoulders drooped. She had known he'd be angry but she had counted on seeing the eager welcome leap into his eyes once he had scolded her. She knew she would get no welcome. On the contrary, what she saw was total rejection. "I'm tired . . . I need a bath," she said unhappily.

"I will summon the palace steward to prepare a chamber for you."

Eleanor bit her lip. He wanted separate chambers. For one blinding instant she thought of rushing to Oxford Castle and asking the king to dissolve her marriage, but after a moment's consideration she knew her marriage to Simon de Montfort was the most precious thing in her life. "I'll return home on the morrow," she said softly. She went from him and he did not try to stop her.

At Oxford Castle, Henry was being besieged by the queen, by the Savoys, and by his half brothers. They insisted that he take a high hand with the barons and with the traitorous de Montfort, but Henry was deeply in debt, mainly due to these same relatives who were urging him on to recklessness. He had put pressure on the monasteries and the Jews, bled them dry, and now the only place left was Parliament and direct taxation.

On the second day of Parliament the barons presented the "provisions" they had drawn up for the king's signature. They demanded a permanent council to advise him on all policy with the right of veto. As well, the crown was to resume control of all royal castles.

William of Valence was on his feet before they got to the third provision. "I shall never give up my castles . . . I am uncle to the Queen of England!" he shouted arrogantly.

William de Lusignan added his effeminate voice. "My brother the King of England gave me Chepstowe and Pembroke. You are speaking to a member of the royal family, de Montfort!"

Simon relished the confrontation. "Not one drop of royal blood runs in your veins. You may have had the same mother as the king, but may I remind you that not one drop of royal blood runs in her veins either." Then he raised his black eyes to stare down William de Valence. "You and I have a more personal score to settle."

The two Williams were in a rage. "Traitor!" they cried, and drew their swords, but de Montfort's steel was out first.

The giant advanced upon Valence and Lusignan. "Hold this for sure: Either you give up your castles or you lose your heads!"

Valence backed down, but William de Lusignan, purple in the face, turned to Henry.

Roger Bigod, the marshal, coughed. "There is one more provision." He paused, then plunged on. "Exile for the Lusignans."

A gasp arose from the king's men and a great murmur of approval arose from the barons. Henry was too weak and feckless to stand against such fierce pressure. Reluctantly, bitterly, Henry yielded and signed the Provisions of Oxford, then turned accusing eyes upon Simon de Montfort. "I never thought I would see the day when I had to fear you more than any other man."

"You should not fear me, Henry. My sole desire is to pre-

serve England from ruin and you from the destruction that
your false counselors are preparing for you."

The barons were satisfied that their rights as peers of the
realm would be upheld. Simon de Montfort wanted to take
things one step further. He argued that the Magna Carta laid
down that the rights of the peers be extended to their depen-
dents. The common man must be protected. He argued that the
king should be the servant of the people, not their master.

Not all the barons agreed with him, so for the nonce de
Montfort had to be satisfied. He had taken up the reins of
power and allowed Henry to retain the semblance of kingship.

Simon returned to Kenilworth knowing he had been re-
prieved. His marriage was still intact. Yet he knew this was just
the lull before the storm. When the cataclysm came, would it
tear them asunder?

The barons, knowing that it was second nature for King
Henry to dissemble and make lying promises, kept their
knights and men-at-arms ready. Under the leadership of Simon
de Montfort they had assembled the largest army in England's
history.

As Simon and his men thundered along the earthen causeway to Kenilworth's portcullis, his eyes scanned the walls and
gatehouse. He saw only guards and he experienced a small
pang of disappointment that she had not run to meet him. Last
time she had met him with whip and longbows, but at least she
had met him.

Once inside the impregnable stronghold, he was greeted so
warmly by all including Eleanor that his mood lifted.

As the days passed he had taken to watching her. To him she
seemed more beautiful than ever. She laughed more often, her
eyes sparkled brighter, her gowns were prettier, her movements
more graceful, and yet it seemed to him she was the tiniest bit
cool and distant. Oh, she was passionate enough whenever he
initiated it, but a yearning, a longing had grown inside of him.
He wanted more. He wondered if there was such a thing as a
"soulmate" as the poets rhapsodized, or was he just lovesick?
Was he actually jealous of the love she bore her brother? No, it
wasn't jealousy, he decided. Rather it was a need to have her

commit to him totally, unconditionally, without question. If she would pledge her trust, he would be a happy man.

That night, after a fierce loving, she lay upon him in slumber. He gazed at her in wonder. How small and silken were her limbs. The contrast with his own body was unbelievable. Where he was huge, she was tiny. Where he was hard, she was soft. Where he was dark, she was pale. Where he was hairy, she was silken. Where he was coarse, she was fine. His fingertips traced the down upon her cheek, the tiny blue veins in her eyelids. He brought her small hand to his lips and marveled at the perfection of her pink oval nails. Why had man and woman been created so differently? At this moment it seemed an impossibility that a great giant of a male could mate with such a petite female. How on earth had one so fragile borne him lusty sons?

Desire for her flared in him hot and savage, yet at the same time his need to protect her was stronger than his lust. He loved this woman with all his heart and soul. He sighed. If one of them must love more than the other, thank God it was he.

The calm lasted for many months, then on a blustery day of autumn, Rickard de Burgh rode in hard on a lathered destrier.

Simon gave his lieutenant hot buttered ale and prepared himself to hear the worst.

"Henry has drawn up a long list of charges against you. He has sent to the Pope for an absolution of his oath to observe the Provisions of Oxford and he has decreed that he has resumed royal power."

Simon's eyes were fixed moodily on a far-off point. Finally he said, "And so it begins."

"Henry brought in a great body of mercenary troops and London became so incensed, he had to move into the Tower for safekeeping."

"He hasn't the brains of a piss-stone," Simon said sadly. "He acts like a child waving a tin sword." He quaffed down his ale, wiped his mouth, and announced quietly, "I will call a Council of War."

He sent messages to Oxford, Gloucester, Norfolk, Chester, Derby, Surrey, Northumberland, the Marcher Lords, and the Cinque Ports. There was one other, however, whom he knew he must inform, and it was what he had dreaded and postponed for what seemed like years. He saddled one of his horses and rode out alone into the hills. He loved this countryside, loved all of England; he deeply regretted that it had come down to civil war. It would not only divide the country, it would divide families, possibly his own.

De Montfort had come too far to compromise. Strict adherence to the terms of the Great Charter was the only acceptable course. There must be no more squandering of national wealth or land or heiresses upon foreigners or royal relatives from abroad. No more levying of illegal taxes.

He did not turn his horse for home until the last of the light had faded from the chill afternoon. He never felt the cold, yet as he rode across the windswept causeway he gathered his red wool cloak more closely. Kenilworth's welcoming lights beckoned him, yet the dread he felt in his heart prevented the warmth of his home from comforting him.

Eleanor was in the solar surrounded by her women, but the moment she saw him she quickly reminded the nurses it was time to feed the children. Her other women tactfully withdrew to allow the countess privacy with the earl.

He swallowed hard and indicated a chair by the fire. "Eleanor, we have to talk."

Her eyes never left his dark, serious face as she sat down. A small bubble of panic rose in her breast and her hair bristled on the nape of her neck. At every crisis in her life Rickard de Burgh had appeared.

Simon found he could not wrap it up in a prettily disguised package. Here was his moment of truth. He tried to conquer his fear, for had he not always said you get what you fear in this life? "Eleanor, we are two very strong personalities, and God knows we have clashed over and over since the day we decided to scorn convention and marry. We are both expert at male/female games wherein you enjoy flouting my authority and I strive to keep you in your woman's place. I think you are wise enough to know they are only games. Both of us know you are my equal."

Her eyes widened. She had known it and deep down she realized he too had always known it, but she had never thought to hear him admit it aloud.

He took a step closer and impatiently threw back the scarlet cloak from his wide shoulders so it would not impede him. "Physically we are one. You have always submitted your body to me. Now I must have more. Today we will have it out one way or the other. I want full commitment. I demand the personal morality of loyalty, friendship, and honesty from you. I am asking for a pact of chivalry from you to me for what I am about to do."

His words almost overwhelmed her. They showed her with crystal clarity that though this magnificent man did not need permission from her to do what was right, he was asking for her approval, her commitment to him not only as a Plantagenet and a princess but also as a wife, a mate, an equal. Unless they stood together, attuned in body, mind, and soul, he could not go forward with anything but a heavy heart. But go forward he would.

She arose from her chair to face him. How like him it was to ask her to commit to him without question, without full explanation of what it was he was about to do. She saw him for what he was and ambition was no small part of him. This past year she had not gone about blind, deaf, and dumb to what had been happening. She knew he led the barons in opposition to the crown. She knew he plotted against the Plantagenets.

The time was at hand for her to look at her brother Henry honestly and see him for being weak and childish. Now she admitted he was at the core of everything that was wrong with England. Simon was asking her to choose, but in truth there was no choice. There never would be a choice between right and wrong, good and evil, justice and injustice. To England Simon de Montfort was a symbol, to the barons he was an instrument, but to her he was everything: breath, blood, strength, life, love . . . love eternal. He was the magnificent standard of manhood by which she hoped their sons would measure themselves. This man had taken her and taught her the meaning of love as a woman, not as a child, and now he was giving her free choice to pledge to him as every one of his fighting men had pledged to him. She felt honored. It would be her privilege to pledge her life to him and follow him to the ends of the earth.

She stepped close and raised her hand. For one horrific moment he thought she would strike him, but then she sank to her knees before him and grasped his wrist for the pledge. "I am your woman, my lord of Leicester."

Tears stood in his black eyes as he lifted her from her knees. He embraced her tightly. "I am afraid it is war, my darling, but I swear to you no physical harm shall come to Henry. I have a signed pledge from all the barons that Prince Edward will be brought up to the kingship. We shall see to it that he is the best king that England has ever known. Eleanor, thank God you see my ambition is not a personal one for the crown; my ambition is for England."

She marveled that he never doubted the outcome. The idea of failure never entered his head. She smiled and touched his face. The rough shadow of his beard pricked her fingertips. "You once told me, 'Never look back, your past is gone. Always look ahead, embrace your future!' "

He turned her palm toward his mouth and his lips traced her life line and heart line, which ran together. "You are the only Plantagenet fit to rule."

The haggard look had left his face and had been replaced by one of infinite tenderness. He held her lovely sapphire eyes with his. This woman meant more to him than life. She probably meant more to him than saving England, but thanks to her generosity he did not have to make the choice. "I pledge to you this newfound bond between us shall never be broken. You shall have equal say in all I do. I pledge you my protection, my love, my life." He felt like a god. It was what he had always desired of her. Total commitment. This bond was deeper than anything physical. It was a deep, mystical experience that filled his senses to overflowing, yet strangely it humbled him. Quickly he sealed their vows with a gentle kiss and strode from the room with every ounce of his strength restored.

Rickard de Burgh climbed to the solar. Eleanor stood by the window in the shadows. She said quietly, "There is no other way?"

He shook his head. "War is inevitable. I don't suppose he

told you Henry has issued an endless list of charges against him and has asked Rome to absolve him from his oath?"

She shook her head and lit the candles. "Oh, Rickard, he doesn't know what fear is. He is so sure of himself."

"He is sure of himself, but he does know what fear is . . . he wasn't sure of you."

She smiled at him hauntingly. "Justice is his passion . . . and he is mine."

"Do not be afraid, Eleanor. Youth predominates in the baronial ranks. Young men find him irresistible. He has a magnetic appeal to their sense of idealism."

Her eyes were filled with her love and understanding. "The choice between a knight in shining armor and a weak king is not a difficult one."

"Do you remember that day long ago when Henry's bride arrived? I had a vision that day of the London mob stoning her barge and pelting her with filthy names. A few days ago it came to pass. She is hated more heartily than any other queen in history."

Eleanor shuddered. She could never celebrate another woman's suffering, and yet the woman had brought it upon herself. She had hated the Londoners long before they had hated her.

"How long do I have before he goes from me?"

"Two days perhaps. You know how thorough he is. All is ready."

"Then let us go down to dinner. I want to spend what time is left to me at his side."

48

Simon de Montfort acted with speed and fury. His forces and those of his barons descended upon Oxford, then struck westward to secure command of the Severn River and the Marches of Wales. Bristol and Gloucester immediately opened their city gates to him. Hereford, which was known to be Royalist, was plundered and the magnates of Hereford were imprisoned. Any who supported the king had their fields burned and their livestock seized to feed de Montfort's army.

He wasted no time besieging castles. He knew London must be secured, then the Cinque Ports, which meant command of the sea. In a panic, Henry wanted a peaceful settlement and sent for his brother Richard, now King of the Romans, to handle negotiations. Richard Plantagenet and his men rode furiously to Oxford, but they were too late. De Montfort had not allowed the barons to pause. Richard then rode to Reading but again he was too late. All he got was dust in the face raised by the barons' marching feet.

De Montfort avoided London and instead drove straight into Kent, which was supposed to be a stronghold of the king. The earl had calculated well, for the men of Kent came out to welcome his army and the barons of the Cinque Ports rallied to his side, as Hubert de Burgh had promised him. Simon now had control of the English Channel.

Many of the king's adherents fled to France and the continent. The London mobs now openly defied the king, and the royal family did not dare to leave the Tower. Simon de Montfort, ever shrewd and decisive, took only three days to set up a provisional government. He appointed a new chief justiciar and took custody of the great seal. Foreign owners of all castles were ordered to vacate.

The Pope lost no time condemning Simon de Montfort. A legation was sent from Rome excommunicating the Earl of Leicester and condemning the barons' action. Simon met the delegation at Dover and threw the papal bull into the sea.

Then finally Louis of France offered to arbitrate between Henry and his people. After long thought Simon agreed to this because he saw some of his younger men break away to form a party of their own in support of Henry's young son, Edward.

Simon de Montfort took this respite for a quick visit to Kenilworth. He cared not one way or the other what King Louis of France decided. If the decision was favorable to de Montfort and the barons then there was an end to it, but if the decision favored Henry then it meant all-out war.

When the decision came, England and especially London was stunned. Louis was favorable to Henry on every point. He declared the Provisions of Oxford null and void and that the King of England might rule as he saw fit and appoint his own ministers.

Simon de Montfort had no intention of accepting the ruling. He knew that this diplomatic defeat of the barons would again unite them. The city of London would not be dictated to by France, and the Cinque Ports were up in arms over the decision.

When Simon rode into Kenilworth, Eleanor was alarmed that he had received a wound in his leg. The war lord was a veteran of such minor hurts, which he considered no more than a scratch. Her alarm lessened somewhat when she saw his wound did not impede him in any way, but when he immediately began to undress her, she protested firmly and told him such outrageous activity was out of the question.

"Splendor of God, Eleanor, I can still copulate!" he shouted.

She sent his squires to fetch in the bath. "When you have bathed and I have dressed the wound, *I* will decide if you will indulge in sexual athletics," she informed him firmly.

He stood with legs firmly planted apart until the bath was filled and all the servants had departed. Then she saw him sag and rushed to his side to aid him. "You were just putting on a show of strength before the others," she scolded. "Sit while I undress you."

Simon was secretly amused. She seemed to have no idea how ridiculous it was for a six-and-a-half-foot man to lean upon a woman who stood less than five feet tall in high heels.

His squires had taken his armor, so she gently eased him from his padded gambeson and wool tunic. Her eyes examined his bared chest for more wounds, then just to be certain she ran her fingers through the thick, dark pelt.

"Ah, that feels so good," he said huskily, and she wondered if his voice masked unbearable pain.

Her eyes sought his. "You must rest, Simon. Promise me?" she implored.

"I shall stay abed all day tomorrow," he offered weakly. His face was a careful mask, hiding his wicked intent. He really was weak at the knees, but it was her closeness that was doing it to him. Each time she bent to aid him he was given tantalizing glimpses that made his fingers itch to play with her delicious breasts. Some intoxicating fragrance wafted over him. He did not even try to identify it; to him it was woman. She always smelled and tasted like a creature from an exotic paradise. Sometimes he suspected she had been bestowed upon him by the gods. He managed with a grimace to remove his sword and scabbard, then fell back to allow her to remove his boots, unbuckle his belt, and ease him from his chausses. He carefully observed her reaction through lowered lashes. She had forgotten that he always wore the black leather sheath to protect his large genitals whenever he spent days in the saddle.

He saw her eyes widen and her cheeks grow pale with desire. Her pink tongue came out to moisten her lips and he had to stop himself from ravishing her then and there. "I'm sorry, darling, I really thought I was strong enough to make love," he teased.

She forced her eyes from the black leather sheath and lifted them to his. He saw they were dilated with pleasure.

"You weren't eager for bed play, were you?" he asked.

"No, no, of course not," she assured him.

He threw back his head and the laughter rolled out. "Liar! You haven't even glanced at my wound. Your eyes can't get past my swollen cock." He whooped.

"You devil!"

He picked her up and dropped her into the tub.

"You bugger! You . . . you Frenchman!"

He said with a leer, "I can't think of a faster way to get you out of your clothes."

She pretended outrage, but she was relieved that his wound was minor and excited that they would be able to spend the night making love in the wide bed.

They exchanged places and Simon bathed while Eleanor removed her wet clothes and rubbed herself with a big towel.

"You shouldn't have done that yet. I like you all wet and slippery."

"You like me heated before the fire, you like me under you, over you . . . admit the truth, you'd like me stood on my damn head," she said, laughing.

He was out of the water the moment he had scrubbed himself. He refused to allow her to tend his wound because it would mean a further delay. He poured her a large goblet of wine, picked her up in his arms, stood her upon the bed, and held it to her lips. "Drink deeply of the dragonsblood, my darling," he ordered.

"I hope you know what to expect if I drink the whole goblet," she warned him.

"Insatiable?" he whispered hopefully.

Over the rim of the cup her eyes sparkled like sapphires and devils danced in their depth. When she drained the cup he tossed it over his shoulder and she launched herself into his waiting arms. Their mouths fused, her legs twined about his strong body, and they slid to the bed, not separating for the next twelve hours. Both of them knew he could not remain long. The barons had decided upon all-out war, and Eleanor knew once her husband departed he would be engaged in many battles.

The darkly beautiful princess shivered beneath her transparent robe as she stepped into the privacy of the castle bedchamber. Her breath caught in her throat as she saw her lover naked upon the great bed. One step closer and the whisper of her garment would have awakened him, for he had the disciplined sleeping habits of a hardened soldier, falling asleep and awakening instantly to meet any challenge.

She paused just inside the arched portal and let her eyes avidly enjoy his male beauty. He lay supine with one arm thrown above his head. His shoulders were so impossibly wide they took up most of the bed. The column of his neck was thick with corded muscle and the strong slant of his jaw was shadowed blue even though he'd shaved that day. The firelight turned his deeply bronzed skin to flame, accentuating every muscle and sinew of his powerful torso.

The corners of her mouth lifted in a smile. The fire was a concession to her; he needed none, but since it enabled her to walk about in a finespun bedgown, he tolerated it. His tousled hair upon the white pillow was black as a witch's cat, even darker than his black magnetic eyes that could lure a woman to commit any sin.

He was much more than her lover, he was her strength and her weakness, her wisdom and her folly. He was her hero . . . her god. She would never tell him; he'd be too big for his britches. She smiled at her choice of words and her sapphire eyes were drawn down the superb flanks to what nestled between them. How innocent and harmless it looked in repose, but make no mistake it was a weapon, one he wielded with exquisite expertise. She shivered but it was not from cold.

He was a man in a million, towering over other men, yet it was not only in size. Most of England thought him a godlike hero—the barons, the masses. For one brief second a stab of fear pierced her heart. Tomorrow meant another battle. Of course he would emerge victorious. The fear vanished; she was incapable of doubting him. Still, she must take care not to awaken him for if she did and he saw her within arm's reach, he would spend his magnificent strength bringing pleasure to her body.

He would laugh at her protests that he must conserve his strength for the battle. He was a war lord . . . a warrior god. He had laughed at her protests since the day they had met. Oh, how she had protested! He had conspired with Fate itself to make them lovers. When had it all begun? She closed her eyes and her mind took wing.

"Come and lie with me."

Eleanor's eyes flew open. How long had he been awake, watching her daydream? "Sim, no. We were at it all night. I'm not saying no to tease you."

"Kathe, please love, come and lie with me."

She had learned to obey him in all things. She stretched her tiny body beside his and he stroked her hair. "I must be gone within the hour," he told her softly. "This time the fighting won't cease until they are my prisoners. I shall demand total capitulation. The royal standard will be torn down."

"I know that, Sim," she said softly. "We are equal partners in this."

"I want your signature on all state documents."

She closed her eyes and lifted her mouth to him. His kiss was so tender it filled her with awe. "When you return, for all intents and purposes, you will be king."

He held her against his heart. "And you will always be the King's Precious Jewel."

AUTHOR'S NOTE

After the Battle of Lewes, Simon de Montfort ruled England for over two years. During that time he realized his dream of seeing plain men sit in Parliament. From each city and borough he had summoned two to four good and loyal men to sit with the peers, the barons, the bishops, and the knights to discuss the business of the realm.

The story of Simon and Eleanor is one of the great love stories of the thirteenth century. They had five sons and then a daughter.

After the Battle of Lewes men wrote poems in praise of Simon de Montfort.

Earl Simon's faith and faithfulness all England's peace
   secure.
He smites the rebels, calms the realm and drooping hearts
   makes sure.
And how does he keep down the proud? I trow 'tis not by
   praise
But the red juice he squeezes out in battle's stubborn frays.
He felt he must fight for truth or else must truth betray
To truth he gave his right hand brave, and trod the rugged
   way.
Read, read, ye men of England, of Lewes' fight my lay;
For guarded by that fight ye live securely at this day.